The Unforgettable Loretta Darling

The Unforgettable Loretta Darling

A NOVEL

KATHERINE BLAKE

HARPER

NEW YORK • LONDON • TORONTO • SYDNEY

HARPER

Originally published in Great Britain in 2024 by
Penguin Random House UK.

HarperCollins books may be purchased for educational, business, or sales promotional use. For information, please email the Special Markets Department at SPsales@harpercollins.com.

FIRST US EDITION

Library of Congress Cataloging-in-Publication Data

Names: Blake, Katherine, 1970- author.
Title: The unforgettable Loretta Darling : a novel / Katherine Blake.
Description: First US edition. | New York : HarperCollins Publishers, 2024.
Identifiers: LCCN 2023044270 | ISBN 9780063342200 (trade paperback) |
ISBN 9780063342231 (ebook)
Subjects: LCSH: Hollywood (Los Angeles, Calif.)--History--20th century--Fiction. |
LCGFT: Thrillers (Fiction) | Novels.
Classification: LCC PR6102.L3434 U54 2024 | DDC 823/.92--dc23/eng/20240202
LC record available at https://lccn.loc.gov/2023044270

ISBN 978-0-06-334220-0 (pbk.)

24 25 26 27 28 LBC 5 4 3 2 1

To Ella

'Everything in the world is about sex, except scx.
Sex is about power.'

Oscar Wilde

The Unforgettable Loretta Darling

PART ONE

I

Jimmie patted down his pockets, then froze, glaring at me. 'You!'

'Me?'

'You stole my passport, you little bitch. Give it back!'

Frankly, I couldn't believe it had taken Jimmie this long to notice. We'd already collected our luggage, thankfully deemed unsuspicious by the customs officers who'd sailed out to meet the liner and go through our belongings onboard.

A passing woman in a fur stole threw us a stony glance.

'Darling, the other passengers are staring,' I said from behind a frozen smile. 'Let's not make a scene.'

'Don't you *darling* me! Where is it?' He pulled me to one side and I stumbled, still wobbly from the ocean crossing.

'Get your hands off me.'

Reluctantly, he let go. From over his shoulder, I could see a liner steward watching. I wondered how many marital arguments he'd witnessed in his time. Only, me and Jimmie weren't married.

I'd first bumped into him at Morecambe's Winter Gardens. Albert Modley and the Sandow Sisters were playing. He was leaning against the wall as though he was in some sort of funk, but I went over and asked him to buy me a drink. Some men like that – cheek. It made them think that I was naughty, which I am, and that meant they'd hope I'd sleep with them, which I wouldn't.

'What's got you in such a bad mood, anyway?' I asked, sipping my Coca-Cola through a straw.

'You wouldn't understand,' he said, hands sulking in his pockets.

'Oh, come on. Try me.' I'd already noticed that he had an American accent and I was curious. Teeth like a row of condemned houses, which seemed odd for a Yank, but still.

'I'm having problems with your guys in Liverpool.'

'My guys?'

'Customs.'

'Oh.' I took him in then, good and proper. The wide lapels, the thin moustache and greased-back hair. Clichés are usually there for a reason.

'You're a spiv,' I said over the music.

He glanced around. 'Keep your voice down!'

I couldn't help laughing. Didn't have the heart to break it to Jimmie that one look at his dodgy suit and anyone could see exactly what he was.

'What do you deal in?' I asked.

'Stockings.' Pointedly, he glanced at my bare legs. 'Maybe you've heard of them?'

A thought prickled my skin. 'So, what's the problem with our men in Liverpool? They suspicious?'

Jimmie took a long drink of his beer and nodded. My

thought was joined by a few more thoughts, and quickly became a plan.

'You know what you need?' I said. He stared, clearly confused. 'A mule.'

'Hey, what did you say your name was?'

'Margaret.'

He frowned again. 'I don't get you, lady.'

'Listen.' I took a last, noisy suck on my straw and indicated for another Coca-Cola. Jimmie would be paying. 'What you need is a nice little wife to travel with you.' Surely, that had to be better than fake bottoms in suitcases. 'A cover. The veneer of respectability.' I'd already checked out his ring finger. 'Now, you already have one, I know, but . . . we can pretend that I'm your wife.'

He swallowed hard. 'She's dead.'

'Oh.' I smiled. 'Even better.'

His eyes widened. 'How can my dead wife be a good thing?'

I spoke even quicker then. 'I simply mean that she won't get annoyed at someone else travelling under her name. What *was* her name?'

'Loretta.'

I liked it.

'It's a good plan, don't you think?' I coaxed.

He looked me up and down. 'Are all the girls in this town like you?'

I grinned. 'Oh no. There's only one of me.'

'Thank God.' He adjusted the collar of his shirt.

It took a little more persuading, but after a while

Jimmie saw my point – for me to come out with him as part of his black-market smuggling, travelling under the dual passport he shared with his dead wife. If anyone stopped him, why shouldn't his missus want a bunch of stockings?

That had been the plan I'd first shared with Jimmie. The plan that had been perfect for both of us. My plan. But I had to look after myself. My dreams were too important to risk losing and, right now as we stood by the exit gate, that passport was hidden inside my unmentionables.

'Anyone could have taken your passport!' I pointed out, trying not to wriggle with the booklet's corner jutting into my derrière.

'It never left our cabin.' His hand twitched like he wanted to slap me – I knew the signs – so I was pretty glad of that nosy steward keeping an eye on us. If you're going to blackmail someone, it's best to do it out in public. I let out a sigh, as though tired of this little game, when really I was enjoying it immensely.

'Listen, as it happens, I do have your passport and—'

'You!'

'You really must stop saying that, Jimmie. It's becoming boring.'

'After everything I've done for—'

'For me?' I finished for him. 'What do you want? An award for a young woman joining you in a gig that could see her end up in jail?'

His mouth dropped open. 'Are you for real?'

6

I allowed myself to laugh. 'You'd better believe it, brother!'

He drew his chin in. 'Is that your attempt at an American accent?'

'No good?' I asked, reverting to my northern vowels. 'Lousy.'

'See, Jimmie? Even in a situation like this, you can still have a joke with me.' I patted him on the arm. 'You really are one in a million.'

He shook his head slowly. 'You're stealing from me! Is there anything you won't do?'

'Oh, shush,' I said. 'I'm not stealing; I've just been looking after it for you.' Before he could say anything else, I pushed on. 'Now, listen. Here's what's going to happen. You're going to take me with you all the way to California.' That's the address he had in his passport; it had been the greatest stroke of luck.

'But I don't need to! The stockings are here!' He glanced around and lowered his voice at the sight of a port patrol officer stationed at the gate. 'We just hang around a couple of days and then get the next liner back to Liverpool. That's what we agreed.'

'I know, but I've changed my mind,' I explained patiently. 'I want to go to Hollywood and you're going to take me there. Once you've safely deposited me, you'll get your passport back.'

'What is it with women changing their minds all the time?' He shook his head mournfully. 'I'll miss my contact for the stockings.'

'I don't give a flying flip about the stockings, Jimmie,

and I won't be coming back with you. Do you under-stand? You're taking me to Hollywood and leaving me there. If you do all that, you get your passport back.'

'Why don't I just give you the money to get there by yourself?'

'Because I haven't a clue how to go about that, and I need someone to help.' I wasn't totally deluded. A twenty-year-old northern lass on her own in America with barely any money and no friends? That was asking for trouble.

Besides, I still needed time to nick whatever else he had on him. 'Just get me safely there and then you never have to see me again.'

'You are the most despicable human being I have ever met. You know that?'

'Thank you!' I said brightly. 'Now, shall we crack on?' The crowds had faded away, already through passport control and out into the streets of New York City. 'I just need to nip to the bathroom.' I looked around and spot-ted a public convenience. 'Back in a mo!'

I went to dig the passport out of my undercrackers and had a quick piss while I was there. As I washed my hands, I looked at myself in the small bathroom mirror above the sink. I felt jubilant. No, more than that – victorious.

'You're Loretta now,' I told myself. 'And welcome to your brand-new flipping life.'

2

We'd been travelling for six days straight when we arrived in Hollywood. It was 23 May 1950 – no one and nothing will ever make me forget that date. From that day on, I'd never have to see Jimmie again. Thank goodness. Travelling with someone who hated me had been . . . a trial.

But now, we'd arrived. I'd never been so exhilarated in my life. As I climbed down from the train, I couldn't help gawping. The station platform was a thrill, buzzing with people in sharp suits and nipped-in dresses. The segregated cars and what I'd learnt to call 'jerkwater' towns of our journey faded away like a bad memory and I suddenly no longer cared that I'd been wearing the same dress for nearly a week.

Jimmie and I stood opposite each other as I held out a hand. 'Pleasure doing business with you.'

He ignored my gesture. 'Where *is* it?' he spat.

I sighed and knelt beside my beauty case; I'd given up on the whole knickers thing, not wanting the passport to totally disintegrate. Before I could even get back to my feet, he snatched it from me, tucking it away inside his breast pocket.

'If I ever see you again, you'd better run fast.'

'Hollywood's a small town.' I had no idea what size it was.

'Exactly. And you'd better hope you see me first.'

As he stalked away, I called an ironic fond farewell after him, which prompted him to raise two hostile fingers. I laughed and gave him one back as he disappeared inside a taxi.

So much for goodbyes. I wondered how long it would take him to realize that I'd liberated him of one of the larger dollar notes in his wallet. Well, when I say one, I meant two. Three, actually.

I followed the other travellers out onto the pavement. Correction: sidewalk. It was *just* like in the news reels that played before the main feature, back in Morecambe's Odeon cinema. I'd sat in the dark there so many times with Enid, the two of us soaking up all the glamour and me secretly dreaming of being there one day. Palm trees swayed in a soft, warm breeze. There were hills to the north, etched in tones of blue and grey. The day's warmth seeped into my tired bones and I hung around for a bit, picking through leaflets in the station foyer, spending a few precious cents on a bottle of Coca-Cola, which came with its own straw. It was strange, but I was almost reluctant to start on the next part of the adventure. I didn't want to be disappointed; I couldn't bear it if Hollywood ended up being tired and dull, rather than the most glamorous town in the whole world. I hadn't come this far to be let down. Eventually, though, I had to get going. The station master was starting to watch me.

I stepped back out onto the sidewalk, but with no idea which way to head. I didn't want to stand there for too long, with my mouth hung open and a virtual sign around my neck saying, 'Please take all my worldly goods'.

I spotted a sign for Sunset Boulevard. As good a place to start as any. Ignoring the pinch of my shoes, I headed off with a confident stride that was as fake as the line on the 'nylons' Ma used to draw during the war. It struck me that I might have been the only person in the world ever to have *walked* into Hollywood, but that long, straight road unfurled ahead of me like an invitation, punctuated with flag posts that reached up to the sky, posters advertising Schlitz Beer or Wallichs Music City. There was the scent of lemons that drifted from groves that dotted the sidewalks. *I am in California and there are actual lemon trees!* Was I dreaming?

I caught sight of myself in a department-store window. *You made it. You're here!* My spirits soared. I shouldn't have worried. It was clear that Hollywood was not going to disappoint me at all. I wanted to break out into a run, or grab someone and hug them, but this wasn't *Meet Me in St. Louis* and I didn't fancy getting arrested quite yet.

This place was like nothing I'd ever seen before! Everything was so new. And big. New and big. Billboards towered over me. Even the occasional church had clearly been thrown up in a heartbeat, built like a vast concrete monument to the importance of size, palm trees studded around the grounds.

And the sidewalks! People swarmed out of nowhere and everywhere, like extras filling a scene. Buoyed up, I went into a drug store and bought a postcard and stamp to scribble a message back home, leaning on top of a mailbox:

My dearest Enid (That would have given her a laugh.)

Arrived by motor car to Beverly Hills. It couldn't be better!
(A lie.)
    Having fun! (Another lie.) *The trees are so tall and the sky is really blue and it's so warm. I should have left my cardigans at home for you.*
    I wish you were here to see all this. I miss you so much. I'll write again when I'm more settled.

Lots of love, Margaret xxx

Hesitating, I added a final PS.

Forgive me.

I licked the stamp and turned over the postcard to gaze at the picture – rows of cars on the Hollywood freeway. Four whole lanes! How a simple trip out to the beach didn't end up in mass carnage, I had no idea. I noticed a woman with a baby strolling past. She looked friendly enough.

'Hello!' I called out to her. 'Do you know any rooms to rent?'

Without a word, she quickened her pace. Nearby, a man was leaning against a wall. He pushed himself off and came towards me, bringing out a rolled-up newspaper from beneath his arm. 'Here, check out the small ads.'

I hesitated. 'Where's cheap?'

'Nowhere!' He grinned and moved off down the sidewalk.

I found a bench and smoothed the paper out on my lap to scan the ads boasting all sorts of features – air conditioning with individual room control, modern kitchens, private parking . . . The words swam expensively before my eyes. A shadow passed over me and I looked up to find a woman wearing a satin dress that seemed out-of-place in the middle of the day. She was holding several large paper shopping bags. She reached into her clutch, balancing a hip against the weight of the bags, and after a moment held out a piece of gum.

'Thank you . . .'

'English?' she said.

I felt my eyes widen in shock. 'How do you know?'

'The accent, dummy!' She leant over to move my beauty case out of the way and I shifted along the bench for her to sit. We must have made a strange pair – me all dishevelled, and her the picture of glamour.

'Let me guess.' She nodded towards the railway station. 'You're here to make your dreams come true. Am I right?'

'You make it sound so predictable.'

She gave me an amused stare. 'It *is* so predictable.'

I began to gather my things, but she put out a hand. 'Listen, I know a room that's going. Apartment block next to mine. You're lucky we met like this!' She leant in. 'There's no rent control, and the cockroaches are beyond crazy, but . . .' She shrugged. 'It's cheap and you'll be left alone.'

Rent control? Cockroaches? She was speaking another language, but I understood the word 'cheap' all right.

'Do you have an address?' I asked.

She looked me up and down, as though she was trying to decide. 'You got cash?'

'Yes.' Those would be the dollars I'd stolen from Jimmie, stuffed damply inside my bralette.

Without warning, she shot up. 'Cab's on you!'

'Now, wait a minute—'

But she was already out on the kerb, whistling down a taxi. She opened the back door and slid in, then wound down the window with a judder of glass against rubber and rested her arm on the sill.

'You coming or what?' She was smiling so much that I couldn't help smiling back.

The cab driver leant long and hard on his horn. 'Get a move on, lady!'

I leapt off the bench and clambered into the back with my beauty case and a small holdall as my new friend gave an address. The cab driver swore softly beneath his breath and yanked down hard on the steering wheel. After a few moments of being thrown about in the back of the car, we stopped at a junction, the driver leaning out to exchange powerful swear words with another fellow.

'I'm Primrose, by the way.' She held out a hand, ignoring the exchange going on in the front.

I shoved my case beneath my armpit. 'Hi. Loretta.'

'So, what are you?'

What was I? 'A make-up artist.' I wasn't. Not yet, not even close. But she didn't need to know that and, besides, I would be one day. I had to be, otherwise I could never have justified to myself everything I'd done to get here and the people I'd left behind.

She nodded. 'Cute.'

'And *what* . . . are you?'

'Me?' I saw her exchange a glance in the rear-view mirror. Laughter trilled. 'Oh, honey, I'm a prostitute.'

3

The landlord assured me the place was a steal. A furnished apartment for $37 a month, a number that made my heart leap into my mouth. I had enough for the deposit and the first two weeks. After that . . .

'I can't be too fussy with the rent,' my new host explained, as though he was doing me some big favour. Turned out that I was moving in bang next door to the most famous brothel in California, the Hacienda Arms – which I discovered just happened to be owned by my new friend. He handed over a box of what turned out to be roach traps. 'Keep on top of things and you'll be fine. Don't let them climb the walls.'

I spent the first few days sleeping. God, did I sleep! There were the nightmares, of course, but I was used to those.

After a while, I gathered myself and went out job hunting. I found myself a position at a diner called Van de Kamp's, no questions asked and cash in hand.

'What's your name?' the manager asked, leaning over an order form for uniforms.

'Loretta.' It was already rolling off the tongue, just like I'd been saying it my entire life.

He wrote down the name. 'Should be ready Wednesday. Until then, you're Bertha.' The manager passed me an over-sized uniform. I wore it for three days straight, livid on the inside. I mean, did I *look* like a Bertha?

But what a day when my own personalized outfit arrived! Here I was, *Loretta*. I had an embroidered kerchief to prove it, so it had to be true. My new uniform was two-tone, pink and turquoise with contrasting collar flaps and cuffs, and a personalized hankie that sat in the cutest little breast pocket.

'Make yourself pretty,' the manager told me. 'Customers like that.'

Each morning, I'd do my make-up before the cracked bathroom mirror in my apartment. I'd paint the subtlest pink glow over the apples of my cheeks, draw in my eyebrows, take a mascara block and spit in it.

The make-up worked. I went down a storm! Often, I'd end up working two six-hour shifts, back to back. Diners rested their chins on their hands, asking if I'd ever met the king. You couldn't make it up! Let me tell you – some of these people? They were a milk bottle short of a full crate.

On the first few mornings, I'd get in extra early so that I could learn about all the different orders.

'You see this?' Jake said, holding up an egg. He'd been a short-order cook here for twenty years. He always said, 'Find a job you love and you'll never work a day in your life.' Jake must have *really* loved making fifty pancakes a day.

I shrugged. 'It's an egg, Jake.'

He shook his head. 'Wrong.' He cracked the shell with a kitchen knife and tipped the egg out onto the griddle, where it sizzled and spat. He pointed the knife at me. 'It can be sunny side up, over easy, medium easy, hard scrambled, soft scrambled, poached or shirred.' He took up a spatula and flipped the egg over. 'And I haven't even started on frittatas!'

'I never knew it was such a science,' I said faintly.

'Well, you need to learn all this stuff,' he warned, taking two slices of bread and smearing them with thick wedges of butter. He slid the egg onto one of the slices and pressed the other down on top, handing the plate to me. 'Ketchup's over there.'

I went to sit across from him, and Jake watched closely as I took my first bite.

'Oh, it's incredible,' I moaned, butter dripping down my fingers. It really was. Eggs were still rationed back home.

All the free food gave me the perfect figure to fill out a bikini and, on our days off, a bunch of us waitresses would go to the beach to hang out with Primrose's gang beneath the sweet Californian sun. I never did tan; just grew more freckles. But I was starting to learn how this town worked. It was full of hierarchy, but when you were stuck at the bottom nobody cared. Prostitutes . . . waitresses . . . we were all friends and that helped. I was able to practise, practise, practise! Faces – I couldn't get enough of them. But it was the prostitutes and their bodies that taught me a lot. If you think that handing out sex for a living is all about lying on your back, you're wrong. These girls worked hard at their craft.

'Listen,' Primrose told me after one day at the beach,

once we'd all showered off in my bathroom. She drew a girl towards me, naked as the day she was born with the body of an angel, and a mouth so filthy that I couldn't even repeat the words, no matter how hard you asked me. 'Make her look beautiful. And I mean *all* of her.'

I took in every detail of Rosa. I had no idea if that was her real name; they weren't usually. But the rosebud lips, nipples that looked like ripe pillows, the hips that curved into a tiny waist! Whatever was swimming around in America's gene pool . . . Boy, did it work.

As the sun faded towards the golden hour, light shone off her body as though it was greased in Vaseline. Rosa angled a hip in a pure S of the most perfect curves.

'Get up on this stool for me.' I took out my largest make-up brush and began to paint. Because that's what it felt like – really painting. I was making a woman beautiful.

First, I added an extra blush to her nipples, then white chalk to hide the stretch marks on her stomach. Her calves were to die for, finessed from the constant wear of high heels, and I shaded them to accentuate their shape. More white chalk in the dimples behind her ankles and then darker powder to accentuate the comforting crease between her breasts. Breasts that any man would love to dive into. Any woman, too. Rosa had it all – except I could give her more. That's when I finally understood the power of make-up.

In Morecambe, working on the Woolies make-up counter, I'd thought it was all about getting one over on the customer – convincing them to buy an extra lipstick for good measure, or insisting that coral was absolutely their colour when it actually made them look clownish. I'd always loved the stuff – the make-up, I mean – but now I was starting to truly understand its power. A make-up artist wasn't just altering the surface; she was changing how people felt in their hearts, their souls. How these women behaved. Back then, as I'd watch a customer leave Woolworths, carrying that little bag of tissue-wrapped products, I'd see a person pulling their shoulders back, ready to confront a husband or maybe ask for a pay rise from a boss. For the price of a lipstick, I was changing people's lives. Helping them see the best version of themselves. Did that make me a saint? No, it did not. I was changing my life, too. But it made me useful, especially in a place like Hollywood. I'd found my dream – other people's dreams – and there was no way on God's sweet earth that I would give up on that.

Especially not now.

I was Loretta, darling. Let anyone try to stop me.

4

The first time I ever set eyes on Raphael Goddard, I'd already served ten breakfasts.

Customers had been in and out all morning and I was rushed off my feet, so I didn't take much notice of the door slamming shut. But after a moment, the usual noise of the diner grew quieter. I paused in stacking the napkins. Mothers were staring, their children forgotten. Fathers were frowning. But almost everyone was looking. That's when I spotted him walking towards me, his silhouette outlined in gold from the sun streaking through the glass door.

Blond curls like a cherub's and a face to match. I wouldn't have been surprised if an angelic chorus had set up at his arrival. Honestly, I don't think he'd have been surprised either. He always did have an arrogance to him, the way his hands stayed firmly in his pockets and how his upper lip had a slight curl to it. He slid onto a stool at the counter and revealed a smile that lit up the entire diner. If I'm making this all sound religious, that's how it felt. There are some moments when you know that your life is about to change forever and, on this occasion, I knew because a fire had set up in the region of my knickers. Talk about Moses and the burning bush.

Despite the whole Bible story that was going on in my

nether regions, I just about managed to hold out a laminated menu. He didn't even bother looking.

'Chocolate milkshake.'

I hesitated, unsure I'd heard right. 'For breakfast?'

He gave me a look. 'Yes, for breakfast.'

I moved to the blender and held up a silver scoop. 'You want ice cream in that?'

'Naturally.'

A few moments later, I slid a shake across the counter, the glass misting with cold. I waited for him to take it, wondering if – hoping that – our fingers might touch.

'Gonna throw in the mud?'

I reached over to the chocolate syrup and squeezed out a generous portion.

He didn't break my gaze. 'And I'll have a couple of those crackers, while you're there.'

I reached to the graham-cracker box, snapped a cracker in two and placed the pieces around the edge of the saucer.

Finally, he seemed satisfied. 'Thank you.'

I gave a faux little bob of a curtsy. 'You're welcome.'

There was a glint of silver – a cufflink – as he reached for the glass, and a watch that looked hefty. And by 'hefty', I meant expensive.

He noticed my glance and reached out his arm, pulling back the cuff. 'It's an Omega Seamaster. Give them to the sporty types.'

He may as well have been talking French. 'Sounds fancy.'

'And my shirt is a silk-linen mix, while you're taking

notes. Finest Italian.' He straightened out his cuffs, those dots of silver still glinting. 'Like what you see?'

'Maybe. You sure are sure of yourself, aren't you?'

He didn't miss a beat. 'Always.'

What an ego! I left him to it and went back to my surreptitious reading beneath the counter. I was trying to learn the studio system, but it seemed to be full of secret codes and handshakes that an outsider like me would never understand. Still, I tried. I'd cut out Hedda Hopper's Hollywood column from an old copy of the *LA Times* that some customer had left behind.

> UNFAIR! Paramount admits Phyllis Loughton is wonderful. Only reason they won't make her a fully fledged director is, so I'm told, they're afraid the men won't take orders from a lady. Since when, fellows, since when?

'You a fan of Hedda's?'

He was leaning over the counter, brazenly checking out my reading material, so close I could detect the fresh cedarwood of his cologne. Flustered, I folded the paper up into a tight, little square and shoved it into my apron pocket. 'None of your business.'

I moved down the counter, refreshing people's coffees. When I returned, he'd finished his shake. I handed him his bill. 'You can pay at the door.'

Instead of moving off, he rested his chin on his hand, staring at me hard, his brow furrowed.

My hand stilled over a glass cake dome. 'What?'

'I've figured it out.' He pointed a red-and-white straw at my little waitress cap. 'It's the hair.'

A hand flew to the nape of my neck. 'What's wrong with it?'

'Take a look around.'

I studied the other customers.

He leant over the counter again and summoned me with a wave of his hand. 'Let me whisper.'

I checked over my shoulder for my manager, then reached up on tiptoe.

'It's Audrey Hepburn,' he whispered, his breath hot in my ear. 'She changed her bangs last Thursday. They taper down to the ears now.' He sat back and tapped the side of his nose.

My eyes darted around. He was right! It was so obvious now. All the women had subtly restyled their pixie cuts. I licked my fingers and hastily rearranged my fringe. Watching me, he gave a crooked kind of smile. Immediately, the blood rushed up my chest. Part of me hated him already. But that's exactly how long it took for a beam to spread across his goddamn handsome face. He had me in that moment, and he knew it. I did, too.

'You blushing?'

'No.'

'Looks like it to me. New in town?'

'I couldn't possibly say.'

'Parents?'

Who did he think he was? 'None of your business.'

'Miss?' Another customer called over, pointing at his plate. I went to the chef to pile on more greasy bacon.

When I'd finished, my new friend was still there. He slid a business card across the counter: *Raphael Goddard, Booker, Blue Book Modeling Agency*.

My skin prickled. 'Blue Book?' I asked loftily. 'Never heard of it.' Of course I'd heard of it! But I wasn't going to let him know that. Blue Book was advertised in all the magazines as a way for a young model to start her career.

'You must be as green as they come.' His eyes sparked with amusement, as though he saw through my fib straight away. 'We have all the best models on our books. Cut your bangs, and you'd fit right in.'

'Who says I want to be a model?' I could feel my cheeks flaming.

'All right, so what *do* you want to be? Let me guess. A starlet? We can help with that, too, you know.'

I gave a thin smile. 'Not at all. I'm not in the game of paying to chase hopeless dreams.'

This seemed to amuse him. 'Come on, now . . . What do you really want?'

I looked at him from across the counter, my body melting as our eyes challenged each other. Talk about a loaded conversation. 'I'm going to be a make-up artist,' I said, answering the most obvious question. 'To the stars.'

He gave a low, impressed whistle and started to take back his business card. 'You certainly don't need me, then.'

I put out a hand to stop him and felt his forearm flex. 'Leave that with me,' I said, slipping the card into my apron pocket.

He glanced around the diner. 'But you already have a job.' His eyes twinkled, as though he didn't really believe in my dreams.

'I like to keep my options open,' I said.

He cocked his head. 'Always sensible. Are you?' He paused. 'Sensible?'

'What do you think?'

He leant back on his bar stool. 'I kind of hope not.'

'Boring?'

'Deathly.'

He made a big point of looking at the name on my kerchief. 'Well, *Loretta*, maybe we can talk.'

'When?'

'Loretta, table six is waiting!'

Reluctantly, I started to move away.

'You have my number. Call me.' He slapped a couple of dollar notes on the counter, before heading out. Two whole dollars! Before I could say anything else, he strolled out onto the sidewalk.

'Table six, Loretta!'

Impatiently, I headed towards a family of four, the dad with a Brownie camera hanging conspicuously around his neck. Tourists.

As I scribbled down their order, I watched through the window while Raphael Goddard sauntered fluidly down the sidewalk, like he didn't have a care in the world. As though his heart wasn't hammering, like mine was. As if he wasn't feeling unnaturally hot and flustered, like I was. He must have been one heck of a kidder, and that made me like him even more. I know, crazy, right? But what the heart wants, the brain ignores. And as he turned the corner and disappeared out of sight, I knew that I wanted that man like I'd never wanted any man before. And I would be making darn sure we'd be seeing each other again.

5

The hotel was set back from a long lawn, flanked by apartments, flags whipping from turrets, palm trees reaching up to the sky. This wasn't simply a hotel; it was a whole complex. A golf course, ballroom, theatre, parrots in the porch and more white-gloved staff than I could even begin to count. It took me half an hour just to locate the lobby and by then my feet hurt like hell.

He had taken over a sofa in the Cocoanut Grove. Was that Judy Garland sitting at the bar? I checked out her shoes, but they weren't red or sequinned. Disappointing. Instead, she wore some sort of backless mules with a low heel that looked far too comfortable for a movie star.

'You've had your bangs trimmed,' Raphael said by way of a greeting.

'I have?' I tried to sound casual, but a hand flew to my brow, betraying me. I'd stopped off at Primrose's on the way over here and she'd given me a quick restyle, using her sewing shears with a tea towel draped across my shoulders.

He took in the rest of me as I sank onto a chair opposite him. Earlier, I'd picked out my beaded cardigan and sweater set, carefully teaming them with a circle skirt to cinch in my waist. My make-up was subtle – a touch of pink across my upper brow, the same shade to colour in my cheeks. The lightest powder and a few drawn-in freckles. But the fake eyelashes had been a nightmare, the glue refusing to stick in this heat. Still, I was glad I'd taken the time. I felt proper enough for such an establishment.

A large, marble coffee table stretched between us over the thick, white carpet that was hoovered into straight lines like a rich person's lawn. Raphael felt very far away.

He lifted a cocktail glass and crooked a finger at a passing waiter. 'Another one of these,' he said, tapping a fingernail against the rim.

'Don't you ever say please?' I asked, after the waiter had departed.

Raphael laughed. 'Not if I can help it.'

'So, why did you want to meet?'

'You called me, remember?'

'You gave me your card, remember?'

'You were watching me out of the diner window, remember?'

Damn.

The waiter returned and placed a cocktail glass before me, something small and green floating in the clear liquid.

'It's called an olive,' he explained.

'I know.' I took a gulp and quickly swallowed down the choke that rose in my throat.

He raised his glass in a toast. 'And you're drinking a martini.'

'I'm not a total idiot.' I glanced around the room as though expecting to spot to a friend.

Unfazed, he waited for me to take another sip – smaller this time. 'You like it?'

'It's divine.' It was horrific. What was he trying to do? Kill me?

His lips quirked in amusement. 'You don't have to drink it, you know.'

'I like it.' I exploded into a fresh fit of coughing. Eyes red and watering, I inspected his infuriatingly symmetrical features. 'Why are you even doing this? Meeting up with a waitress from a no-mark diner?'

'Kid, you make me laugh.' It seemed like no explanation at all, but the way he said it felt like the world's greatest compliment.

Three hours and two martinis later, we were upstairs in a hotel bedroom. He had me naked and my new haircut all mussed up. My cheeks flushed as he pulled the Egyptian cotton bed sheet back to expose my curves, making my skin prickle with goosebumps.

'What do you want?' I asked. My desperate hope was to be ravished. It always sounded pretty splendid in the dime novels.

His face was so close that I could make out every individual eyelash. The rest of his face looked like an arrangement of circles – the pillows of his cheeks, the dimple in the plumpness of his chin, a freshness that still spoke of youth. Nothing sagged, nothing creased. I wondered how long that would last. A few more years, at most. If he wanted to break out as an actor – everyone here did – it would need to be soon.

He bent to kiss my throat. 'Everything.'

That sounded like . . . a lot. But whatever he was offering, I wanted it. He was so entirely different to anything I'd had before. I mean, not that I'd had a lot: a few fumblings down the alley beside the Winter Gardens or inside doorways – it's amazing what can be achieved when you're still living at home but impatient to grow up. But this was different. No street lamps, no wet, dark pavements, no catcalls from passing strangers. This was heat and light and glamour and sophistication, all tied up in one gorgeous man. I wanted to taste every bit of him.

He traced a finger down my jawline. 'You ready?'

I couldn't help laughing. 'You asking for permission?'

He slid a hand between my legs and received all the answer he needed.

6

Weak morning light broke through the curtains. Still groggy, I turned over on my pillow to gaze at the wonder of Raphael asleep. Men don't like to be told they're beautiful, as though it's some sort of insult to their levels of testosterone, but Raphael was. He was beautiful, his face all lines and angles as though carved from marble.

He must have sensed the weight of my gaze. He gave a sleepy groan and reached out for me. I scrambled over and dug my nose into the crook of his arm, drinking in the morning scent of his body.

Raphael laughed softly into my hair. 'You trying to wake me up?'

'No!'

He kissed the tip of my nose, and drew a finger across my brow, pushing the curls out of my face. 'Last night was nice, huh?'

'Nice?' I could think of other words. I moved closer, hoping for a sign, but a phone jangled. *A telephone! Right here, beside the bed!*

He hooked the receiver out of the cradle, leaving me to sulk from across the expanse of mattress. 'Hey, Mick,' he drawled. 'What's the score?'

I heard an urgent voice down the other end of the line. Raphael hung up, immediately swinging his legs out.

'Come on, sugar tits. Rise and shine!' He strode over towards the bathroom, rubbing his lower back.

'Sugar tits?' I untangled my body from the sheets and wriggled to the edge of the mattress.

There was a gurgle of water, then he peered round the bathroom door and grinned, still groggy from sleep, a toothbrush clenched between his teeth. 'Get dressed.' At least, that's what I think he said. He disappeared back behind the door, and I heard a flamboyant spit into the sink. Then he strode out, wiping his face down with a towel. He was still entirely naked. What a beautiful sight.

'We need to get out of here, pronto.' He was already marching around the room. 'Mick can only cover for so long. The maids will be here soon.'

Understanding prickled beneath my skin. I stood up, clutching the sheet around my body. 'You have to be kidding me.'

By now, Raphael was climbing into his pants. He tucked his shirt tails into his waistband. 'What?'

'You know what.'

'Oh. You don't like being called Sugar Tits? Yeah, sure, whatever – I apologize.'

My mouth twitched in a smile. 'Not that.'

'Oh good. Because you sure do have them.' He gave me a long, assessing glance as I stood there with the sheet tucked up to my chin. 'You're not one of those who goes all coy in the morning, are you?'

I dropped the sheet and ran across the room to throw myself at him, beating him with my fists. 'Tell me we paid for this room!'

He squinted up at me from where he was crouched, protecting his manhood. 'No, Loretta. We did not pay for this room.' He gently pushed me off to grab his jacket.

'Why the hell not?'

He went to the window and peeked out of the curtains, assessing the sidewalk. 'Mick and I do favours for each other.'

From beyond the bedroom door, there was the sound of an elevator pinging. Then voices gossiping softly and trolley wheels squeaking past. Raphael bugged his eyes at me, jabbing a finger at the door. 'Maids. Now we *really* need to go.'

'I can't believe you've put me in this position,' I hissed.

'Well, suck it up, kid.'

'But you signed in,' I reminded him. 'They'll know who you are.'

His mouth twitched. 'Fake name.' He looked me up and down. 'Better get dressed.'

I could tell that he expected me to drag on my clothes quickly like every other woman he'd had.

Instead, I stood there as bare as the day I was born.

'You need to get dressed,' he said.

'Or what?' I placed my hands on my hips, no longer caring what he could see – or what anyone else might.

There was the trundle of a laundry trolley and keys chiming from outside the door. He looked over at me, his tone anxious now. 'Come on, Loretta. This isn't a game any more.'

'That's what we're doing? Playing a game?'

'Oh, come on!' He'd run out of patience now, tripping up as he dragged his trousers over his ankles, hopping to one side with the effort. His eyes glared, as he fell back against the mattress. 'I mean it!'

The whole spectacle was laughable. This was the man who'd impressed me with his expensive watch and Hollywood contacts? I sauntered around the hotel room, slowly picking up my skirt, my sweater, taking my own sweet time . . . I glanced around, looking for my beaded cardigan, my eyes skimming the drained martini glass beside Raphael's side of the bed. The cardigan had fallen behind a chair. I leant over to rescue it, a cloud of sweat and sex billowing up off my body. I hadn't even had a chance to brush my hair or teeth.

'What now?' I said to Raphael.

'Now we make a run for it.'

He held a finger to his lips. I gave him a nod, and we tiptoed to the door. Raphael eased the handle down and poked his head out to check, then we slipped into the corridor. He hung the 'Do Not Disturb' sign on the handle, left the keys in the other side of the lock for Mick to find – then we ran for our lives.

There was a fire door at the end of the corridor. Ignoring the 'Staff Only' notice, Raphael led me down a set of concrete stairs. We skirted the hotel kitchens and burst out into the bright morning sunlight. *Oof.* I hadn't removed last night's make-up or even my eyelashes. I didn't want to think about how I looked. But Raphael didn't seem to notice. He scooped me up off my feet and swung me around, laughing into my hair in a pure, uninhibited way. Like a kid really. A kid who didn't care who heard, the laughter turning into a spurt of coughing as he leant over to be sick into the sloped alley that led to the hotel refuse bins. It was kind of romantic, if you didn't mind the rats and Raphael throwing his guts up.

'Are you OK?' I asked.

He wiped the last strands of bile that hung from his lips, nodding.

'You've done this before, haven't you?' I asked.

He lifted my hand and began to kiss my fingertips, one by one. I pulled away from the distinct smell of steaming vomit.

'That was a cheap trick,' I said.

He rolled his eyes. 'What did you think? That I'm a Hollywood millionaire?'

'I didn't expect you to be a thief.'

'Come on, I'm ravenous.' He glanced around as though this was all so ordinary. 'Let's get breakfast.'

I had to admit, I was hungry. Together, we broke into another run, up that litter-strewn alley and out onto the boulevard.

Whoever tells you that LA looks grim in the morning light hasn't seen it like I've seen it. It was glorious, in all its bawdy beauty, the neon lights switched off, the empty bottles in the street, overflowing bins, homeless sleepers and all. The wide sidewalks, palm trees reaching into the sky, the occasional red-tailed hawk circling in the clear morning sky. I loved every inch of it.

We turned down the sidewalk and slowed to a stroll, both of us silent as we breathed hard from our exertions.

'I didn't even have a chance to brush my teeth back there!' I protested, even though I was having the best fun in the world.

'Oh, don't worry about that.' Raphael slid a hand into his breast pocket to reveal a couple of items – one pink and one baby blue. 'Your friendly dentist here stole the toothbrushes.'

7

Raphael wasn't all I'd hoped he would be, but still – he was fun! – and we kept playing our games. He took me to a cinema, only for me to find out that it was dedicated to dirty movies. I took him to a real-live boxing match that I knew was rigged and watched him bet on the wrong man. You know, all the normal 'getting to know each other' stuff.

After each excursion, we'd retire to my bed, flip each other over and start tussling. But eventually the kidding around would stop and things would become serious. Intimate. I knew that it was a big deal to open up my heart to Raphael, as well as my legs, and it made me nervous as hell – which made it more exciting, which made it more scary, which made it more romantic. I was caught up in a big, endless circle of lust and . . . I don't want to say love exactly, but it was something close to that. And I sensed that Raphael felt something like it, too. With our limbs intertwined and our noses almost touching, we'd gaze into each other's faces as our hands explored.

'You know me better than anyone else in this whole damn world,' Raphael would murmur. Which meant that by the time that he turned up on my doorstep, carrying a cardboard box, he had me, good and proper.

That morning, I was painting my nails. When the doorbell rang, I levered myself up, trying not to touch anything, and awkwardly opened the door with the pads of my fingers, before running down the stairs to see who it was.

Through the panes of glass, I saw Raphael. He shifted the box to one side, freeing up a hand to wave at me. Then he pointed at the door lock, indicating for me to be quick.

I stepped aside. 'What are you doing here?'

'That's not much of a welcome. Here, take this.' He reached inside the overflowing box and thrust a bottle of wine into my hands so quickly that I had no choice but to take it. 'And this.' With it, came a corkscrew.

He moved towards the stairs, and I traipsed after him. 'What's going on?'

'We're celebrating.'

'And just what are we celebrating?'

'Us. Moving in together.'

I felt a flutter of nerves. 'Ha, ha – very funny.'

'No, I mean it.' He turned back. 'I'm moving in.'

I nearly dropped the bottle. 'You're what?'

He waved a finger between the two of us. 'You. Me. We're living together now.'

I shook my head, then broke into a run up the stairs after him, slamming the apartment door shut behind me. He owed me a manicure.

'This is crazy! We've only known each other a month!

And besides, I'm not allowed to sub-let,' I said, still not even sure if he was serious. But he had already placed the box on a kitchen counter and was reaching for the wine, which I was still holding. He gripped the bottle between his thighs and pulled on the corkscrew until the stopper emerged with a pop. A smug look of satisfaction on his face, he began to search through cupboards, slamming doors as he looked for wine glasses.

'To the right of the sink,' I said, too stunned to think straight.

'Ah, yes!' He handed me a glass. 'To us!'

'Raphael, what is going on?'

His mouth turned down. 'Nothing's going on. I just couldn't bear to be apart from you a moment longer. Speaking of which . . .'

He took hold of my spare hand and led me towards the bed.

'No,' I said. 'No, no, no . . .'

He raised a finger to his lips. 'Shush now.'

'You don't get it that easily!' But already I was laughing.

'What? What don't I get?' His smile teased me. It was always a game with Raphael.

'You don't get to just move in!'

He drew me into his embrace, kissing me on the lips. 'What don't I get?'

'You don't get to—'

He hooked a strap down my shoulder and kissed it.

Then he looked me straight in the eye. 'I don't get anything?'

'No, you don't!'

It wasn't going to take long for him to prove me wrong.

8

Not long after Raphael moved in, he wangled me a job, working in the mornings on Miss Snively's head shots – 'to help groom girls for careers in motion pictures' as the Blue Book Modeling Agency's catalogue said. My first in, and I grabbed it with both hands. Raphael was right; I could learn professional make-up *and* get paid for it, all at the same time.

The agency was run by a Miss Emmeline Snively, based in a retail outlet on the casino floor of the Ambassador Hotel.

'I have a young lady for you,' Raphael announced to the receptionist. He'd come to accompany me to the interview. I kept my smile fixed in place as Raphael shook my hand, pretending that he barely knew me.

'Best of luck,' he said, then turned and disappeared into some mysterious room, where he was greeted by a gale of delighted female cries. I was beginning to understand why he liked this job so much.

The receptionist was still looking after where Raphael had been a moment ago. Pointedly, I cleared my throat.

'Ah, yes!' She jolted back, before turning to her ledger. 'Now, Miss . . . ?'

'Miss Darling,' I repeated.

'That's right, you have an appointment at ten a.m.'

'I know,' I replied. Her glance darted up at me, testing to see if I was being sarcastic. I was, but I gave her my best winning smile. 'I do hope I'm on time.'

She picked up a telephone receiver and pressed a button. There was a rustle and then the faint sound of a voice. 'A . . . Loretta is here to see you,' the receptionist announced, before replacing the receiver. 'Second door on the left.'

I'd been more than a little excited to meet Miss Snively, the woman from the magazines who turned models into movie stars. I'd imagined all sorts of glamour – a mahogany desk, drapes at the window, Grecian columns – after all, I'd seen the photos of Hollywood execs' offices in the motion-picture magazines. By now, I considered myself an expert. So it was something of a surprise when I climbed some rickety stairs, the floor sloping towards the rear wall. She sat at a desk that was far too big for the room – second-hand? – and was tucking a lace-trimmed handkerchief up her sleeve, eyes bloodshot above a red nose. Someone – herself, most likely – had given her a very bad dye job, which made her hair look like a helmet. On the wall behind her was a corkboard covered in photos of cover girls from magazines.

She didn't bother to smile. 'Please, sit.'

Out of nowhere, nerves began to squirm in my stomach as I realized how badly I wanted this job. Working as a waitress to pay the bills was all well and dandy, but it wasn't why I'd blackmailed my way out here. This was my chance.

'So . . .' She read through notes. 'Mr Goddard says that you're a make-up artist.'

'Well, I certainly have a great passion for it,' I said, my mouth suddenly dry.

'Qualifications?'

'Self-taught.'

She raised an eyebrow. 'Cheap, then.'

I didn't say anything to that. She had my number. I was just about resigned to getting up and leaving after the shortest job interview in the history of the world, but then she held out a hand.

'Résumé.'

I reached into my pocketbook and handed her the résumé that Raphael had helped me pull together. One of Primrose's girls – an ex-secretary – had typed it up for me. We had lied through our teeth, inventing jobs back in Morecambe. Revamping working as an assistant on the Woolies make-up counter, selling lipsticks on commission that none of those women actually needed – at least that bit was true. Graduating to doing the make-up for musical acts at the Winter Gardens. Not so true. Coming out to Hollywood with the specific dream of working with Miss Snively. The biggest whopper of them all. I'd just wanted to escape.

She scanned my sheets of paper and then cast them aside. 'Accent's cute. Done your own make-up?'

'Yes.'

'Come here.' She wheeled her chair back from her desk. 'Bend down.'

I did as I was told, looking to one side as she inspected

my face. I'd been extra careful that morning, taking time over grooming my eyebrows and applying the freckles. I'd used an especially fine powder to set my base and my favourite trick of extending the lipstick just past my lip line. Primrose had even trimmed my bangs for me.

'You'll do. Go back and sit down.' I felt like a cadet in the army. 'Now, here's the deal.' She leant forward on the desk, her chair creaking dangerously and her arms folded primly. 'I have thirty girls on my books. You'll do the make-up for their head shots. Blondes are best – easy, you know. We get all sorts through these doors, so you'll have your work cut out for you. Just tell all of them how beautiful they are. I provide the make-up supplies, so go easy. Are we clear?'

I nodded dumbly.

'I'll pay your wages weekly on a Friday.' She named a sum that was a tiny bit more than I earned at Van de Kamp's. 'You can start next week.' She passed my résumé back to me.

'Thank . . . thank you,' I stuttered.

She flapped a hand, indicating that I should leave. 'You're lucky. Kelly quit yesterday and I need someone fast.'

Despite her thinly veiled insult, I floated out of that office, down the hallway and past the receptionist.

'Did it work out?' she called after me, as I headed to the main door.

I turned and grinned. 'It did. I'm your new make-up artist.'

'Sweet! You're gonna love it here. Miss Snively is just the best.'

Did I detect sarcasm? It was always so hard to judge out here; Americans always came across as sincere even when they weren't. Whatever. We'd done it; Raphael and I had pulled it off. My entry into the world of professional make-up had begun.

9

Dear Enid,

I have a brand-new job as a make-up artist! You'd be so proud of me!!

> *The place is run by a Miss Snively — and yes, she's as dour as her name . . . It's not the most glamorous establishment but my patent leather pump, or should I say your patent leather pump (thanks for the loan!), is firmly in the door. Well, a toe at least!*

> *I hope you and the baby are doing just fine. I haven't heard from you in a while. (Read, ever.)*

> *Let me know if you need a return envelope or some money or something. I can spare it now. (I couldn't.)*

> *Send my love to everyone.*

Margaret x

Miss Snively was quite the education. She taught lessons in visual grooming and professional presentation. Models were shown how to make a good first impression, put wardrobes together, and pull a pleasing expression. She'd give them mock interviews, posing tips and personality counselling – this largely involved telling the girls to keep quiet. My favourite lesson was 'how to be outstanding'. I mean, these girls could have paid me to show them that!

As a general rule, Miss Snively preferred her models to be single.

'Christ!' she'd screech. 'If I need to deal with one more over-protective husband or another shitty nappy, I'll pay for the divorce and abortion myself!'

She'd keep notes on each new model, written in a sloping hand: *Blue eyes, blonde, curly hair, crooked teeth. Better undergarments required.*

Every girl was reduced to a column of statistics. They were expected to have their own wardrobes, to change the colour of their hair at the drop of a hat, and if they didn't have the money to pay her fees, she'd take them out of future earnings.

No doubt about it, these girls were trapped, from the moment they signed on the bottom line. Some – some! – of Miss Snively's models had managed to feature on the front of *Time*, *Life* and *People* magazines. More often than not, though, our clients would end up as small-fry hostesses, standing at gambling tables or trying out for beauty contests. I couldn't see how anyone was going to make their fame and fortune from these gigs. Was *I* a fool to hope for more?

My role was to make up the models for their head shots. And I was learning how to curl hair that hadn't been washed in a week, to sculpt cheeks for the camera with a creamy layer of pancake with dustings of powder to set. It would never have worked out on the street, but it did in front of a studio camera, where the women were taught to hold a pose, reclining on a chair or wearing a bathing suit. We were taught to make the starlets glamorous, exaggerating their small smiles, or make someone look wholesome even if they weren't. We had to work around their wonky teeth or frizzy hair. There would be props as the models carried a candle, wore a swimming cap or held a surfer's board. All of them working for five dollars an hour. Miss Snively liked what she called 'natural awareness' – the ability to cross legs just right or angle a head, occasionally flicking hair.

It could have been so easy to forget the make-up, but we never did. We were turning these people from rank amateurs to somewhat professionals – if we did our job right. Bangs were cut, chests were exposed, and Hawaiian garlands worn.

But none of that meant anything without make-up. We needed moist lips, open eyes, camouflage and strong eyebrows. I knew how to do all that.

The rest of the make-up artists and I employed some of the new techniques that we'd learnt. Then there were the brow pencils, the lip liners . . . It was art, really. I came to love blondes as much as Miss Snively – they could be photographed in any light, the girls so excited to have an actual professional make-up job.

Bless their deluded little hearts. And all the time, we were being watched by posters on the wall.

'Tell me about this guy,' I said to a girl one day. I pointed to one of the images. Small guy, moustache. 'Petraś something?'

My model glanced up from beneath the bleach that was undoubtedly frying her hair. 'Alecs Petraś? Only the greatest make-up artist in Hollywood!'

'Polish royalty,' called over one of the other models. 'A prince!'

I didn't even know the Poles *had* royalty.

'Yes, thank you, Marcy. I can take it from here.' My model sat up straighter in her chair, clearly annoyed at having her moment interrupted. 'He fled to America from Poland in 1918 when the royal family was abolished over there.' This girl had really done her homework. 'He'd lost all his money and connections, so started as a pharmacist, but then became a full-on make-up artist.'

'All the actresses want him!' the other model interrupted again. 'Oh, to have Alecs Petraś do your make-up!' She gazed into the middle distance as though she was having some sort of religious moment.

I glanced between the two of them. If Petraś inspired this level of devotion from people who had never even met him . . . I wanted in! How hard could it be? Here was I, here was he. We were in the same old, same small town. Hollywood was notorious for chance encounters. Me and this Petraś guy? It was destiny that we'd bump into each other! Or if it wasn't destiny, I'd make it happen, sure as my ma had ever promised me that I was born to be something, or someone. Definitely, someone. Definitely, a friend of Petraś. Because to think otherwise was impossible. It was the whole reason I'd come out here! All I had to do was find my chance . . . as long as I wasn't distracted.

Distraction. The worst, most evil word in Hollywood ever. Ask me how I know.

10

Every morning, I'd work on the models. Afternoons and evenings, I'd be at Van de Kamp's, wearing my little embroidered kerchief and collecting my tips. Often, I'd get home in the small hours of the morning with Raphael waiting up for me. We'd place candles along the windowsill and sit on the fire escape to eat slices of pizza, wiping the grease from our chins, slugging beer and talking until the candles guttered and blinked out.

One night, he sat with his socked feet up on the windowsill, forearms resting on his knees, and he looked at me.

'So, what *are* your dreams?' He nudged my thigh with his toe.

'Dreams?'

'All right, plans. How do you expect to take over the world? I mean, that's why you're here, isn't it ?'

'I just want to be a make-up artist.'

He sent his head back and roared with laughter, clearly mocking me. 'My fucking ass!'

I grinned. 'I don't know how your *arse* fucks.'

His eyelids lowered and he gave me a straight stare. 'Don't kid a kidder, Loretta. Come on, we've known each other long enough by now.'

'Well, obviously, if I'm going to make it here, I need

legal status.' I couldn't rely on cash wages if I was going to build my career.

'Now we're getting somewhere.' He reached for a slice of pizza. 'So, you need me. Agreed?'

'Well, it doesn't have to be you.' I shrugged. 'It could be anyone.'

His pizza paused halfway to his mouth. 'Jeez, you're confident.'

'And what about you? What do you want?'

'You know what I want.' I reached over to slide a hand down his thigh. 'No, not that. I mean, sure – that. But the other stuff. I want to be an actor. A big one – not one of those bit-part players.'

'Can I help?'

He considered. 'You could. I need someone by my side who understands the game – and I think you do. Someone I can be honest with, who won't get upset when I have to go to auditions or be out filming on the other side of the world.'

I couldn't help it; I thought his plans were racing far ahead of what he was actually capable of. He was still working for Miss Snively, for goodness' sake! But I wasn't about to point that out to him: the handsome boy who'd come to Hollywood to turn himself into a star.

'And you think that should be me?' I said. 'The wife who'd go along with your plans?'

'Wife?' He nearly choked on his beer, but I could tell it was an act. A bad one at that.

'I thought that's what we were discussing. You do me a favour; I support your career. If you don't like it, you can always go back to Mick's.' Here, he got rent-free accommodation and sex on tap. Plus, I was helping him tone down his look – fewer of the gaudy suits and more sophistication. He needed my eye; I needed his name. It was such a simple transaction.

'All right, then,' he said. 'I'll think about it.' He brushed the pizza crumbs off his shirt and reached across for dessert – me. I pretended to fight him off, but it was a half-hearted fight and he knew it. He scooped me up by my waist and carried me over to the bed. As soon as he let go, I ran round to the other side, raising my fists into mock punches.

'You'll think about it?' I challenged.

He leapt onto the bed and strode across the mattress, his body rolling and swerving above the tired springs, the lampshade swinging wildly from where his head knocked into it. Then he grabbed my wrist and pulled me down beside him.

'I'll think about it. Now, come here.' He leant over and dragged his cheek across mine, the stubble stinging my skin just as he knew it would.

'Ow! Get off!' I tried to push him off me, but he was stronger. I wriggled and twisted my face from side to side, trying to avoid his teasing. Finally, he had my wrists pinned down either side of my throat.

'You don't want me?' he asked.

'I don't want you. I need you,' I said, my breath coming out in abrupt pants.

We both knew what was going on. He let go of my wrist to slide a hand up my skirt and between my thighs, and then he released my other wrist, too, his arms enfolding my body, suddenly tender. It was the tenderness that did me in. I'd never had that, not in those back alleys. Raphael might have been a bit of a bastard at times, but he was *my* bastard, and he always knew what to do at just the right time. He understood me then, that I needed the needing.

In the morning, we'd fuck again. I'd wake up extra early. It didn't take much – as soon as he sensed my body moving, he'd unfurl and grow hard. His hand would tuck beneath my hair and, without sharing a single word, we'd begin. Often, it was silent. I'd listen to the sounds of the rest of the apartment block waking up, the radiators ticking, the garbage men shouting to each other from the back yard. It wasn't what you'd call romantic, but I didn't need it to be.

Afterwards, I'd get up and pad around the apartment, picking up my discarded uniform and sneaking into the bathroom to dress. He'd fall asleep and start snoring again. I'd pause by the bed and watch him, his lips loose, his face creased up against the pillow. I loved those moments, knowing that he couldn't sense me watching.

One particular morning, I emerged from the bathroom to find him propped up in bed, arms folded across that gorgeous expanse of chest. His hair was tousled, and I had to fight every urge in my body not to climb onto his lap and straddle him.

'I was thinking,' he began.

'Yes?'

'About your suggestion.' Casually, he picked an invisible fleck of dust off the eiderdown. 'You're right. We should make this arrangement more formal.'

'Are we talking about . . . marriage?' I placed a dramatic hand against my brow and pretended to swoon.

He laughed and patted the edge of the mattress. 'Get over here, kiddo. Let me explain.'

No way. If I let him get hold of me, there'd be absolutely no way of getting to work on time. 'Just tell me.'

'You sure you want to stay all the way over there?'

'Quite sure.' I made a big point of glancing at my wristwatch.

He held up his hands in mock surrender. 'All right, all right, have it your way. So, I was talking to a few of the fellas in the Screen Actors Guild.'

'And?'

'And apparently the studios like their actors to have a nice wife. A man who doesn't have a family is missing something . . .'

'You're asking me to get pregnant!'

'No! But you know . . . there's the Hays Code.' When he saw my blank face, he gave another sigh. 'Morals, Loretta. We all need to be seen as whiter than white, right now.'

'OK, I get that.' Honestly, I wasn't convinced that Raphael had a political thought in his head, other than how to get ahead. 'But is this about us or is it about politics?' I said, crossing my arms.

'It's about us! This is a mutually beneficial arrangement. Just look at Danny Kaye and Sylvia Fine. It worked fine for them.'

I blinked. 'I didn't know you were that way inclined.'

'Ha, ha, very funny. You know what I mean.' He gave an immaculately lazy grin. 'This is our chance, Loretta, to build our careers together and you'll be legal. Isn't that what you've always wanted?'

Legitimacy. Everything I'd ever hoped for.

I couldn't stand it any more. 'I'll take that!'

I burst out into a run and leapt onto the bed, near about ready to break it and screeching with delight. I flung my arms around him, dragging him on top of me, wanting to be pinned down by the weight of his body.

He gave me a long kiss and then pulled away. 'Thought you were all worried about the politics.'

'Fuck politics.' Already I was halfway out of my uniform.

'Snively will be furious,' he said, watching me wriggle to get naked.

I straddled him. 'There's only one model booked and it will take at least two hours to get her hair right.' We both grinned. Then I pulled my soon-to-be husband close and we sank back between the sheets.

11

Enid! I'm getting married – and on my twenty-first birthday! I
hope you're thrilled for me, but you're not allowed to tell anyone
because Miss Snively wouldn't give me the day off, so I'm going
to call in sick – ha, ha! I so wish you could be here for the
wedding, but . . . Well, it's a long way, isn't it, and there's Ma
to think of. Do you remember my eighteenth in the church hall,
when I slapped that uncle for feeling me up? Ma still hasn't
forgiven me . . . has she? I wish she would. How are you? I
miss you. It would be good to hear your news. Any wedding bells
of your own ringing? You never know!

Margaret x

On my twenty-first birthday, I wore an oatmeal linen suit
that I'd retrieved from the depths of a thrift store. With
a Peter Pan collar, mother-of-pearl buttons and a belted
jacket, it felt right somehow: not too ostentatious for a
bride who was going to call into work sick. I didn't have
a wedding bouquet. Raphael said the flowers would only
wilt in the heat, and I tried not to mind too much. I was
going to wear pale make-up to suit my skin, but then in
the end I went for a bright-red lipstick and killer eyelashes. I mean, you only get married once, right?

The ceremony was performed by Father Cornelius

McCoy – known for not asking too many questions. He claimed he had Irish heritage, as though drinking in Tom Bergin's was some sort of proof. Anyone could sit in a booth beneath a paper shamrock, so I told him all about Da's relatives across the water in Galway. Characterful bunch. Almost too funny to be true. Father McCoy didn't seem to notice that the names of half of them changed according to whether or not I was on my first or third half pint of Guinness.

Mick had already faked the paperwork, just like Raphael had said he would. He acted as witness, along with Primrose.

'Married?' she'd asked when I first told her about our plans. 'You certain?'

'He makes me happy.'

'Good in bed?'

I grinned shamelessly. 'Crazy good.'

She lit a Lucky Strike, and a thin column of blue smoke curled up towards the ceiling, her eyes narrowing. 'Baby, you know – you can get off without needing to get hitched. You pregnant?'

'No!

'You sure? I could help with that.'

'Yes! I mean, no! I mean . . . What is this? You training for the Gestapo?'

'Then . . . why?' She brushed a hand across my brow, making me feel very young. Her voice softened. 'You're a pretty girl. Clever to boot. Why don't you wait a bit?'

I took her hand in mine. 'He's good for me, and I'm good for him.'

She hesitated. 'You know, I don't think he's all that he seems.'

'Which of us is?' I said, bristling.

'Talk to me,' she coaxed.

'We ... we support each other. I help get him all suited and booted for Hollywood; he gives me legal status.'

Primrose looked doubtful. 'And love? Does that come into it at all?'

In that moment, I wanted to hug her. There was some part of her despite all she'd seen, all she'd experienced, that stayed so deliciously romantic.

Instead, I ground out my cigarette. 'Love isn't really part of the plan,' I explained.

'That's a shame.'

I felt my face harden. 'Is it?'

'Oh, darling.' She stroked a hand down my cheek. 'Some day you'll find out that it really should be.'

I turned my face and kissed the palm of her hand. 'You can help me organize the reception if you like.'

Her brow furrowed. 'Sounds expensive.'

'Don't worry. We'll hold it at my place.'

'OK, then,' she said softly. 'It would be my honour to help.'

The plan was agreed. Primrose gave up on her protestations and for the next three weeks we had every waitress at Van de Kamp's stealing beer.

I 2

Primrose and I stared at the bathtub, filled to the rim. I plucked a beer bottle out of the dripping water and used the opener tied with string to the faucet. I eased away the cap in a hiss of gas. Music drifted through from Raphael's turntable. It was gone midnight. If the neighbours hadn't already called the cops, they surely would soon.

Primrose came to sit on the side of the bath. 'How does it feel?'

'Grand.' Actually, the ceremony had been small and over so quickly that I wasn't sure how it had felt. I knew that I'd missed Ma and Enid being there.

I went to the mirror to refresh my lipstick. I had a little cosmetic case that lived beneath the sink. Raphael would often complain about the lack of space in the studio he barely paid rent on. He had his sights set on a bigger apartment, one with an actual bedroom. For myself, I didn't care. I loved our little space, a clothes rail rescued from the sidewalk, a sewing machine borrowed from the agency tucked into the corner by the window. Compared to my bedroom back home, this was a palace.

The music snapped off.

'Loretta? Could you come out, please?'

Primrose winked at me. After a final, refreshing sweep

of red, I felt my confidence return and popped the lid back on my lipstick to follow her out into the main room. The lights had been switched off and people burst into song as they gathered round a cake. The number *21* was curled in loops of icing.

Raphael held the cake out, his beautiful face lit up from below by the candles. He'd done this for me? The great Raphael Goddard had gone to all the trouble to find me a birthday cake? Our eyes met over the candles and it was as though everyone else in the room faded away.

'My darling husband,' I said, my throat suddenly thick with emotion. What was wrong with me?

'My darling wife,' he said softly, and for once his acting skills were top-notch. Or maybe he actually meant it. Then he broke my glance and looked around the room. 'Come on, guys!'

He launched into singing 'Happy Birthday', the others quickly joining in. Some of them stumbled when it came to my name – not everyone here was a close friend exactly – but I didn't mind. Or, at least, I tried not to mind.

'Blow 'em out!' he cried, as the singing faltered to an end.

I closed my eyes and paused for a moment to take it all in. I knew what I had in this little room was more than most people could dream of. But I blew on the candles and made a wish for more anyway.

Everyone cheered again and someone put a new record on the turntable as Raphael and I gazed into each other's eyes once more. Our pact was official. The ring was on my finger now, and no one could ever take it away.

'Thank you,' I said.

He grinned crookedly. 'Oh, there's more!'

Before I could ask what he meant, a friend of ours came to link an arm through Raphael's and dragged him off to dance – he only just had time to place the cake on a side table. Her partner scooped me up and circled me round, my head twisting. I couldn't take my eyes off my shiny new husband.

Raphael abandoned his partner – I admit to a spurt of satisfaction – and leapt onto the bed. He caught up a tumbler and raised it in the air.

'To Mrs Goddard!'

Everyone cheered for what felt like the nth time that evening. He held out his glass towards me, whisky spilling onto the bedding. 'And now? A surprise.'

'Another one?' Why did I feel so uncertain?

'But, of course.'

If he'd noticed that anything was wrong, he didn't show it. Resplendent in his pink suit, Raphael herded us out of our apartment to a volley of cars. All we needed were trotting horses wearing plumes of feathers to make the Cinderella scene complete.

'You sit here, Loretta.' He snapped his fingers. 'Come.'

'Where exactly are we headed?' My feet wobbled in my satin heels as I slid into the passenger seat. I'd borrowed the shoes from Primrose, but she hadn't had much time to teach me how to walk in them. Let's be frank, she very rarely *walked* in them herself.

'You'll see.' Raphael took his place behind the wheel and I felt a ripple of excitement flow through me. He shouldn't have been in a motor car at all – he'd been drinking since breakfast – but I was way past caring. I snuggled up next to him as we swung out of the drive, leading the others in a carnival train as wedding guests leant out of windows, whooping and hollering.

We drove out beyond the perimeters into that Californian night, stars hanging over us like crystals threaded in our hair. The city noises faded away as we drew a long, lazy streak across the tarmac, white-wall wheels eating up the road as headlights sliced through the dark towards the Hollywood hills. It felt as though we were the original gold diggers, our spades thrown into the trunk. All we needed was a glint of magic to make us turn off the road, churning up clouds of dust behind us. *This is an evening for fantasies*, I thought. I should have been careful what I wished for.

The first warning sign was the jazz. That, and the girls dancing naked in the turrets.

Raphael pulled in and came round to my side, gallantly opening the door. He held out a hand. 'My darling wife, we've arrived.' His voice slurred.

Hesitantly, I took his hand and slid out of the car, turning my hips for discretion's sake as my skirt rode up across my stockings – my last decent pair. I gazed up at the huge, white stuccoed walls of . . . What should I have called it? A mansion? A folly? It was a Mexican-style villa, unlike anything I'd ever seen before, sprinklers cascading over an emerald lawn that surely didn't belong out here in the desert. Beyond them, the low, uneven foothills of Californian mountains.

A partygoer, wearing only a feather boa to cover her modesty, ran over to welcome us. Through Primrose and the girls, I'd become very familiar with the female anatomy, but in this cool California evening she looked . . . well, chilly. As she drew closer, I concentrated on keeping my eyes fixed on her face. Raphael wasn't so circumspect.

Laughter trilled out. 'Hi!' she said brightly. 'I'm Daisy.' She looked me up and down. 'Hey, you're cute.'

I gave a thin smile and held out a hand, but she wrinkled her nose and shook her boa in my face instead. Raphael was already moving ahead. Daisy ran to catch up with him and linked an arm through his, raising up on tiptoe to kiss his cheek.

Watching their silhouettes move towards the house, I blinked. They knew each other.

I called Raphael back. 'Hey!'

He patted Daisy on the rump, shooing her ahead.

He strolled back. 'Yeah, honey?'

I jerked my chin towards the villa. 'What the hell is this?' The others were already running ahead, laughing. 'Were they in on this?'

Raphael reached out for me, but I stepped away.

'I wanted it to be a surprise.' There was an unexpected desperation in his face. 'Listen.' He experimented with shuffling along the car, closer to me. 'I had no idea that the dates would clash, but we . . .' He smiled fixedly. 'We really need to be here.'

'We?'

He at least had the ability to look shame-faced. 'OK, me . . .'

I looked down at my wedding suit, the oatmeal lit up by the moon. My corsage was already flagging. 'Look, I know we had an arrangement, but this? You just slapped a girl on her naked arse! It's . . . humiliating.'

He took hold of my hands. 'It shouldn't feel that way. It's just, I dunno, negotiation.'

'With a bunch of people who are half out of their minds? They're not going to remember any conversation you have tonight.' I pulled my hands free.

Another car drew up and a crowd of people merrily spilled out, calling to Raphael as they ran past. He waved back, but his smile dropped the moment he turned back to me.

'Stanley Hughes will be here. You know, the director?' He must have seen the blank look on my face. 'Remember, sweetie?' His voice wheedled now. 'I told you about him.' He saw my hesitation, and his face turned dark. 'What? Now a guy can't even surprise his wife on her wedding day?'

'Oh, so you're doing this for me?' I took a step back, suddenly wanting to be nowhere near him. I strode round the other side of the car, keeping a careful distance between the two of us as he stalked after me, the two of us drawing a tight circle. 'An orgy? This is your grand plan for success?'

Raphael was starting to look around. 'I hate it when you talk like this,' he muttered. 'Why do you always have to be so . . . direct?'

'Oh, I'm sorry. Am I embarrassing you?'

'Actually, Loretta, yes.' He grabbed my arm. 'Remember where you are. This party is a big deal, and it could do you some favours, too, you know.'

I shook him off. 'Oh, yes, I forgot. All those prostitutes! Guess I can give them a free makeover.'

He pointed a finger in my face. 'Well, so what? You do that now, anyway.'

'For my friends,' I blurted. 'Not for . . .' I flung out a hand to the girl wearing a feather boa. 'I don't even know who she is!'

'Does that make her less than Primrose?'

'Primrose has nothing to do with this! She warned me about you, and I—'

'Oh, how delightful. Glad you two have had a chance to bitch about me.'

'We weren't bitching, it was just . . .' What to say? That Primrose had been right all along? I didn't want to believe it. I was all for building my career, but I very much doubted that my personal advantages would come about by attending a sex-fuelled party.

'Don't play this game,' he growled dangerously. 'We made a pact.'

'Not one that involved sex!' I said. 'At least not sex with strangers.'

'I'm not asking either of us to have sex with strangers. I'm just asking that we attend. Mingle. See who we end up talking to.' He shook his head in disbelief. 'I thought you were ambitious, Loretta.'

This was all another game to him. Well, if that was the

case, it was one I wasn't going to lose. I straightened the flowers in my lapel. 'Come on. I guess if we're doing this, we're doing it.'

Relief broke out across Raphael's face. 'I knew you'd understand. We're two of a kind, you and I.'

'Well, good job because we're married now.'

There was a shout from up ahead, and a man waved.

'Hey, you rogue! How ya been?' Raphael called back. He held out the crook of his elbow to me. 'Come on. Come and meet everyone. Honestly, once you're in there, you'll like it. It'll be fun.'

'You go ahead.' I needed time to think. 'Just gonna fix my make-up.'

Raphael gave me a hasty kiss on the cheek. 'Good idea. Make yourself pretty, but don't be too long. I want to introduce you.' He broke out into a jog towards his friend, hooting with laughter when he inevitably stumbled. They slapped each other on the back and disappeared inside.

Make myself pretty? What a joke he was. Still, I reached into the car for my handbag. There was the sound of a door slamming. Primrose. Clearly, she'd been fixing her own make-up – red lipstick to match her dress – in one of the other vehicles. She must have heard the whole conversation.

She looked at me. 'He has a high opinion of prostitutes, huh?'

I snapped the lid back on my lipstick. 'Well, he can go to hell with his opinions.' I linked arms with hers.

'You have more sass than he has in his little finger,

Loretta.' Her arm came around my shoulder and she pulled me into her, kissing my brow. 'Oh, honey.'

I couldn't stop staring after where Raphael had been, just a moment ago.

'Whose party is it, anyway?' I asked bleakly.

'An actor. Apparently he calls himself the Emperor of Hollywood.'

'And that's his coliseum,' I muttered, taking in the crazy turrets and parapets all over again. At last they made sense.

'Well, let's look on the bright side,' Primrose said. She tapped her toe as music floated out towards us. 'Tonight may finally be my night to be discovered, too.' She let go of me to make jazz hands and turned a tiny pirouette. Despite myself, laughter bubbled up in my throat.

Her body stilled beside me. 'Come on, let's do this.' She held out her hand.

After a moment's hesitation, I threaded my fingers between hers and the two of us walked towards the entrance. I could just make out a set of glass doors and then the aquamarine oblong of a swimming pool, with people bobbing about in the water. That was one thing I learnt on my wedding day, at least. *Never* go swimming at an orgy.

13

I never expected my first orgy to be quite this glamorous. It was full of actors, actresses, directors, producers, writers – all looking for distraction. And, boy, had they found it. The stars worked their butts off during the week, but on a weekend they partied hard.

Still, nothing had prepared me for this.

The smiles were painted on as thick as the Silver Stone No. 2 body paint some of the naked girls were smothered in as they paraded around in their swimsuits and feather headdresses. Clouds of blue cigar smoke billowed above our heads. Have you ever heard the rattle of a studio executive's laughter? I tell you, it sends a chill down your spine.

I walked past a tight clutch of men in suits, one of them loudly complaining, 'I brought the son of a bitch over from Europe, paid for his passage, and all he does is tell me that the story I paid eighty thousand for is no good.' As one, the group turned and stared darkly at the oblivious young actor who was kissing a woman by the pool.

Primrose was still holding my hand and my grip tightened as we gazed around.

'Keep smiling,' she said from between clenched teeth. 'Just keep smiling!'

An older woman walked past, tits hanging like spaniel ears. She sat on a young waiter's lap, and he squeezed the crêpey skin of her thighs. Another waiter appeared with a tray of shimmering martinis. I grabbed a drink, watching the scene over the rim of my glass. Primrose and I backed into the shadows beside the tennis court.

Have you any idea what a middle-aged man's derrière looks like in the buff? It's not for the faint-hearted. And the hair! It was everywhere. There was one man with a head as bald and shiny as a billiard ball but with a pubic region that could have claimed national park status.

'Don't these guys ever groom?' Primrose whispered out of the side of her mouth, after a man in a flapping silk kimono walked past, nodding hopefully at us. Beneath his kimono bobbed a large but bent erection, nestled in what looked like a bird's nest.

A cigarette girl wearing a satin corset approached us. Instead of popcorn and cigarettes, her tray was full of . . . other stuff.

'Joy powder?' she offered. 'Or maybe a girl-on-girl surprise?' She held up something ribbed that wobbled merrily in her hand.

'Er, no . . . thank you,' I replied.

Her mouth fell open. 'That accent!' She turned and waved a hand over her shoulder. 'Hey, Hank! Come and meet this one! She's from *Europe*!'

Arms suddenly grabbed me from behind as a wet mouth kissed my ear.

'Hey there,' my husband whispered. He took hold of my hand and raised it above my head, forcing me round in a twirl. I couldn't decide if I wanted to kiss him or throw him into the pool.

'Enjoying yourself?' he asked.

'Not yet. You found your guy?'

Raphael's smile turned into a grimace. 'Working on it.'

Primrose tapped me on the shoulder.

'Oh, hey, look!' Raphael said. 'The prom queen's here!' He pretended to look around. 'Where's your beau?'

Primrose ignored his bad attempt at a joke and I shot my new husband a filthy look, which he ignored. 'I'm gonna check out the piano player,' was her reply.

'That's my pal you're talking to!' I hissed, as Primrose stalked away. 'You know, the one who helped organize our wedding?'

'Yeah, yeah, whatever.' Without looking back, he jogged after a waiter carrying a cocktail shaker. I found myself alone and feeling awkward. *Come on, Loretta. Go and explore. How bad can it be?*

The heat hit me the instant I stepped through the floor-to-ceiling glass doors, sweat prickling my armpits. I shrugged off my jacket and tossed it over a sofa, the petals of my wedding corsage crumpling.

I gazed around, taking in the sunken floor. One, two, three . . . six, seven, eight . . . After ten, I gave up counting the bodies. More than I could keep in my head, limbs slippery with sweat. My mother would have been down there with a bottle of bleach in two shakes of a lamb's tail, but I wasn't sure there was enough detergent in the world to tackle those people.

There was a gale of laughter from above and I glanced

up the stairs, desperate for something – anything! – that didn't involve bodily fluids. Spotting a stairwell, I pushed past the dancing girls and the men tipping out little dots of white powder.

I wandered up, following the slow hiss of a record player's needle as it repeatedly caught in a groove. As I placed a foot on the top step, a new record dropped down and I recognized the jazz lullaby immediately. 'Hush Little Baby'. Ma had sung it to Enid and me as the three of us huddled up together beneath her eiderdown.

A woman – I guessed in her mid-thirties – stood on top of a grand piano, her heels scratching the varnish as a column of cigarette ash fell from the tip of an ebony cigarette holder. She looked vaguely familiar, the loops of pearls casting a glow beneath the tilt of her chin and then I realized who it was. Louise Brooks, star of the silent screen. I only recognized her because Ma had adored her European films. But now – *lord*. Her eyes had dark shadows beneath them and the shingled bob badly needed a trim. She looked so alone. A star fallen from the galaxy, drowning in a martini glass.

'She's a courtesan now,' someone whispered in my ear, as they walked past.

I turned to see who had spoken but they'd disappeared into a small crowd gathered around something on the other side of the room. As the silent-movie star turned another pirouette, I wandered over, unable to watch any longer.

At our feet was what looked to be an oblong of reinforced glass in the mezzanine floor. Below the glass, a bed. On the bed, a couple. I felt my palms suddenly turn damp as I watched the bouncing motion of a pair of buttocks, skin downy as peaches with an odd little birthmark by the dimple above his left cheek. Beneath the pounding lay a woman, her eyes rolling back in her head as she reached a languid hand out across the bed and caught up a red, polished fingernail of cocaine, tipping it across her lover's broad shoulder to sniff.

'Jesus,' a man muttered. 'Does Stanley know he's being used as a snuff bullet?'

Stanley? The director Raphael was so desperate to meet?

The woman lifted her face from the spectacle, her own glance dead and hollow. There were so many of us, silently watching the scene play out below our feet. It must have been one-way glass – the man had no idea he was being observed. But from the way his lover's eyes stared up at their ceiling – our floor – I guessed that she did. I fleetingly wondered how much she was being paid, or if she was being paid at all.

'Clear the way!' a voice boomed, as a door slammed shut and a tall, broad man strode over, wearing a billowing silk shirt and silver cufflinks that flashed beneath the lights. He looked kind of young, despite the scar on his brow and his lavish clothes. There was a high sheen of sweat across his face and a limp lock of hair that suggested he'd been drinking for hours. Our host, I guessed. The Emperor.

He came to join our party, a sly grin splitting his face. Then he raised a warning finger to his lips. Once we'd all gone quiet, he stamped his foot against the parquet floor. The buttocks beneath us froze in shock, before resuming their piston speed. Our host roared with laughter and the rest of us hastily joined in, but mine came out false and brittle. I backed away and reached towards a dish of olives, spearing one of them with a wooden toothpick.

'Show not good enough?' asked a voice. I glanced back over my shoulder to find a man watching with a wry smile. He nodded at the glass floor. 'I mean, it beats listening to the World Service.'

I popped the olive in my mouth. 'I don't think he's doing *her* world any service.'

His head tilted. 'I think you might be right.'

We shared a grim smile. Scooping up the dish of olives, I went to join him. We wandered over to a balcony that overlooked the garden. There were those stars again, far too majestic to hang in a sky like ours. I gripped the handrail and felt my heartbeat slow down.

There was a sudden orange flare as I watched him light a cigarette, exhaling smoke that curled away into an updraught. He was a sidekick type of man – the one whose better-looking friend always hooked the girl.

'You're hanging back,' he said.

'So?'

'So, most of the Emperor's guests make a point of introducing themselves to their host.'

'My first orgy.'

'Ah.' He gave a sympathetic smile. 'They say that you never forget your first.'

'Well, they're right,' I said, finding somewhere to

deposit the dish. 'Those images are scarred onto my eye-balls for life.'

There was a fresh burst of laughter from behind us. I turned and leant my elbows on the balcony rail. Below, the crowd had dispersed to reveal another sofa covered in bodies.

'Dare I look?' He'd fixed his gaze on the swimming pool, probably counting nipples.

'Depends.'

'I've an idea.' He drew a hand across an invisible canvas. 'Paint me a picture with words.'

I considered the scene playing out below. 'Well, there's a woman going down on a man.'

'Hair colour?'

'Red.'

'Man?'

'Bald.'

'Ah. Maxine and Nowak. Interesting. Last week she was giving him a hand job. She must be going up in the world. Carry on.'

My glance caught on something being held aloft. 'And there's a . . . I think it's a dildo being . . .' I took a sharp intake of breath. 'Is there a doctor in the house?'

He laughed. 'Lord.' He couldn't resist any longer and swivelled round. Blinked once. 'You don't see that in the rushes.'

My skin prickled with interest. 'You a studio man?'

He cupped a hand around his cigarette. 'Something like that.'

'Tell me more.'

He let out a long sigh. 'I didn't introduce myself to bore you to death.'

'You didn't introduce yourself at all,' I reminded him, holding out a hand. 'Loretta. Loretta Goddard.'

He held up both palms, not yet prepared to shake on it. 'Real name?' He saw me hesitate. 'Come on, half the people in this city have made-up names.' The corners of his mouth turned down in mock hurt. 'If we're gonna be pals, we must be clear with each other.'

I folded my arms. 'And who said we're going to be friends?'

'Don't go all English on me now.'

'Margaret,' I said quietly.

'Did your parents hate you at birth?'

'Fuck you,' I said, softly enough so that he knew I didn't mean it.

'Fuck you, too.' He made it sound like the opposite. 'You know, you're not exactly dressed for an orgy.'

I glanced at my oatmeal skirt. 'When I woke up this morning, I didn't *exactly* know I'd be coming here.'

'What did you think would happen?'

'That by now I'd be in my wedding bed.' I held up my left hand, wiggling the sparkling new gold on my fourth finger.

'No!' There was something strangely satisfying about seeing the look of shock that passed over his face.

'Yes.'

'Ouch.'

'Ouch, indeed.'

He scanned the room. 'So, where is he?'

'I have no idea.' For the first time, my voice nearly broke.

He watched my face carefully.

'Don't you dare be kind,' I warned. Suddenly I didn't want to talk about my marriage any more. 'So, what are you doing here?'

He raised an eyebrow. 'You really wanna know?'

'I really want to know.'

He shrugged. 'I have to be.'

'Why?' I'd never heard of anyone being forced to go to a party before.

'For work.'

'It's in your contract?'

'Not exactly, but . . .' He ran a finger around the rim of his glass. 'It just . . . it's part of the job.'

'This is a really strange town.' I drained the last of my martini.

Immediately, he flagged down a passing waiter. 'Two double gins, if that's all right? Neat.'

Waiting, we watched Louise again. She'd climbed down from the piano and was gently snoring now, propped up on a chaise longue, legs splayed as people navigated their way around her kicked-off shoes.

'Is it true she's a courtesan now?' I said.

The man took in a deep, regretful breath. 'Apparently, her voice didn't suit talking pictures, but I think it was more than that. Hollywood found her . . . difficult.'

'Heaven forfend a woman should be that,' I said, as the pieces fell into place in my mind. 'She probably asked for milk with her tea.'

'Or a raise,' he said more seriously. 'The male actors don't like that.'

'Good lord.' I was glad when the waiter returned. 'Thank you.' I took my tumbler.

'Chin, chin.' My new friend raised a toast and gave an adorable short, stiff bow.

I took a sip. 'You know, you still haven't told me *your* name.'

'Eliot. Scott Eliot.' He reached out a hand and we formally shook, just as a naked girl on roller skates sped past.

'Hey!' A familiar voice called up from the sunken floor below. It was my husband, waving up at me, a couple of women draped across him. One of them was dark-haired; the other was a blonde. Our host was standing over Raphael, watching the two women kiss each other across my husband's chest. 'Come and join us!'

I waved back rigidly. Looked like Raphael was working *really* hard on tracking down Stanley Hughes.

'That your husband?' Eliot asked.

'That's him.'

From our bird's-eye view, I could see the dark roots starting to encroach along Raphael's parting.

'*Why* did he bring you here on your wedding day?' Eliot asked, clearly mystified.

'He knows somebody who knows somebody.'

'You guys didn't have anything better to do?'

'Well . . .' I felt suddenly tired and ashamed. 'He really wants to get into the movies.'

'Bad enough to bring his brand-new wife to an orgy?'

I watched Raphael wave up at me again. There was a look on his face I didn't like – an urgency. I could sense the message: *Get down here. Quick.*

Weakly, I waved again. 'I should go.'

My new friend caught my elbow as I began to move away. 'Don't do anything you don't want to.' His face had turned pale beneath the deep Californian tan. 'Seriously, sleeping with a handsome actor won't get your new husband a part in a movie. It doesn't work that way. They just want you to think it does.'

I felt my face turn rigid. 'Who said anything about sleeping with an actor? You've got the wrong end of the stick.'

We'd only just started talking. Why should I listen to a word he said? 'You know, you're almost managing to spoil my wedding day . . .'

'I'm sorry. That wasn't my intention.'

'Well, just be careful with those clever words of yours,' I said. 'They could hurt someone.'

He began to speak, but then there was another call from below.

'I have to go now,' I said, too stubborn to apologize for my outburst.

'Sure.' He reached out to shake my hand. 'May you have a long and happy marriage.'

'I intend to,' I said, giving an awkward shake.

'Your husband's a lucky man.'

'I know.' I dropped my hand and started to walk away. Then I paused and turned back. 'Why do you care, anyway? We've only just met.'

He didn't miss a beat. 'Ah, you sense it, too, then?'

I frowned, unsure what he meant.

'Well, I think we could be friends, at least.'

I forced a laugh. 'I don't think my husband would care for me making new friends like you.' It was a cruel jibe and an unnecessary one.

He looked at me as though what I'd just said was beneath me. It was. 'Well, we'd better respect his wishes,' he said after a moment. 'Run along, Loretta. Your attention is required.'

Raphael's voice hollered up again. '*Loretta!*'

Eliot and I gazed at each other for one last time, silent messages passing between us that I understood all too well. That I was worth more than this, that Raphael was a monster, that I needed friends like Eliot. I wanted to order him to stop feeling sorry for me, that I was perfectly fine – more than fine, happy. Deliriously happy! So why was my breath so tight in my chest?

Eliot began to sing ironically, something about meeting a loved one in familiar places.

I stamped my foot and repeated. 'We've only just met!'

'I know,' he agreed. 'Which makes it odd, doesn't it? That we get on so well?'

And then he turned away before I could even answer.

14

Back downstairs, Raphael made the introductions.

The Emperor took my hand and hooked it up above my head to make me turn on the spot. I craned my neck back towards the balcony, hoping that Eliot couldn't see this latest humiliation. Thankfully, he'd disappeared.

'Let me show you around, sweetheart.' Our host's arm snaked round my waist.

I glanced at Raphael to see if he'd do anything. When he reached out for his drink, I had my answer.

'Sure.' I could look after myself just fine.

'Good girl.'

He steered me through the party, pressing his body against mine, as guests watched slyly over shoulders or stared with open jealousy. I couldn't see Primrose anywhere.

He kept his hand on the small of my back and nodded hellos as he pointed out details. 'I had the whole place torn down and built again from scratch,' he said with more than a hint of pride. 'It was old, you know – built in 1930 or something like that, I forget. Art Deco.'

'Wow, really old,' I murmured. 'You know *all* these people?'

'How many do you figure there are?' he asked greedily.

'Maybe . . . I don't know, a hundred?'

'Oh,' he said shortly. 'I'd say much more.'

We stepped outside. Among the long grasses that skirted the pool, there were bodies moving. At one end, day beds had been arranged beneath billowing muslin sheets draped over wooden frames, and as the fabric danced in the warm breeze, I'd catch glimpses of limbs. A jazz trio played on a podium as a girl in a golden dress reached drinks up to them.

He pointed to a girl in the pool; she couldn't have been more than sixteen. 'See her? Waitress. I got her in on a package deal with two other actresses. She's going to be a hundred-thousand-dollars-a-year star.' A pause. 'If she fucks the right people.'

I swallowed hard. 'You're very charitable.'

'Sure am, honey!' He laughed filthily and my stomach roiled.

I still didn't recognize him from any movies, not even up close. I guessed he was what they called one of those new 'Look at me' actors – working on his physique. He was stunningly handsome. The camera would need close-ups and tricks to make him work, carrying the whole movie on his looks, but I recognized the type. The type of actor that Raphael wanted to be.

We returned inside, straight into a vast kitchen. Staff in crisp uniforms moved about, making way for us. I noticed a male guest watching from the door. His hand slid up a waitress's skirt and I swear she didn't even flinch. My hands twitched to slap the man as I watched the waitress move away. I felt suddenly light-headed.

Only just twenty-one and trying to play with the grown-ups. All for the sake of my husband who was nowhere to be seen. I wished I hadn't agreed, but, by then, it was too late. Far, far too late.

'And here's the conclusion of our tour!' my generous host quipped, as he led me up another flight of stairs. I slowed down, glancing over my shoulder at the crowds below, looking for a face – any face – to come and rescue me. I didn't recognize a soul.

His hand tightened round my arm. 'Just this way.' He reached to a solid gold doorknob and threw the door open, steering me inside before kicking the door shut behind us, the noise of the party fading away.

There was a mahogany bed frame with an inlaid rose-wood pattern, satin drapes at the window and a mirror on the ceiling. Onyx bathroom off to one side. He only seemed to be in his late twenties, but this room felt as though it belonged to a much older person.

There was another man in the room. As I was led past a set of discarded lingerie, my feet sank into the deep carpet. I knew immediately that this was all wrong – that these men were all wrong. The other person was the man we'd watched through the glass ceiling; I recognized the bulk of him, the broad expanse of his naked shoulders. Stanley. The director my husband was so desperate to impress. He sat on a velvet stool, a towel wrapped around his waist, whisky tumbler gripped on his knee.

I looked between their faces and caught a discreet, complicit nod. *Oh, lord. Oh no.* I felt all so immediately sober.

'Stanley, meet Mrs Goddard. Congratulate her, Stanley – she got married today.'

'Happy for you,' Stanley said, sounding bored. He took a long draught from his glass and sat back to assess me. From the frown on his face, his conclusions didn't look that great.

'Nice . . . nice room,' I said, attempting to look around in an interested manner.

Out of nowhere, the Emperor took hold of me and forced me over to his friend. Stanley stood up, his towel dropping to the floor. I tried not to scream.

I felt the hand still in the small of my back, an uncomfortable heat radiating off it.

'We should celebrate,' Stanley said.

My eyes swept the room to spot anywhere there might be a lock to slide open, another door or a window to climb out of. But we were two floors up.

'Relax,' the Emperor ordered. As though anyone could relax around him.

I caught the dense woody aroma of the cologne.

'She's a beautiful bride, isn't she, Stanley?' His voice emerged cold and calculating. There wasn't any acting involved; the sincerity of threat hung between us. Suddenly hands gripped me from behind, twisting hard so that my wrists felt as though they were going to pop.

'Hey!' I tried to shake him off, to laugh. I failed.

Stanley's eyes burned as he watched. He came over

and pushed his tumbler against my lips, my teeth jarring against the glass, as burning amber liquid was forced down my throat.

I exploded into a fit of coughing, doubled up. The Emperor had no choice but to loosen his grip, giving me just enough time to wrestle free. I ran to the window, slapping my hands against the glass and calling down, looking for a single face in the crowd below that I recognized.

No one. Nothing. Not a person looked up, my shrieks drowned out by the band.

'Hey, if that's what you want.' He came up behind me and pushed me against the windowsill, a hand cupping the back of my head to force me over. I stared out into the abyss as a hand travelled up my skirt.

Come on. My mind whirled. I'd always managed to look after myself before. *Come on. You can handle this.*

I turned back round, placing my palms against a warm chest. 'Now, now, boys.' I threw Stanley a desperate glance, hoping that he'd stop whatever the Emperor had started, but he just stood there.

'Kneel.'

I couldn't speak.

'Kneel,' the Emperor ordered again, face twisted in loathing. 'Kneel at my feet, you tramp.'

There was a heavy glass tumbler beside me on the windowsill. 'Fuck you!'

I lunged for it and threw it at my host, but my aim was all wrong and it bounced off his chest. We all stared at it in silence for a moment. Stanley looked at me as though I'd made the most terrible mistake.

'Quite the ball of fire, isn't she, Stanley?'

The director said nothing.

Suddenly the Emperor was manhandling me into the bathroom. Hands were all over me in an instant. I caught a flash of silver cufflinks; fingers pressed against my mouth so hard that I felt my lips cut on my teeth. No one could possibly have heard my muffled scream. I couldn't tell where I ended and they began. Hands moving around my body. Stockings pinging free of suspenders. Corset rolled over hips. Buttons ripping from my blouse.

Bloody hell, Margaret. What have you gone and done now?

Not my fault, I wanted to tell Enid. Definitely not my fault this time.

Then fight, you bugger!

I began to struggle, tried again to scream.

'Keep still.'

But I didn't. I didn't keep still, my sister's words filling my head. I bit down hard, teeth driving into knuckles. The iron tang of blood exploded in my mouth. A hand pulled away and slapped my face so hard that my head whipped back. But I could scream now and did, my lungs filling with air. I kicked and I punched, aiming for anywhere that would really hurt.

But there were two of them, and only one of me. Soon enough – far too soon – I was doubled over the edge of the gold-plated bath, manicured nails clawing at me as I found my skirt hiked up around my waist. I stared at my blurred reflection in the gold plate. The fight was over. I'd lost. I seemed to float off above myself as through the open bathroom door the sound of jazz grew louder. The band had been joined by a singer, her voice low and husky. She was singing a funny song but in an oddly slow and mournful way, strange for a party like this.

'*Oh, cherished love of mine . . .*'

Hands tore my knickers down my legs.

'*Your face is so divine . . .*'

Fingers threaded in my hair and yanked back so hard that pain exploded across my skull.

'*When you talk, you take my heart . . .*'

A hand reached over the bathtub and squeezed my breast so hard I cried out.

'*I can't bear to be apart . . .*'

Feet kicked my legs apart and there was the hiss of a metal zip being undone, accompanied by words that were ugly and violent.

'*When you're so smart.*'

Everything started to turn fuzzy. Then there was a loud slam and everything stopped. Hands froze. Three pairs of eyes looked at each other, some of them cold and my own desperate, bulging above a hand slapped over my mouth.

Someone else was in the room.

15

I collapsed back against the bathtub's hard marble rim. There was a grunt and that zip again, then the sound of feet marching out.

Stanley grabbed my hair and pulled me to standing. 'Tidy yourself up,' he whispered. I might have been mistaken, but for a moment there it sounded as though he pitied me.

I did as I was told and pulled my skirt back down. The torn stockings would have to wait. In the mirror I could see my left cheek glowing from the slap and my lips swollen. Nothing I could do about that, but I could fix my make-up. With a trembling hand, I ran a finger around my mouth, neatening the outline. Then I tidied up my eyes with the pad of my little finger, wiping away the flakes of mascara that had fallen and bled into streaks through my tears. I ran a hand over my head and picked off the stray hairs from my shoulders from where they'd been ripped out. I concentrated on each small task. Eventually, my hand dropped to my side. The trembling subsided.

There. All better.

I went out to join the others, feeling as though my legs could buckle beneath me any moment. I leant a steadying hand against a side table.

Eliot was standing beside the pristine bed; he flashed me a glance that warned me to keep quiet. Raphael hovered behind him, staring at the wound on the Emperor's hand.

Our host's eyes bulged with petulant fury. 'What are you doing in my bedroom?' he demanded.

Raphael stared beseechingly. 'I'm sorry, I—'

My husband looked as though he was about to pass out from fright. My husband. The man I'd trusted with my life.

Eliot cut him off. 'We were looking for Loretta. Seems we've found her.'

'Seems you have.' The Emperor looked Eliot up and down. 'You're that writer guy, aren't you?'

Eliot nodded.

'Well, write your way out of here!' He pointed at the open door, his voice rising dangerously. 'And get this tramp out of my sight.'

'S-sweetheart,' Raphael stuttered. He held out his hand and it took all my self-control to walk over, rather than run into his arms.

'Well, thanks for taking care of her,' Eliot said. He turned to me and Raphael. 'Shall we call it a night? Leave these gentlemen to it?'

Stanley had retired back to his chair.

Raphael nodded quickly.

'Well,' our host said, gathering himself. 'Real nice to meet the bride.' His eyes caught mine and I felt a spurt of fury that I didn't dare show. 'She has spirit, huh?'

Raphael laughed shakily. 'She sure does.'

I made to leave, but Raphael held me back. 'Darling, haven't you forgotten something? You need to thank our host.'

The final humiliation. Reluctantly, I turned back, my cheek still throbbing. 'Thank you.'

He grinned. 'You're welcome.'

Raphael turned to Stanley. 'Speak soon?'

I slid a glance at my husband. He was smiling like a prize chump, still hoping that Stanley would provide him with his big break.

'Sure,' Stanley grunted. Anyone could tell that he didn't mean it. Anyone, except Raphael.

We moved towards the door, jostling to stand back for each other in some show of ridiculous politeness. As I passed the wardrobe, I noticed the vast collection of suits – there must have been thirty of them in there, all in a rainbow of colours. This was the man who had everything, a god among us mere mortals, but he hadn't had me. Not tonight.

From behind the bedroom door, we heard the two of them immediately start yelling at each other. I had some pretty urgent questions of my own and squared up to my husband. 'What the hell was that?'

He bugged his eyes. 'What the hell was *what*?'

I indicated the door. 'Do you have any idea what they were about to do to me?'

'I didn't make you go in there with them!'

What was he even trying to say? 'Not much you didn't!'

'Oh, stop being so dramatic.' He looked to Eliot for support, but he was staring hard at the floor.

'I'll leave you guys to—'

'No, stay.' Then I dug a finger into Raphael's chest. 'You traded me like a poker chip. That *isn't* what we agreed.'

Raphael's face sank. 'Honestly, this isn't what I—'

'Wanted to happen?' Eliot muttered beneath his breath.

'Excuse me?' Raphael turned on him. 'Who the hell gives you the right to—'

'To rescue your wife?' Eliot jerked a thumb over his shoulder. 'She'd still be in there now if I hadn't found her. If I hadn't made you find her!'

I stared at my new husband: hands shoved into the pockets of his gaudy pink suit. He couldn't meet my eye.

'You're pathetic,' I told him.

'And you're an ungrateful little bitch,' he snapped back.

I shook my head. 'I never should have trusted you. I mean, I knew I couldn't trust you – not properly and not for long—'

'Just long enough to get your Green Card, huh?'

'—but all this. On our wedding day.' My voice cracked and instantly I hated myself, almost as much as I hated Raphael in that moment. Almost.

Raphael took a deep breath, visibly stopping himself from trading another insult. 'I'll wait in the car. Get your things.' He pushed past Eliot and fled down the staircase.

Eliot and I stood alone, allowing the energy to settle around us. He was the first to speak. 'You OK?'

I laughed shakily, pushing the hair out of my eyes. 'Oh, sure.'

His eyebrows pinched. 'Sure you're sure?'

I swallowed, saying nothing.

He took a cigarette from his case, lit it and passed it to me. Then he lit a second for himself. We smoked in silence, leaning against the wall. Eventually, I took a last deep inhale and enjoyed grinding the stub against the expensive parquet floor. 'Say, how d'you get away with talking to the Emperor like that? I can't believe he didn't knock you out on the spot.'

'I'm a scribe.' Eliot gave a sad sort of a smile. 'I write the scripts. Without me, even the emperors count for nothing – and he knows it. Also, I'm a weakling.' He lifted an arm and pretended to flex a puny muscle. 'Only cowards hit men like me.'

'Well, I think you're pretty marvellous,' I said. 'Thanks for . . .' I waved a hand in the direction of the bedroom. '. . . everything.'

Eliot shrugged.

'I'm sorry about earlier. I didn't mean to hurt your feelings.'

There was a whoop and a cheer from down below. I jerked my chin towards the stairs. 'Go on. Go and join your friends.'

'I'm not leaving you here on your own.'

Surprising even myself, I slipped my hand into his. His fingers were long and elegant, the skin cool despite the party's heat. Together, we moved towards the stairs.

'We must do this again sometime.' I hesitated. 'Friends, right?'

'Absolutely.'

At the bottom of the stairs, he squeezed my hand. After a few heartbeats, we pulled apart, his fingertips drifting across mine. His expression was unreadable.

'Take care of yourself, Loretta.'

I watched him disappear, moving among the crowd. It almost broke my heart to let him go, the party fading away around me. I'd never met a man quite like Scott Eliot before. But after a moment or two someone shoved past me, his hand brushing my backside. Definitely time to go. I went to find my wedding jacket in a pile of discarded clothes. Beside them, Primrose was slumped over the sofa. 'Come on, sweetie.' I hooked a hand beneath her armpit and dragged her up to standing as her head lolled. 'Time to go home.'

No one rushed to help, but somehow I managed to get her out to the motor car. Raphael was seated at the front wheel, evidently in a tremendous sulk.

I tipped Primrose into the back, like a drunk Norma Desmond, very much not ready for her close-up.

'Watch the upholstery,' Raphael muttered, glaring in the rear-view mirror.

I sank into the front passenger seat, keeping my glance fixed straight ahead. 'Let's go.'

As the car pulled off, beams arced through the night, and I finally turned to look at my husband.

'What?' He indicated left, an amber spot winking in the night. I dug my fingernails into the palms of my hands.

Against the silence, he reached to snap on the radio. I reached to switch it back off.

'It wasn't my fault,' he said at last and oh-so inevitably.

'What wasn't?' My voice emerged, clipped and cold.

'Whatever happened back there . . . I don't know.' Oh, sure. He didn't know.

I pretended to consider. 'You didn't know that there would be cocaine or sex or . . . what? That a new bride might be a novel experience?'

'I would never do that! Don't make me out to be the snake,' he growled. 'I was trying to show you a good time. Just like I promised!'

Was he kidding?

There was a curve in the road up ahead, where we followed the coast route and the head beams cut across a layby on the cliff side.

'Stop the car,' I commanded, indicating the layby.

'What?'

'I said, *stop the car*!'

He pulled over, swerving dangerously close to the edge.

'Christ, you can't even park right!' I spat, clambering out.

'What are you doing?' Raphael protested.

In the sudden silence, I could hear the cicadas playing in the long grasses on the other side of the road. I marched around the front of the car, my wedding suit lit up by the lamps, then I came round to Raphael's side and leant over to take the keys from the ignition.

'Hey! What are you doing?'

I stepped back. 'Get out.'

'What?'

'Loretta!' His face turned pale as he understood. 'You're not going to leave me here, are you? You can't be serious. You can't even drive!'

'I'm sure it can't be that hard. You manage it, after all.' I took another step back, keys raised aloft. 'I'm waiting.'

He threw the driver's door open and leapt out, lunging to grab the keys – but I held them out over the cliff edge.

'Come one step closer and you'll fall,' I warned him. 'I want you out of the apartment by the end of the weekend,' I announced, heading for the driver's seat.

'Listen, we're—'

'Not any more.' I started to scratch at my hand and hurled my wedding ring at him.

He didn't move and it clattered in the dirt. Behind us, Primrose was finally waking up, her head swinging groggily as she levered herself up on the bench seat.

'What's going on?'

Raphael and I stared at each other.

'We're breaking up,' I said.

She frowned, like a child presented with a particularly hard maths sum. 'Already?'

'We don't need to do this,' Raphael pleaded.

'We were just getting started,' I said, choking on my own words. 'We could have built something together – something good – but not any more.'

I climbed into the car, the seat still warm, and scrambled to insert the key in the ignition, hands shaking. The engine came to life. I released the hand brake and hit the accelerator. With a squeal of tyres, the car jerked forward and I felt myself thrown back in the seat, Primrose screeching in shock behind me. I glanced in the rearview mirror to see Raphael watching. Soon he became nothing more than a tiny pinhead of a man, and that was nothing – entirely nothing! – more than he deserved.

16

Hedda Hopper's Hollywood

Last night, Hollywood transformed into a showcase of the great and the good! At a venue that we could not even dare to name, the stars came out in their legions. With all the pomp of any Academy Award ceremony, the host showed everyone a good time. Plenty of models and actresses, and a mysterious Cinderella figure, being led around by the infamous host. The Emperor proved that he doesn't need the system to show the talent a good time. But who IS the Emperor? You'll have to guess!

All we can say is that the cocktails tasted mighty fine. Be warned, dear readers – negronis make you naughty!

I cast the morning papers aside. Hedda Hopper had got the story out before any of the other syndicated movie columnists. Someone on the inside, clearly.

I got up and had a long and satisfying piss – all over Raphael's gaudy suits. There hadn't been any sign of him yet, and I hoped against hope that he was still walking into town. More likely, he'd have had the chance to flag down a lift from someone. One by one, I threw the suits out of the apartment window, leaning out to watch as they billowed into the garbage bins in clouds of pink, cream and orange. Who in their right mind would wear an orange suit? Raphael Goddard, that's who.

I sank onto the windowsill, waiting for any sign of life from the Hacienda Arms. I guessed that Primrose would be having a *long* lie-in. Tears pricked my eyes, but I didn't let them fall – behind me, the remains of the party looked so sad. Ashtrays piled with stub ends, bottles discarded on the floor.

'Come on,' I chided, rolling up my pyjama sleeves. 'Stop being daft.'

I moved around quickly. I drained the bath of beer bottles. The cake went in the trash. I returned the vinyls to their sleeves and lined them up next to the record player on the floor. Windows were flung open, and endless bags of clinking bottles thrown down the garbage chute.

Once I was done, I drew a bath, plumes of water thundering against chipped enamel. I lay there for a long time, skin turning red and mottled, head tipped back against the rim and . . . I waited. I waited to hear the music. Some sign that across the way, prostitutes were waking up. And did I need a prostitute to wake up right about now. Primrose, specifically.

After half an hour there was still no sound of movement from next door. Giving up, I lifted the plug chain between my toes, watching the water descend. The ancient plumbing gurgled. Dripping and listless, I stepped out and dried myself on a threadbare towel. I went to the mirror above the sink and stared. What a clown.

Mascara bled down my cheeks. There was still a faint

stain of lipstick, and wet ropes of hair hung around my face. I was back to being that silly, reckless girl from home, standing in front of the mirror in a dank, dark bathroom. I'd worked my arse off to get to Hollywood and build my dream to be a make-up artist, and now here I stood – a sorry-looking mess of a woman. Had everything been for *this*? Before I had more time to feel sorry for myself, I pulled off the Ey-teb strip eyelashes, carefully returning them to their little red box alongside the miniature bottle of glue. Next, I took a face towel and held it out beneath the water that sparkled out of the faucet, before tipping my head back to drape the cloth over my pores. I stayed there for a moment, drinking in the heat. Then I rubbed my face in circles, finally dropping the cloth to stare at myself – fully naked before the mirror, a flash of dark hair around my most private parts.

The make-up had gone – all gone.

Hello, Margaret. Not seen you for a while . . .

I reached for a jar of cold cream and slathered it on, until my face and neck were shiny and thick with grease. As I wiped the cream off, I watched myself in the mirror. This was me, Margaret. No make-up. No gloss. Back to being nothing.

I got dressed and went round to knock at the Hacienda Arms. Primrose's face appeared in the doorway, shamelessly assessing my damp hair and hasty outfit.

'I wondered how long it would take,' she said around a long yawn. 'Come on in.'

She stood back and I followed her into the lobby.

There was a silver bucket filled with ice and jars of Russian caviar. Work must have been good. I slipped into one of the easy chairs, curling my legs up beneath me.

She reached to turn the opera music down. 'Quite a night, huh?' She gave me a pointed look over the top of her sunglasses.

I rested my head on the back of the chair and let out a breath. 'How much do you remember?'

'Well, I remember that you and Raphael have . . .'

'Separated,' I finished for her, lifting my head back up.

Primrose studied my face carefully. 'Wanna tell me about it?'

She pulled a bottle of tequila out of a side cabinet and poured us a couple of shots, then passed a glass to me.

I knocked back the drink in one, wincing at the taste this early, and then I started to talk.

'The pig!' she exclaimed, once the whole sorry story had reached its conclusion. She shook her head. 'I've seen a lot, but Raphael selling his wife for a bit part in a movie. Christ!'

I snorted. 'I doubt he'll even get that. Extra, maybe, if he's lucky. I'm done with him. He's out.' I leant forward, resting my elbows on my knees. 'Is this what men are like in Hollywood?'

She picked a piece of fluff off her dressing gown. 'It's not . . . unusual.'

I felt my foot jiggling. 'And everyone just accepts it?'

Primrose poured herself another shot, but there was a sudden impatient knock at the door. She swore under her breath. 'He's early.' She downed the shot and gasped, then quickly hid the bottle back in the cabinet. She plucked a mint from a glass bowl full of them and popped it into her mouth. 'Could you hang about?' she whispered. 'The other girls are still sleeping, but the clients like to find the place busy.'

'Sure . . .'

Primrose headed towards the heavy oak door with its wrought-iron studs and trimmings. 'Peter!'

A man stepped into the front room, glancing around as though he owned the place. He looked me up and down and didn't seem at all convinced that I was a lady of the night. With my tired make-up and slacks, I didn't blame him. How did Primrose keep this up all the time? It must have been exhausting!

Primrose tried to give him a kiss, but he pushed her away.

He settled into a chair beside the fireplace and flipped his trilby between his hands. A spark of concern tightened my chest; he seemed angry in some way. I looked at Primrose questioningly, but she gave a tiny shake of her head.

'Would you like a drink?' I asked, as Primrose went to sit on his knee. He gave a curt nod and I moved towards the grog tray that had been set up in a corner. I was glad to have my back to them so that Peter couldn't see my face. Before me, the bottles glistened in a rainbow of colours, reflected in the silver tray. There was a bowl of lemons and a little jar of ruby-red cherries. An Aladdin's cave of neat alcohol.

I called back over my shoulder. 'Fancy a cocktail, Peter?'

'Sure.'

I reached for the bottle of vibrant, green liquid and poured it into a cut-glass coupe. I sliced a sliver of lemon peel, the knife sharp enough to skin a man. Then added some dry vermouth and popped open a bottle of champagne that had been resting in its own bucket of ice.

I carried over the glass, careful not to spill any liquid, and placed it down on the side table beside him. He leant over without acknowledging me and took a sip.

'Thank you, Loretta,' Primrose said. 'You can leave us now.'

17

I kept an eye on the Hacienda Arms all through that morning, windows thrown wide so that I could listen out for any trouble. It didn't take long. After an hour or so, the Hacienda's front door was flung open and I spotted Primrose struggling with something slumped over her shoulders. Not something – someone! It was Peter, drunk as the proverbial skunk.

I slipped on some shoes and skittered down the main stairwell of my building, but I was too late. A man with a small paunch stood on the other side of Primrose and was helping her steer Peter down onto the sidewalk. He wore a Stetson and one of those leather thongs at his throat, a flashy pair of cowboy boots with pointed toes and chunky heel, along with a gingham shirt with red piping around the yoke. He looked just about ready to yee-haw.

'Are you OK?' I gasped as I ran over.

'Now, little lady, don't you come too near!' The stranger held out a hand in warning. 'This fella . . . Well, I don't like to say it, but he looks juiced up!'

Primrose looked up at me from beneath the arm draped over her shoulder and narrowed her eyes. *This was your doing, Loretta!* Maybe I had been a little heavy-handed with the spirits.

I didn't want to give us away – Primrose or me – so did as the man bid and kept a distance. I hovered around them as they dragged their load to a bench by a bus stop and deposited him there.

The other man dusted his hands off, shaking his head in disgust. 'There I am, just driving to the gas station and there *he* is!' It was only now that I spotted the truck parked haphazardly across the sidewalk, pedestrians weaving past. 'Stood on the doorstep hollering, calling this young woman names that . . . Well, I wouldn't like to repeat.'

Young woman?

Primrose threw me another warning glance.

'Are you OK, Primrose?' I gasped. Peter was slumped, arms spread across the back of the bench, already snoring loudly.

'I am now, thanks to this fine gentleman.' She gave him a shy smile. Lauren Bacall could eat her heart out!

He shoved the Stetson back on his head. 'Arthur's the name.' He shook hands with both of us but couldn't tear his eyes away from Primrose. 'What was he doing at your place?'

'Yes, Primrose. What *was* he doing there?' I asked.

'Uncle!' she blurted. 'Uncle Peter! I'm sorry, he does tend to become a bit . . . over-excited.'

Arthur shook his head. 'You can say that again! It's not even midday!'

For a moment, all three of us stared at poor old Uncle Peter. By this time, he'd slid further down the bench.

'Now, are you going to be all right, little lady?'

'Oh, I'll be fine!' She flapped a hand. 'I'll lock the doors and by tomorrow he won't remember a thing. Harmless really.'

Arthur inclined his head. 'Well, you take care.' He took out a wallet and handed over a business card. 'Any problems, just let me know.' He turned to me. 'You take care, too. Some of these men . . . I just don't know what's wrong with them.'

'Me neither,' I said. 'Don't worry, I'm a friend. I'll make sure Primrose stays safe.'

'Primrose,' he breathed, drawing in a breath as though he could inhale the scent on the smog-ridden Californian air. 'A perfect name for a pretty gal.'

I smiled. 'Isn't it?'

'Well, I'll be off. Mighty fine meeting you girls.'

'It was just lovely to meet you, too,' Primrose said, suddenly sounding like Zelda Fitzgerald or one of those other Southern belles, dressed in flounces of white.

The two of us watched Arthur climb back into his truck and with a wave he drove off, horns blaring as he swerved back into the traffic.

'You a virgin now?' I asked, as the car disappeared out of sight.

'You know me, the prom queen.'

'Do you think he's Texan?' I was starting to spot the accents out here.

'Definitely Texan.' Primrose nodded.

'Looks good for you.'

'Well, what did you expect?' She turned to me. 'Now, what's good for you?'

'A new start,' I said without hesitation.

'Well, I think you've started on the new start.' She looked pointedly at my naked fourth finger. 'But what's next?'

'Oh, you know. Building my career in a studio.'

She laughed. 'Like it's that easy.'

'Oh, Primrose.' I smiled back. 'You underestimate me.'

'Fine, I get it. But what are you going to call yourself now? You can't be Loretta Goddard any more.'

I thought back across all the names that people had called me. Darling this and darling that. Wasn't this the whole town of reinvention? 'Loretta Darling!'

'I love it!' Primrose cried. 'You sound like a movie star already.'

I didn't want to be one of those, but it certainly sounded romantic.

Loretta Darling. Who would mess with her?

Monday, I handed my notice in at the Blue Book Modeling Agency. Of course, it was the law of sod that when I went in with my resignation note Raphael was already there, wheeling in the latest bright-eyed candidate for the books. Tufts of honeyed hair sprang out of his open shirt collar. He looked as blond and beautiful as ever, as though nothing at all had ruffled his feathers. I noticed that he wasn't wearing his wedding ring either and cursed myself for the hurt that blossomed in my chest.

When he saw me, he left the latest would-be model with the receptionist and steered me down the stairs and out into the back yard, apparently determined we should speak. I expected him to beg or plead or . . . something. But it wasn't like that.

'I'm staying with Mick,' he said stiffly, avoiding my eyes. 'Can you get my stuff sent over?'

So, that's all it was.

I folded my arms. 'Actually, I can't. I've thrown everything out.'

There was a shocked silence. 'All of it?'

I nodded. 'All the shirts, all the suits.' His face turned visibly paler. 'And you may as well know that I've handed my notice in.'

At this, his eyes flickered. 'But what will you do for money?'

I shrugged, pretending not to care much. 'More shifts at Van de Kamp's?'

'Seriously?'

'It'll mean I never have to see you again,' I said, in a tone as though it should have been perfectly obvious.

He didn't say anything to that. I watched a flame sputter and die before my eyes. There was no going back now.

He recovered pretty quickly, reaching out a hand to shake. 'Well, have a nice life, whoever you are. Because you do know, you're nothing without me.'

'Oh, didn't you hear? I'm Miss Darling now.'

He laughed. Actually laughed. 'Good luck with that.'

I felt the burning of tears, but I was damned if I'd give him the satisfaction of seeing me cry. He turned and walked back into the studio, retreating into the gloom until he finally disappeared. Raphael had promised to stick with me through thick and thin, and that promise had been about as substantial as a lipstick with too much beeswax.

I stood all alone in the yard, gathering myself and swore to myself that day would be the last day he or any man would ever get to hurt me. Then I walked away from Miss Snively's and out of my husband's life. I'd already wasted too much time. Now was the time to build the rest of my life – and Loretta Darling? Goddamn, she was ready for that!

PART TWO

18

Dear Enid,

*Can you believe this? Miss Snively has said I am TOO
GOOD at what I do and has given me a month's wages to
leave and MAKE MY FORTUNE elsewhere. Talk about
laugh of the century. I am going to try with someone called
Alecs Petraś. He's a bona fide GENIUS and an actual
PRINCE! Wish me luck persuading him that Miss Snively
is right! Ha, ha!*

*Seriously, though . . . How are you and the baby? I wish
I could see you again.*

Best,
Margaret x

I turned the postcard over and gazed at the front: *Greetings
from Hollywood, California!* So chirpy, so larger than life. I'd
been in America for over nine months already. Enough
time to have a baby or build a career. And how much had
I achieved of my grand plan? Close to nothing.

But I hadn't forgotten Petraś, my Polish prince. I'd
done some digging. Rumour had it that Marlene Dietrich
had given him two – two! – sets of diamond cufflinks
after he'd worked with her. Ida May had delivered an ele-
phant to his front yard as a Christmas gift, tied up with a

ribbon at the poor creature's neck. But it wasn't all rumours and legend. There was substance behind it. Everyone loved him – the man behind the white spot in the corner of an eye that made an actress's gaze look instantly wider; the way that he'd paint in the fake shadow of a long eyelash beneath the cheek; his brand-new potions that rescued actors from looking gaunt and greasy beneath the harsh, new glare of Technicolor. The man was a genius, as well as having royal blood.

I'd at least managed to familiarize myself with the studios and where they were located. That hadn't been much of an effort; they studded the streets on every other block. Turn down any avenue, and a person would stumble upon the backlots behind the fakery of the studios' tall white pillars. Here was where the palm trees disappeared, and the garbage trucks parked up. I sometimes wondered if, hoped even, I'd bump into the man from the party, Scott Eliot.

Gate 3, Olive Avenue was where it all began for real. This was the back entrance to the studio lots. I'd also been scouring the dailies and had figured out that this was where Petraś's royal empire sat. My route to work suddenly diverted. Each morning on my way to Van de Kamp's, I'd scout out the joint. It soon became clear that there were only two uniformed men who worked security. One of them was young and cute but impervious to my charms. The other was older but friendlier. I got into the habit of taking him a steaming black coffee and found out his name: Biff.

I'd get up extra early each morning and hover by Biff's

kiosk. It was too early for anyone to care; even Biff was still half asleep, yawning over his coffee. After a while, chauffeur-driven cars would start to arrive. I was able to glimpse beyond the smoked glass as windows were rolled down – spotting the occasional flash of a stockinged leg or a compact mirror clouded with powder as lipstick was applied. I'd politely hang back as each car entered the lot, then I'd approach Biff's kiosk again, asking him questions – gently, at first. Who was the most fun on set? Could a girl take a look around? How did someone get a job as a make-up artist here?

'Look, kid,' he said one morning. 'I'm not letting you in, no matter how many coffees you bring me.' He spotted the look on my face and then his own face crumpled. 'OK, I'll tell you what.' He turned to wave at a couple of girls walking past one of the other guards, gaily showing their coveted passes. 'Hey, you two! Get over here!'

They shared a bemused glance and then weaved between cars to join us. Hastily, I leapt off the barrier where I'd been sitting and smoothed a hand down over my hair, my heart beating against my chest. An in!

'This is Loretta,' Biff said to them. 'She wants to know how to make it as a make-up artist. Any advice?'

The smaller girl's face flushed with pleasure above her neat pussy-bow collar. 'Oh, my! You're asking me for tips?'

'Alice, don't be such a schmuck,' chastised the other. I took a dislike to her instantly. Still, Biff gave me an encouraging nod and I swallowed down my pride.

'I hope you don't mind,' I said, feeling as though I

should curtsy or something. 'It's just that I'd love it if you could help. I'd really love to meet with Mr Petraś.'

'Well!' The girl called Alice started to speak, her blonde curls bobbing as she nodded along at her own words. 'What you need to do is—'

'What you need to do is stop hanging around like some sort of tourist,' the other one said, acid pouring out of her voice as her glance travelled up and down me. 'It's not a good look.'

'Debra!' her companion protested. 'Don't be so mean.'

'I'm not being mean,' Debra said, snapping her gum. 'I'm just telling her the truth.' She turned back to me. 'If you really want to work the other side of this barrier, I'd suggest that you get to know the people who matter.' She didn't even look at Biff, who suddenly busied himself polishing a silver crest. 'You need to know somebody who knows somebody who knows somebody.' She stared at me, still chewing. 'Do you? I mean, know somebody?'

My mouth opened and then I shut it again. Anger flared inside me. So badly I wanted to tell her what she looked like with her mouth going ten to the dozen – like some sort of heifer in a dress, but I wasn't dumb enough to make enemies. Not yet. 'I mean, no – not really.'

The Debra girl snorted. 'Check out her accent! Of course, she doesn't. Limeys!' With a flip of her starched white petticoat, she turned and flounced away like Doris Day's evil twin.

Clearly embarrassed, Alice hung back. 'I'm sorry

about that,' she said after a moment. 'My friend's kind of confident.'

'She sure is,' I said, watching as Debra stopped at the corner of a lot and furiously circled a hand, urging Alice to keep up.

'Anything else?' Biff asked weakly. 'You're one of the good ones, Alice, and Loretta here – she's been hanging around for a while now. You know what it's like. Everyone in this town has a dream!' He tried to make it sound joyful, but it all sounded so depressing . . . which it was.

She struggled for a few moments, and then . . . 'Have you trained in make-up at all?' she asked hopefully.

'I worked at Miss Snively's!'

'Well, that's a start! Keep doing what you're doing, Loretta.' She waved a hand and hastily ran after Debra, whose face was dark with menace. As we watched her escape, she kicked up her heels like a schoolgirl and then rushed to apologize as Debra seemed to be spitting out something that looked awfully like curses.

The silence brooded between Biff and me for a few moments.

'Thank you,' I said eventually. 'That was good of you.'

'No problem.'

We couldn't meet each other's eyes. He returned to his cabin, and I went back to my perch, watching the cars drive by as though I was invisible, in the same way that they had done for weeks. So much for girls looking out for one another. That hadn't worked. I guess I needed . . . a man?

19

After witnessing my humiliation with that snooty Debra, Biff gave in. He began to answer my relentless questions, helped me understand the hierarchy and the jockeying for position. At the top were the men who played God: the studio executives. Biff would hustle me out of sight when they drove through. Then there were the producers – more powerful than the directors – who could either get a movie made or tear up the script. Writers, stars, actors, chippies – I was surprised to learn that even stars came somewhat down the pecking order – there was a whole list of people who fought to keep their heads afloat in these shark-infested waters. You'd have thought it might put me off, but I became more determined than ever. I wanted in. I wanted to show them all what I could do. If some of the girls from Miss Snively's agency could become stars, why couldn't I become a professional make-up artist? All I needed was my lucky break, and wasn't Hollywood meant to be full of lucky breaks?

Biff continued to let me sit on the metal fence that surrounded his kiosk and I'd swing my legs, watching the comings and goings as cars delivered their mysterious passengers. After a while, there was one car that stood out. It wasn't a Corvette or a Chevy, like the others.

It was bulky with a huge, battered fender and an engine that wheezed like a bronchial seaside landlady.

Then, out of the blue, the driver of the old car ignored Biff's wave through and paused beside us. I felt my skin prickle as the window wound down with a judder of the rubber seal. A face appeared, eyes unreadable behind Ray-Bans.

'Well, look who it is,' he said. 'The English Muffin.'

My heart nearly jumped out of my chest.

'Good morning, Mr Eliot!' Biff was suddenly all smiles. Enthusiastically, the two of them shook hands across the window. Sunglasses were eased back over a widow's peak to reveal laughing eyes, flecked green. It was the man who'd saved me. Scott Eliot.

'Hello, Loretta. We meet again.'

'Oh, hi!' I waved a shaky hand. 'Long time . . . no see.' Memories flashed behind my eyes. That party felt like a lifetime ago and it was strange, seeing Eliot in daylight.

'It sure is.' He lit a cigarette with a silver lighter and beckoned for me to come forward, an elbow hanging off the car window. A script covered in spidery scrawls sat on the passenger seat beside him.

I hastily smoothed hands down my outfit and checked my hair. *Let me in*, I silently begged. *Just one last favour.*

Eliot raised his eyebrows. 'Biff, this is a friend of mine.'

'Sir.' Biff pushed his cap back on his head, frowning at the line of cars that were piling up behind Eliot. 'I'll have to ask you to—'

'Come on, jump in,' Eliot said, looking up at me with

a lazy grin that made my heart melt as he reached to open the passenger door.

I raced round that car faster than I'd ever run any-where in my life. The leather of the passenger seat sagged with the shape of a body it was already used to. Fleetingly, I wondered if Eliot had a girlfriend, but not long enough to argue.

'Mr Eliot, sir! Now, just a—'

Eliot reached a couple of dollar notes through the driver's window and Biff's mouth clamped shut. He leant into his cabin and pressed the green button to raise the barrier, hastily glancing around to see if anyone had noticed. As the car pulled away, I pressed my body back against the leather seat and tried to make myself invisible.

'No one's going to arrest you, you know. Would you like a tour?'

'Oh, I don't think—'

Too late. He yanked down on the steering wheel and the car swung heavily into one of the rows of avenues that ran between the studios with their domed roofs. Immediately, we had to swerve to avoid a golf cart carry-ing an actress. She was wearing a fawn-coloured mackintosh and rain hat, and carried a black umbrella, which was at odds with the blazing Californian sun.

'Morning!' Eliot called. The actress waved back charmingly, her driver scowling at us.

'Was that Debbie Reynolds?' I remembered seeing her in *Three Little Words* with my sister, Enid. Fred Astaire had had a much bigger role, but I'd found Debbie to be unforgettably cute in her sailor dress.

'That's the one,' Eliot confirmed. 'She's filming something new now with Gene Kelly.' He leant close and whispered. 'Apparently, Gene hates that she's in the movie.' She looked so fresh and wholesome that I couldn't imagine anyone hating her.

We turned a corner into the backlot and my mouth fell open in shock. There was a whole cowboy town set up here, complete with dusty streets and a real-life horse tied up to a post. A saloon sat opposite a church, and there was a general store and a haberdasher's . . . They even had a fake mountain painted onto a backdrop that hung in front of a warehouse.

'This is crazy!' I said, squeezing myself with delight.

'This is Hollywood,' Eliot corrected, 'and yes, it is crazy.'

'Oh, come on. You're enjoying this,' I said.

His mouth quirked. 'Well, I'm enjoying you enjoying it.' He swung round and we found a parking space. He switched off the engine, then finally pushed his sunglasses back off his face, turning to me. His arm stretched along the bench seat. 'You only get to lose your Hollywood virginity once. I'm glad I could be part of it.'

I felt my cheeks flush. 'You think I'm naive to be impressed?'

'Remember that those stores have no interiors. They're just that – a front.'

'Wow, you've just turned a cowboy town into a lecture on architecture.'

He raised his eyebrows. 'So, you like the big words, do you?'

'I know a couple of others – "condescending" and "pompous" are two of them.'

He raised his hands in defeat. 'You're right, I'm sorry. That was rude of me. I've been up all night and I'm tired.'

He reached down into my footwell. The script had fallen there, and I leaned to pick it up. As I handed it over, I noticed that his fingers were stained by typewriter ink, a stubby pencil behind an ear, his shirt creased. He looked as though he'd been up all night.

'Have you been writing?' I asked.

He laughed joylessly. 'For my sins.'

'What you working on?'

'A flop.'

'I'm sure it isn't!' My good mood couldn't be punctured.

'I'm sure it is.' He climbed out of the car, then came round to my side. I took his hand and unfolded my body out of the car.

'See you later, then.' Abruptly, he dropped my hand and began to walk off towards one of the lots.

Alarmed, I ran after him. I wasn't about to let him go just yet. 'Thanks again!'

Eliot was rifling through his script, distracted. I reached up on tiptoe, trying to see over his shoulder. The pages were covered in pencil scribbles.

'Not going so well?' I ventured.

He let out a low growl. 'Seventh rewrite, and the kings still aren't happy. If I have to sit through another story conference, I'll die.'

'Maybe you need a new typewriter,' I suggested, pointing out all the missing 'S's.

'Maybe I need a new brain.'

'I wondered . . . just asking . . . but I don't suppose you know an Alecs Petraś?'

He barked a laugh of disbelief. 'Do I *know* an Alecs Petraś? I know *of* him.' He stopped and folded his arms, stuffing the pages under his armpit. 'He's a living legend in these parts. You know that, right?' He leant to stage-whisper to me from behind his hand. 'Kind of a big deal.'

'I just . . .' I gulped. 'I need to talk to him.'

Eliot began to walk away. 'Good luck! Say hi to Biff when you get kicked out.'

I took his arm. 'Please. Just tell me. Where can I find him? Please? I'll never ask anything from you, ever again. I promise.'

'You sure about that?'

'No.' I grinned.

We'd arrived at a door and Eliot swung it open to reveal a long corridor. A man was leaning against the wall, flirting with a young woman gripping a clipboard to her chest. He spotted us and sent her away with a slap on the rump.

'Hey, Eliot! Get in here! Farrow's sent us more editorial notes overnight.'

'Fucking notes. When will fucking directors learn that they're not fucking writers?'

I quickly caught the door after him. 'Please.' I was begging now. 'Where do I find Petraś?'

Digging his fists into his pockets, Eliot turned back to me. He seemed to consider for a moment.

'Last favour, OK?'

'OK.'

'And you don't mention my name for getting you in here?'

'Who are you again?'

The corner of his mouth peeled up in a smile. 'All right, then.' He steered me round and pointed over my shoulder. 'Lot thirty-nine. Ask for his PA, Arvella Hoffman.'

His colleague called impatiently. It looked like it was time for Eliot to begin the eighth rewrite.

I swallowed. 'Do I need to get past any lions or tigers or anything?'

'Nah. Just Arvella. She has a certain reputation round these parts.'

'Thanks,' I said. 'I owe you. Oh, and I hope your flop is a great success!'

His mouth twitched. 'Go on. Go get 'em.'

'I'll try.' I gave a little salute, then stepped out into the blistering heat.

I began to walk down between two rows of tall buildings – the stages – and as I passed each lot, I couldn't help peering in. One was nothing more than a gnarled mess of wires, pipes, ladders and lights, scenery flats propped up against a bare wall. Another housed some sort of nineteenth-century townhouse, and a third was being transformed into what looked like a palace interior, hammers echoing as men in dungarees crawled over the set like ants.

Lot 36, 37, 38 . . .

And there it was. Lot 39. I came to a halt before a set of aluminium steps that led to a modest door, beside which was a sign with curlicue gold lettering:

Alecs Petraś
Beauty Studio

20

'I told you to bring me the dark hair! Are we *trying* to make her look like a corpse?'

A young woman – twenty or so – scurried past a row of hairpieces set on canvas head blocks. As I entered, she flashed me a humiliated glance, her eyelashes wet with tears. The door swung shut noisily behind me.

A man with a tidy, short moustache wheeled round and stared. Above his open white coat, he was wearing the most ridiculous, drapey bow tie of clementine silk.

He glared at me. 'Who the hell are you?'

I walked over, holding out my hand. 'I'm Loretta, Mr Petraś. Loretta Darling.'

He stared, then laughed in my face. 'Mr Petraś!' He looked around at his colleagues. 'Did you hear that?'

The others tittered nervously.

He pointed to a large, framed photograph hanging behind a desk. 'That's Mr Petraś. I'm Mr Klein. I look after the wigs.'

'The . . . wigs?' I suddenly had to work very hard indeed not to stare at Klein's head, smooth and shiny as an egg.

'Who signed *her* in?' a clipped voice demanded. A woman stood in a doorway, clutching a clipboard to her bony chest, glasses dangling on a gold chain over a wine-coloured suit. Her hair was coiffed within an inch of its life and her face so made up that it looked glacial, as though it would crack if she smiled. And she certainly wasn't smiling at me. She was staring. Hard.

'Miss Hoffman? I . . . I was sent by the agency.' My heart was beating so loudly in my chest I felt sure they could hear it.

The woman didn't react. She continued staring at me, her lips pursed. After a long moment, she frowned down at her clipboard. 'We didn't send for anyone.'

Before I could reply, the girl from earlier arrived back by Mr Klein's side, holding out a shallow aluminium pan. He snatched it from her and glared at it.

'What is this?' The girl's face paled. 'What is THIS?'

He threw the tin back at her. As she scrambled to catch it, the older woman held out her hand to me. 'Day pass.'

Day pass? I made a big show of searching my pockets. 'Oh, my goodness! I must have lost it.'

She gave a sigh, as though this was all too familiar. 'Come with me.' She turned on her heel and marched quickly away, leaving me to scurry after her.

We entered another room, some sort of salon, where a blonde actress sat before a mirror. The door swung shut behind us and Klein's shouts faded. The actress glanced up from her romance novel. 'He in a bad mood again, Arvella?'

Standing next to her was a man, frowning at her face in concentration.

It was the man in the photograph. The genius behind the velvet curtain. Petraś.

His face was soft and fleshy, younger-looking than his grey hair, swept back from a severe parting. He looked less imposing than his photograph and yet there was a quiet air of authority about him that made me want to curtsy or genuflect or something.

'Sandra is crying again,' Arvella uttered with a sigh. I stood, frozen to the spot, not daring to move as all three of us women watched Petraś to see what he'd do next. He was staring hard at the actress's face, tapping a forefinger against his lip. He wore a small gold signet ring on his little finger, with some sort of crest engraved. Probably some sort of royal symbol.

At last, he spoke without looking up. 'Who've you brought me?'

Arvella gave another exaggerated sigh. 'Apparently, she was sent by the agency, but she has some sort of accent, and—'

He crooked a finger. 'Over here.'

Arvella nodded furiously at me.

I walked over to stand on the opposite side of the salon chair to Petraś, the actress seated between us. Another blonde young woman appeared carrying a tray covered in palettes and brushes. It was that girl – Alice!

Arvella's eyes narrowed.

'Now, tell me,' Petraś said, finally glancing up at me. 'This face. What would you use?'

I could see the actress's expression warning me: *Get this wrong, and you're toast, baby.*

'Petraś, I don't think she—' Arvella began.

Her employer held up a hand.

Hopefully, all my practising with the girls was about to pay off. With the flat of my hand, I gently lifted the young woman's chin and turned her face from side to side until a cheekbone caught the light. Interesting. Eyes the colour of melted chocolate. A honey tone to her skin. I turned her face the other way and picked up on the fine, dark down on her upper lip. That blonde hair was telling lies.

My mind scrolled. Miss Snively bought her make-up supplies from the prestigious Pantages building where the Alecs Petraś company had set up shop. Hopefully, we'd be speaking the same language.

'I'd go for Amber Rose,' I said. 'Something that brings out the warmth of her skin tone without clashing with the blonde.' I hesitated to suggest that it was a dye job – not in front of the talent.

'Anything else?'

I thought quickly. 'A line of white down the centre of the nose to stop it flattening out on screen.' I'd learnt that trick from the model shots at Blue Book. 'Light make-up over the lid of the eye, merging into darker grease towards the eyebrow. That'll give a long, full lid – like Garbo.'

The actress flushed with pleasure.

Petraś was less easy to impress. 'Brushes?'

I answered back like a shot. 'Angled Canadian squirrel for the dark.' I pondered. 'Sable for the lighter – it holds product well.' The only brushes I'd ever used were pony. Pony brushes were cheap, any old hair mixed. Nerves were making my hands clammy, and I let go of the actress's face. Alice flashed me an encouraging glance from the other side of the chair.

'You haven't even mentioned blush,' Petraś said gravely.

'Well, it's risky, but I'd save that till the very last. Dampen my hands, then take the pillows of my fingers, dip them in the rouge and go over anywhere in the face I wanted to look naturally flushed.'

'A wet rouge? That *is* risky.'

'It's the only way.' His nostrils flared at that. 'In my opinion, at least.' I gripped my hands behind my back. All four of us waited for Petraś's reaction. The silence stretched on so long I thought I'd burst.

At last, he spoke. 'Who taught you?'

A lie or the truth? I only had seconds to decide. I decided to risk the truth. 'I . . . I taught myself.'

A sharp inhale from Arvella. The actress raised an eyebrow. Alice's tray wobbled. Petraś said nothing and the silence stretched out taut as a high rope in the dark. I felt like I was about to lose my footing and tumble into the sawdust.

Arvella took a step forward, tapping a finger at her clipboard. 'I'm so sorry, Petraś. I don't know how she got past security. What a waste of your—'

'She's good,' he said. 'What's your name again?'

'Loretta. Loretta Darling.'

He clicked his fingers at Arvella. 'Well, Miss Darling, let's find you a uniform.'

Her face screwed up as she blustered. 'You can't just hire any girl who walks in off the street!'

'I think you'll find I can do whatever I like.'

Arvella threw her hands into the air in surrender and marched out.

'How long has it been now?' he asked suddenly.

'How long what?'

'How long have you been hanging around Biff? Six or . . . is it eight weeks?'

All this time, he'd known. My face flushed. 'I can't recall, sir.'

Alice melted away and, just like that, people were swirling around me. A white coat was shoved into my hands. From somewhere, a wheeled stool was brought to my side and someone else held out a form. I signed it blindly.

The actress winked at me in the mirror. 'Welcome to the team,' she said, reaching a hand over her shoulder for an awkward shake. 'Grace Riley.'

'Hello, Miss Riley. I'm Loretta.'

She winked. 'Just call me Grace.'

A starlet asking me to use her first name!

Petraś smoothed the drape down over Grace's shoulders. 'Miss Riley here is on a new contract for five new films, isn't that right?'

'Little old me!' she said.

Petraś tucked a lock of hair behind her ear, and she smiled at him as though he was God and her daddy all rolled into one. 'We're going to make her into a star.'

She kissed his hand. 'You're too kind.'

Arvella leant into the salon, holding a phone's mouthpiece to her chest. 'Petraś, it's Sally.'

He went to leave, taking the cradle from her. The three of us were left alone; Arvella was staring hard at me.

'Miss Hoffman . . .' I began.

Grace hopped out of her salon chair swiftly. 'Just going to powder my nose.'

Arvella folded her arms and allowed the silence to settle around us. 'You're not with an agency, are you?'

'No.'

She gave a deep sigh, as though this was all so predictable. 'And are you at least a union member?'

I shook my head.

She sank into one of the salon chairs. 'How old even are you?'

'Twenty-one.'

'At least you're legal. If you put one foot wrong, I'm calling security and they'll march you off the studio lot. Understand?'

'Yes. Thank you.' I hesitated. 'I'm sorry if I've done something to offend you.'

She raised an eyebrow. 'Offend me? You flatter yourself, Miss Darling.'

We stared at each other until Grace poked her head round the door.

'All done?' she asked brightly.

Arvella didn't take her eyes off me. 'All done.'

21

Arvella Hoffman could kiss my arse. By the end of the day, I'd learnt more with Alecs Petraś than I had in six months with Miss Emmeline Snively.

We worked for three hours straight. I learnt how to slather on a thin layer of Vaseline before any pancake was applied – that made Grace's skin glow like glass beneath the camera lens. Darker shading towards the temples. Then we drew in her eyebrows – no face had a frame without eyebrows. A dot of white eyeshadow in the inner corner of each eye – to make them pop, Petraś explained. He even let me do my line of white down the nose. Then lip liner, a ritualistic sweep from a bullet of lipstick and finally a well-placed beauty spot. Petraś left me to choose where it should go. I pencilled it in, one inch below the left corner of her mouth to accentuate her full, lush lips. Grace had *great* lips – you could imagine them muttering the most delicious filth. Hollywood was all about the filth. Finally, the wig was put in place.

'Good.' I felt as though I was about to burst with pride.

Throughout the whole session, Grace wasn't permitted to use the bathroom. Her novel remained unopened in her lap. She watched in fascination. I could see her mind whirring, trying to remember the tricks. Petraś never wrote anything down for exactly this reason.

After a while, a young man poked his head round the door. He caught sight of Grace and gave a low, appreciative whistle.

Petraś threw him a scalding look, despite Grace's laughter. 'We don't whistle at the talent, young man.'

His face coloured. 'Mr Wyler is ready for you now.'

Grace slid out of the chair and gave Petraś an extravagant air kiss on both cheeks.

'Darling, you've made me beautiful, just like you promised.' Her personality had become exaggerated along with her looks. She turned to me and held out her hand. 'Thank you, Loretta.' She took a final glance in the mirror, smoothing down her dress after the drape was removed by Arvella.

The three of us watched as Grace took the young man's hand and then we followed them out. They emerged into the harsh sunlight, before turning left.

'I hope she gets into the shade,' I said. All that hard work, ready to melt beneath the sun.

'She will if she knows what's good for her,' Arvella growled.

Grace picked her way across the tarmac, laughing and flirting.

'She's going to be a star, then?' I asked.

Petraś smiled. 'Well, she's already thick in a romance with one of the studio's other actors.'

'That's a good thing, right?'

Arvella snorted. 'If she gets into trouble, the studio will at least organize an abortion.'

'Arvella,' Petraś said, flashing a glance at me. 'Less of the gossip, please.'

Grace disappeared inside an aircraft-hangar-sized door, the froth of her petticoats bouncing with every step.

Petraś turned back inside. 'Be back here for seven in the morning tomorrow.'

I looked at Arvella.

'Well, he's not talking to me.'

I headed back indoors and found Petraś sitting at his desk. He handed me a note. 'Your wages will be twelve dollars fifty a week. Give this to the cashier. You'll pick your wages up after you've completed your first week.'

I did some rapid calculations in my head: this was far more than I'd ever earned before.

'First week up front?'

He stared. 'You have any family out here?'

I pulled back my shoulders. 'No.'

'Figures. All right, then, up front.' He peeled off notes from a fat bundle that appeared out of one of his pockets. 'You have chutzpah, I'll give you that.'

'What's *shoospa*?'

He smiled and held out the dollar bills. 'You'll find out. Now, get out of here before I change my mind.'

Back in the studio lot, I waltzed towards Biff's cabin, outlined by the sun that was starting to set behind the palm trees.

'You did it, then?' Biff called.

'I really did!' I said breathlessly.

He beamed. 'I always knew you had it in you.'

'That girl Alice was there!'

Biff's eyes bugged. 'Did she say anything?'

'She's not the one I need to worry about. You know Arvella Hoffman?'

Biff rubbed the stubble on his chin, thinking. 'Gossipy but kinda snooty-looking, like she has a rod up her . . . ?'

'That's the one. She hates me already!'

'What's to hate about you?'

Some people could have written him a list. 'I'm not going to let her spoil this for me. I'm in, Biff. I'm really in!' The words came out all in a rush.

This was it. I'd done it. I'd made my dreams come true, just like I'd said I would. Wage, boss, dollars in my pocket. I floated back towards my apartment, where I stood in front of the bathroom mirror and took out my tube of Rascal Red. The wax had nearly run out, but this modest little lipstick had travelled with me all the way from Morecambe like some sort of good-luck charm. I swiped it across my lips, admiring yet again the deep red in the mirror's reflection. I'd never have to pay for another lipstick in my life, I knew that much. But I wasn't done yet. Not by a long way.

22

Dear Enid,

I pulled it off! Can you believe it? I'm working with that prince, Alecs Petraś. I'm being paid to hang out with him! Life is on the up and up. I'd love it if you came out to see me.

Let me know your news.

Margaret x

On my first day, I was given two pristine, white coats – Petraś was the only person in Hollywood who made his staff wear a uniform. We were happy to wear them, proud to be instantly recognizable as one of Petraś's Pearls: a silly name given to us by our grateful actors, but one we couldn't help embracing. We were pearls, all growing inside the shell that Petraś carefully gave us. We should have had that name embroidered onto our kerchiefs, like at Van de Kamp's! Petraś looked after us. But I quickly discovered that, as the newest pearl, it was my job to launder everyone's coats and keep them spotless. Not the easiest task when everyone was using highly coloured pigments every single moment of their day.

Each morning, Petraś made a point of inspecting our cuffs and collars, so I quickly became familiar with every type of detergent – *Tide: a new washing miracle!* – boiling those coats on the stove, in lieu of cooking supper. I didn't care – I was happier than I'd ever been.

Except as busy as I was, I couldn't shake Raphael Goddard out of my head. I'd vowed never to spare my ex-husband another thought, but the opposite had proven to be true. I'd find myself going around the apartment, looking for any last signs of him – a crushed cigarette packet behind a pile of books, or some forgotten cologne, dusty from talcum powder in the bathroom cabinet. It wasn't that I was still in love with him – I'm not sure I ever truly was. It was more that I couldn't forgive him. To trade me like that. Was I worth so very little to him? And then of course I wanted him to know that I was succeeding.

Thank goodness for Alice. She loved to go out to the bars, and this made her a great distraction. I spent half my time running up and down stairs to the telephone in the lobby as she invited me out to one shindig or another. It was only a matter of time before she and Primrose met.

'You have to come to Ciro's!' Alice announced breathlessly, early one evening. Ciro's was a nightclub, the walls famously painted a deep crimson, the colour of passion and excitement, lending itself to discreet corner booths where the light was flattering up close, but no one else could see what was going on. The colour choice had worked. There might have been fights out on the dance floor, but in those booths the rich and the famous could find some sort of discretion. Perfect for Hollywood. Everyone who was anyone went there, even John

F. Kennedy. 'Ella Fitzgerald is playing a secret gig! I know the doorman; he can get us in.'

'Ella . . .' I swallowed. She was one of my favourite singers, the queen of jazz found singing in the streets of Harlem. Not that I particularly knew what Harlem was. 'That's incredible, Alice. How did you find out?'

'Oh, I was talking to Mr Wallichs in Music City.'

'*The* Mr Wallichs?'

'He and Dad went to high school together.' Alice had grown up in Hollywood, and half of what I found amazing she took for granted. 'Anyway, meet you outside at seven?'

I only had one problem. Primrose had turned up, and I knew it would hurt her feelings to be dumped.

'Can I bring a friend?' I asked.

'If she can pay her way, sure,' Alice said.

I grinned. 'Don't you worry about that.'

I turned up outside Ciro's wearing a cute little two-piece – a cropped top and dress skirt with a sash bow tied at my waist, in colours of navy and white.

'Ahoy, sailor!' Alice said, giving me a stiff little salute as she greeted me on the sidewalk. She wore a violet ostrich-feather bolero over a floor-length gown and silver heels.

Primrose stepped out of the drug store next door, where she'd gone for some gum. 'Well, hello. I'm Primrose.'

She wore her own impressive outfit: a dress of Chinese silk and some sort of tortoiseshell fan comb in her hair. As she and Alice shook hands, I considered that between them, these two women owned more clothes than I could wear in three lifetimes.

Alice and Primrose were already talking as though they were old friends.

'You live in Silver Lake? I know that area!'

'Oh yeah, how?'

'Hey, ladies,' I interrupted. 'Let's get inside before we're thrown off the sidewalk.'

Already, there was a line forming outside the night-club, along the curved walkway, excited couples chatting animatedly, hoping to get in. The nightclub's name was picked out in giant curly neon script on the roof and a doorman stood at the entrance. He had the typical door-man stature: imposing. Reminded me of the guy back at the Winter Gardens in Morecambe. But there was one big difference. This guy wore the most immaculate tux I'd ever seen. It was all handstitched buttonholes and a made-to-measure fit.

'Keep with me,' Alice whispered.

Primrose side-eyed me as Alice led the way. 'Is she with the Mafia?'

'No, she just parties a lot.'

'Good girl. I like her already.'

We went to join Alice at the top of the line.

'Well, surely you remember me? I was here last month with some friends,' Alice pleaded. She pushed her chest forward in the naive hope that could help jog his memory. Bless Alice for trying.

'Isn't everyone?' the doorman said, looking past her in a bored manner.

'And you said you could get me in any time I wanted. Remember?'

'I don't say that to no one,' he growled.

'Are you sure it's the same doorman, Alice?' I whispered. But before she could respond, a voice rang out.

'Tommie!'

The doorman's eyes nearly popped out of his head. 'As I live and breathe!' He pushed past Alice to scoop Primrose into a hug. 'How ya doing?'

'Fine, just fine.' She patted him on the chest and then removed an imaginary speck of dust before smoothing a hand over his jacket. 'Looking dapper, Tommie.'

He blushed! The big brute of a man actually blushed. 'Well, you know I like my threads.' He straightened his cuffs. 'What do you think?'

Primrose nodded in approval. 'Your ma would be proud.'

Tommie's face turned an even deeper shade of red. 'Now, don't start me off, Primrose.'

'I know, I know. She was a good woman.'

By this time, everyone in the line was listening. Who needed movies?

'So, what's happening with you?' Tommie asked. 'Any beaus?'

Primrose blushed, and she tapped a finger against his chest. 'Oh, you! Stop it, now.' She nodded past her friend. 'You going to let me and my friends in?'

'Of course!' He stepped aside, and Primrose crooked her finger at me and Alice. 'You coming or what?'

Tommie beamed after Primrose as she stepped through the hallowed doors. 'What a dame,' he whispered.

Alice kept close to me as we followed. 'Primrose is well connected, huh? Lucky us!'

I smiled at Alice's wide, innocent beam. 'She sure is.'

Soon, we were seated on a row of stools, hugging our martinis. Beside the bar, Ella was crooning into the microphone, her voice like honey. Tables studded the floor, people crowded around them, women sat on their fellas' knees. Normally, the place would have been a cacophony of noise, but tonight you could have heard a pin drop as we hung on Ella's every soul-infused word.

Well, apart from the barfly sat next to us. He kept calling the bartender over to refill his glass and would knock into us as he slid off his stool for the umpteenth time.

I elbowed Primrose. 'Got any tranquillizers with you?' I whispered. 'We could slip one into his drink.'

Primrose whispered back sternly. 'You can't just go around messing with people's drinks, Loretta.'

'I'm kidding!' I spluttered.

Just then, one of the staff came over to have a quiet word in the man's ear and he was led away between songs.

We watched him leave. 'And that,' Primrose said, 'is why we need gentlemen in our lives!'

Alice nodded with the deep knowing that only several martinis could give a person, her nod morphing into a sad shake of the head.

I lifted my glass. 'Here's to the actual gentlemen!' Not that I knew many, and I wasn't sure Primrose did either. Messily, we clunked glasses, and then slid round to see what else was going on.

Primrose pointed a cigarette through the crowd. 'Check it out. Dean Martin.'

Alice screeched when she spotted the deeply tanned, tall man clutching a tumbler of whisky. 'Oh my goodness, he's just teamed up with Jerry Lewis! Is Jerry here? Is he here!'

'Calm down, Alice.' I laid a hand on her arm. 'Stay cool, remember?'

And that's when it happened. A figure, spotted across the room. Stanley. The man with the birthmark. The man who'd watched, who'd helped the self-styled Emperor steer me into a marble bathroom.

My glass slammed down on the bar. 'We need to go.' I scrambled around for my jacket, before remembering that I'd left it in the cloakroom.

'What's wrong, Loretta?'

My eyes skittered past Primrose's anxious face, just in time to see Stanley spot me. 'I'm leaving. You girls stay if you like.'

'No!' Alice leapt from her stool, tottering unsteadily as she thrust her glass in the air. 'The three amigos!'

We pushed through the crowd towards the exit, but Alice was leading the way and obliviously took us closer and closer to Stanley's table. With Primrose bringing up the rear, I was trapped. He reached out a firm hand to stop me.

'Good to see you again, Mrs Goddard,' he said, forcing me to look down into his face. That bloated, leery face. And yet there was something else I could see there. Something pleading.

'I'm Miss Darling now,' I choked out, shaking off his hand.

He looked past me. 'Hi, Primrose.'

'Oh, hi, Stanley.' Of course, Primrose knew everyone in Hollywood, even if she'd been too drunk to see him assault me. I couldn't blame her for that. She gave him one of her sweetest smiles and we spilled out onto the sidewalk. I couldn't get away from him fast enough. That man? He didn't deserve to know my name. Any name.

23

'Who's up?' The next day, I arrived bright and early at the studio, carrying my pile of perfectly starched white coats. I hadn't slept all night, pondering the ghosts from my past. They were hanging about far too much for my liking.

'Sally Dee,' Petraś said. 'We're using compressed gold – sixty dollars an ounce.'

'Sally Dee! She's one of my ma's favourites!'

'Let me give you a piece of advice,' Petraś said, looking at me over the top of his spectacles. 'Don't try telling Sally how much your *mother* loves her. She doesn't appreciate being made to feel old.'

'Of . . . of course.'

Arvella's head appeared round the door. 'She's here.'

'Mood?' Petraś asked.

Arvella grimaced. 'Screaming already.' She slipped further into the room and lowered her voice. 'Sally's contract isn't being renewed.'

Petraś paused in what he was doing. 'Does she know?'

Arvella shook her head. 'I don't think so, not yet.'

'Then let's keep it that way.' He turned back to his jars and bottles.

I'd already learnt that the motion-picture contract system was a gilded cage built on the foundations of ritual and hierarchy. The producers, writers, directors, actors – all shackled to a studio, until they weren't. And bottom of that hierarchy? The actors. They were chess pieces, moved from one movie to another on a whim. They had no say in the matter. The agents were their manipulators, and the business managers their babysitters. Everyone taking a cut, until there was nothing left. Depending on success or failure, the people surrounding an actor could fade away like wisps of smoke, leaving them to look around, blinking in confusion, wondering why their name was no longer in lights.

'Well, darlings,' said Petraś, glancing at me and Arvella, 'shall we begin?'

Arvella went to collect Sally, while Petraś disappeared into an anteroom to gather supplies. I was left on my own, dabbing my damp hands on my uniform and praying that I wouldn't make a fool of myself. I was about to breathe the same air as Sally Dee!

The door swung open, and she stood silhouetted in the frame. She wore a neat navy suit and white gloves, as well groomed as a president's wife. Every bit the Oscar-nominated star. Three times nominated that is, but never a winner.

I moved forward, my hand held out to shake hers.

She glared. 'Who the fuck is this?'

Arvella gave a sigh. 'Some girl who's inveigled her way into Petraś's team.'

Sally cocked her head. 'Impressive. It takes a lot to get under his skin.'

She reached into her handbag and drew out a

cigarette case, handing it to me. It was black leather with a gold trim and had a weight to it that suggested the gold trim was real.

'Miss Dee would like a cigarette,' Arvella hissed.

'Oh!'

I fumbled to open the case and take a cigarette out from the elastic. Was I meant to place it between her actual lips? Tentatively, I started to raise the cigarette to her face, her lips suddenly taking up all my vision, but she snatched it away with a curse that would have made a sailor proud.

'Where did Petraś find her?' she drawled.

From behind Sally, Arvella was shooting me a withering look. I bet she had every make-up artist in this studio running scared. Sally brought out a lighter and I went to help again.

'Don't bother,' she said, snapping a flare of orange. She took a deep inhale, the tobacco crackling in her lungs as she sent out twin plumes from her nostrils.

'Sally, dear,' Petraś said, reappearing from the anteroom. 'Wonderful to see you.' He went to kiss her hand. 'This is Loretta, my new apprentice. She'll work with us today.'

'I know. Arvella says she's a creep.'

'I didn't—' Arvella began to protest.

'Mix Miss Dee's martini, would you?' Petraś said, cutting her off with a warning look.

With a scowl, Arvella went over to a drinks trolley. It wasn't yet 10 a.m., but who was I to judge?

When Arvella returned, Sally peeled off her gloves

and expertly received the glass without spilling a precious drop. All three of us watched as she took a sip, then paused before uttering, 'It'll do.'

Palpable relief flooded the room.

Petraś steered Sally towards the workstation. As Sally lowered herself into a salon chair, a secret look passed between them as he smoothed the drape over her shoulders. I flashed a glance at Arvella, to see that she was watching them as closely as I was, but her lips were curled in a way that I couldn't interpret.

Petraś began to smooth wisps of hair away from Sally's face, in preparation for the skull cap. 'I see your mood has improved.'

She raised her glass in an ironic toast. 'Fuck you.'

I'd known of Sally Dee ever since I was a child. Ma adored her – we'd seen every one of her movies. But it was something else entirely to see the reality, up close. As my mentor began to work, a tiny brass vial sat in her lap. It had a lid that she'd flick back; there were tiny holes in the end that allowed her to tip white powder onto the back of her hand. Every now and then, she'd take a snort.

Petraś busied himself removing her day make-up and applying the tape – an instant face lift that most actresses insisted upon – and then he was ready. He waited for her glass to be refilled for a second time, then: 'Shall we apply the gold?'

'Give me the works,' Sally rasped, leaning her head back and closing her eyes.

I crept nearer, having hoovered up the script the night

before. Sally was playing the deluded landlady of a haunted desert inn but had insisted on a bizarre Cleopatra vibe.

Carefully, Arvella carried over a tray. On it was the sixty-dollar gold leaf, pressed between sheets of tissue paper.

Petraś had already talced any exposed skin on his arms to avoid the foil catching, and now wore white cotton gloves. He peeled back a layer of paper and then took a pair of tweezers to tear off a strip of gold. He'd applied Vaseline to Sally's eyelids, bringing out the fragile blue of her eyeline even more. The suspended gold leaf danced in a stream of cool air from a vent.

'Turn the air con off,' he ordered.

Arvella ran to do as he said. We watched the gold tremble, then it stilled.

'Get on with it,' Sally growled.

What happened next was nothing less than delicious. Arvella rolled her eyes behind Sally's back – just as the legendary actress opened her eyes a sliver.

Instantly a voice floated up from the salon chair. 'I can see what you're doing, you know.'

Arvella's cheeks drained of blood and from the look on Petraś's face I guessed that his assistant had just lost that year's bonus.

'Sally, I'm so—' Arvella gabbled.

'Oh, shut up!' Sally threw a glance at Petraś. 'Get rid of her, will you?'

'You'd better leave,' Petraś said.

Arvella's cheeks flushed. 'I apologize.'

A growl emerged from deep in Sally's throat. 'Your apologies mean shit to me.'

Arvella's face was a mask of hatred. 'I really don't think—'

'You don't get paid to think,' Sally said, cutting her off. 'Get out!'

As the door creaked shut after Arvella's departing figure, Sally turned to me, holding out her drained glass. 'Mix me another.'

Now that the distraction was over, Petraś carefully draped gold leaf over an eyelid with the tweezers. It was the tiniest piece, small as a flake of snow, angled into the crease of her socket, and he stippled it there with the end of a firm brush. Over and over, gold leaf was applied in tiny flakes. I found myself holding my breath as the gold accentuated every pillow and crease of Sally's eyelids. It was like watching human flesh transformed into art, but nothing prepared me for what would happen when Sally finally opened her eyes.

Our queen. Hollywood's golden star. She deserved the accolade. She was like royalty, sitting in that chair – and she knew it. Noble, her back straight, a wired hairband pulling her face taut so that she looked immediately ten years younger. This was more than make-up – it was magic.

After a few moments of taking in her face from every angle, she gave a nod of approval and eased herself out of the chair, unknotting the drape. An assistant had appeared from nowhere and held out her costume – a landlady's nasty polyester housecoat. She shouldered it on, and the ghoulish transformation was complete.

'Darling.' Petraś kissed the back of her hand. She held herself as if she was the most beautiful woman in the world, which she was. Then he steered her towards the wings, telling her, 'Kill 'em dead.'

Sally didn't even acknowledge him. He didn't need it. The two of us watched her glide away, the director's assistant running to greet her.

'Tell that bastard he's putting my speech back in.' Her legendary voice carried over. 'If he thinks he can cut my part the night before, he's a damn fool.'

Petraś must have seen the astonishment on my face.

'Never underestimate a star,' he whispered, in obvious awe. 'No one can light up a screen like Sally Dee.'

24

A month flew past. I worked hard, enjoying the fact that my new job could help me hide. There's a strange detail to becoming part of the system; you become invisible. It was all so big! The studio liked to put up statistics every week on a green felt board. *Sixty million people went to the movies this week!* I should have been intimidated, but I didn't care about those numbers. There was only a single number important to me – the number one. Loretta Darling. I was going to make it!

In the meantime, all I needed to do was be humble, turn up on time and keep my mouth shut. Shame I couldn't manage the last detail; I could never quite stop myself from giving pointers to the other Petras's Pearls. Despite their training, they didn't seem to understand make-up in the way I did. I wasn't being arrogant; I was just better. And they should have thanked me!

I'd coach them on how to judge an eyebrow, or what to look for when you were judging a chin. Let me tell you, there are all sorts of chins out there: square, pointed, narrow – or the worst, weak. It was up to us to give a person's face a frame, and that meant the whole face! If they were just going to shadow in the cheeks, then the other Pearls were fools! Of course, they didn't appreciate my advice.

I avoided everyone else around the studio. After my unfortunate encounter with Stanley flipping Hughes, I needed to keep my head down and clear.

I reassured myself by sending gossip to Enid. It was amazing who would just walk the sidewalks out here! I was invisible to them, but I could spot a star from a ten-mile radius.

Dear Enid,

You would not believe what happened today. There I was, walking down the sidewalk (pavement) when guess who came out of a store (shop) and bumped right into me . . . Only Lauren flipping Bacall! Remember her in 'Key Largo'? Oh, didn't we both want to be Miss Bacall, hiding from a hurricane? Like we knew what a hurricane was!

Your loving sister, Margaret xxx

I relished this quieter life – watching and not being watched. I'd be in bed by eight thirty sharp, with an eye mask and ear plugs with little silk tassels. Alice was appalled at my lack of social life. I only let her drag me out on the occasional weekend. Heck, I was living like a nun, bang next door to a brothel! Primrose had been out a lot in the evenings, but occasionally she would come by, asking about Alice and sometimes Sally. Mostly, about Sally.

'So, what's it like, working with a bona-fide star?'

'I'm not allowed to say. You know that!'

Primrose would give me a long, straight stare. 'Excuse me?'

Then we'd both laugh, and I'd say, 'OK. You really want to know?'

'I really want to know.' She'd point a long, painted fingernail at me. 'And don't give me any of the studio bullshit.'

We'd descend into gossip. 'Obviously, a raging alcoholic.'

'Obviously.'

'Beautiful in a crinkled kind of way.'

'Plastic surgery?'

I'd think back to the unnaturally narrowed cat eyes and the scars behind her ears. 'Maybe.'

Primrose would nod, hugging herself. 'So, at least one face lift, then?'

And yet I did want to protect Sally. Sure, she'd had plastic surgery. Hadn't all of them? Hadn't every woman in this town been forced to endure the fragile skin of their face being cut apart, hairlines reduced with electrolysis, flesh sliced from their noses?

'Now tell me . . .' Primrose said one time, leaning forward. 'What's her home life like?'

'I have no idea,' I said honestly. 'Sally just turns up on set, we mix her a pre-breakfast martini . . . For her, the rest of the day is a blur – until the cameras start rolling.'

Primrose flumped back in the chair I'd rescued from a thrift store. 'Well, that's disappointing.'

It wasn't. There was nothing about Sally that could be considered disappointing. It wasn't just her fame. The two of us had nothing in common and yet it felt as though we understood each other. The old dame and the ingénue. Both of us wanting the camera to be turned away until we were ready.

Unfortunately, there was an eye that one of us couldn't escape, no matter how hard I tried. Arvella had been watching me like a hawk ever since I'd turned up at Lot 39. Most people would let one little white lie go, but not Arvella. Oh no. Seemed like she wanted to know *everything*. I'd worked my backside off for her, turning up early and leaving late, keeping my head down – and even that wasn't enough.

One day she took me aside. 'You know, Loretta . . . You don't have to be so ambitious all the time.'

'I don't think I have been,' I protested genuinely. 'I haven't tried to be anything.'

'Yet you keep doing more than your strict hours and really . . . you're making the other girls feel uncomfortable.'

I looked back over my shoulder. Everyone's heads suddenly dipped over their clients, all apart from Alice who threw me a sympathetic glance. Kind, sweet Alice.

'It's just that everyone has their rota,' she continued, professional to a fault through the ice of her words. 'It doesn't work when someone breaks the rules. Unions, you know.'

I was being ordered to work *less* hard?

'Anyway,' said Arvella, 'the good news is that you've finished your turn on the coats. Debra will take over now.'

She gave a little wave and Debra scowled back.

'Loretta, can you show Debra how it works?' Arvella clicked her fingers and Debra came running over.

Debra's smile fell from her face the minute Arvella's back was turned. 'You haven't been sacked yet, then?'

'Why would I be sacked?'

'You have a reputation, you know.'

'Over here.' I ignored Debra's tone and led her to the cloakroom, the walls lined with jackets and cardigans on hooks. In a corner was a large laundry trolley where we'd toss our coats at the end of each day. 'You take them home, boil-wash them, bring them back in when they're dry and ironed. Simple as.'

Debra's eyes bugged. 'I can't do that! I don't even know where our laundry room is!'

'You have a laundry room?'

Debra shrugged. 'Apparently. Our housekeeper deals with that.' Her eyes lit up. 'Hey, that's it! The housekeeper can do it!'

'You have a laundry room *and* a housekeeper?' My stomach roiled with sudden jealousy.

As I showed Debra where the laundry bags were and the best way to fold a coat, it all came out. Her father was an entertainment lawyer and a quiet word in the right ear had landed Debra a job. And she called me a sham! 'I mean, why not? I don't have anything else to do until I get married.' She didn't actually have a boyfriend; just took it for granted that she'd get hitched one day. She already knew the names she'd give her babies (two – a boy and a girl). In the meantime, she was turning up late and berating the rest of us for trying to forge our careers. What a punk!

As long as I let her talk about other people, she was happy, always so full of studio gossip. Once we'd finished, she slipped an oblong of cards out of her pocket. 'I get these. I mean, it's a bore sometimes – receiving so many party invitations – but you know what these indulged stars are like.'

I didn't, but I recognized gold dust when I saw it. 'How did you—'

She slid through the cards, casting them aside. Actually throwing them on the floor!

'Gregory Peck – past it. Rita Hayworth, whatever. God, it's boring!'

I'd have loved to have been so tired by Hollywood in the way that Debra was. Actually, I wouldn't. Who the heck did she think she was?

'How do you even get these invitations?' I asked.

'Spares from Daddy. The ones they can't get rid of.' She tucked the last invitation away, clearly enjoying the jealous look on my face. 'I went to a hideous one last year. New actor – lord, he was so desperate. Calls himself the Emperor. You heard of him?'

My skin prickled. 'You were there?'

'Of course I was! You as well? Oh, you poor thing.' She looked me up and down doubtfully, as though the entire party had been a wash-out. Without waiting for my response, she stalked away.

Right then and there a flip switched in my head. Enough with hiding! Enough of being invisible and building my way from the ground up. I was going to get back out there. But how? Almost instantly, a name occurred to me. The person I hadn't seen in weeks, who liked being invisible himself but somehow – somehow! – seemed to hold this whole town in his fist. The man who'd spotted a no-mark at a party and introduced himself. He had to know people. He'd got me into Hollywood, after all. Scott flipping Eliot. I was going to find him!

25

It didn't take much for me to bribe Eliot's telephone number out of Biff; by now, the man adored me.

I called him from my building's lobby and invited myself out. If he was surprised, he didn't show it. Not long after, Eliot picked me up from my apartment, discreetly ignoring the nails in the wall from which my clothes hung, and the dripping bathroom tap with its brown water from the rusted plumbing. Primrose and Alice had come round to help me get ready and it had been fun to watch people meet – consciously – the first time.

'You're the writer,' she'd said, shaking his hand.

'And you're the . . .'

'Prostitute,' she finished for him. 'We met at the Emperor's, though I think I had passed out by then.'

I was impressed at how smoothly Eliot moved the conversation on. 'Well, it's going to be something entirely different tonight.'

'Romantic?' Alice prompted, making my face flush.

'Oh, the Garden of Allah is nothing less,' Eliot said. He held out the crook of his arm. 'Are you ready, Miss Darling?'

'She's always ready!' Primrose said.

I shot her an evil look behind Eliot's back and she

instantly drew an invisible zip across her mouth. She and Alice were enjoying this far too much! Why had I ever allowed them to come round here?

Eliot led me down to his car. 'You have the best friends,' he said, opening the passenger door.

'Can we just get there? I want to see what *romantic* looks like.'

He went round to the driver's seat. 'Oh, you'll see.'

And damn him, he'd been right. The Garden of Allah was a complex of twenty-five Spanish stucco villas.

Starlets wandered around the pool, silhouetted by underwater lights. A band leader played a piano beneath the semi-tropical trees.

'F. Scott Fitzgerald used to stay here.' Eliot glanced at me. 'You know who he was, right?'

I shrugged. 'Wrote a book about parties?'

Eliot laughed quietly. 'Something like that.'

A woman ran out to greet us as Eliot climbed out of his car.

'Hello, Christine. This is Loretta.'

'Well, aren't you cute?'

As I got out, Christine looked at me as though I was something she'd won at a fair. Her glance shifted back to Eliot and there was a flicker of something.

'Come on – come in and meet everyone.'

Her accent was English, but nothing like mine. She reminded me of Princess Margaret – she wore the same regal lip colour and heavy kohl. Her frock was red rayon covered in black daisies, nipped in at the waist and with a pegged hem so that she sashayed as she led us inside, the lining hissing against her thighs. Her hair must have been cut every six weeks on the dot. Once inside, she kicked off her satin heels and padded down the hallway in her stockinged feet.

'Dorothy Parker was here, but you just missed her.'

Eliot took my hand and I felt my skin spark along with the glint of Christine's exposed metal zipper. From the room beyond floated the sound of a record player. A haze of cigarette smoke billowed out to greet us.

'Everyone!' Christine announced. 'Eliot's here – and he's brought a young lady!'

All the men turned like sheep. Half of them wore spectacles. One of them was actually smoking a pipe.

'Why are they staring?' I whispered.

'Don't worry about it.' Eliot stroked the pad of his thumb across the back of my hand. 'They're just jealous that I'm with the prettiest woman in the room.'

'Prettier than Grace Riley?'

'Never heard of her,' he joked. 'Come on,' he said. 'Let's get a drink.'

We squeezed between guests towards the kitchen as the conversation started to pick up again and found a giant cut-glass punch bowl sitting on the Formica top. The contents looked nuclear.

Eliot filled a punch cup, passing it to me. He watched as I took a hesitant sip. It was so obnoxiously sweet from pineapple juice and coconut that my face scrunched up.

'Jeez Louise!'

'Christine's favourite recipe,' he said.

'No taste, then?'

'Taste enough to invite us.' Eliot reached for a glass tumbler and poured some whisky from a flask he'd procured out of his pocket.

'Hey, hey, hey!' I protested. 'I thought we were drinking punch?' He clinked his glass against mine and took a sip. 'Well?' I said.

'Oh, I've had Christine's punch before. I just wanted to see what you thought.'

I suddenly understood why the bowl was still so full of the violently yellow liquid, despite the number of guests.

I screwed up my face. 'Are you teasing me, Mr Eliot?'

He took the punch cup from me and poured the contents down the sink.

'Let me get you something else,' he said, moving towards the bucket of wine bottles. 'Then I'll introduce you to the others.'

26

As Eliot led me to the pool, a voice carried over. 'And they say Jean Muir is a sympathizer!'

'That broad? A commie?'

'You never can tell. Gotta keep your eyes peeled, folks.'

The group's conversation stopped abruptly as we drew closer.

'Everyone, this is Loretta Darling, all the way from Blighty,' announced Eliot. He drew me into the light. 'Loretta, this is Paul, James, Otto . . .'

I shook everyone's hands. 'Hello, nice to meet you. Hello, how wonderful.' I was never going to remember all these names.

Christine narrowed her eyes against a thread of cigarette smoke. 'You work with Petraś, right?'

'That's right,' I replied. 'I don't think I've seen you, though.'

Otto snickered. 'She sneaks around, this one.'

Christine kicked him in the ankle. 'Oh, shush you! I don't sneak around.' She cast a fleeting look at Eliot, then turned back to me. 'I've heard about you, that's all.'

At a glass table, some of the men were building a pyramid of cards.

'Hey, there's Charlie, my co-writer. Hey, Charlie!' Eliot took me by the arm. 'Come and say hi.'

As we moved away, I looked back over my shoulder. Christine was still watching Eliot as he touched Charlie's shoulder, who grunted in acknowledgement, concentrating hard as he added more cards to the pyramid, which wobbled dangerously.

'. . . and he said that the whole sequence was trash. Threw it back in my face!' said one of the men as he balanced a horizontal card on top of the teetering pile.

'Bastard!'

'He wouldn't understand good dialogue even if it was Shakespeare!'

'Oh, come on! Who here understands Shakespeare?'

The men laughed in agreement and the conversation moved on.

'Say, you heard about this new actress Grace Riley?'

Grace. She was the one I'd first made up, the day that Eliot had snuck me into the studio.

'The blonde one?' someone asked. 'Yeah, some makeup artist or other was spreading rumours about her. Won't she be starring in *The Witch* with the witch?'

'That's her,' the other man continued. 'Dating James Luke.'

One of them gave a low whistle. 'That's brave.'

'Brave or dumb,' Charlie said.

Christine crushed her cigarette out and came over to join us.

'So!' she said, turning to Eliot. 'How's it going with *The Misbelievers*?'

Eliot's eye twitched. 'Good, good.'

'You got the finance?'

'I hope so.' He flashed a glance at the other writers. Christine's eyes twinkled with amusement, and she rolled her eyes.

There was a sudden cry as the pyramid of cards collapsed. 'McLellan, you dickwad!'

McLellan shrugged in apology as Charlie laughed in resignation and stood up to greet Eliot, smacking fists with him.

'Hey! Good to see you.'

'You, too.'

The men at the table returned to their gossiping. '. . . and besides, the Emperor can do whatever he wants.' Instinctively, I edged closer to Eliot.

Charlie rolled his eyes. 'God, they never stop,' he muttered.

'Rumour has it, he took a girl out for a drive,' said McLellan. He looked around. 'Up into the hills.'

Everyone groaned.

'And?' Christine's voice interrupted, sharp and cold.

'He came back with scratches all over his face. New girl in town. She didn't understand the rules. Next day, she was on the train out. Escorted to the station, no less.'

The men all laughed.

'I don't think that's very funny,' I found myself saying. Everyone at the table looked up in surprise.

McLellan's smile didn't falter. 'Who said I was trying to be funny?' He blew a cloud of blue smoke into the air. 'Just telling it like it is.'

Fury thundered in my ears.

'Come on, Loretta,' Christine said. 'Let's find a drink.'

She took my arm and threw the men a filthy look as we headed back inside.

'Thank you,' I whispered.

She gave my arm a squeeze. 'No worries. Small dicks, every single one of them.'

Inside, the jazz had given way to rock 'n' roll and people were dancing. Well, trying to. They were writers, after all. Christine pushed past her guests and grabbed a misted bottle from the refrigerator, then rinsed a couple of glasses in the sink to slosh wine into them. She passed a glass to me.

'Bottoms up.' She took a slug. 'Christ! Sometimes McLellan drives me so mad I could kill him.' She looked at me over the rim of her glass. 'So, how long have you and Eliot known each other?'

'A few months.'

'So, not that long then?'

'What about you?'

'Oh, pretty long. We've been there for each other, you know? Through thick and thin.'

Good for her.

She nudged her shoulder against mine. 'So, you're the Lip Girl?'

'Well, it's nice to hear my reputation's getting about,' I said with a grin. 'What's the deal with Grace and James?'

Christine lit another cigarette and filled me in. James had been discovered working as a gardener on one of those difficult-to-maintain Hollywood lawns. 'He slept in the shed. Didn't have a dime to his name.'

Despite being third-generation American Japanese,

his family had been interned in an airfield trailer park during the war. 'Imagine that,' Christine said, shaking her head. Apparently, when James's family had finally been released, he'd come straight to Hollywood. James was lucky; his looks were difficult to interpret. He had one other advantage – startling blue eyes. His agent had changed his name and hawked him as a white man.

'The problem is,' Christine finished, 'the studio might sell him as white, but they don't want him near their women. If they found out he and Grace were dating, they'd run her straight out of town. Him, too.'

'But if people here know, surely the execs do?' I asked.

'Not necessarily. The higher you get, the less you know. Grace could get away with it – if she's lucky. And if she's really lucky, she'll fall out of love with him and move on.'

I shook my head. 'This town . . . it's really something.' But I couldn't help wondering: was Grace lucky or clever? Maybe I'd underestimated her. Maybe.

'Come on.' Christine drained her glass. 'Let's see what the guys are up to. Probably exchanging jokes about minors.'

'You OK?' Eliot asked, once we returned.

I nodded.

'Wanna leave?'

I nodded again.

He took my elbow. 'We're off,' he announced.

'Already?' Christine pulled a sad little moue of a smile.

'Another party,' Eliot explained. 'You know how it is. Come on, Loretta.'

Christine called goodbye as we slipped away down the side of the house.

'Do we really have another party to go to?' I asked, as Eliot held the car door open for me.

His eyes danced in the dark. 'What do you think?'

I leant my elbows on the door. 'I think you're a very bad man, Mr Eliot.'

'Oh, call me that again,' he said, grinning. 'I like it.'

Then he turned on the ignition. It only took three attempts.

27

The apartment wasn't entirely as I'd expected. I'd imagined toppling piles of books and overflowing ashtrays. Instead, Eliot's place was all open plan and oh-so tidy: oak floors polished to a high beeswax shine, neat drapes at the windows, and doorways that seemed to disappear into nowhere. Did he have a spare-time job as a housekeeper?

He strolled around, switching on soft globes of light. There was a window that had been left open for cool evening air, and muslin shades billowed like ghosts.

Wordlessly, he placed a record on the turntable and brought out iced martinis from the refrigerator, glasses misting perfectly.

'You don't have any books.'

He lit a cigarette. 'People collect books to make a statement about themselves.'

'But you're a writer.'

He sank into a chair, raising his glass in a toast. 'There are two types of scribes. The kind who wants to be immortal, and . . . the other sort.'

'The other sort?' I sat opposite him, folding my legs beneath me.

'The ones who realize that it's all nonsense.'

'Is that you?'

'Yes.'

'I don't buy it.' I leant forward, elbows on my knees. 'I don't believe for a moment that you don't care.'

He gave me a level gaze. 'Do you ever stop?'

'Stop what?'

'Being so persistent. Let's talk about you instead.'

'Go for it.'

He paused, thinking. 'I liked seeing your digs.'

'I think you'll discover that those digs – as you call them – were listed as having water throughout and soundproof floors.'

'And do they?'

'Well, I have running water.'

'And what was with all those colours?'

Darn it, he'd spotted the lipstick samples out on my kitchen counter. 'Stuff.'

'Stuff?'

'What do you want me to say? I'm ambitious, all right?'

'Does your boss know?'

'Who cares? I don't answer to him!'

'Like I said, your *boss*.' He gave far too much emphasis to that last word.

'Whatever. Did you ever let anyone stop you from writing your first story?'

He inclined his head. 'No.'

'Well, then.' I glanced around. 'Got any snacks?'

'All right, all right.' He held up his hands. 'Just saying, it might help sometime if you got permission.'

'Permission to do what? Be myself, have a dream? Jeez!' I took a sip of my drink. 'I thought you'd believe in all that stuff.' I bugged my eyes at him, waiting for an answer. Who was he, the make-up police?

'OK, OK – ignore me.' He drained the last of his martini and held up his glass. 'Another?'

But just then, the record came to an end in a hiss of needle and I shook my head. One martini was more than enough.

'Would you like me to show you around?' he said instead.

'I thought you'd never ask.' Poking around in other people's homes was one of my favourite hobbies.

As we got to our feet, the whole apartment fell quiet, apart from the cicadas singing from beyond the billowing curtains. He took my hand and drew me along behind him. I liked it.

'This is the kitchen – there's a terrace just off it – and here's the dining room. This is the guest bedroom and there's mine. Oh! I need to find you some pyjamas – hold on.'

I blinked. 'I'm staying over?'

'Sure you're staying over. I'm not driving you home after this martini. You don't mind, do you?'

'Of course I don't mind.'

'Then it's decided.'

He went back down the hallway and pulled open the doors to a built-in closet, fumbling through piles of clothes.

Abandoned on the threshold of his bedroom, I couldn't help stepping inside. A bedside lamp cast a warm glow over the immaculately made bed and the drapes that hung rod-straight. I spotted a framed photograph on the bedside table – of a woman. She gazed right down the camera lens, confident of her place in the world, almost challenging the photographer. I felt my mouth turn dry. Behind the frame stood a mahogany book trough and my gaze scrolled down the row of cracked spines in various shades of pink and cream. The titles were either sentimental or racy, the type of novels Enid would have loved. *You Have Chosen*, *Odd Girl Out*, *Darling, I Hate You*.

I heard a noise behind me as Eliot entered the room.

'So, you do have some books!' I said.

His face was dark. 'Some.' Stiffly, he held out the pyjamas. 'Here.'

'Eliot, I'm sorry – I didn't mean to intrude.'

'The bathroom's just along there.' He nodded down the hallway. 'And the bed is made up in the spare room.'

I wanted to take his face in my hands, to smooth away the frown. Instead, I said a quiet goodnight. Seemed safer.

'Thank you.' I stepped back out into the hallway.

'Your toothbrush is pink,' he said. 'There's one in the bathroom cabinet.'

'I'll see you in the morning?'

But, by then, Eliot had already closed his bedroom door.

28

The next morning, I helped Debra fetch the coats from her new shiny red Chevy. 'A birthday present,' she'd smugly disclosed. 'Daddy knows how hard I've been working.' The car was gaudy as hell and suited Debra down to a T.

We each carried a laundry bag so huge that we could barely see over the top of them. As we struggled across the lot, I swerved to avoid a speeding golf cart – and bumped straight into someone coming the other way, the coats falling from the bag into a pile at my feet.

'Oh, my goodness!' I bent to retrieve them, with Debra going on about how I was such a pinhead and her housekeeper had worked through the night, and might I be more careful?

'Let me,' offered a deep, gravelly voice as someone knelt beside me. Not the type of voice that cared about make-up artists' white coats.

It was the Emperor.

I froze as he scooped up the coats, bundling them against his chest. The overpowering woody aroma of cologne carried over to me.

'Loretta, what's wrong? I'm so terribly sorry, sir. My friend was dropped on her head as a baby, and she's never been the same since.'

Debra's voice broke into my daze as she fussed around him, taking the coats. She roughly shoved them into my arms, and I felt a flush of relief as my face became half-hidden. Still, I could feel my whole body trembling and I wasn't sure I was even capable of walking away.

Debra was still talking: '. . . and you might know my father. He's the legal eagle around here. Would you sign my hand? My mother's your biggest fan. So, I work for Alecs Petraś – you know him? You should ask for me to do your make-up sometime . . .'

'No!'

Suddenly I'd found my voice. Debra's head snapped in my direction as the Emperor's eyes locked on mine with a bemused smile. There was that same lock of hair falling over his brow, the faint scar, the dimples. The broad shoulders, the thick torso, the hands that could hold a girl down. Yet his face had lost the angry, florid ruddiness of heavy drinking. The man was taking care of himself, his youthful good looks returned.

'I mean, I'm sure our actor friend is very busy,' I continued desperately, 'and doesn't need us taking up any more of his time.'

Debra glared at me as though I was insane, but I wasn't having her or any woman I knew anywhere near this man.

'Come on, Debra. They'll be missing us.'

'Well, it was nice to meet you, ladies. Here.' He passed me the last of the coats.

'Thank you.'

'You're most welcome.' He *looked* like the perfect

gentleman; he *sounded* like the perfect gentleman. But he wasn't.

Debra and I watched as he walked away. Once he was round the corner, she turned on me, stamping her foot. 'What did you go and do that for? I nearly had him!'

'Oh, don't be so ridiculous.'

Despite my words, Debra quickly brightened. 'We met the actual Oscar Romero! Wait till we tell everyone. Come on.'

'Oscar Romero,' I repeated, turning the words over in my mouth as Debra raced towards the beauty studio. Not an emperor at all. Just some man, with some name, who'd happened to somehow try to rape me. But now I knew who he was.

29

During the long make-up shifts, Petraś and Sally would entertain me with stories about the legends they'd both worked with. I was sworn to secrecy, of course. Josephine and her fabulous skin tone. Clara and the eyebrows plucked and then re-drawn at a rakish angle. Theda's vampiric, kohl-rimmed eyes. And then there were the scandals. The jailbait and all those matinee idols with secrets to hide. They told me about the star who had done can-cans for Soviet leaders, the studio-created glamour model who was known as the Erector, and the silent-movie star who'd ended up dealing dynamite, otherwise known as heroin. A person's face could have turned pale at the thought – if that person hadn't been me. I loved it all!

One morning, after a particularly salacious story, Petraś pointed a make-up brush at me. 'Loretta, trust me. Stay away from the parties.'

Too late for that.

'Now, are we going to get this gold leaf on?'

I ran to bring over the tray. As Sally waited for Petraś and me to pull on our cotton gloves, she took a long inhale on a cigarette, her cheeks hollowing. Moments later, she was deep in a coughing fit. Petraś and I waited for her to gather herself, my boss watching anxiously.

Then he looked pointedly at me over the top of Sally's head. I could tell exactly what he was thinking. *And don't start smoking, either.*

But I couldn't help blurting, 'Tell me about Oscar Romero.'

'That cowboy?' Sally's glance flew towards Petraś, but he didn't say anything. Sally took a deep breath and continued. 'Chancer, new boy. Terrible reputation. A war hero, if you believe it, but it made him . . . not a good man.'

Were any of them?

Not long afterwards, Sally glided off to set and we cleared up our workstation. Petraś was always insistent on tidiness, and I respected the way that he would always hang back to help.

'So, Oscar . . .' I began.

'Don't you concern yourself with him.' Petraś's voice was sharp and to the point. Time to change the subject.

'What was it like back in Poland?' I asked instead.

His face softened immediately. 'Hard, but there were good times, too. My matka used to take me out foraging.'

'My mother, too,' I said, surprised.

His eyes gleamed. 'Interesting. What would you gather?'

The English hedgerows of my childhood scrolled behind my eyes. 'There would be rosehips and camomile, roses obviously. Oakmoss . . .'

'Oakmoss?'

'Oh, yes.' I thought back to watching Ma steam

it – the deep, earthy aroma that filled the kitchen. 'We'd use it to make aftershave lotion for my da.'

He nodded in agreement. 'Droga, you are just like me.'

I shook my head, daring to contradict him. 'We aren't alike at all. You're royalty and my ma grew up in a Gypsy caravan.' I glanced at the signet ring on his pinkie. 'Isn't that your royal crest?'

Petraś's mouth twitched. 'Would you like to know a secret?'

I felt a prickle of intrigue and in that moment I guessed. 'You're not royal at all, are you?'

He shook his head, shoulders rolling with laughter. 'This ring that everyone admires so much? I bought it in a pawnbroker's in St Louis. I am – what's the phrase you use? – common as muck.'

My eyes widened in shock and delight. 'You little . . .' I couldn't say out loud what I was thinking. 'You made the whole thing up. You've hoodwinked Hollywood!'

'Marketing, Loretta. Please, call it marketing.'

A new thought occurred to me. 'Does Sally know?'

'She's the one who suggested it. I was new in my career, but she understood the studios so much better than me. We met at a party. I remember: she was wearing a fox fur and a dress of diaphanous gold silk. She looked like a goddess, and I looked like a nobody. She told me as much within five minutes of our meeting. Said I had to create an image.'

'What was Sally like back then?'

He gave a deep, luxuriant sigh. 'She was beautiful.

The whole room would fall silent when she entered. People hardly dared to speak to her, they were so overawed.'

'And she picked you out as her friend?'

'Yes, and . . . well, the rest is history. She became a movie star and I became the mysterious European prince who could make American women look like queens.' He wiped his hands down on a discarded face cloth. 'Now, you can finish up in here. And remember: that is a big secret so no gossiping. I need to go and check my diary.'

Petraś's diary was a thing of legend – full of stars and glamorous trips away. Everyone wanted Petraś to do their make-up. The man was a living legend, a genius . . . an illusion.

And yet again, he was right. The two of us had more in common than I could have hoped for. I felt inspired all over again, more than I ever had been before. I felt the hunger and ambition solidify in my belly. We'd both come from nothing in Europe. We'd both created new versions of ourselves, liberated by the fact that no one knew anything about us. And if he had launched a whole industry out of foraging in the hedgerows, then surely it only made sense that the girl who'd once stood, bored and listless, behind a Woolworths make-up counter could do the same. Some things were meant to be. Some people were meant to be.

Loretta Darling? She was meant to be!

30

Dear Enid

Oh, lord! Remember Sally Dee? How we used to dress up like her with Ma? All that kohl that we'd paint in with burnt matches? I'm only working with her now! Sally (she actually asked me to call her that!) is still a Big Noise (just!) and I am beyond thrilled. She's not exactly happy in the mornings, if you get my drift. Reminds me of Da sometimes. Don't you ever start on that stuff! Though I must admit, last night I had a daiquiri and I could get used to rum.

Yours,
Margaret xxx

Sally Dee's next movie, *The Witch,* was just dark enough to keep the studios happy. Horror was the new fad, and everyone was there for it. Well, apart from Alice. She said it was too scary, but more fool her because she was missing out on the performance of a lifetime.

Sally was magnificent.

Her character was a twisted woman-child and she channelled all her Hollywood bitterness into the part. In return, the cinematographer worked his own magic, painting with darkness in incredible cinematic tableaus. Even Sally would turn quiet when we watched the rushes.

As I'd done a good job for Sally's previous movie, Petraś trusted me with the final touches of Sally's make-up – the powder, one more spit and polish from the cake of mascara, and a final tweak of the wig. I knew how privileged I was to share this time with her. The stories would roll out. Hollywood – talk about an education!

One time, after regaling me with the details about her affair with a famously happily married actor, her eyes misted over. 'You know, Loretta, I haven't slept with a man in ten years.'

But surely even women in their forties still had sex? I thought.

'Men are good for one thing, and one thing only. Money,' Sally informed me.

She went on to outline each and every one of her divorce settlements. She'd made some good investments, unlike her actress friend who had spent $40,000 buying a house from someone who wasn't even its owner. 'Fool!'

But my favourite stories were about her weddings. She sounded less caustic then. She still wore a ring on her wedding finger – a grotesquely huge emerald, encased in a cluster of diamonds. Claimed she couldn't get it past the knuckle any more.

One day, Sally noticed me surreptitiously watching the jewel's glint. She nudged the ring with her thumb.

'Nikolai gave me this one,' she said with a hint of wistfulness. Nikolai had been her second – or was it third? – husband. Of course the Russian prince's real name was Nick Baxter, and he'd grown up at the dodgy end of Mass. Av. in Boston.

Sally leant back in her salon chair. 'I had to marry four

jackasses to make my fortune.' She pointed at me. 'But you? You have talent.'

'Thank you.' In my mind, I agreed.

'You found Petraś and made him give you a leg-up. I had to do exactly the same to find my first break in Hollywood. Although in that case it was my legs that were up and around his back.' She cackled. 'Did more for me than my parents.' Her eyes opened, as I stood back. 'Say, where are yours, anyway?'

'In the north of England, a place called Morecambe. You know England?'

'I mean, vaguely.' Clumsily, she repeated the pronunciation of my hometown. Accents were not her forte.

'It's a small seaside town.' I thought back to the pavements slick with rain, the fortune teller's stall and the cocklers out with their horses and carts, dodging the treacherous quicksands. It hadn't been a pretty place to grow up, but I still loved it despite the foul weather and piles of dog shit. It was my town, the one with chip shops and funfair rides, dance halls and cinemas. It's what had made me. You get like that when you leave a place. Sentimental. And then, of course, there was Enid.

'Like Venice Beach?'

I smiled. 'No, not like Venice Beach at all.'

'You miss them?'

'My da – my father – he's dead.'

'Bad luck.'

'Isn't it?'

'And your mother?'

'She's still alive. Sells her own stuff.' I thought back to

all those lotions and potions sold door to door, along with the wooden pegs she'd carve herself. Such a little life, all hand to mouth. I was amazed we'd ever survived.

'Sisters? Brothers?'

'A sister. Enid. Did you ever have children?'

'Actually, I did. Managed to hide the pregnancy from the studios for months, but then I had a miscarriage. It was in the middle of my first divorce.'

I tried to imagine Sally with a small hard tummy. 'I'm sorry. That must have been awful.'

'Pah! That's what everyone says.' But even as she spoke, I could see the sadness cracking her face, the way her glance skittered about looking for her martini glass.

I thought about all those rumours that Primrose had shared with me about the fixers. How they'd arranged things for Marlon Brando's girlfriends and the like. So many babies, lost or living.

'Does Petraś know?'

She drew her chin in. 'Why would he?'

'I don't know. You two seem close.'

'Close as I'll get with anyone, which isn't pretty close. We enter this world on our own and we leave it on our own. What we do in the meantime is up to us. So, you go with whatever plans you have. Make them happen, and don't ever let anyone distract you – especially the men. Your ambitions are the only happiness you'll ever have.'

I didn't understand why we were suddenly talking about my plans. I hadn't shared any of them with her. But she saw right through me, guessing that they existed. She was good like that.

'Say, wanna come back to mine later? We could talk some more.'

See inside a movie star's actual home? 'Yes, please!'

She gave a nicotine-stained smile. 'Good. Meet my chauffeur outside at six.'

We arrived at a Spanish-looking bungalow in Beverly Hills. A maid met us, politely asking Sally how her day had been.

'Enough of that, Romina!'

Sally pushed past into the entrance hall, which was huge and tiled. To one side, there was a marble-topped table and a couple of shimmering martinis on a silver platter.

'Come on.' She flung out a hand to indicate the house, nearly spilling her drink. 'Knock yourself out.'

Wobbling on her heels, the lines of her stockings askew, Sally led me through to a living room with a sunken space surrounding the fireplace, which had three – three! – sofas, arranged around it and was almost as tall as me. The carpet was deep and expansive, and there were vases of fresh flowers everywhere. Sally's dogs lounged around in various parts of the room, wagging happy tails at our arrival. A couple of gold awards were on the mantelpiece but had been turned towards the wall. Gilt-framed oil paintings alternated with swathes of drapes at the windows. Bulging lamp stands sat on occasional tables, their silk shades casting spots of golden light around the room. There was even a miniature grand piano with a three-pronged candelabra atop it. Part of me doubted Sally even knew how to play the piano. But the deeper we walked into the bungalow, the less I realized I knew of my host, my mind hastily storing away snapshots.

'You should check out the jewels while you're here. Come on.'

She led me into a small anteroom with watered silk wallpaper and thick, velvet drapes.

'Hedda always wants to come back here,' Sally said. 'I love telling her no.'

The room was lined with wall-to-wall cabinets, each with its own key. She went to ease open a drawer. Rows of necklaces rested on a long, padded cushion. One of them showed two strands of strung pearls, a silver clasp holding a small jewel in its heart. She threw open another drawer and another, revealing piles of rhinestones, rubies and diamonds.

Sally watched from a distance as I moved from drawer to drawer. 'Sixty carats,' she'd call over, seeing me inspect a ring. 'First husband gave me that one.' Or, when I picked up a wristwatch: 'Solid gold! Kept it in my third divorce settlement.'

Then suddenly her mood turned and she started to slam shut the drawers, one by one. She stalked out of the room, but I hung back. Quietly, I turned the key in each of the drawers to lock them.

I followed to find her leaning heavily by some French doors overlooking a majestic garden. Swifts darted in the deepening amber sky above a gardener who lazily skimmed leaves from a pool that had an actual waterfall cascading into it. She tucked back the linen drapes to let the cool evening air envelop us as she nodded at the gardener.

'We had an affair, back in . . . 1940, I think it was.' She sighed wistfully. 'Biggest dick I've ever seen. My darling Federico.'

'Were you in love?' He looked so bent and crooked now I could barely imagine it.

'Hard to recall. Maybe.'

I didn't believe her.

'His manhood leant to one side. Painful, you know.' She took a deep breath. 'Still, I like to keep him in wages. Makes me feel better about myself.'

Sally Dee had a *conscience*? About a giant dick?

'Good for you,' I said faintly.

'Now!' She turned back into the room, clapping her hands together. 'Wanna see the real deal?'

31

We sat on the champagne-coloured carpet of Sally's dressing room. I mean, I had to lever her down somewhat and she bellowed at me when her martini spilled. And when I say dressing room, I mean a space larger than the whole of my apartment. It was lined wall to wall with dresses spilling out of cabinets in a rainbow of colours. It was a bit like being in a big Fabergé egg, only with more gilt.

Now Sally stroked the dusty album that sat between us. She'd rescued it from the back of an armoire – one of those posh wardrobes.

'I keep this for my memoirs,' she said. 'If I ever get round to writing them. The fans like photos, you know.' The album creaked open with a rustle of paper and her expression softened.

'This is me as a baby.' I saw a child with a lick of blonde hair, wearing a pristine christening outfit, seated in a photographer's studio. 'My father was a vaudeville actor and my mother a seamstress. Show-business Gypsies, travelling from town to town. We boarded in basement rooms and slept on sofas.' She turned another page to show me a photo of a stiff-looking couple, staring straight into the camera. 'As a child, they'd stand me on a table and get me to do tap dances.'

'Did you like it?'

'Of course! By the time I was four years old, I was already auditioning.'

Four years old. I bet she couldn't even read then, and certainly not a contract.

'And did you? Make your parents happy?'

'Not so sure about that.'

We continued through the album, sipping our martinis. Newspaper clippings, theatre stubs, more and more photos of Sally in an all-girl tap-dancing troupe, or sitting with her grandmother on a train, dance bag on her lap. Apparently, Mrs Dee made all the costumes, and her husband negotiated the contracts. All so innocent, all so wholesome. An entirely devoted set of parents. Lucky Sally.

'And then we came to Hollywood.' She turned another page to reveal her first publicity shot. The hair had grown lighter and been straightened.

'How did you find it here?' I thought back to my own first time, stepping down from the train, waving good-bye to Jimmie as he'd stalked away.

'Nest of vipers. Everything changed. The studios wanted me to lose weight, cast my parents aside, gave me feature parts and an apartment. None of it helped. They said I was a fish out of water and that my stage experience had ruined me. I *acted* too much. Ha! After six months, my contract was cancelled. Wouldn't even loan me out to another studio.'

'So what happened then?'

'I gave them hell! What did they expect me to do?

Move back to Wisconsin? No, I fought my way back and, once I was powerful enough, I made sure that the person who'd cancelled my contract never worked in Hollywood again.'

'Sally, why are you showing me all this?'

'Don't you see?' She cast out a hand towards all the photographs of her younger self. 'You're in danger of letting everything slip through your fingers!'

Before I could open my mouth to protest, she picked up. 'Petraś this and Petraś that!' she said in a mocking sing-song voice. 'You're so far up his backside, all I can see are your toes wiggling.'

I was more than a little stunned. 'I thought you liked him?'

She placed a hand over mine. 'Honey, you can like a man. Doesn't mean he gets to own you. You only have one life, Loretta. Make it count.'

'Arvella says the opposite – that I should stop trying so hard.'

'Oh, Arvella. That woman sucked a whole bag of lemons after she was born and she's never been the same since. Plus, the woman can't keep her mouth shut. What you gonna do? Be Petraś's sidekick all your life just like her?'

'He's been good to me.'

She rubbed knuckles into her eyes. 'Boohoo! Pass me a handkerchief, why don't you?' Then her face turned serious. 'All these men, these husbands, the affairs . . . They're distractions. Don't let that happen, Loretta. Time's running out.'

'Time's running out? I'm twenty-one, Sally!'

'And I was four,' she countered. 'There's a whole line of girls behind you, all waiting to grab their chance. And I can promise you that they're not letting the men in this town distract them. Here!' She flipped back to the photo of a tiny, tap-dancing girl. She prised a fingernail beneath a corner and it popped out, the glue so brittle it barely existed any more. 'For you.'

I recoiled. 'I can't! It's yours. It's too much.'

'Take it,' she growled.

Hesitantly, I took the photograph and turned it over to see a little stamp on the back from the photographer's studio. 'You really mean it?'

'Yes, I mean it. It can remind you to hold on to that ambition. Don't let anyone stop you.' She paused. 'And when you're ready to set up on your own, you can sell it. Should be worth a few dollars, don't you think?' She burst out into a fit of coughing.

'It's priceless,' I said, once she'd recovered. 'I'd never sell it.'

Sally narrowed her eyes at me. 'Oh yes, you will. One day. One day, you will. OK, help me up.' I steered her to her feet. 'Now, the bedroom.'

On wobbling feet, she led me down the long hallway towards another room, off to the right. It was large, and the air conditioning made the room frigid. I'd always thought that a bedroom should be small and cosy, remembering how Enid and I would curl up together in our small bed like dormice in a nest. How did anyone ever sleep in a place like this, with its gold cornicing and the pristine drapes that looked so formal?

Sally lowered herself onto the edge of the mattress before succumbing to another coughing fit.

'So, what do you think?' she asked.

'Well, it's . . .' I took the plunge and was honest with her. 'It's not what I would choose.'

She laughed again. 'Me, neither. But the studios . . . they like glamour.' She patted the bed. 'Come, sit.'

I sat down beside her, my whole body rigid. I sensed we were about to have another uncomfortable conversation.

'Seen any other bedrooms like this?' Closely, she watched me.

I stalled. 'What do you mean?'

'You know what I mean, Loretta. I see you. You're so on guard, like a little marionette. I know the signs. What happened? And don't try to fool me because I can always find out other ways.'

'There was something,' I began. It was almost as though I didn't have the language. Oscar and his pal standing there, the cold tiles of the bathroom, the jazz — and then the way that Eliot had rescued me.

'You're not the first woman, and you won't be the last. Which douchebag was it?'

'Oscar Romero,' I said, staring at my hands. 'It was at one of his parties.'

'Oh, Jesus Christ, you went there! Why didn't anyone warn you? So that's why you were asking about him!'

'I guess people assumed I knew.' I couldn't bear to

mention my husband of only a few hours – I didn't want to see her face when she understood what he'd done, what I'd let him do.

'Oh, honey.' She wrapped a bony arm around my shoulders and pulled me to her as I did my best to ignore the stink of gin and cigarettes.

She leant back and took in my face, a nicotine-stained finger tracing my brow. I felt stupidly grateful, turning my face into her palm. I closed my eyes, thinking of my own ma. Her stiffness around Enid and me, how she couldn't bear it if we tried to climb into bed with her and Da, or scolded us when we scraped our knees. Hers had been a cold type of love.

After a moment, I pulled away. 'It doesn't matter,' I said. 'Things happen.' I didn't even believe my words; I could feel the low flames of anger reigniting at the back of my mind.

'They sure do,' she said. 'Just make sure that they don't happen again.'

'How?' I asked. 'I can't lock myself away.'

'Oh, you don't have to do *that*. Besides, why let them stop you in your tracks?' She shook her head. 'I remember when I found out my third husband was having an affair; I sprinkled amphetamines in his morning coffee for a week. He liked it nice and strong. By Friday, he'd been ordered by his office to go on a sabbatical and sort himself out. His lover dumped him shortly after. He dumped me not long after that.'

'You'd be up in time to make him coffee?' Frankly, that was more of a shock than the amphetamines.

'I know, ridiculous. I was trying on being a housewife for size. Didn't work out.'

'I bet!'

'But that's not the point, Loretta. The point is, I let men take from me, and then I made mistakes. It all cost me big.' She gazed at me; her mascara had flaked beneath her eyes. 'Don't go looking for revenge. It doesn't work.'

She gave a yawn, as though suddenly bored, and I realized that my time with her was up. I got to my feet, my eyes flitting towards her bedside table, which contained a cacophony of bottles of all shapes and sizes.

'You don't sleep so good?' I asked.

'Not since 1945,' she answered matter-of-factly.

My mind scrolled back to Ma and her concoctions. I used to watch from the kitchen window as she moved about our small scrap of a garden, carrying the trug she'd made from woven willow. There was nothing she grew that wasn't useful.

'Why don't you try some lavender in your pillow?'

'Will do, Nurse Darling,' Sally said dismissively as she lay down on top of the satin eiderdown, her head resting on a humungous pillow. Already, she'd shut her eyes.

My audience was over, but I lingered a little to take her in. Her body was tiny, decades of starvation making her knees, her collarbones, even the joints on her fingers all stand out. There were no breasts to speak of. A hand twitched by her side, as though it was agony simply to stay still. I bet she'd never taken a vacation in her life. Her closed eyes were sunk deep in their sockets, and her cheekbones sliced through the air like razors. Despite the wonky wig, she was still beautiful in a ghoulish sort of way. I felt a pulse of affection for her.

'You gonna stand there forever?'

'No, Sally.' I planted a kiss on her forehead. I half expected her to tell me to fuck off, but she didn't say a word. 'Goodbye, Sally.'

I turned towards the bedroom door, spotting a shadow pass beneath its sweep. A figure moved silently across the deep carpet beyond. I went to look, but there was no one there. Quietly, I pulled the door shut behind me and walked slowly back down the hallway, past all the pieces of art, and into the living room.

Romina was waiting for me. 'The chauffeur will drive you home.'

Not long after, as I sat in the back of the car, watching the houses grow smaller, I thought back over our time together. *You only have one life, Loretta.* Sally was right. It was all down to me, and I had to make everything count.

32

The next morning, I got into the studio nice and early. Fortunately, Biff was already on duty to let me through. Unfortunately, I also had a chance to spot Scott Eliot with Christine, waving him off at the entrance. Didn't she ever take a day off?

'What are you doing here?' Arvella asked from her desk.

'Good morning.' I passed her the greasy bag of doughnuts that I'd picked up on the way in as a breakfast gift.

She took the bag between forefinger and thumb, holding it away from her silk dress, to deposit in her trash basket. 'Sugar isn't good in the mornings.'

I didn't bite. 'Is Petraś in?'

She opened her mouth to speak when a voice came from behind the glass-panelled doors where his name was picked out in gold leaf. 'Who is it?'

I raised an eyebrow at her. She glared at me, then called out, 'It's Loretta, Mr Petraś.'

'Well, send her in!'

I entered the office and let the door swing shut behind me, leaving Arvella as a ghostly shape beyond the ribbed glass. It was all I could do not to put my thumb to my nose and stick my tongue out.

Petraś was watching me from above a steaming cup of coffee. A half-eaten doughnut sat on a plate beside a napkin.

I fixed a smile to my face. 'Good morning, Mr Petraś.'

He indicated for me to sit down and leant back in his own chair, swivelling one way and then the other as he contemplated me. 'What are you doing here so early?'

'Well, you see, I wanted to talk to you about something and I didn't want to cut into my working day, I'm conscientious like that and—'

'Cut to the chase,' he interrupted.

'I want my own actress and my own movie.'

He paused. 'I don't give my trainees their own gig until at least a year in.'

'Make an exception.'

His lip quirked with amusement. 'Why should I?'

'You know why. I'm excellent at what I do – I'm quick and I'm clever.'

He watched me from behind hooded eyes. 'You don't need to tell me, Loretta. Do you know why I hired you in the first place?'

'Because you thought I had chutzpah?'

He pulled over a ledger, flicking through the pages until he found what he was looking for. Trailing a finger down a column of names, he paused at the bottom and cleared his throat. 'As it happens, we do have a new starlet on set.'

'Starlet? I was thinking more of an actress.' There were hostesses, magazine models, bit parts, starlets, character actors, third leads, second leads, leads . . . stars. I wanted an actor – at least a second lead.

'Come on,' I coaxed. 'Give me a challenge!'

He gave me a long stare. 'You've some nerve, Loretta.' After a moment, his finger rose back up the column.

'All right, you can have Grace Riley.' The starlet with the not-so-secret boyfriend. After scanning the details, he slammed the ledger shut and leant on his elbows. 'Hard worker. A few bit parts so far, but *The Witch* is her first big break – or that's the theory, at least. Cute. Plays wholesome. A bit bland, if you ask me, but that's where you come in.' He pointed a pen at me. 'Don't mess it up, Loretta.'

I gave a cheery salute. 'I won't!'

'You'll be sharing a salon with me and Sally,' he warned. 'We'll be keeping an eye on the two of you.'

33

I had underestimated Grace Riley. In fact, the whole town had. The studio publicists – or flacks as I'd learnt to call them – were circulating the notion that she was a sweet farm girl from Hudson Valley with an eager smile and ample bosom. The truth was somewhat different. She'd grown up in Brooklyn tenements, the tip of her nose had gone under the scalpel, and she'd had her hairline pushed back during a series of painful electrolysis sessions squeezed in between acting classes.

That first morning, Sally watched Grace in the mirror as the younger actress chatted with another make-up artist, throwing her head back in laughter.

Sally snorted. 'Too pretty.'

I was folding towels. 'What do you mean?'

'She's all perfect symmetry. Won't work in front of the camera.'

Before Sally could say anything else, one of my colleagues led Grace over. 'Loretta, your actress is here.'

As soon as Grace spotted Sally, she went straight over. 'Oh, my goodness! Miss Dee!' She clutched her hands to her chest. 'I had no idea we'd be made up together. I'm honoured. Truly!'

Sally gave a glacial smile. 'Aren't you the lucky one?'

I waited for them to finish shaking hands and then settled Grace into her chair. 'I'm so pleased to be working with you.'

'I know *you*! Loretta, right?' I couldn't believe she still remembered my name from our one meeting. 'You're the Lip Girl! Talks back, makes the lips work. Everyone knows!'

I politely ignored the sound of Sally's sniggering from behind her magazine.

Grace had a small wicker basket in her lap, covered by a square of gingham. 'This is for you, by the way.'

I took the basket and peeked inside. Cold chicken, with a golden crispy skin. A fat wedge of tortilla, the potato and onion a startling white. A flask of what looked like homemade lemonade and a slice of fruit cake. There was even a cutlery set, wrapped in a napkin.

'Now, pop that in the refrigerator and we can get started.'

I looked up at her. 'You did all this for me?'

'I love cooking.' She placed a hand on top of mine and squeezed. 'I just know that we're going to become the best of friends. Besides . . .' She leant close and whispered, 'If I keep you sweet, you'll keep me looking pretty!'

That was Grace all over. She was perfectly open about her tactics for getting ahead. She had nothing to hide – well, apart from one man-shaped secret. I liked that about her; she wore her ambition on her sleeve.

Each day from then on, Grace would bring me a

different treat – chicken pie for one, meatloaf, devilled eggs . . . After a while, I had to ask her to stop.

'I'm going to swell up like a balloon!' I said. 'And besides, you don't need to bribe me to give you my best work.'

Her plan had worked; I'd have done anything for Grace Riley.

'Oh, Loretta, you really are one in a million. Utterly unforgettable. Hey! You're the unforgettable Loretta Darling!' She drew a hand through the air, as though she could see my name up in lights already.

From one side of us, Sally made a poor attempt at covering up a laugh, but Grace and I were used to her derision by now.

'Funny,' I said, pretending to laugh.

'Not just funny – perfect!' Grace said. 'One day, I'll be able to say that I knew Loretta Darling before she was famous!'

'*Famous?*' I almost choked! I wasn't so keen on being known; I just wanted to sell make-up. Lots of it. But then I thought about Petraś and his whole shtick about being a Polish prince. That had worked and then some. Maybe I did need to put my face out there?

Even the thought of it gave me a shiver down my spine. I'd come here to escape, and now I had to consider the idea of having my face slapped on every poster in the universe. Was this for real? *Could* it be for real? But I knew in my gut that Grace was right. She dreamt big for everyone, not just herself. That's what I'd always liked about her. She wasn't like one of those men, only daring to imagine their own selves writ large on a six-foot poster. She wanted both of us – me! – to succeed. And it occurred to me then that . . . who was I to disappoint her? And Grace Riley liked me. It was just about the biggest compliment a girl could have.

34

The two of us settled into an easy rhythm. I worked, she talked. I'd stopped looking out for Eliot and Christine because – whatever.

I'd ask Grace about her upbringing, her ambitions – to be a star, of course – and her dog, Betsy. Most actresses had a dog; they were good accessories for publicity shots and made the actresses seem relatable. Betsy wasn't like most other Hollywood dogs. Grace had found her in a pound and the dog had a missing eye. But that was the least of Betsy's worries.

'No one seems to like her!' Grace would cry. 'I mean, she only barks at the delivery man. People who ride bicycles. Anyone wearing a hat. Maybe some people who carry a walking stick. Is that so bad?'

She brought in snapshots to show me. It *was* so bad. A one-eyed dog of indeterminable age, with coarse fur and missing teeth? Hell's bells, I could have found a dog like that for free in a backstreet– and I wouldn't have been feeding her steak.

I was more interested in James Luke than I was in Betsy. Grace's supposed beau, who I'd heard about at the writers' party. But whenever I tried to ask about her romantic life, she swiftly changed the subject.

To draw her out, I'd tell her about home. The Winter

Gardens where I went dancing, the promenade and the pier, Morecambe bay, Mrs Atkinson who ran the fish-and-chip shop.

'You're so cute!' Grace would say. But I knew that she was hiding from me. Didn't we all have secrets?

In the meantime, Grace gave me the best detail a make-up artist could wish for – a blank canvas.

I'd tie her hair back with a length of silk ribbon, clean her face and allow my hands to rest against her collar-bones. We'd gaze at each other in the mirror, and then her face would clear, as she realized that we were about to set to.

'You ready for your make-up?' I'd ask, as we'd been taught to. But Grace was born ready.

My hands, warmed from spreading the lotions, would move around her face. Am I allowed to say that it was almost erotic? Because it was. Women aren't meant to say that, right? But with Grace, it was. She would lean back in her chair and submit herself to me. My hands would weave and thread around, her eyes closed, which allowed me to watch her more intensely than I'd ever watched any woman before.

People like to imagine that stars are born beautiful, but Grace and I both knew better than that. Grace wasn't a Betsy exactly, but she wasn't flawless either. There was the corner of an eye that was slightly crooked, the scar in her bottom lip from a childhood accident. Sally was wrong. Grace wasn't too pretty. She was perfectly imperfect. Everything that a star should be.

I led her out on set that first time, with all the lights

set up, and the cameras ready to roll. Right on cue, she lit up from inside, her eyes like jewels. Every word dropped from her lips like a gift and we were all mesmerized, even her fellow actor who nearly missed his cue.

'Do you think it went OK, Loretta?' Grace asked afterwards.

I laid a hand on her shoulder. 'You just became a star.'

'You really think so?' But her eyes sparkled like she knew. Oh, she knew.

Word spread. The runner started to allow the crew to gather and watch. The cinematographer, Norman, had just about fallen in love and would go the extra mile for her close-ups, with an intricate arrangement of Chinese lanterns, smearing Vaseline on the camera's optical flat to make her glow.

But here's the thing. Clark Stuart, the male lead, didn't like her shining, not one little bit. So he began a quiet rebellion. At first, I didn't understand what was going on but it was my job to scrutinize the actors' faces, ensuring their make-up was immaculate, and soon I clocked what he was doing. He had a tell.

Eye twitch – he'd fail to hit his mark.

Eye twitch – he'd cut in too early.

Eye twitch – he'd change a line of dialogue.

By now, Grace had figured it out, too. She abandoned her usual breezy demeanour, marching off set with a face like thunder, straight into the salon.

'Can you believe that guy?'

And when he'd cut in too early: 'What a rattlebrain!'

Then: 'He can't do this to me!'

In response to that last complaint, a voice called out from the other salon chair. 'Sure, he can.'

In that moment, even *I* hated Sally. Grace clenched her hands into fists and turned on her heel, staring me straight in the face so that she didn't have to look at Sally. 'I've tried so hard,' she hissed, 'but if either of them push me one bit more . . .'

'What you gonna do?' Sally called over. Her hearing always was immaculate. 'Call the Keystone Cops?'

Grace's eyes bugged in frustration.

Billy Trapido, the director, came into the salon, looking around. 'Are we doing this or what?'

'I'm so sorry,' Grace said. 'My head must be screwed on all wrong today!' She turned on that innocent act full blast.

Clark Stuart had appeared behind Billy and gave an exaggerated sigh. 'Shall we try it one more time, Grace? I don't want you to feel bad about getting it all wrong.' He came closer. 'But listen, Norman is going crazy. It's crucial that you hit your mark. If you're just off a bit, you disappear.' The lighting was so brooding, so dark, it relied on very specific spots of light for the actors. One step in the wrong direction and the shot was ruined.

Grace nodded stiffly. I was the only one who saw the tears brimming as Billy departed.

'Don't you dare cry,' I whispered. 'Don't give Clark the satisfaction.'

She gave a trembling smile and dashed the back of a hand across her eyes. 'I wouldn't want to ruin the make-up.'

'Good girl.'

'He's a bastard.'

'He sure is. And the others can't see it because they're all bastards too.' I followed her back out, unsure that this was the way make-up artists and actresses usually talked together.

Grace went to her mark. The clapperboard sounded and Clark started . . . well, I guess it was technically still called acting.

'I don't even understand you any more!' A moment ago, it had been 'I don't even know you these days!' which would have been Grace's cue, but instead she glanced at Billy in confusion.

'Cut!' Billy sat back in his canvas chair, megaphone hanging limply from his hand.

'Those . . . that wasn't his line,' Grace tried to protest.

'It's called improvisation, Grace,' Clark explained as though to a dolt. 'Ever heard of the Actors Studio? It's one of the best.'

'But—'

'Oh, forget it.' Feigning weariness, Clark nodded to Billy. 'Let's go again.'

I felt my insides churn with anger. Who the hell did he think he was?

Grace held a hand to her eyes and tried to see beyond the lights, squinting. I gave a little wave and her face smoothed out in a smile as she spotted me. *I'm here for you, Grace.* I don't know why I cared so much, but I damn sure wasn't going to just stand here in the dark, watching helplessly while some man humiliated her.

Once filming was moving along smoothly again, I headed back to the make-up room – just in time to catch Sally slipping a silver hip flask from the pocket of her fur coat, which was hanging off the back of her chair. She started, but when she realized it was only me, she raised the flask to her lips and took a nip.

'Oh, hello, Little Miss Snoop.'

If she'd been caught, she'd have been marched off set. Officially, the studio had banned Sally from drinking during working hours.

I went to pull up a stool. 'Sally . . .'

'What?' she asked suspiciously.

'Who said I wanted anything?'

She looked me up and down. 'Just being near you is making me itch.'

I laughed. It was almost impossible for Sally's insults to strike home these days. I saw them more as terms of affection. 'I was just thinking . . . Say you were working on a movie, and say the male lead was being a pain and say you wanted to make that stop. What would you do about it?'

She stared at me. 'You wanna start talking English?'

I sighed. 'You heard Grace before. What can she do?'

Sally smoothed out the drape over her skirt. 'Nothing.'

'What? Why not?'

'If she challenges Clark, he'll deny it. They'll be paying him more, so if there's tension between the two leads, who do you think they'll get rid of?'

My heart plummeted. 'Grace?' She nodded. 'But surely . . . Isn't there something we can do? He's making her look like a buffoon!'

'Why do you even care?' Sally asked. 'You're still getting paid.'

I got up off the stool, tired of her dark mood. 'Well, thanks anyway.'

At that moment, Petraś entered the room carrying a bunch of hairnets in different shades of brown and blonde. He paused and glanced between the two of us. 'Everything OK here, ladies?'

'Everything's fine,' I said, quickly shifting to stand in front of Sally, giving her time to slip the flask back into her coat pocket. 'I was—'

'We don't bother the talent,' Petraś said. 'You know that, Loretta.'

'Oh, she wasn't bothering me.' Sally caught my glance in the mirror's reflection. 'Loretta was just leaving.'

35

That evening, Primrose and I sat facing each other on the windowsill, slugging from beer bottles. She was wearing a burnt-orange silk dress with a scattered print of hydrangea. There was a side flounce to the skirt that draped over the side of the windowsill and gathered in a pool of silk on the floor. As always, she looked magnificent. Beside her, I felt grubby.

'You're quiet tonight,' she said, poking me with her stockinged toe. 'Got stuff on your mind?'

'Sally was drinking at the studio today.'

'Uh-oh. Do people know?'

'Everyone knows. She's already had her next contract cancelled; she just doesn't know it yet.' My hands twitched with irritation.

Primrose cocked her head on one side. 'Why do you like her so much?'

'She's good to me.' A disbelieving laugh escaped her lips. 'In her own way,' I said, laughing back, but then I paused. 'Primrose, do you think all men are bad?'

'You're asking a prostitute if all men are bad? No, I don't, actually.'

'Why not? Oscar Romero is. Raphael is.'

'Your writer guy isn't. Petraś isn't.' She opened her mouth, then abruptly stopped.

'My writer guy still isn't talking to me. And who else were you going to say?' I prompted.

'Oh, there was that fella who rescued me from Peter that time.'

'Oh! The cowboy with the truck? But what do you do when a man *is* bothering you?'

She cocked her head. 'Well, there are a few basic rules. Never judge, just listen ... and when they cry, don't make them feel foolish.'

'But what if you don't want to help them?'

'Then we *do* make them feel foolish. Simple.'

I nodded, then turned to the window, my gaze settling on the middle distance.

'What are you thinking?' asked Primrose. 'I can see that brain of yours turning over.'

'Oh, nothing. I'm just tired.'

I reached for another couple of bottles and passed one to her. We popped off the caps against the side of the sill and leant back against the window frame as we each took a gulp of beer.

'Was it difficult, setting up on your own?' I asked. Primrose's brothel was one of the most famous in California, after all.

'I saved up for years,' she said. 'Dollar notes underneath the mattress, unlike most of the other girls who were getting high or struggling to raise kids on their own.' She laughed at the memory. 'They used to get so jittery around those envelopes stuffed full of notes. Still do.' I could imagine. 'But I was lucky.' Sternly, she pointed her bottle at me. 'Don't get high and don't get pregnant.'

'Anything else I should know?'

She pulled a surprised face. 'You thinking of setting up?'

'Maybe.'

'Now, this is more like it.' She scrambled into a cross-legged position – difficult in a dress like hers – and leant forward, forearms on knees and eyes wide. 'Tell me everything!'

Her enthusiasm was infectious, and I couldn't help smiling as my own mood lifted. 'It's just an idea . . .'

'Oh, phooey.' She batted a hand through the air. 'I bet you've been planning this from before you even arrived in Hollywood!'

Actually, I hadn't. The biggest dream a girl from Morecambe dared to have was simply to escape. But hanging around Petraś had made me hope for more. Money. And not just from doing the stars' make-up. He had endorsements, private clients and public events, his own line of cosmetics . . . There was more to make-up than I'd realized, and I wanted in. I wanted to do more than survive. I wanted to make myself untouchable.

I found myself pacing the floor of my apartment as I laid out my plans. 'Well, they call me the Lip Girl . . .' I reached one wall and swivelled. 'It's kind of cute and memorable . . .' Swivel. 'I could trademark it and launch a range of . . .'

'Lipsticks! *Loretta Darling's Lipsticks!* Or – no – *the Lip Girl's Lipsticks!* Or *the Lip Girl's Darling Lipsticks.* Oh, so many options!' Maybe too many options. But Primrose leapt to her feet and twirled me around, nearly knocking me from my feet. Then she leapt up onto the windowsill and leant dangerously far out of the window.

'My friend's going to be rich!' she cried. 'She's going to make a bunch of lipsticks, and you're all going to wear them!'

'Not me, lady!' a gruff male voice called back up from the sidewalk.

She hopped down and the two of us fell onto the bed.

'Calm down!' I laughed. 'It might not even come to anything. I still need to choose shades.'

She elbowed herself up. 'Oh, this will come to something. If I know anything about you, it will.'

But in the meantime I was thinking about something else, something much more urgent. Clark Stuart. Primrose didn't know it, but she'd given me an idea for bringing him down. I needed to work on him – literally. There was only one problem: that bitch Debra was his make-up artist.

36

'Hello, I'm Loretta. Your make-up artist for today!'

Clark glanced around. 'Where's the other one?'

'Debra is seeing to Grace.'

'Grace?' he echoed. 'Why?'

'Petraś thinks I'd be best to do your make-up for this big scene. He's asked Debra to work on Grace instead – just for today. I'm good with the details and all those close-ups . . .'

He gave a grunt and went back to his dime novel. Really, he didn't deserve to breathe the same air as Grace, never mind share a screen, but my ruse had worked. I'd got in extra early to explain everything to Debra and she was more than happy to swap places when she realized she was going to work on Grace.

Do you know how intimate it is to touch someone's face? To be so close to another person that you can tell whether they showered that morning or what aftershave they use? Sometimes I liked to test myself to see if I could figure out what the talent had had for dinner the night before. Skin lives and breathes. It tells its own story, and Clark's story stank. He doused himself in Old Spice and wore so much Brylcreem that it stained the collar of his shirt. I had to remove his own foundation before applying the right stuff for the cameras. Plus, he was exceptionally rude.

'You done yet?' he'd drawl, or knock my hand away when he wanted to take a glug of coffee. Still, I kept going with what I needed to do.

You deserve everything that's coming your way.

By the time I was done, he looked magnificent. Everyone said so. The filming went according to plan, but the big scene was set for the late afternoon. It wasn't ideal, but I wasn't in charge of the schedule. By that stage, we were all dead on our feet so I felt pretty confident that no one would be watching too closely.

'Cup of tea?' I asked, as Clark and I sat through another interminable stint of patiently waiting for him to be called up.

'*Cup of tea?*' He mimicked my English accent, raising an imaginary cup and saucer and holding out his pinkie. His most convincing performance yet.

'Milk and sugar?'

'Both.'

I nodded to one of the assistants, and she moved away to the kitchen area. A few moments later, she returned, carrying a trembling cup that had already spilled into the saucer.

'Here. Let me.' I carried the tea over to a counter where my beauty case sat, and wiped it down, then I took it over to Clark.

He took a sip and grimaced. 'Too much sugar.'

'Should I bring you another one?' the assistant asked.

'Don't bother,' Clark said, throwing a filthy glance.

I held out a couple of pan sticks. 'Now, what do we think? Thirty-two or fifty-six?'

37

Clark got through the scene well enough. Afterwards, he shrugged on his jacket without even looking at me and left, weaving slightly.

'Goodbye, Mr Stuart!' I called after him.

He waved a hand over his shoulder.

Others trailed into the salon, and I drifted through to the actresses' area, where Grace sat down to have her make-up removed.

'How did it go?' I asked.

'OK, I think,' she said. 'We had to do a couple of retakes. Clark forgot a couple of lines, but – you know – it's been a long day.' She yawned like a cat and leant back in her chair, as Debra set to with the cold cream. Grace seemed calmer and that made me glad. On the aluminium roof, there was the sudden drum of rain. 'Wow, actual rain,' Grace murmured, closing her eyes. 'Miracles do happen.'

A head appeared round the door.

'Eliot!' I exclaimed. 'What are you doing here?'

'Hello, Loretta. Nice welcome.'

He stepped into the make-up studio. Debra was already gawking like a prize idiot and Grace twisted round in her chair, both of them clearly delighted.

'I thought I'd take Loretta out for something to eat

once she's done here.' He sank into a salon chair, crossing his legs. 'Don't mind me. I'll wait until you're all done.'

Debra and Grace's faces swivelled to me, eyes wide with questions, and I felt my own face colour.

'Loretta?' Grace prompted. 'Aren't you going to introduce us?'

'Oh . . . yes. This is Scott Eliot. He's a writer – you know, gifted.' He flashed me a look that I very much enjoyed. 'Scott, this is Grace Riley – a star in the making – and this is my colleague Debra.'

'Charmed, I'm sure.' Grace held out a hand for Eliot to take.

He reached over, but instead of shaking, he kissed it. Scott Eliot was . . . was he flirting? Christine's face flashed behind my eyes, the way that she'd looked at him – so predatory. Warning me off.

'I've heard so much about you,' he said, straightening up.

'All good, I hope!' Grace laughed nervously. 'Now, where are you two lovebirds off to?'

'Oh, we're not—' I began.

'I haven't decided yet,' Eliot said. 'Loretta can choose.'

All three of them turned to look at me.

'Well, I'm not sure I can . . .'

'Oh, shoo!' Grace said. 'We're nearly done here, and Clark's left already. If anyone asks, I'll just say that you'd finished up for the day.'

'All right . . .' I slipped my Sweet Sixteen compact into my pocket. I could return it to my beauty case later. 'Ready!' I said with a shaky smile.

'Have fun,' Debra said less than graciously. If I knew

anything about her, the gossip would be all round the rest of the make-up girls within twenty-four hours.

Eliot shook her hand.

'It's been really nice meeting you,' he said to Grace with genuine warmth in his voice. He liked her, I could tell.

'You, too! Now, you take good care of Loretta.'

'We should get going,' I said. For some reason, I suddenly found it really difficult to find the arm holes in my cardigan as I tried to shrug it on. All this attention!

'Allow me.' Eliot came and helped me as Debra and Grace continued to stare, then he gave them a little mock salute. 'I'll see you again, I hope.'

Debra looked just about ready to faint on the spot. I gave a weak wave and the two of us left to make our way down the corridor.

'Well, you all seemed delighted to meet each other,' I commented.

'It's called being polite, Loretta. You should try it sometime.'

'Looked more like flirting to me.'

His grin broadened. 'You jealous?'

'Never!'

He opened the side door and light flooded in. The flash storm had ended as quickly as it had begun, puddles gently steaming beneath the sun. I couldn't help my mood lifting.

'How did today go, anyway?' he asked.

'OK. Could have been better.' I followed him to his car. 'Clark forgot his lines, apparently.'

'Oh, that,' Eliot said. 'Happens all the time.'

As I climbed into his car, my powder compact fell out of my pocket and into the footwell. Eliot and I both scrambled to rescue it, but I got there first, shoving it back firmly into my pocket.

He turned a key in the ignition. 'Now, Cocoanut Grove or Miceli's?'

We chose Cocoanut Grove. It was all red chairs and tablecloths beneath an ink-blue ceiling made to look like the night sky with lights like stars.

I was still feeling rattled and reached for some of the free tacos to calm my mood.

'Is everything OK, Loretta?' Eliot asked as our plates arrived.

I tossed my napkin down on the table. 'So, what's really going on with you two?'

Eliot frowned. 'You're going to have to share a bit more information.'

'You and Christine.'

His eyes widened. 'Me and . . . Christine-from-the-party Christine?'

'How many Christines are there?' I demanded. He started to crack another joke, but I cut in. 'Don't answer that!' I tipped my chin in the air. 'It's clear as vodka that something's going on.'

He leant back in the booth. 'Oh, this is gonna be good. Really good.'

I didn't like his tone.

'Well, obviously she's your lover!'

'Obviously.' He nodded in ironic agreement.

'And you didn't tell me, didn't even warn me when we went to that party, not even when we went back to your house and, honestly, I think—'

'What do you think, Loretta?'

I slammed my hands against the table, feeling my face flush with self-righteous outrage. 'I think that you're an awful liar and that you could have warned me!'

'About what?'

'You! Sleeping with Christine, flirting with Grace, that photograph on your bedside table just waiting for me to see it! How many women are there? What, are you waiting for the right time to seduce me, too? Or am I not good enough for you?'

For some reason, that final thought made me burst into a sudden storm of scalding tears. There was a small noise to one side of us and when I dared to peek, a waiter stood there, holding out a napkin, his face averted. I took it and blew my nose noisily. When I looked back up, Eliot's smile had collapsed.

'That's what you think?' he asked.

'Well, all the evidence is there.' My voice sounded stretched like an over-tuned violin string.

'Oh, Loretta. That photo is of my wife.'

So! He was an adulterer on top of everything else.

'She died, Loretta.'

The heat drained from my tear-stained face. 'I didn't know,' I said stiffly.

'Right. You didn't know. You assumed.' He stood up from our table. 'I think what you mean to say is "I'm sorry for your loss, Eliot" or "That's tragic, Eliot".'

People were staring now, a waitress whispering to the chef.

'I'm sorry for your loss,' I mumbled.

'Too late.' Fumbling for his wallet with trembling hands and his face twisted with hurt, he tossed down a fistful of dollar bills. 'Enjoy the rest of your life, Loretta Darling.'

38

Boy, was I miserable. The next morning, I dragged myself out of bed and immediately checked for the powder compact – the one that contained the powder I'd prepared and slipped into Clark's tea. But the tranquillizers hadn't even worked. My whole plan had been a waste of time.

Distracting myself from my funk, I gathered last night's free newspaper and spread it across the kitchen counter. The Lip Girl's Lipsticks still needed some stand-out shades. Most of the ingredients could be bought for a few dollars from a pharmacy, which was exactly what I'd done. Some sort of beeswax for shape, oil so that the lipstick could spread – lanolin or jojoba would work. The only thing I was missing were the lipstick moulds, but I could make do with some screw-lid pots for now.

I set my Sweet Sixteen compact on the counter to one side, thankfully empty and scrubbed clean. My thoughts flickered to Ma. Immediately, my chest grew tight. I'd caught my love of make-up from Ma, before Enid had even been born. It was strange to think that we couldn't speak any more. But back then, it had all been about Ma. The cucumber water for oily skin, burnt cork to draw in her eyebrows, and charcoal for her lashes. I'd help her gather geranium petals from the garden to colour her cheeks, and she'd take me on trips to dig up roots from the hedgerows for lip salve. All the tricks she'd learnt during the war. She'd even make my face up too sometimes, as a treat. Then we'd scrub off the make-up before Da got home.

For the time being, I just wanted to practise mixing my base, making sure I got the quantities right and that the texture worked. As I set to, my eyes caught the newspaper's trumpeting headline.

BRILLIANT YOUNG STAR IN COCONUT CRASH DISASTER!

Well, readers, it never rains but it pours. After recent rumours of Ingrid Bergman's scandalous affair, the wheels have come off another Hollywood train! Only this week, up-and-coming star and ex-athlete Clark Stuart's convertible had a nose (drive!) with a coconut palm, as he drove home in the storm after a movie shoot.

Stuart is currently working with Grace Riley on their new two-parter, *The Witch*. Grace said, 'Clark is one of the most dedicated actors in town, and I know he'll be back to work just as soon as he is able.'

Clark had been driving himself home in a second-hand Ford convertible with dodgy brakes. This wasn't exactly what I'd planned and I read faster and faster, hoping that nothing serious had happened. I may have made a slight miscalculation with the powder.

I allowed myself to breathe again once I reached the end of the article. Thankfully, Clark's injuries hadn't been substantial. Still, it gave me food for thought. I needed to be more careful, more scientific. *Or maybe just don't try to pull this type of hoax again, Loretta.* Yes, it was time to listen to Sally – really listen. She was the wisest person I knew.

Correct, came her voice in my ear. *And don't you forget it.*

If Sally Dee wanted me to be a good girl, that's what I'd be. The incident with Clark had been too close for my liking.

A week later, I saw Sally at the studio canteen. She was sitting at a table, pushing a salad around with a fork as she listened to some executives back-slapping each other.

When she spotted me, she eased herself off the bench and trailed after me as I carried my tray towards a booth. 'Filming going well?'

I smiled brightly. 'Couldn't be better.'

'I bet. Clark Stuart behaving himself? I hear he had a motor accident.' I found her watching my face carefully. 'Terrible. Really terrible.'

'Yes, terrible . . .' I repeated, my skin prickling – she couldn't know, surely? Time to change the subject. 'So, your movie is all done and dusted.' I nodded over at the execs. 'Good meeting?'

'Yes, that movie is all done – and so am I.' She glanced at the table of men in suits waiting for her. 'People only want to meet in a public space when there's bad news to share. Less crying.'

Before I had a chance to respond, a male voice rang out across the canteen, calling Sally's name. 'Ah, listen!' She raised a hand to cup her ear. 'God speaks!'

'Are you OK, Sally?' Up close, she looked tired beneath the make-up.

She rolled her eyes. 'Still not sleeping.'

I could sense the diners around us, observing, their confusion palpable. The movie star and the make-up girl. What could they possibly have to do with each other? Then I watched her weave between tables, hips sashaying, towards the execs who were about to stab her in the back.

I wanted to go after her and explain that I hadn't planned to hurt Clark Stuart, but we never did get to have that conversation. She was too busy shaking hands, smile fixed in place for the photographs. And by the next morning Sally Dee would be dead.

39

A hammering on my door woke me. It couldn't be one of the neighbours; Primrose was the only one who ever called round and she had her own key. For a moment, I hoped it might be Eliot, but when I went to answer, it was the last person I would expect to see there. Petraś.

Seeing him standing outside my crummy apartment was a shock, especially with all the lipstick samples taking up space in my kitchen.

'What are you doing here?' I blurted, shoving a hand through my hair. 'I'm sorry, that's rude. I . . . thought you were in New York?'

'Can I come in?' Not even a *Hello, Loretta*. There was a crease in his shirt front, so I knew immediately that something had to be seriously wrong.

I stepped back to allow him to enter, aware that my face must be red and splotchy from sleep. I moved ahead of him and quickly shut the kitchen door as he stepped past me into the apartment. Clothes on the floor, guttered candles on the windowsill, takeaway cartons on the bedside table. The long hours at the studio hadn't improved my domestic skills.

He hooked a finger through the arm strap of a damp swimsuit from where I'd dropped it days ago. He hung it over the back of a chair. 'You know, your mother wouldn't be impressed.'

I still hadn't said anything – couldn't. I was too frightened about what was coming next.

He indicated a chair. 'Would you like to sit down?'

'No.'

'All right, then.' He sighed and rubbed a hand over his brow. 'It's Sally. She died in the night.'

I dropped like a stone into the chair. 'Oh, God. What happened?'

'Her gardener called me. The maid was too upset.'

Federico and Romina. What would happen to them? To all her dogs? The knowledge sat like a heavy stone in my stomach, weighing me down.

'She left a note. Asked specifically for you.'

'Does anyone else know what's happened?'

'Only Arvella. No one else, hopefully, unless the news has leaked out already. The note asked for you to make her up one last time. They've worked on her overnight at the morgue.'

'Fast work.'

'Have to with the stars. This place is 24/7. Get your beauty case.' He turned towards the door. 'I'll wait for you downstairs.'

I raced around the apartment, climbing into the first clothes I could find. Whatever games I'd been playing with Grace Riley and Clark Stuart, they were forgotten now. I went to the little mirror in the bathroom and dragged a brush through my hair, staring at my reflection, trying not to think too much. Yesterday Sally had been on set and now she was in a funeral parlour. My hand fell to my side, but I couldn't stop looking at myself in the mirror.

'Just stay calm, Loretta,' I told myself.

I grabbed my beauty case, then ran out of the open front door and down the stairs after Petraś.

For all the skills he had, driving wasn't one of them. We swerved wildly round other cars, a trail of blaring horns tracking our route. It wasn't my place to tell him to slow the heck down. Instead, I clung on to the dashboard and listened carefully as he filled me in.

'Federico found her with bottles of pills.' We swerved round a junction.

I swallowed. 'What type of pills?'

His hands tightened on the steering wheel, knuckles white.

'Some sort of herbalist nonsense,' Petraś said vaguely. 'I'm sorry if I gave you a shock, calling round so early,' he added, clearly trying to change the subject. But I wasn't having any of that.

'What happened when they found her?' I asked.

'You really want to know?'

'I really want to know.'

'OK, but listen, if you don't like what you hear, I can turn the car around any time and take you straight back home. You don't have to be involved.' His voice sounded flat and resigned.

'Involve me,' I said dryly.

He cleared his throat. 'The studio . . . I phoned one of the executives from Sally's bedroom. He didn't appreciate being woken up.'

'Why did you phone an executive?' I asked.

'I should clarify, I phoned an ambulance first.'

I looked at my boss. It made my heart ache that he even felt the need to say that. 'Of course you did,' I said softly. 'Now, why did you phone an executive? And which one?'

He gave a sigh. 'You won't know him.'

'Try me.' I didn't usually talk back to him this way, but this felt important.

'A talent manager.' His hands twitched on the steering wheel. 'The studio was determined to get Sally through this movie. She was drinking on set. So they gave her some – *ahem* – pills.'

'Oh, lord.' I turned my head away.

Petraś gave a grim half-laugh. 'She washed them down with whisky.'

I had nothing to say. Absolutely nothing. We were a part of this, Petraś and myself. Colluding even by driving to the funeral parlour.

'You did ask,' Petraś said.

The sound of our engine disturbed a cluster of starlings, and a black cloud lifted out of a tree, shifting across the brazen blue sky.

Petraś slowed down, then a single bird rose high out of sight, a jubilant song filling the cobalt air. Maybe that was Sally, finally free of all her pain.

Who are you kidding? I imagined her saying. *I'd be an eagle.*

I had to bite my lip to stop myself from laughing. Or crying.

Petraś swerved past a wooden sign – FOREST LAWN MEMORIAL PARK – and finally slowed down to a respectful crawl. As we advanced up the drive, I glanced around.

Petraś swore quietly beneath his breath. 'They're here already.'

'Who?'

He nodded towards a crowd, cameras slung around necks. 'The ambulance chasers.'

He parked off to one side. I grabbed my beauty case and we climbed out, the two of us gazing at each other across the soft top as we braced ourselves for what would come next.

'Just ignore them,' he advised, 'and whatever happens, don't talk to them. Now, are you ready?'

There was something I had to ask before we moved off. 'Why me? Why not you?'

Petraś smiled with something that looked like pride. 'I appreciate it may be hard to believe, Loretta, but she didn't just like you – she respected you. So do I. I wouldn't trust anyone else with what I've just told you.'

'Not even Arvella?'

'Too uptight. Secrets send her crazy.'

He took my elbow and led me towards the entrance. I wanted to run away, but it was too late now – from inside the main building, I could hear the faint sound of funereal organ music. But almost immediately it was drowned out by the clatter of running feet and the newshounds jostling around us.

'Mr Petraś? Mr Petraś! Will you be doing Sally's final make-up?'

'How did she die, Mr Petraś? Overdose?'

'Or razor in the bath?'

Petraś threw the owner of that last question a filthy look, but the reporter just laughed.

'Oh, come on. It's usually one of the two. Don't worry, you can be an anonymous source.'

A bulb popped. 'Who's the little lady?'

'All in good time, *gentlemen*.'

The funeral director was waiting to greet us.

'She's already been embalmed. We started straight away,' he said by way of introduction. He glanced at me. 'This the one she asked for?'

Petraś nodded, then turned to me. 'Don't try to make her look alive. Just make her look . . . less dead.' He shook a finger. 'Paler foundation than usual. Pink undertone. Her skin will be dry, so apply a layer of Vaseline first. You won't be able to work in the foundation otherwise. You have Vaseline, right?'

I nodded.

'Her lips will have thinned out, you'll have to—'

'What if I can't do this?' I interrupted, pulling my cardigan tighter as fear skittered across my skin.

'If you're *ready*, I'll show you through,' the funeral director said, clearly impatient.

Petraś placed a hand on my arm. 'I believe in you.' I could only hope that Sally did too. 'Don't forget the eyebrows!' he called after me.

Darlings, I *never* forgot the eyebrows.

40

Organ music piped out of hidden speakers. I took a deep, calming breath, and placed my beauty case on the sideboard. Then I turned to finally look at the open casket. It was mahogany, studded with ornate gold handles and lined in powder-pink satin. At either end stood unlit candles on sconces. To one side of the casket was a gaudy display of pink roses.

Pink? Do I look like a dead poodle?

I drew closer and my glance reluctantly shifted to Sally's face, already knowing what I'd see there. This wasn't my first corpse. The familiar scent of formaldehyde drifted out – I recognized it from the preservative some of the make-up artists used, though Petraś had banned it from his formulas. Someone had closed Sally's eyes, but the rest of her was a mess. Her dress was dishevelled, her wig crooked. That broke my heart – she'd always been so proud of her collections of jewellery and art. Even the baby photos.

'It's all right, Sally,' I whispered. 'I'm here now.'

Don't fuck it up.

'No, Sally.'

First, I straightened the wig and pinned it into place – not an easy task. With the back of her skull resting against the underside of the casket, the wig kept pushing forward over her brow, but with some tape and extra pins I managed to get it to lie right. I took a deep breath. One job done.

Next was the incision in her neck where I guessed the formaldehyde had been added through a vein. I pasted strips of facelift tape over the wound and then added concealer. No one would ever know.

There was no avoiding it any longer. The only task left was her face. I'd been informed that her eyes had been glued shut, but there was something odd about the way she looked. Her legendary cheekbones had disappeared. A short rummage around revealed wads of cotton stuffed inside her cheeks to plump them up. I tossed the damp cotton wads in a waste bin.

Rubbing the Vaseline into her skin was like massaging butter into a turkey. I had to look away, steadying my glance on the sideboard and a blue bottle left out along with a syringe. The formaldehyde.

After that, things got a tad more palatable. I started to convince myself that Sally was still with me, that this was just another day in Petraś's salon, that all she needed was another glug of vodka to go on set and knock 'em dead. My mind drifted back to all our conversations, and I couldn't help asking myself again – why had she chosen me? Was she trying to send me some sort of message? She'd warned me about the men in Hollywood, seemed to encourage me to stand up to them. But then she'd dropped all those heavy hints about Clark, as though she knew what I'd done. And now involving me in this had drawn me even closer to

Petraś with our shared secret, when she'd urged me to spread my wings.

'What are you doing to me, Sally?' I asked beneath my breath. She'd probably have told me to stop making the whole situation all about me. I was going to miss her nuggets of advice and wisdom. I thought back to the child in the photograph that Sally had given me. I'd do her proud, help her to leave this world as larger than life as she'd always been.

I checked over her face with my tweezers for any unwanted hairs. Foundation with the pink undertone to lift her skin, as Petraś had advised. Then the finest dusting of powder. An extra sweep of blusher to add a touch of warmth, but the lack of body heat made it difficult to blend. After that, a spot of white in the corner of each eye for youth. Subtle shading around her jawline.

Petraś had given me a pale pink lipstick. No way. I went to my beauty case, where one of my sample pots lay. It was a deep red, made from rose petals, that I'd wanted to try on Primrose. Maybe . . . I took the pot and went to Sally's side.

'My gift to you,' I said.

I took up some of the lipstick on the pad of my little finger and dabbed at her lips. The sheen from the extra oil worked perfectly. I stood back and admired my work. If it could make a corpse look this good, I was on to a winner.

The false eyelashes proved to be more tricky – there was no give in her eyelids. Then, finally, those killer eyebrows. Her real ones were non-existent. She used to joke that they'd run for the hills when she was twenty-two, after a misguided make-up artist had experimented with burning them off with matches. 'And I let her!' Sally had hooted.

I watched her face reveal itself again. The lips that had become pinched and narrow returning with the aid of a lip pencil shaped in above the natural lip line. Theatrical make-up that would remove the look of jaundice. At last I stood back. Her face was complete.

I glanced down her body. Her gown was all bunched up. I began to move around the casket straightening Sally's collar, the tie at her waist and the row of satin buttons. She felt tiny and fragile beneath my hands, a body half-starved by order of the studios.

'Good luck, Sally,' I said sincerely. 'Wherever it is you're headed.'

I started to pack up, jars rattling. There was the sound of footsteps and a knock at the door.

The funeral director poked his head round. 'How are you getting on?'

'All done.'

He went to inspect my work. 'Not bad. I'll settle up with Petraś.'

As the door swung shut, I crossed the room to say my last goodbye – and a silent thank you – to Sally. But when I arrived beside the casket, I found it suddenly empty. Whatever was laid in there, with its painted eyelids and pencilled brows, it wasn't my friend. She'd finally gone. *Can't go through the pearly gates without a full face, Loretta!*

I smiled to myself. 'You show them, Sally.'

As Petraś and I stepped back outside, I turned to him. 'I meant to ask. When did you call for the ambulance?'

'Just before the reporters found out.' He had that to be proud of, and I was proud of him.

41

The funeral took place on a sunny day. Would you believe it if I told you I was starting to miss the seasons?

Petraś couldn't make it – some actress in New York needed him for an award ceremony, and no matter how he felt about Sally, Petraś never turned down a job. Still, I couldn't help scanning the gathered faces for a sign of anyone I knew. In particular, the slender stroke of a man who I had to thank for saving me.

The writer.

This had felt like the longest I'd ever gone without talking to Eliot, although I knew that couldn't possibly be true.

Crowds sheltered beneath the cypress trees. I spotted Federico, cap wrung between his hands. Then my glance caught on another man, strolling past, hands in his pockets. The Emperor, Oscar Romero. He went to join a pal. I risked another look from beneath my lashes. I felt my body start to tremble. He scanned the crowd and quickly I backed away, hiding behind black-clad strangers ... Fortunately, by then, the ceremony had started and as the coffin was lowered into the ground, I took the time to calm myself.

Afterwards, a sympathetic figure appeared by my side. 'How are you?' Deep tan, Ray-Bans, open-neck shirt and unconventional suede brogues. Billy Trapido, director of *The Witch*.

'Oh, I'm fine, thank you.'

We began to walk after the clusters of mourners moving beetle-black across the grass.

'You've seen one funeral, you've seen them all. You're the Lip Girl, right?' He hooked his arm through mine. 'I know this isn't really the time but . . .' He leant closer. '*The Witch* is in the can, and filming starts next week on *The Quarter Ball Hit*. Maybe you've heard word about the script? It's a ball-breaker!'

I winced at his language. I'd heard, of course. Debra couldn't stop talking about it – admittedly in less florid language – but I wasn't about to stoke Billy's ego by letting him know that.

'We need a really great make-up artist. And a little birdy told me that the Lip Girl is the best.' He slid his Ray-Bans down his nose and gave me a long, significant look.

Did I have this right? Billy Trapido was actually offering me an actual job? At an actual funeral?

We'd arrived beside his car and a driver opened the door. He wore a ridiculously over-the-top uniform, like a film studio's idea of what a chauffeur should be. Heck, the whole outfit was probably borrowed from a costume department.

'Need a ride?' asked Billy.

I looked over his Chrysler – sleek, dark metallic green with one of those silver-winged hood ornaments on its bonnet. Sally would have approved.

'Sure,' I said. 'Why not?'

As we drove, Billy talked me through the plot. The billiard star who throws a game. The love of his life who shopped him. The gunshot masked by the sound of billiard balls smacking off each other.

'We have a newish actor as the lead. Handsome in a pretty-boy way. And a top-notch writer!'

He reached into the door's side compartment and handed me a script. I flipped through it. All the 'S's were missing.

'Let me guess,' I said. 'Is the writer you mention Scott Eliot by any chance?'

'That's the one!' He clicked his fingers. 'Say, you know everyone.'

My skin prickled. I sure did.

After a long soak in the tub, I went to sit on the windowsill. Primrose had come round with a new girl, Cora, so I could teach her how to do her make-up properly. Apparently, she'd left the Eleven Whispers because of something no one wanted to whisper about. Venereal disease.

'Are you sleeping with Billy?' Primrose asked, chin propped on her knee as she drank a bottle of beer, watching me apply Cora's lipstick. I didn't care what she may have caught; it made no difference to me.

I snorted. 'Of course I'm not. I have my eye on someone else and you know it.'

Primrose gave a wry smirk before removing her cigarette from its holder and flicking the butt out of the open window. 'So, tell us about this latest movie.'

I nodded to where I'd left the large brown envelope. 'Take a look for yourself.'

Primrose plucked up the parcel, pulling on a string knot. Idly, she flipped through, then looked at me. 'You seen this?'

'No. Why?' I said, as I finished Cora's lips.

Cora went to stand behind Primrose and she read out loud from over her shoulder. 'Oh, hey – I know this guy! Raphael Goddard; height, six foot two; shoe size . . .' Her voice drifted on.

Primrose and I stared at each other. My ex-husband. The dope was back – and he was working with Scott Eliot.

'I don't think I can do this,' I said, sinking into a chair.

'Why not?' said Primrose.

'Well, for starters, there's my ex-husband to worry about!'

'And that's a problem . . . because?'

'Because I don't want to see *him* again!' Even as the words exploded out of my mouth, I knew that I was lying – or half lying, at least.

From the look on her face, Primrose knew it, too. 'Yeah, I get that. The man who fucked you sideways, backwards and every which way. We could hear the screams from the Hacienda Arms!' She shook her head in apparent misunderstanding. 'Why would any woman want to see a sex bomb like that again?'

'I thought you didn't approve of him? He betrayed me, Primrose!'

'And you don't want to see what he's up to, at least?

Push your tits into his face while you're doing his make-up?'

'Would you?' I demanded.

'Revenge,' she announced, looking into the middle distance like a university philosopher who'd been smoking something suspicious, 'is a dish best eaten cold.' She snapped her glance back at me. 'They're the words, right?'

'You been reading the big books again?'

She shrugged, impervious to my jibes. 'Even whores use the library. We just don't take the books back.'

I hated her in that moment! I mean, really hated her. Yet again, she was right.

I snatched the script back. 'I'm doing this, aren't I?'

'Oh, darling. You were *always* going to do this.'

'Am I that predictable?'

'You're anything but,' she replied, laying a conciliatory hand on my knee. 'Could you ever have predicted that one day you'd be working on a brand-new movie with a brilliant director?'

'No,' I said, sulking and staring into my lap.

'There you go, then.' She laughed. 'People don't get offers like this every day! The director tracked you down at Sally Dee's funeral. Do you know what that means?'

'No.'

'It means you're going places.' She gave one last shrug and reached for another cigarette. 'What a terrible position to be in.'

42

Things moved fast after that. I said yes, just as Primrose had predicted, and Raphael and I were reintroduced when we gathered for a make-up screen test. It was a Sunday and the studio was relatively empty – just us, the camera man and a few chippies knocking together a set. And Arvella, though I couldn't understand why she was so dressed up. She wore a two-piece dress and jacket in what looked like cashmere.

Arvella raised her voice above the noise. 'Mr Goddard, this will be your make-up artist.' She frowned, as though it caused her great personal pain to even acknowledge my existence. 'If she does anything – and I mean *anything* – to offend you, don't hesitate to let me know.'

Raphael looked different yet nauseatingly familiar. The same handsome face, same haircut – but everything was ever so slightly more refined.

He held out a hand, swallowing hard. 'Hello, Miss . . . ?'

'Miss Darling,' Arvella finished for him. She tapped her clipboard. 'But we have her down as technician thirteen.'

I held out my hand. 'Unlucky for some. So, how've you been keeping, Mr Goddard?' I whipped back a drape and it billowed around him.

'Er, fine?' He made it sound like a question, clearly alarmed at my peppiness.

'That's great.' I placed a hand on his shoulder. 'We'll start with testing base colours against your skin and taking short films of different looks. I'll keep a record of what works best in front of the camera, and we'll use that as your template for the screen.' My hand squeezed. 'We want you to look your best and that will mean bespoke creations. We mix it from scratch.'

'You're quite the expert.'

'Oh, don't let her fool you, Mr Goddard,' Arvella snapped, before turning on her heel.

Once she'd gone, he immediately dropped the act.

'So, she's a bunch of fun,' he quipped. I didn't reply. 'Look, Loretta. This is awkward as hell. Maybe you should get someone else to step in – like technician twelve or, I dunno, fourteen?'

'Raphael, this is a small town. We were bound to bump into each other sooner or later.' I patted him on the shoulder. 'We can be civil, can't we?'

He shifted in his salon chair. 'Well, that's very good of you, Loretta.'

'Now, close your eyes.'

As I worked lotion into his skin, I kept up the act. Talked about how we both needed to move on, that we had our careers to think about and should get used to working together. How he needed me, how I knew just what he needed, how Petraś's tailored approach gave actors the edge they needed to make it big. His initial suspicion faded away and soon he was sharing stories. They were nowhere near as entertaining as Eliot's; unsurprisingly they were all about him, him, him. How he had a new girlfriend. How her name was Lucinda and she worked as a hostess at a hotel I'd never heard of. How Oscar Romero had got him the screen test for this movie.

I held out a hand, forcing a smile. 'Where's my cut, then?'

'That was a long time ago, Loretta,' he said stiffly.

Ever the professional, I picked up the conversation. I told Raphael all about Petraś and my job, shared gossip from the Hacienda Arms. By the time we'd finished for the day – dead on noon – my ex-husband genuinely thought we'd become friends again. The fool.

'You know, I'm really glad we've been able to put everything behind us,' he said, as he climbed out of his chair. 'Just one thing. You won't . . . I mean, it would be good if we could . . . That night at Oscar's party. It would be good if we kept that between the two of us.'

Anger unfurled inside me again like a dragon's tongue, but my mask stayed set.

'Like you say, it was a long time ago.'

His shoulders dropped in visible relief.

'I really appreciate it, Loretta.' He swallowed. 'You're one of the good ones.'

'I like to think so.' I flapped my hands at him. 'Go on – go! You have a screen test to get to. Knock them dead!'

He grinned, saluting in the way that had once been a standing joke between the two of us. I lifted a stiff hand to my brow and saluted back before he disappeared through the door. In an instant, the hand dropped to my side and my smile fell away.

I'd had Raphael down as lots of things. Vain. Self-centred. Utterly without morals. But I'd never figured he was dumb. Not really. If he thought I was going to do anything at all to help his career, he was even more stupid than I'd realized. Didn't he know me at all?

I gazed at the empty space where he'd been stood, moments ago.

Raphael Goddard?

I was going to destroy him.

43

For our trail walk – my suggestion – I wore a cute little gingham two-piece with a matching headscarf. Eliot wore shorts that made him look like an Austrian yodeller. He drove us into the hills, his beaten-up car coughing in protest, and we parked on Lake Hollywood Drive near a hiking trail called the Wisdom Tree.

'You wanna go hard or easy?' Eliot asked, as we faced the dusty red steps.

'Easy.'

We set off up a dirt path between outcrops of rock, the sun beating down relentlessly. After a while, the path levelled out and finally I caught my breath enough to be able to hold a conversation.

'So, how are things going?'

'Great.' His voice was clipped.

'Eliot, I wanted to say—'

'You don't have to say anything.'

'Oh, come on.' I tried to link my arm through his, but he wasn't having any of it. 'Eliot!'

He paused and gave a great big sigh. 'What is it, Loretta?'

We stared at each other. 'You really gonna be like this? I'm sorry, OK! I'm sorry that I got the whole wrong end of the stick with your wife. I'm sorry that I acted like such a blockhead. I'm sorry it's taken me weeks to work up a reason to apologize.' Then I softened my voice. 'I really am sorry. Do you know how much it cost me to call you?'

'Five cents?'

What a crummy joke. 'I missed you!'

He let out a small puff of air, then, after a moment, held out a hand. 'I missed you too. And shall we stop calling her "my wife"? Her name was Agatha.'

'Nice name. Saintly.'

Eliot smiled sadly. 'Believe me, she was no saint.'

I couldn't tell if that was meant to be a good or bad thing and didn't dare ask in case I said the wrong thing yet again.

'I've spent five years grieving, Loretta. I'd only just started to get back out that first time we met and, funnily enough, I didn't want my conversations with a new friend – that's you, by the way – to be all about Agatha. Maybe I just wanted to have some fun for a change?'

'Would you like to talk about her – I mean, Agatha – now?' I asked.

'Would *you* like to talk about her?'

'I do have some questions,' I admitted.

He dug his fists into his pockets. 'Shoot.'

I just asked whatever rose to the surface first. 'What did she die of?'

'A road accident.'

I nodded. 'Do you miss her?'

'Every day.'

That gave me a pang of recognition, or maybe something else. 'I don't.'

He pulled his chin in. 'What do you mean?'

My stride quickened, feet hitting the ground heavily. 'I don't miss Da, not at all. Good riddance.'

'Your father's dead?'

'He fell.'

Eliot put out a hand to slow me down, forcing me to look at him. 'Loretta, I'm so sorry. Why didn't you tell me before?'

'Well, you know.' My voice wobbled, but I couldn't seem to stop talking now that I'd started. 'He was a cruel bastard and was pushing all of us around. He had it coming.'

I saw the shock and confusion in Eliot's face.

Too much, Loretta.

A hummingbird buzzed past our faces. I followed its flight and took in the heart-stopping views across the canyons and mountains. We were higher up now, closer to the sky, and it felt sort of freeing. Maybe too freeing.

He opened his mouth to say something, but I got there first.

'Come on,' I said, before either of us could ask any more questions. 'Let's keep walking.'

As we set off again, I listened to the tramp of our feet, the buzz of cicadas and the faint bell chimes that floated up from a church far below. Eliot took the lead, and I followed him past the long grasses, spiky brushes, honeysuckle.

'Why do you care who I sleep with, anyway?' He threw the words carelessly back over his shoulder.

I slowed. 'What *is* going on between you and Christine?

'Nothing.'

'Nothing? But the way she looked at you, the way you looked at her—'

'She was Agatha's best friend, Loretta.' His voice was hard.

'Ah.'

'Ah, indeed.'

'So,' I began, looking for a way to start over.

'So.' He sighed.

'I have a new gig.'

'That's great!' He stopped in his tracks, smile overly bright. 'What is it?'

'*The Quarter Ball Hit.*'

His brow pinched in a crease. 'Oh, that's good.'

'Good? It's great!'

'Yes, I'm glad for you.' He didn't sound it.

I set off again, staring at the ground. Everything I said seemed to be wrong, or else he was saying the wrong thing back. Why couldn't we return to how we had been? I found myself surrounded by white clouds of flowers, clusters of pink. Reminders of home.

'We should stick together,' Eliot called. 'The wildlife here can be dangerous. Bears and stuff.'

'Oh, I know! The wildlife, huh? All those unpredict-able wolves.'

'There aren't any wolves in Hollywood, Loretta.'

'You sure about that?' I asked, reaching to grab a handful of flowers.

'Not really.'

I straightened up, my knapsack already swinging back over my shoulder.

Eliot paused in the path and snorted. '*Come for a hike!* she said. *It'll be fun!* she said. Jeez, Loretta, I thought we were making friends here!'

'We are. Just . . . can you stop patronizing me? *Oh, good for you, Loretta! I'm really pleased for you, Loretta. Do you think it might be too much* work, *Loretta?*

We glared at each other.

'You're honestly doing this? I just thought that—'

'Thought what?'

He shook his head. 'No. It doesn't matter now.'

'It matters to me!' By this point I had no idea what we were arguing about – Eliot's ex-wife, his new movie, my new movie? But Eliot had something in his head – I could tell.

'Listen,' he said after a moment. He reached out. 'I am really and honestly glad that you phoned. And I'm glad that you have this opportunity.'

My own anger faded a little. 'You mean it?'

'Of course I mean it. Do you know how difficult it's been, not having anyone to tease?'

I glanced up at him. 'You don't have to make it seem so easy. Teasing me all the time.'

'Like you don't tease me back?'

'Only sometimes.'

'Only sometimes!' he called out into the air, raising his

hands as though begging God for help. 'Only sometimes does this woman drive me crazy!'

I shrugged my backpack round to do up the buttons, shoving the flowers beneath its flap. Then I glanced around. 'Now, can we get going? The wolves will be here soon, and I don't want to be eaten alive.'

'Any wolves won't eat you, Loretta,' he said, taking me in. 'You'd cut them open from the inside.'

'Well, I'm glad we can agree on that,' I said, threading my fingers between his.

He grinned and squeezed my hand back as we resumed our walk. 'So am I.'

44

The next time Raphael and I met at the studio, he looked jittery as hell.

'You gotta help me, Lorctta!' He held out trembling hands. Who knew what was running through his body? I eased him into his salon chair.

'Can you get me a drink?' He pulled a pretty-boy begging face.

'Sit down. I know the perfect thing.'

When I arrived back at the salon, he took the milkshake. 'You remembered! You always did know how to look after me.'

A choke threatened at the back of my throat, but I managed to place a cape around him. He pulled out his battered script, lips moving silently along with his lines.

I sprayed rosehip water onto a cloth and wiped down Raphael's skin; he tended to oil. Then I moisturized, and after that applied the face base.

I brought out a jar from my beauty case. 'I've been studying the results of your film test and I have the right base for you now.'

'You worked over the weekend, just for me?' he asked.

'Sure did.'

Fuck you, Raphael.

He sat back in his chair and I set to, carefully using a

sponge to apply the base. Then concealer, rouge, powder, Vaseline on the brows and eyelashes, a pencil of white in the corner of each eye, and the palest pink on his lips, just enough to bring them to life. He looked like an angel sent down from heaven. I almost hated myself for making him look so good.

'I'm done.'

He held out a tentative hand. The trembling had stopped – almost.

'No one would ever know,' I said.

'I owe you,' he said.

Already, Raphael's co-star, Vivien, was making her way out onto set. She paused beside his chair. 'Look at you, you handsome devil!' She wagged a finger at me. 'Stop being so good at your job, young lady!'

We all laughed in a fake kind of way.

She crooked the same finger at Raphael. 'You coming?'

He leered. 'For you? Always.'

Vivien looked faintly nauseous at the innuendo, and I had to turn my head away to hide my laugh. I watched in the mirror as the two of them left the studio, Raphael standing back to allow her to lead the way. Always the gentleman. It was only as I turned round from my counter that I spotted Arvella observing from the doorway.

'Everything OK?' I asked.

'You tell me.' Her voice carried across the salon as she folded her arms, watching me. Always watching me.

'Oh, sure,' I said. 'Just dandy.'

*

The Movie Production Code was full of odd rules – no pointed profanity, excessive or lustful kissing – and absolutely no couples together in a bed. So Eliot had been clever. To avoid the annoying bed detail, he'd set his seduction scene across a billiard table. Neat, huh?

Vivien and Raphael were already laid across it. The costume designer was rearranging Vivien's blouse so that it looked torn open. Her hair had been dishevelled. Arvella was back out from the salon, her eyes scouring the whole scene. Beside her stood Hedda Hopper, which was never a good sign. Who'd invited *her* on set? Arvella?

'Ready, people? Off set!' called Billy.

'And . . . action!' A clapperboard snapped shut.

```
                    BRETT

    'You think you have it all sorted,
    don't you? You and your mother!'


                    JULES

    'No, Brett, don't—'


                    BRETT

    'I'm your husband, goddamnit! You do as
    I say.'

    Jules twists her head out of his hand.

    Brett pushes her back against the
    billiard table, and lifts her hips onto
    it.


                    BRETT

    'I'm telling you, you'd better start
    listening . . .'
```

This was Eliot's work? I mean, sure, if you liked rape dressed up as romance.

He'd come to stand beside me. 'The next bit's better,' he whispered anxiously.

'Sure.'

'Jeez, what's wrong with *him*.'

I followed the line of Eliot's glance. He was right; our leading man looked flushed.

'Cut!' roared Billy.

The director went to give Vivien some directions around hitching her skirt up higher. Raphael motioned to me and I ran over. Up close, I saw that his eyes were already red and swollen.

'I feel strange,' he croaked. 'How do I look?' I hesitated just long enough to let his panic rise. 'Do you think it was the milkshake? Maybe I'm allergic to milk!'

Our eyes met as he yanked at the knot in his tie, loosening it. 'I . . . can't . . .' His eyes widened. 'Oh, God, I'm dying!'

'You're not dying.' At least, I hoped he wasn't. 'You're just . . . suffering.' My eyes ranged over his face.

'Show me,' he said.

'You certain?'

'Show me!'

I scrambled in my pocket for a compact and held the mirror up to him. He immediately gave a small yelp. There were angry red blotches all over his face and neck.

Billy marched over from where Vivien was adjusting the tops of her stockings. He glared at Raphael. 'You look like a clown! Jesus, sort him out.' Then he headed towards the rear of the studio. 'Take a break! Ten minutes!'

There was almost a stampede for the refreshments table.

'Come on,' I whispered to Raphael. 'The beauty studio. Now.'

45

Raphael threw himself into a salon chair and stared at his reflection. 'What the hell is happening to me?' He leant forward, frantically turning his face from one side to the other in front of the mirror as he reached to undo the top button of his shirt.

'Oh. Oh dear.' My voice went down a notch as I spotted Alice following us into the salon. She pretended to tidy up some towels, but I knew she was here to make sure I was OK.

'What do you mean, *oh dear*?'

'That's bad.' I stepped back.

He looked as though he was about to burst into tears. 'Loretta, you have to tell me. What's going on here?'

'What did you get up to this weekend?'

His breathing worsened. 'Why?'

'It's just that . . .' I peered closer. 'This rash. It reminds me of—'

'Oh, God!' he wailed, pushing me off and digging his head into his hands.

'Is everything OK?' Alice asked, coming over.

'It's fine,' I said, ushering her away. She didn't need to be involved.

As her footsteps faded, Raphael looked up at me from between his fingers.

'The weekend,' I said calmly. 'Just tell me.'

'We may have . . . had a party.'

'Well, that's wonderful! Social relaxation always helps an actor.'

'You don't understand!'

Oh, I did. 'Tell me,' I coaxed.

He glanced around and then indicated that I should come closer. I leant down.

'There may have been some prostitutes.'

'Oh, Raphael,' I said, doing my best impression of a Sunday-school teacher. 'And . . .'

He nodded. 'And I may have slept with one of them.'

'Where were they from?'

'The Eleven Whispers.' Bingo! 'You know any of the girls from there?'

I pretended to gather myself. 'That's where Primrose's new girl came from. I'm sorry to say she had syphilis. And her rash . . .' I allowed my glance to drop to Raphael's crotch.

'Jesus Christ,' he whispered. 'What have I done?'

Billy's runner poked his head round the door.

'You guys ready?' he asked. 'He's getting angry.'

The boy's eyes widened when he saw Raphael's face and he scarpered. Clearly, he recognized trouble when he saw it.

Then there was the sound of marching feet and Billy himself appeared, framed in the doorway, Arvella behind him and peering over his shoulder.

'What the fucking hell are you guys—' His words dried up when he saw Raphael, who by this time was cowering in his salon chair, trying to make himself disappear.

Alice watched with wide eyes as Billy marched over. 'What the hell is happening?'

If Raphael had expected sympathy, he was going to be sorely disappointed. Billy's voice raised a notch. 'You have single-handedly fucked up my entire schedule! You absolute dickwad!' The director clicked his fingers and Arvella appeared by his side. 'Get the studio doctor. Now!'

'I certainly shall.' She ran off, struggling to hide her mouth turning up at the corners as she slipped past Alice towards the door. Alice and I shared an eye-roll. Why did Arvella have to be around *all* the time?

Billy pointed at Raphael's face. 'If we need to pack up for the day it's on you!' Then he jabbed the same finger at me. 'Sort it out!'

Vivien came to stand beside us, her lip curling in disgust. 'His hands have been all over me!'

Through the doorway, I saw a white coat flapping. The studio quack, with Arvella tailing him. This had not been part of my plan.

'I need to go,' I said, quickly shouldering on my jacket.

'No!' Raphael clung onto my arm. 'Stay!'

'Do as he says!' Billy ordered, before striding out.

I placed the jacket back down. The doctor clutched a clipboard to his chest. A stethoscope hung round his neck. His hair was shiny with Brylcreem and he looked about twelve years old.

'This is our studio doctor,' Arvella announced. 'One of the very best.'

From behind her, Debra was peeking into the room. Great – now we had the whole gang of blabbermouths.

'Ah, Mr Goddard. I'm Dr Altman.' He smoothed down his hair. 'What can I do for you?'

Raphael dragged open the collar of his shirt. 'Can't you see? It was this one! She gave me milk!' Arvella's eyes snapped to mine in silent accusation. *You, again!*

The doctor took a cautious step closer. 'Yes, indeed.' He pushed his spectacles up the bridge of his nose. 'Pretty nasty, I would say.'

'I know that! What I want to know is how do I get rid of it!'

Dr Altman consulted his clipboard, blindly flicking between sheets of paper.

I stepped forward. 'Dr Altman, I'm Loretta Darling. I don't think this is an allergy.'

He glanced at me, surprised. 'And what relationship do you have with the, ahem, patient?'

'She's my ex-wife,' Raphael wheezed. Arvella's eyebrows disappeared off the top of her face.

'I'm his make-up artist,' I corrected. 'The thing is, Doctor . . . Raphael had a party this weekend.' I lowered my voice. 'With prostitutes.' I felt a spurt of satisfaction to see Arvella's face colour like a beetroot.

'Ah!' Altman's face brightened. 'A venereal disease!' he said in a voice loud enough to wake the dead. 'Now that I do know.'

'Yes,' I said. 'One of the prostitutes had syphilis.'

'You slept with her?' the doctor enquired.

Raphael nodded glumly. Arvella looked outraged.

'Excellent!' Doctor Altman began scribbling. 'Penicillin. You'll be right as rain in twenty-four hours. An injection is what you need!'

Raphael face darted up. 'An injection?'

Altman nodded. 'Into the buttocks. Trust me, it's the quickest way, but please don't have sex for at least seven days afterwards. Now, if you'd like to come with me, the nurses' office is just down here.'

Raphael threw me a beseeching look.

'It's for the best,' I said, patting his shoulder. Then I walked the two of them to the salon door, politely asking Arvella to get out of the damn way. 'You been graduated long?' I asked, as I shook hands with Altman.

'Oh, I'm not graduated,' he said, sounding surprised. 'I have three more years of medical school, but Pa knows someone who knows someone. Summer job.' He smiled. 'You know how it is. All good experience under the belt!'

As he steered Raphael out, Arvella came to my side and raised a finger. 'I'm watching you, Miss Darling.'

My smile spread. 'I know. I'm fascinating, that way.'

Her mouth fell open. 'Fascinating? You should be so lucky. You're lucky that I . . .' Her mouth trembled.

'Goodbye, Arvella.' I indicated the open salon door. 'Remember, don't snoop too much! And try not to talk to Hedda Hopper!'

Cheeks aflame, she marched out of the room, skirts flapping behind her. I waited until the door had swung shut and then laughed to myself. I'd just taken the perfect revenge on a man who fully deserved it. And what did Arvella think she was going to do now? Stop me?

46

Moo-ving Drama For Actor On Trapido's Flick!

New film *The Quarter Ball Hit* nearly scored a Kill Shot when up-and-coming actor, Raphael Goddard, fell dramatically ill on set. Our young sources say that a studio doctor was on hand to assess him, and a dairy allergy was quickly diagnosed. A literally red-faced Goddard told us, 'It was a shock, I can tell you!' We're pleased to report, dear readers, that filming is now back on schedule and Goddard has a clean bill of health – so long as he can avoid the glasses of milk! Is he . . . too wholesome for this script? We say no, readers! And don't worry, you'll soon be able to catch this dramatic story of lust in a billiard room at a cinema near you. It should be udderly fabulous!

An interesting fact about Baby's Breath I learnt from Ma. It grows in areas with lots of grit, much like the rocky hill trails Eliot and I hiked a few short days ago. Another curious fact, the sap they contain, gyposenin, is a toxin that causes diarrhoea and vomiting if consumed. But that's not all this mighty little plant has to offer. Say, for example, if someone extracted that sap, slicing those thin stems and scraping it painstakingly into a tiny glass pot, and say that tiny glass pot got muddled with another glass pot, it could give someone a nasty rash, if they weren't careful.

I slid the morning's newspaper back across Petraś's desk from where I'd been reading it, the other girls having crowded round. The studios had sent Raphael straight home to his cottage, tail between his legs, and told him to keep a low profile for a few days. Vivien was refusing to do any more scenes with him; the studio had been forced to draft in another actor. Then I discovered another piece of gossip that made my heart soar.

'Did you hear?' one of the girls whispered, giddy with scandal. 'They say his agent's dropped him!'

'Shame,' Debra drawled.

Another girl gave a low whistle. Without an agent to secure a package, an actor became nothing. I'm not going to say I'd enjoyed all this, but I'm not *not* going to say it either. Raphael would be fine. Raphael Goddard was always fine.

'Quick! Arvella's coming!'

The whisper tore round the room, and we leapt up, hastily putting Petraś's desk to rights and straightening our uniforms. I took my place at the edge of the room. Debra shuffled along the wall to let me stand beside her.

The voices fell as Arvella made her entrance, clutching a pile of manila folders to her chest. Twenty pairs of eyes hungrily took in her outfit – for all the things I hated about Arvella, the woman knew how to dress. This morning, it was a silk sleeveless dress, navy blue with white polka dots. There was a spring in her step. This was going to be bad.

She took us in with a patient smile, waiting for silence. She cleared her throat and a final pair of girls abandoned their whispers to each other.

'Petraś isn't with us this morning so I'll be handing out the next work rota.' She patted her manila folders as though they were the keys to the White House. At each team meeting we checked in on projects. Sometimes we'd shift make-up artists between movies if there was a particular issue at hand – an actor with wandering hands or creative tensions. Petraś was good at looking after us like that.

Arvella pulled out his chair and sat down with a superior air, Petraś's kingdom temporarily hers. A few of us girls shared sly glances, as her head bent over a ledger.

After a moment, she picked out a fountain pen, screwing off the lid oh-so slowly. Then she began to read through our names as though she was taking a school attendance. Of course, my name was first up.

'Darling, Loretta.' She gave a small, tight smile as she reached to a folder and held it out for me. 'Well done for your work on *Quarter Ball*. Obviously, there were issues, but . . .'

I slid off the cabinet and picked my way across the carpet, moving between the other girls. I took the folder with a small thank you and went back to my place, opening it up. The script was something called *Widow in the City*. I flipped a page and checked out the cast list. Nobody, nobody and another nobody. I hadn't heard of a single one of these actors. I looked at Arvella over the top. We both knew what she'd done.

'Pack your bags, Debra,' came the next announcement. 'You're on location.'

Everyone gave a sharp gasp. Of all people, Debra?

As I watched, open-mouthed, Debra returned to stand next to me. Jealously, I watched over her shoulder as she peeled open the folder. Unbelievable. Her new movie was Eliot's *The Misbelievers*.

A girl on the other side of Debra had also been reading over her shoulder. 'No! You lucky thing!' She elbowed her companion. 'Look – in the Alabama Hills! And working on the star – no less!' Word quickly spread around the room.

'The Dow Hotel!'

'Gig of a lifetime.'

'Swap, Debra?'

Debra looked fit to burst, grinning shamelessly. Alice shot me a sorrowful glance.

'All right, all right! Quieten down!' Arvella had one last folder to hand out. 'Alice?' My friend ran over. 'You'll be going with Debra, too.' Alice looked near about ready to faint, but before she could voice her thanks, Arvella slammed shut the ledger. 'My decisions are final.' Her satisfied glance caught my gaze. 'Back to your work, everyone.'

Once we stepped outside, I chased after Debra, the girls parting around us like water.

'Listen,' I began. 'I was wondering . . .'

'No.' She marched away. '–Absolutely not. No way.'

'You don't even know what I'm going to ask!'

She stopped. 'I know exactly what you're going to ask, Loretta Darling, and you're a real deadhead if you think I'd agree. I know you and that writer guy are all loved up and everything, but I have two new swimsuits burning a hole in my bottom drawer. This is my chance to break them out.'

'There's nothing I could do that would make you want to swap at all?'

'Nothing!'

I thought desperately. 'I have two tickets to the Hollywood Bowl! You can have them, if you like.'

She didn't even bite. 'Don't lie, Loretta. It's unbecoming.'

It was true; I didn't have the tickets right at that very moment, but I could get hold of them – somehow. Maybe Raphael's old pal Mick could help.

Debra's eyes narrowed. 'Look, Loretta, I like you – almost a lot. And I'm pleased for you that you're having this success with Petraś.' From the way her mouth pinched, she didn't look pleased at all. 'But all the girls agree that you've become awfully full of yourself.' She looked me up and down. 'Honey, you ain't all that. If anyone deserves to work on *The Misbelievers*, it's me – not you.' She stalked away.

I felt an uncontrollable surge of anger. 'Your dad fixed this, didn't he?'

She turned right back round and stalked towards me, jabbing a manicured nail into my chest. 'He did no such thing!' She glared at me in disgust. 'You think you're so

Hollywood, but you're just a loose-lipped, egotistical, no-talent, loud-mouth hanger-on who deserves to burn in hell!' Gosh, I'd never imagined Debra knew so many big words, but she wasn't done yet. '*The Lip Girl?* Well, that's just about right, isn't it? You can't keep your darn mouth shut, throwing around accusations like that. Who do you think you are!' Her face was so flushed that she looked just about ready to explode.

'Did I touch a nerve, Debra?' My idea of persuading or even bribing her was clearly not going to work, so I didn't give a fig if my taunts upset her even more.

'You . . .'

By some miracle, she managed to control herself, turning on her heel to walk away. As I watched her disappear round the corner of a lot, I thought about what I could do next. Sure, I could try to persuade Alice to give me her place, but I liked her too much; she deserved this break. And Debra didn't.

I felt set on getting her off Eliot's movie. But how? I needed help from someone with influence, who everyone underestimated. Someone good at keeping secrets. Someone more powerful than Debra or even her lousy dad. Someone like Grace Riley.

47

'Where's Grace?' I panted breathlessly, skidding to a halt.

Quickly, Biff checked his notes. 'Studio Twenty-Seven, Lot Fourteen!'

I took off again. Debra wasn't going to get the best of me, no way! I burst through the doors and glanced around.

'I need to see Grace. Now!'

'Well, you're lucky,' a runner drawled. 'She's having a tea break.'

'Grace!' I exclaimed, my voice triumphant.

'Good God, Loretta! What are you doing here?'

'You need to help me!'

She gave a nod and her latest make-up artist backed away tactfully. 'Anything! How? Just tell me!'

'There's this movie I really want to work on. *The Misbelievers*. Except Arvella has put Debra on the gig. She doesn't even care about it. She's just in for the jolly. I offered her anything to take her place, but she's refusing to help, calling me all sorts of names and . . . please.'

'Take a breath.' Grace placed a cool hand on mine.

I started again. 'Can you request Debra to work with you? Please? It would mean the world to me!'

A knowing smile spread across Grace's face. 'I get it.

The Misbelievers. Isn't that one of Scott Eliot's movies?' She raised a suggestive eyebrow. 'Of course I'll help you. But could you do me a favour in return?'

'Anything!'

'Could you arrange for me and James to go out one evening? Like, out in the open? I'm so tired of dates at my kitchen table.' She twisted a curl of hair round a finger. 'You know, I've always thought I'd make a fetching redhead.'

My eyes widened.

'Are you asking me to steal a wig from Mr flipping Klein?'

She squeezed my hands. 'One favour for another. That's how this town works, isn't it?'

I laughed and squeezed her hands back. 'You're outrageous!'

Her eyes glinted. 'Isn't it the best?'

Less than fresh from forty-eight hours in New York, Petraś sat down from unpacking his leather travel case. He removed his spectacles and cleaned them on the end of his tie, tired and owl-eyed.

'I took a phone call this morning,' he said after a moment. 'Apparently, Grace Riley wants Debra to work with her.' He placed the spectacles back on the bridge of his nose. 'Do you have any idea why that might be?'

I shrugged. 'Debra is a very . . . competent . . . make-up artist.'

Petraś cocked his head. 'Well, that means we now have a place going spare on *The Misbelievers*. Quite the coincidence, wouldn't you say?'

I shrugged again.

'Arvella informs me that she had the whole work schedule firmly set. This will all take a certain amount of reorganization. She's disappointed, Loretta.'

Oh, boohoo.

He let out a sigh. 'Unfortunately, we can hardly say no to Miss Riley.'

I leapt out of my chair and clapped my hands together in glee, before quickly remembering myself. I stood to attention.

'I'm sure that will make Grace very happy,' I intoned with over-sincerity.

Petraś gave me a long stare over the top of his spectacles – too long. 'Sit back down.'

I sat so fast that the chair nearly skidded away from beneath me. He waited as I tidied my skirts. 'How have you been? Since Sally and everything?'

'Fine.'

The two of us hadn't talked about any of it since the day we'd left the memorial park. He'd sent me some flowers but other than that we'd tacitly agreed to never again refer to our conversation on the way to the funeral parlour. It was kind of a thrill to share a secret with a legend like Petraś, like being let into some inner sanctum of Hollywood.

'Really? You've had to deal with all that on your own. It's a lot for a young woman.'

'Oh, you've been to one funeral, you've been to them all,' I said weakly, keeping a smile firmly fixed on my face.

He blinked. 'I don't believe you.'

I felt a panic rising up in my chest. 'What do you mean?'

'I don't believe that you're as tough as you like the world to think, Loretta Darling.' He leant back in his chair, polishing his spectacles again. 'I want you to take care of yourself. You work too hard and you play too hard. I know all about your shenanigans.' I felt my eye twitch. He pointed the arms of his glasses at me. 'Take this time away to rest a bit.' Then he indicated the office door. 'Now go. Arvella will be here soon and my guess is that you wouldn't enjoy a run-in with her. Enjoy the Alabama Hills.'

I got to my feet and turned to leave.

'And, Loretta?' Behind his spectacles, his eyes crinkled with amusement. 'You have my permission to enjoy yourself out there.'

I smiled back. 'Oh, I will,' I vowed. 'I definitely will.'

Dearest Enid

I have the most incredible news!

I'm going out on a real-to-life movie shoot on an actual location. In the desert! I didn't know they had those in America, did you? Oh, how I wish you were here with me. Or, maybe not! You've always hated the heat.

Shall I bring you back a memento?

Your loving sister, Margaret xxx

PART THREE

48

At 2 a.m. on the dot, a car drew up.

Alice and I had been watching, too excited to stay in bed from when she'd stopped over. We ran out, waving enthusiastically. I had paired a cute little capri-pant two-piece in an outrageous scarlet with ballet flats and a scarf at my throat. Alice wore a huge petticoat beneath a circle-skirt cotton dress printed with lemons. It was the least practical travel outfit I'd ever seen.

'You know how much dust there is out in the hills?' Eliot asked, a sardonic eyebrow raised.

'Oh, be quiet.' I shoved his suitcases out of the way so that we could cram our belongings into the rear.

After some effort and rearranging, we managed to shut the trunk. Alice scrambled into the back, her petti-coats sticking out from beneath her hem in frothy clouds of pale yellow. I climbed in beside Eliot.

He looked across the bench, from one face to the other. 'Did either of you get any sleep at all?'

'Nope!' Alice said, bobbing up and down.

Eliot shook his head as he turned back to the ignition. 'I'm about to drive into the desert with two of the most hyped-up women in Hollywood.'

'I know! Aren't you lucky?'

Alice laughed, and as we pulled out into the lane, she

waved madly at the Hacienda Arms. 'Goodbye, Primrose! Say, all her lights are on. Surely she can't still be up at this hour?'

Oh, innocent Alice, how I adored her! I didn't dare look at the expression on Eliot's face.

'She's not a good sleeper is Primrose,' was my reply.

After a while, Alice and I settled down. When we turned onto Route 14, the landscape transformed, flattening out. I'd never seen so much open space, with boulders looming out of the dark as the car's headlights pierced the road ahead. It felt like being on the moon. I eased my scarf up and sank into the seat. Behind us, Alice had already started to snore.

I couldn't help wondering what lay before us, or where our futures might go. I glanced back at Alice, knees tucked up against her chin, body covered by a blanket.

'Look,' Eliot said softly.

The slightest dot of amber appeared at the end of the road.

Dawn.

Eliot switched his beams off and we drove into the almost dark, almost nowhere. A long straight highway stretched ahead of us. It felt almost religious.

'Should we wake Alice?' Eliot whispered.

'No, let her sleep.' I wanted it to be just the two of us.

Wordlessly, I reached out a hand and placed it on Eliot's thigh as we gazed at that slowly rising golden dot, the desert coming to life around us. It was beautiful, in the bleakest sort of way. I couldn't believe that this was only a few hours away from Hollywood, the town of dreams and make-believe. It was so stark and brutal.

'People came out here to live?' I asked.

'There's gold in them there hills.'

'People must have really wanted to be rich,' I ventured.

'Or maybe just not to be poor.'

Not to be poor. As good a reason as any.

When we arrived, the first thing I did in room thirty at the Dow Hotel was carry the cockroaches out, one by one, trapped beneath a glass. Here's the thing about cockroaches – you can't simply crush them beneath your shoe. Spreads the eggs. A person has to be more cunning than that. You've got to get real close. That's the only way. As I tipped the last one from my glass, I watched its glistening brown carapace scurry away, antennae feeling the air.

'Good riddance,' I said, shuddering with disgust.

Then I glanced around the courtyard at the other rooms and the main hotel building that stood to one end of the swimming pool. I already knew how it worked out here. These places go down in Hollywood legend. Tourists will pay twenty bucks a night to sleep in the same bed where some famous actor once drunkenly pissed himself. The hotels display grainy black-and-white photos of some director or other, with his arm around the manager, the two of them grinning like idiots. Don't believe any of it. If the Dow Hotel was anything to go by, the reality of life behind the lens was somewhat different. The truth involved cockroaches.

49

The place was buzzing as our crew took over the whole establishment. Doors stood wide open as new friends wandered from room to room, calling out to each other. Alice had been allocated a room opposite mine, and even though it would have been nicer to be next door to each other, we had agreed it would be fun to wave across the pool each morning.

Already, a small group was splashing in the water, beers on the side. A barbecue was on the go and someone was flipping burgers. The only person who looked like he wasn't enjoying himself was the director, Riki Castillo. He was sitting in shorts beneath a parasol, arguing with Eliot, who was still in his tie and shirt. The whole gang of us had already had a short meeting in the hotel lobby, where Castillo had laid out his plans. We had a couple of days to set up, then filming would begin.

I unpacked, shaking out the creases from my dresses and hooking them over bent metal hangers. My toothbrush went into a glass in the bathroom, along with my hair curlers and shower cap. Nightgown on a pillow, slippers by the bed. It was almost starting to feel homely, if I ignored the garish prints of semi-undressed ladies that hung on the wall.

The last thing I eased out of the bottom of my case

was an artists' holdall I'd bought at a garage sale. I used it to hold all my pigments and waxes for the lipstick samples I was working on, along with a notebook. Petraś had taught me that everything lay in the details. If I was going to create my own unique shades, I also needed to keep meticulous notes. But while that was all fine and well in my apartment, it wasn't practical to have a book of secrets in a location where everyone traded in gossip and hearsay. I found a hiding place behind one of the print frames, hanging the notebook's spiral binding from the picture hook. I wiped my hands down and smiled to myself. No one would ever know.

A shout carried across the pool as a figure strode out, clutching a towel around his waist. Someone followed behind, holding a sheaf of papers – Eliot. The others greeted the first man as he dropped the towel to take a naked running jump into the pool, whooping and hollering. I shrank back behind my hotel-room curtains and watched as he reached over to a member of the crew and pushed his head under the water, laughing with aggressive delight.

I knew that laugh. I knew that body. I knew that man.

I dragged the curtains shut, turning into the room, my back sagging against the window. Oscar Romero. What the hell was he doing here and why hadn't Eliot warned me?

Sure enough, a knock sounded at the door. I went to open it.

'Well, don't just stand there. Come on in,' I said, my voice dripping with sarcasm.

Eliot visibly winced as Oscar's shouts carried over from the pool and he quickly shut the door behind him, the noises fading away.

'I'm sorry,' he said in a rush. 'I meant to tell you, but—'

Already I was pacing the room. 'You meant to tell me! When, exactly? On the drive out here or when he tried to rape me again? Jesus, Eliot!' I paused in front of him. 'Are you dumb or just selfish?'

His face flooded with outrage. 'Neither!'

But I was pacing again, unable to stop myself from turning tight circles round the bed. He tried to catch hold of my arm, but I pulled away.

'It was last-minute!' he said. 'Seriously, I only got the call myself last night.'

'Well, lucky for you! Because no one bothered to call me.' I was flooded with righteous indignation. I'd considered Eliot to be my friend and now – this?

He took a deep breath. 'Look, it's fine. We can make it fine.'

'How exactly? I'm stuck in the middle of the desert with a man who tried to rape me. Please, do inform me how that is fine. Or are you going to suggest that I just got the wrong end of the stick at his party?'

He looked disappointed then. In me and by himself. 'I would never suggest that, Loretta. I know what happened.'

'Good!' I stalked right up to his face. 'Because if you even dare to try to tell me that I was hysterical then or now, I swear to God I'll—'

He raised his hands. 'I know, I know. It looks bad.' His

face crumpled and he sank onto the bed. 'Honestly, believe me, it wasn't my decision.'

'It's never anyone's decision,' I said bitterly. 'They just have to go along with things.' I looked up at him. 'Isn't that how the story goes?'

'Loretta, please.' He patted the mattress beside him, indicating that I should sit down, and that made me want to punch him. 'Please,' he said again, more gently.

If it had been anyone else, I'd have told him to go to hell. But it wasn't anyone else; it was Eliot. After a moment's pause, I flumped down, making the entire mattress wobble. 'Why didn't you *say* anything?' My voice came out in a croak.

'Because we can make this work. Loretta, neither of us need to get hung up on this. It's a business transaction, nothing more. He gets to be the star; he makes our movie. My script gets a run at the awards, and you get your name fixed in people's heads.'

'That still doesn't explain why you didn't mention it before.' I wasn't going to let him off the hook that easily.

'Because, Loretta Darling, you are more than a little known for your strong opinions and I figured that you'd tell me to take a long walk off a short plank and renege on the whole movie. Which would have been a mistake.'

Eliot had a point, but I didn't appreciate being manipulated. I hadn't come out here for that, not by him and not by anybody.

A lackey poked his head round the open door and glanced between Eliot and myself. 'Er, Loretta, Riki says you can set up in Romero's room now.'

The make-up test.

'I'd prefer somewhere with better light.'

'I'm not sure Riki—'

I cut him off. 'Natural light is best.'

He glanced at Eliot, who gave a curt nod, and then he ducked back out of the room. I left Eliot to sit on his own and peeked round the door frame to watch the conversation going on out by the pool. I saw Riki's glance flicker over towards my room and then he gestured in frustration. The boy turned and hurried back.

'OK, you can have a corner of the restaurant,' he told me. A holler and a bout of vociferous swearing carried over from the pool where our star male lead had just stripped another man of his trunks. 'But you'll need to be quick. Dinner is at six.'

'Thank you.' I shut the door behind him, then shifted slightly to the side and, with a fingertip, eased back the curtain. Oscar had climbed out of the pool and was towelling himself down. There was the blue ink of an old tattoo on one of his arms, testament to another life. Through the crack in the curtains, I watched as he walked back towards the hotel, leaving a trail of wet footprints behind him. One by one, they evaporated beneath the sun until there was not a single trace of him left behind.

50

'Over there.' The hotel receptionist pointed me towards the restaurant. 'They're waiting for you.'

I carried my beauty case across the marble, past a bookcase filled with a small library of illustrated titles about the area – it didn't look like any of the guests had ever touched them. In the restaurant, the lights were dimmed above a sea of white linen. Silverware glinted like treasure at the bottom of the ocean and seated in the far corner was Oscar Romero with Riki, the two of them hunched together.

I weaved between the tables.

'Where the fuck is she, anyway?' Oscar twisted round in his chair as I approached. 'You the make-up artist?'

'One of them.' I reached to shake his hand. 'Sorry I'm late.' I *wasn't* late.

He kept hold of my hand. 'Hello.' His brow furrowed 'Miss . . . ?'

'Miss Darling. But please . . . call me Loretta.'

His hand squeezed mine again and I felt my stomach squirm. He clearly had no idea who I was.

'Miss Darling,' he repeated. 'You work for Petraś?' I nodded. 'And that bitch Arvella?'

I nodded again.

Riki cleared his throat. 'Mr Romero and I have work to discuss. Go ahead. Just pretend I'm not here.'

'Sure.' I quickly took out a towel. 'If you could . . .' Oscar leant back and closed his eyes as I draped the towel around his throat. 'Thank you.'

He stank of chlorine, and I had a sudden vision of his pool, where the naked girls had frolicked. It was strange, being this close to him again. Not just strange – horrible. I knew this face – the pores, the faint scar above his eyebrow, the way a certain lock of hair fell – the face he'd shoved into mine as he called me names. I took a few rapid, silent breaths to steady my hands.

The two men picked up their conversation as I set to with a sponge and powder.

'I'm telling you,' Riki began, 'the writer refuses to change a word.'

Eliot. My skin prickled. They were talking about Eliot.

'Then tell him again.'

Riki let out a sigh and raised a hand to the bar waiter, who sprang into action. 'A bourbon for me.' He glanced a question at Oscar, whose eyes had snapped open at the mention of alcohol.

'Make that two. Actually, make that four.' Oscar laughed. 'Line them up.'

Riki looked uncomfortable, but a few moments later the cocktail waiter was back with a silver tray and two glasses of amber liquid. I waited as Oscar tipped his back and immediately ordered another. Then he sank his head against the chair once more. 'Carry on.'

I carried on.

'I really think he's set on this,' Riki said, picking up where they'd left off. 'This is his big break.'

Oscar swatted my hand away, sitting up straighter in the chair. 'Listen, you A-hole. I don't care how you fix it, but that man needs to write me a speech.' His knuckles turned white around the tumbler he was holding. 'That doozer is lucky he got me on his script. I made it explicit that I needed at least two speeches. My agent put that in the contract, right?'

From the expression on Riki's face, this was news to him. He heaved a sigh. 'I'll keep trying.'

'You'll do more than try or you can find yourself a new male lead.' Oscar's face was so screwed up and red with righteous outrage that he'd actually turned ugly.

Riki took a deep sigh. 'OK, look. Here's what I suggest. We shoot the smaller scenes first. Gives me time to bring Eliot round. He can rewrite your scenes and . . .' Anything else he had left to say hung silently in the air.

'You finished?' Oscar barked, as I packed up my case.

'Yes, thank you. We should be ready for the screen tests tomorrow.'

'You made me handsome?'

I smiled. 'Oh, you don't need me for that.'

He tore the towel from around his throat. I bent to retrieve it and he slapped my arse so hard that the crack echoed around the restaurant. With a yelp, I shot straight back up. Riki was suddenly intent on studying the script. Coward.

I limped away, determined to keep my head up, past the waiter returning with drinks. He didn't dare look at me, no doubt sensing the fury burned deep inside me, hotter than any desert sun.

'Hey, sweetheart!' Oscar called. I turned round. Riki was still bent over the pages. 'I'm gonna enjoy working with you.'

I waved a hand. 'Me, too!' I called back.

Me, too.

51

Filming didn't go so well at first. The crew were over-heated and so was all the equipment. The location didn't help, but Oscar was our main problem. A diva. He'd get up late every day, his eyes red and body swollen in the heat. In the meantime, Eliot's movie was headed towards the pan.

'Oscar is threatening to bring down the whole show!' Eliot exploded, coming round to my room one evening. We'd got to the stage where we recognized each other's raps on the door. Two sharp raps and we'd let ourselves in without waiting.

'Is it really that bad?' I coaxed.

'At the end of every day, Riki hands me his latest version of the script covered in pencil scrawls. It's insulting!'

'OK, it's insulting. I understand.' I needed to take his mind off things, and stepped closer. It was too good a day to waste on scripts. 'You should cool down. Do you have any swimming trunks?'

He folded his arms. 'I don't swim. It's a rule of mine.'

'You don't swim.' I allowed myself a small eye-roll. 'Is that a New York thing?'

'Obviously.'

'I don't believe you. What about all those summers at the Hamptons?'

'You can believe what you like, but I'm telling you – I haven't brought out any swimwear!'

'Interesting.' I cocked my head towards the pool outside. 'Commando, then?' As if on cue, cries emerged from the rest of the crew, already splashing about.

He sighed, but I could tell his mood was improving. 'Are you *trying* to humiliate me?'

'Always.'

He gave a big sigh. 'OK, OK, I'll borrow some trunks from someone and meet you in fifteen.'

As he walked towards my door, he cast a look around. Colour swatches were littered across the sideboard from where I'd been experimenting with my lipstick shades. 'You know, you should try tidying up some time.'

'Fuck you.'

'Fuck you too, Loretta Darling.'

As the door slammed shut behind him, I grinned and went to dig out the swimsuit from my case.

When I came back out, preening in my violet one-piece, Eliot was waiting for me in the cutest pair of shorts, his hair a mess from the shower. He looked like a flamingo. Admittedly, a very attractive flamingo.

'Nice tan,' I said, indicating his skinny, white legs.

'Nice sunburn,' he said.

'I'm English. Sunburn is what we do.'

We approached the pool, one of us on each side. Eliot dropped his shorts to reveal a pair of trunks that were . . . well, they weren't doing him any favours.

'Who did you borrow them from?' I called over.

'Mind your own business!'

Before I could interrogate Eliot further, a voice called over from one of the crew. 'Come on, Loretta! Get in here!' He struck his hand against the water and aimed a big splash at me.

I lifted my arms above my head and pointed my body and then – with a *splash!* – the crown of my head neatly split the surface. All those times, letting boys train me how to dive off rocks in Morecambe had paid off.

Blue. All blue. It looked pretty for a moment, the yellow husk of the desert forgotten and swallowed up by the silence. I pushed my arms through the water, feeling my muscles burn with effort as I returned to the surface. And yet, for a moment, I never wanted to emerge.

When I did, Eliot was waiting for me. 'I thought you'd almost drowned! The pool is barely deep enough for diving. Are you trying to give me a heart attack?'

He gathered me up and our chests were so close that I could feel his heart beating.

Cries and whistles rang out.

'Go get her, Eliot!'

'Woman overboard!'

'Don't you just love an audience?' I complained under my breath.

He raised a hand to the crew. 'Nothing to see here! Nothing at all!'

'Oh, yes there is!' someone called back.

'You're the one who wanted to do this,' he reminded me, leaning to pull me out of the pool.

I shook off his hand. 'I can do this by myself!'

I started to climb the steps and then fell backwards with a splash. Eliot laughed, watching me struggle as he made no other effort to help. His borrowed trunks sagged around his middle, and he tugged them back up as one of the crew sent out a wolf whistle.

That's when I saw him. Oscar Romero, watching.

Quickly, I climbed out of the pool and dragged a towel around my body. 'I've had enough.'

Eliot's face fell. 'Loretta, hey!'

But then he turned and saw where I was looking and his protests dried up. I hurried back to my room, my swimsuit clinging, rivulets of pool water dripping down my leg. I tried not to think about all the eyes that were watching, tried not to worry that I should never have spent my last measly dollars on this swimsuit. Tried not to mind about the cat calls. Tried, just tried, and constantly tried . . . not to mind.

52

The circus wagons rolled in bright and early. We didn't know how, but word had got back from someone that filming was problematic.

Riki's assistant ran along the doors, knocking for us all to wake up, his voice ringing out: 'The money men are coming!'

Doors flung open as we stumbled out, sleepily knotting dressing-gown belts.

Riki barked down from his balcony, glasses askew: 'Be ready in thirty minutes!'

Soon, there was the roar of showers, radios blaring to wake us up. I still don't know how we managed it but exactly on time we arranged ourselves in an orderly reception line, even if some of us were still picking the sleep out of our eyes.

Riki's boy gave a whistle. 'They're here!'

At first, the line of cars was nothing more than a black dot on the horizon. Slowly, it grew bigger in a cloud of churned-up yellow dust accompanied by the purr of expensive engines. There were four of them. Three Buicks and a Rolls-Royce – that had to be the studio head. And that meant trouble. He never went anywhere without the studio accountant and the head of publicity, so that explained two of the other cars.

They each wore sunglasses that hid their expressions. A tie flapped in a sudden burst of hot wind; a collar was loosened. They walked down the line, ignoring our outstretched hands, until they reached Riki.

'We'll talk inside,' the studio exec said in a low rumble.

Riki hurried to hold open the door. The Suits went in first and the rest of us started to follow, but our leader held up a hand. 'Get ready for set.'

If Riki was going to get a dressing down, he didn't want witnesses. As the final car drew up, a towering figure emerged. The ice queen, herself.

'Hello, Loretta.'

I shielded my eyes. 'What ... what are you doing here?' I blurted. Was it a coincidence that she was coming out here, just as rumours had emerged?

'What a welcome!' Arvella said. 'I've driven four hours straight to see you, young lady.'

'I didn't know you owned a motor car.'

She gave a thin, satisfied smile. 'Petraś lent me his while he's away. One of the perks of the job. I'd love to see where you're staying.'

In that moment, I couldn't think of anything worse than Arvella crossing the threshold of my room.

'Why don't I introduce you to the director first?' I offered.

'We know each other already.'

'The writer, then?'

'I don't care for them.'

Walking as slowly as humanly possible, I led the way round the pool. At my door, I scrambled in my pocket for the key, while Arvella faked friendliness with the crew and indulged them with snippets of gossip. Yes, the rumours were true – Bob Hope had absconded to New York and TV. No, she had no idea why. (Everyone knew why; his movie career was stalling.) As they talked, I fumbled my key into the lock. With an impending sense of doom, I stood to one side.

Arvella paused, inspecting the door frame.

'You keep it locked at night?'

'Always.'

She nodded. 'Good.'

Then she stepped inside and gazed around. The bed was unmade, clothes flung across chairs. The air had a faint taint to it. There were the lipsticks scattered over a sideboard and colour swatches on pieces of card, next to a postcard from Grace.

Arvella began to move around the room, lifting jars and placing them back down, peering at the shades of coral, ruby and magenta. Most incriminating of all, there was my notebook open on my eiderdown, from where I'd fallen asleep sketching imaginary posters for the Lip Girl's Lipsticks. How could I have been so stupid? Arvella picked up the notebook and stared at my scribblings – *The perfect shade for a dream date!* Beside it were some rough sums and even rougher swatches. I was still struggling to find just the right shades, along with a list of suggested ingredients.

'Well, you'll need more money than that.' She tossed the notebook back onto the mattress. 'A hell of a lot more.'

My cheeks flamed. I'd never heard Arvella curse

before. 'If you'd let me know you were coming,' I said, 'I could have written my sums up in a ledger for you.'

'Sarcasm is the lowest form of wit.' She gave me an extremely hard stare, before continuing to inspect my room. 'Quite the set-up you have here.'

I took a deep, calming breath. *Don't let her get to you. You've done nothing wrong.*

'Why are you here, anyway?' I asked, diversion the only trick I had left. Voices carried from outside, calling us for the buses that would take us to the day's filming.

'I have two young make-up artists on a remote location with a crew and cast full of men. Why do you think I'm here?'

Probably to make sure there are no legal cases brought against Petraś. I should have been grateful, but hell was going to freeze over before I'd allow that emotion anywhere near Arvella Hoffman.

'Does Petraś know?' she asked, indicating my swatch cards.

I could have played dumb, but what was the point? 'No.'

'This is a sackable offence,' she said, 'on studio time.'

'They don't own me day and night.'

She sighed. 'Have you even checked your employment contract, young lady? Clause 6a about protecting Petraś's work? He expects the utmost loyalty.' My hands had turned sweaty, and I hid them behind my back. 'Thought not.'

'Why do you hate me so much?' I uttered, surprising even myself with my bluntness.

Her eyebrows rose in surprise. 'I don't hate you, Loretta.'

'You could have fooled me.' I began to move around the room, gathering up my things and clutching them to my chest. 'You never wanted me to work for Petraś in the first place. You hate that I'm his favourite and you do everything you can to give me a hard time.' But the reality of the situation was starting to hit home. 'I might as well pack my bags now.'

'You'll do no such thing.'

I straightened up. 'Excuse me?'

'Petraś's girls never abandon their stations. If you're to leave, that will be his decision.' She wiped her hands down, as though she felt dirty. She stepped towards the sideboard and started picking up the last of my samples and swatches. 'I'm going to have to take these as evidence.'

Over my dead body, she was. I threw my armful into the beauty case. 'Stop that right now.'

I went to take them from her, reaching over her arm to grab them. She fought back and within seconds we'd descended into an unseemly tussle. I forced the final jar out of her grip and staggered back, hastily throwing everything in a pile on top of the others in my beauty case.

She stared at me, shaking her head. 'Physical violence. Now that *is* a sackable offence.'

I felt my whole body shaking. I wanted to blurt out that she'd started it, but knew that would sound childish. How had this escalated so quickly? One moment we'd been exchanging barbed niceties, the next we were virtually pulling hair and scratching at eyes. Oh, why had she come out here, ruining everything? Why couldn't she just leave me alone?

'Your problem is that you don't know how to accept help, and now it's too late.' She crossed the room in a few quick strides, coming so close that I could smell the Parma violets on her breath. 'I'm not in the habit of wrestling with Petraś's employees so, all right, I won't take your precious make-up samples, but he shall be hearing about this.'

She turned to the door. 'Where's Alice?' She eased her sunglasses back on, sliding the arms beneath her silk scarf.

'That way.' I pointed across the pool.

'They didn't put you girls together?' Arvella asked.

'No.'

'Goodbye, Loretta,' she said stiffly.

After all the ways he'd helped me, what would Petraś think of me now? I was done for.

'Yes, Arvella. Goodbye, Arvella.'

I watched as she walked over and knocked on Alice's door, waiting for an answer. There was none. Arvella turned away and scowled back at me, before marching towards her motor car. Where was Alice? It was only as I gathered my things and headed to the coach that I saw Oscar Romero's car pulling ahead, blonde hair flying back from the passenger's seat. What was Alice doing with *him*?

53

The day's filming was slow – one of the younger actors kept wanting to know what his motivations were – and, for once, Riki was too distracted to argue with Eliot over rewrites. I was glad of the rest after all the morning's drama. After a couple of hours with nothing to do, Alice and I went out to sit on the top step of the make-up trailer, watching everything from beneath a tasselled shade as we slugged water. Oscar was gently snoring behind us in the cool, waiting to be called for his scene.

'Nice ride out?' I asked, as we tidied up face flannels on our laps.

'Oh, well, you know . . .' Alice's voice faded away.

'Nope.'

She avoided my glance. 'Nothing much to report.'

'He didn't do anything?'

She dropped a flannel, her face flaring. 'Look, Loretta, there's nothing going on!'

I didn't believe that for one moment. 'Nothing at all? I'm not judging. I just want to make sure that you're all right.'

Arvella's visit had worked in one way, at least – I realized how vulnerable we were. Not just me, Alice too.

Her hands moved quicker than ever, folding those

goddamn flannels. I snatched the latest from her and threw it down. 'Tell me.'

She paused, then gave a big dramatic sigh. 'Why are you making such a fuss? It's kind of tedious.'

'Because if I don't, no one will. I like you, Alice.'

After a moment, she flumped and hid her face in her hands. 'It's not that easy.'

'Yes, it is.' I reached out to lower her hands. She stared straight at me then, her eyes red-ringed with tears.

'He said it would be all right.'

'I bet he did.'

'He said that it was all perfectly normal and that it was all down to – what was that word he used? – testosterone, and that a man had needs that he couldn't control and that I should be more sensitive to that.' Her face crumpled. 'As though it was all my fault for even getting in the car with him.'

Before I could say anything else, a camera man strolled across to stand with us, chewing ruminatively on some gum as he watched Oscar out for the count. He shook his head. 'Getting sober. Worst thing an alcoholic can do in the desert.'

'But the studio insisted,' I pointed out, as Alice turned her face away.

He threw down a cigarette butt. 'Studio knows shit.'

After that, there wasn't much for either Alice or I to do between takes and she didn't want to talk any more, so it was more than a little relief when Eliot wandered over.

'Wanna go for a walk? I found a cave.' He indicated some place behind our trailers. 'Over there.'

'A cave? In the desert?' Alice asked. 'I've never heard of that.'

'That's because it's a *secret cave*!' Eliot whispered melodramatically. 'Underground. Come and see.'

Alice looked doubtful. 'Won't Riki be annoyed?'

Eliot glanced over to where our director was gesticulating with the young actor. 'Nah, he's too busy to notice.'

I leapt up. 'Show us the way, great leader.'

Alice slipped her sunglasses down from her forehead and pulled a scarf over her head.

'Come on.' Eliot circled a hand. 'This way.'

We crept behind the make-up trailer. Once we were out of sight, we began to walk side by side. We didn't talk much, saving our energy for the heat. The weight of it was almost physical. Soon, it became difficult to keep together. Rocks were scattered across the desert ground, along with strange, lumpen plants that seemed prehistoric and terrifying. Trumpeted white flowers raised their heads to soak up the sun.

'It's just some dumb-looking rock,' Alice complained, when we arrived at our destination.

'Patience, little one.' He led us round it and there, windblown into the other side, was a cavern. Eliot peered inside, calling back excitedly. 'Come and see!'

I knelt, the sand biting into my knees. Eliot was right! A horseshoe-shaped cavern, not even tall enough to stand up in. White and caramel stones were embedded in the walls, tunnels leading off to who knew where. The stale heat ballooned around us.

'Why did we never know about this before?' I asked, my voice echoing back to me.

'Well, I guess it's not so necessary for a movie about a bunch of students and their professor.'

I guessed not.

Eliot lay down on his side against a shallow stone entrance. 'I think I could just about . . .' He started to shuffle forward.

'Are you kidding?' I grabbed his arm and pulled him back. 'You are not squeezing in there! What if you can't get out again? Riki would kill you!'

'Oh, don't be such a sourpuss.' He reached out for my hand. 'Are you coming, or not?'

'Not.'

'I said, are you *coming*?' The challenge glared from his eyes.

'All right, all right, but I'm blaming you if we get stuck there.' I glanced towards Alice. 'What about you?'

'No, no! You guys head on. I'll watch out for Riki.'

I threw myself onto the ground, stomach down, and wriggled in until my feet dropped to the cave floor in a puff of dust. I managed to straighten up, just about, beneath the low cave roof and looked Eliot in the eye. 'Now what?'

'Now we explore.'

Crystals glinted all around us. He took my hand, his touch surprisingly cool, and we ducked our heads to wander towards the back of the cave and all those tunnels. We could have turned left, right or anywhere – but instead we found ourselves standing on a shallow rock shelf. It was like being caught in a fairy tale, one of those where the monster comes to find you.

'It's not so great in here,' I said.

'Are you kidding? These are the places where all the best stories are made.' Eliot indicated the various tunnels. 'We could go off down there, or there – or even there!'

'If we wanted to die,' I retorted.

'Where's your sense of adventure?'

'Back with my water bottle.'

He planted his fists on his hips. 'You know, Loretta, you really need to dream a bit. Look around you!' He cast out his hands. 'A whole secret universe!'

'I'd prefer a diner,' I said. But I was only pretending. To be here with Eliot, just the two of us? I didn't even care about the dank air.

I gazed around, and when I looked back, Eliot had drawn closer, both his hands gripping mine.

'Just the two of us,' he said.

'Yeah, just us two! Ain't it great?'

His hands squeezed. 'You still don't like it?'

'Well, if the coyotes come to kill us, I'll know who to blame.' But then his brow creased. I was hurting his feelings. My hands squeezed back. 'It's grand, Eliot. Simply grand.'

'You two done in there?' Alice's anxious face appeared in the cave entrance and our hands slid apart. 'Someone's looking! I think it's Oscar.'

I ran to clamber back out. Eliot wriggled behind me and I helped him to his feet.

'Are you OK?' I asked. Guilt plunged through me that we'd left Alice alone.

'Oh, sure.' She didn't look so sure, a faint patina of sweat across her upper lip.

'Well.' I linked a comforting arm through hers, as we walked back to our station. 'Let's have fun tonight. Just you and me.'

As the three of us marched back to the set, I kept my gaze fixed on the silhouette of a man who was watching. Always watching. And I swore there and then that I wasn't going to leave Alice alone any more.

54

We got back and, as one, we disappeared into our rooms to wash off the dust. I was still wrapped in my towel when I heard a knock. Eliot stood there, very obviously avoiding looking at any part of my body. He held out an aluminium tray. 'Your feast, madam. I thought we could have some supper.'

'Why?'

'I promised I wouldn't watch as they read my script again before a meeting. I need a distraction.'

He lowered the platter onto my side table, pointing out items. 'Olives, salami, bread . . . This is some sort of meatloaf – I think it's past its best, but you know . . .' He pulled out a bottle of wine that had been dragging down his pocket and from somewhere else produced a corkscrew. 'We're all set!'

My stomach roiled with hunger. God, I needed to eat!

I didn't even bother getting changed out of my towel. The two of us lounged across the bed, shovelling food into our mouths, eating in comfortable silence as the grease smeared my fingers. I didn't care how I looked, the towel around my hair collapsing. The other towel around my chest wasn't doing such a good job, either. After a few moments, we lay back against the pillows and emitted a mutual sigh of satisfaction.

I tucked my towel in tighter, then leant across and wiped a breadcrumb from his mouth. 'Had any chance to think more about the script? Happy now that they can't change it?'

'I think about the script, dream about it – and when I'm not doing that, I write the script. They may not be able to change it fundamentally, but they'll still have notes. And we're gonna have to start using giant cue cards for Romero. He can't keep up.'

I flopped back. 'Of course he can't. I get it, he's handsome. But why does everyone think he's such a big deal.'

Eliot rolled onto his side to look at me. 'You haven't seen any of the rushes, have you?' I shook my head. 'That's the thing. When you see him acting in real life, it doesn't seem all that. But the camera does something to him. Watching him back on celluloid, it's like . . .' He shook his head in wonderment. 'He's transformed. I hate to say it, Loretta, but that man is going to be a living legend. I'd bet my salary on it.'

I pulled a face, then checked the clock on my bedside table. 'All right, I need to go check on Alice.'

'Hold on.' He caught my shoulder and I felt myself being eased back onto the bed. I lay there, watching as his eyes ranged over my face. My limbs melted into the eiderdown.

I started to push him away, but only very weakly. 'You have your script meeting. And I need to check in on Alice.' I looked him full in the face. 'I have to.'

After a moment, he groaned with frustration and rolled back. 'You're right.' He gave a loud sigh, staring at the ceiling. 'When this is all over, let's come back here, just the two of us. Have some real fun.'

'You have to be kidding!' I sat up, clutching my towel to my chest. 'Have you seen the roaches? There's absolutely no way I'd spend my own money to come here. If we're going to go away together, you need to do better than this.'

Still, I felt my cheeks flush at what he was suggesting. Already my mind was scrolling forward. Separate bedrooms or twin beds or . . . ?

'All right, all right, I'll see what I can do.' He scooped up the platter and the remains of the food. 'I'll take this back to the kitchen.' He paused, observing my lipstick samples, which he'd tidied to one side. 'How's it going?'

I shuffled to the edge of the bed and stood up beside him. 'Just playing with colours.'

He glanced over the jars. I had to admit, the shades were really starting to work. They looked almost cohesive. 'Plans coming together?' he asked.

'Not really,' I fibbed.

Eliot snorted. 'I'll take that as a yes, then.'

The faint sound of Riki's voice suddenly carried through the air from a hotel balcony. 'Eliot? Get over here, man!'

Eliot rolled his eyes. 'I'm being summoned.'

'Go on.' I shoved him towards the door. Carrying the aluminium foil platter, he looked like a very poor imitation of a waiter.

'Oh, wait, I forgot!' I raced over to my pocketbook and found a half dollar in my purse. Running back, I tucked it into the breast pocket of his shirt, then patted him on the shoulder. 'That's a tip for you. Don't spend it all at once.'

'Ha, ha.'

I burst out laughing and stood watching as he walked back towards the hotel, carrying the platter on extended fingertips at head height. Then he pretended to stumble and I nearly cried out, fooled for a moment, but he rescued the tray in time – of course – and turned back to me, cocking a thumb at his nose. I shook my head, my chest rising and falling with silent laughter, and retreated back into my room, which felt empty in a way it hadn't before. Without Scott Eliot here, my room felt like nothing. Without Scott Eliot, I felt like nothing, too. Don't you just hate it when a man does that to you?

55

After three knocks – no, four! – Alice let me in. Cautious, for some reason.

Her room was nothing like mine, everything in its place. Immaculately tidy. Cashmere cardigans were folded in a neat pile of pastel colours, her make-up station was beyond organized, and the bed sheets had been made so neatly that I had to admire the hospital corners.

We settled down beneath her eiderdown to watch *The Colgate Comedy Hour* – her in light brushed cotton with kitten prints and a baby pink trim, me in scarlet satin that Primrose had pushed on me when she realized Eliot would be on set. It made sense to watch the show together, as the TV sets had a slot for nickels and dimes. The sun was dipping beneath the bark-cloth curtains, and orange light saturated the room.

Above the sound of the TV, we could hear the crew joshing in the pool. Meanwhile on the screen, the fuzzy black-and-white faces of Dean Martin and Jerry Lewis showed off between advertisements for Palmolive soap.

'Remember when we saw him in that nightclub?' I asked, nudging. He looked different on TV, less tall.

'Yes! Dreamy!' She hugged her knees, seeming happy.

Then there was a rattle at the door.

'Oh, Jesus!' Alice leapt up. 'It's him!'

'Him who?' I could make an educated guess, but hoped it wasn't right. I had no chance to ask.

'Hide!' She grabbed and pulled me towards the built-in wardrobe. 'He'll go mad if he sees you here.'

'Alice, stop! What's going on?' But the fist banged again. No four knocks this time. She pushed me into the closet, sliding the door shut just in time. But there was a tiny gap where Alice hadn't closed the door fully. I watched as she gathered herself for a moment, then walked stiffly to answer.

Oscar Romero in his swimming trunks. Water dripping from his hair and a confident smirk on his lips. What a bastard!

'The boys and me want to know if you're coming out for a swim?' he said.

'Sorry, but I'm awfully tired.'

'OK,' he said reluctantly. 'Do you have a towel I could borrow?' He'd wedged his foot in the door as the cheers faded from outside. People making their escape, not wanting to witness. The TV set faded to a sinister silence from where we'd forgotten to slot in extra nickels. As I watched, they moved towards the bathroom and disappeared out of my eyeline. Darn!

I wanted to burst out of the wardrobe then and warn Alice to keep away – well away! – to drag her back and push him out. But how could I?

I dug my fingernails into my palms when I heard the next words. 'Could you help get these off?'

'No.' Alice's voice was so small.

A pause.

'Well, pass me that towel, then.'

Another pause.

'You don't need to look so scared, you know.'

'I know . . .'

A voice, oily in its coaxing. 'So, come here.'

I had to make this stop – now. I spotted a pair of shoes. I picked one of them up. It had a good, strong heel. I cracked open the wardrobe and threw it hard, aiming for the main door. The shoe ricocheted off, just missing the window, and fell behind a chair.

'Someone's at the door!' Alice ran out of the bathroom and I pulled the wardrobe door closed again. 'Hello?'

Of course, no one was there but that wasn't the point. I'd stopped him for now. I'd bought her time.

Then, miracle of all miracles, the phone rang.

Oscar appeared, a towel clutched around his hips, damp trunks sagging from a finger. Alice clutched the earpiece to the side of her head. 'Tomorrow . . . sure . . . I'll let Loretta know, too.' Then she placed the handset back in its cradle. 'That was Riki. He's phoning round all the guys. Wants us to start extra early tomorrow. I think you should leave, Mr Romero. Big day coming up. Your final scenes.'

There was another pause. More footsteps. I watched Oscar walk stiffly towards the main door. Without another word, he exited.

Immediately, Alice came to let me out of the wardrobe. 'I'm so sorry!' she scrambled to explain, 'I didn't want you getting caught up in—'

I pushed straight past her and ran to the door. Some of the crew watched from the pool as I leant out to make sure Oscar was well and truly gone. His figure was silhouetted in gold from the setting sun and he was nearly at the entrance to the bar, but then someone called out from a terrace above my head and he turned back before I had a chance to retreat. His eyes zoned in on mine, freezing me to the spot as we looked at each other, then I ducked back inside to slam the door shut and bolt it.

I turned into the room, where Alice was sat on the edge of the bed.

'Alice, has this happened before? Has he done anything to hurt you?'

Her shoulders sagged. 'No.'

'Alice. The truth, please.'

'He really hasn't.' She gulped back the shine of tears. 'Not yet. A bit of petting and getting me to sit on his lap, tickling. Not anything, really. I mean . . .' She looked up at me hopefully. 'It could be worse, couldn't it?'

Fury rose up my throat like molten lava.

I hadn't paid enough attention. If I hadn't been so caught up in Eliot, in my future plans, then I wouldn't have missed what was happening right in front of my eyes.

'Oh, Alice . . .' I went to hug her. 'It's OK. You don't have to worry. I'll look after you.'

'You don't need to,' she said, pulling back to dab a handkerchief to her waterline, careful not to smudge mascara. 'Really, you don't.' Her eyes were red-rimmed, and they told another story. That she was silently begging me to do the opposite – to look after her.

Just like Enid had.

'It's all fine,' I said smoothly. 'It will all be fine.' My God, I'd make sure it was. For Alice, for me, for Sally, Grace – and for every woman who had to fight off men like him just to survive. 'I have to go now, Alice. Things to do.' God, did I have things to do. I kissed her briskly on the cheek. She was so tiny, so fragile, like a little doll. 'I'm just across the other side. Come and find me if you need to, day or night.'

She came to see me to the door. 'Thank you, Loretta.'

I smiled tightly, the moon watching over us. I hugged her again, squeezing her with all my might. Luck had saved her this time, but next time I couldn't be sure. There was only one way to be sure. To do those things myself.

56

We had twenty-four hours left on set and every moment counted. I marched to my bed and threw myself down, dragging over my pocketbook to dig out the free postcards I'd gathered from the hotel lobby.

Dear Enid,

How to begin? I needed to gather my thoughts. My pen hovered over the postcard as I bit my lip, before starting to scribble.

Work's got messy. (No surprises.)
   There's something I need to do, and I know you'll understand. (She'd better.)
   It's happened again. The men. Always, the men.
   You know me. (Boy, did she.) *Don't hold your breath, but I'm going to do something about this. More soon! And when I say 'more soon', wish me luck.*

Your loving sister, Margaret x

I re-read. Nothing there that a stranger or nosy post-man could interpret, but writing those words down in shaky black ink had helped me think. I leant beneath my bed and hooked out the book I'd borrowed from the hotel library a few days before. I flipped through the pages until I found what maybe I'd always been looking for. There!

Breath catching in my throat, I traced my finger across the words:

Datura stramonium. Nicknamed Devil's Trumpet. A white, flowering plant belonging to the Solanaceae nightshade family.

The author went on to describe that for centuries the flowers had been used to make Devil's Breath – a poison that needed no application more difficult than a swift wipe across the skin.

Datura stramonium. Ma had warned me away from them when we went foraging in the fields and meadows – except the desert variation was even more extravagant, trumpets opening to the moon as dusk fell.

Quickly, I changed out of my pyjamas into a pair of capri pants and soft shoes, fiercely knotting a button-up blouse at my waist. I scrambled through bedside drawers until I found a torch tucked away beside a Gideon's bible, alongside my cotton gloves.

After checking through a chink in my curtains, I slipped outside, using the mat to wedge my door open a tiny crack. I didn't want to risk the noise of the latch behind me. I glanced around the complex – glad to see Alice's lights had gone out – then in a crouch I tiptoed past windows until I reached the gap between the end of our block and the hotel building. I slipped into the shadows and crept along a wall, aware of the faint sound of music coming from the near-empty bar.

The vista opened up ahead of me like an invitation. Nothing but desert. The moon was high and bright; I didn't even need my torch. I paused for a moment, listening to the noises. The crew might have been sleeping already, but the desert certainly wasn't. I could hear the odd scurry of a creature; soft ticks as the ground cooled. Desert crickets played their music and sand danced in a whistling breeze. It was beautiful, the sky's colours fading into a bruised purple against the distant mountains. Best of all, the stars were out. My silent companions and only witnesses.

I took a step away. And another. Disappearing into the desert, allowing it to envelop me. I moved from plant to plant, my eyes exploring, looking for that telltale glow of white. I moved further away from the hotel complex, enjoying the sensation of being entirely alone. If I died out here, no one would find me until the morning. They'd wonder what I'd been doing. A foolish young woman, exploring on her own.

I pulled on the cotton gloves and continued to scour the ground. There was a glimmer up ahead. I quickened my pace, breaking out into a jog. Devil's Trumpet, signalling to me like a friend.

I fell to my knees and snapped off the blooms, laying them carefully on a large linen handkerchief I'd brought out for the job. It didn't take long. I knotted the handkerchief and knotted it again, then folded it away into my pocket, turning back to the hotel.

It only took twenty paces back for me to realize that I wasn't alone. Not any more. There was a tiny orange glow of a cigarette being inhaled and a figure lurched, silhouetted in the gap between the main hotel building and the rooms – my only route back. I knew instantly who it was; who it had to be. The Emperor. Oscar Romero.

I swallowed hard and waited on the spot, willing myself invisible. Mentally, I scanned my body, wondering what I could use as a weapon if I needed to. I tried to think logically. The torch? No, it was a cheap little thing. The only other way back to the hotel was to walk the long way round to the road and come back in by the main entrance, but I didn't like my chances. Too much empty desert, too many opportunities to get lost.

I watched the figure carelessly toss away the cigarette and move back towards the hotel grounds. I let out a long breath of relief, then waited, forcing myself to give him time to retreat. *One, two, three . . . Go!* I broke out into a run.

When I burst through the gap between buildings, there was no sign that anyone had ever been there, other than a discarded cigarette stub, still sending up a miniature plume of smoke. I ground my toe into it, then adopted a casual stroll, congratulating myself on my close escape. I'd done it!

But as I approached my room, I stumbled to a halt. The door stood wide open, guilty light reflected in the calm surface of the pool, inviting everyone in the whole complex to notice. I sure as hell hadn't left it like that, and my heart near about plunged into my shoes. I stepped forward, dread plummeting like a stone to the pit of my stomach. I hadn't got rid of him after all.

57

As I turned into my doorway, standing there was another figure – the one with the green eyes and the pale skin beneath his tan. The man from New York.

I stepped inside. 'Eliot? What are you doing here?'

'I noticed your door was open,' he said. 'Thought I'd check you were OK.'

'I was getting some air.'

He turned to watch me as I moved past him, towards the bathroom, hastily depositing my treasure in the sink before stepping back out.

I wiped my hands down on my capri pants. 'Can I get you anything?'

'No, thank you.' He examined me closely, clearly taking in my sweaty face. 'What are you up to?'

'Up to?'

'I mean, why are you out so late at night? Anyone could have come in here. Oscar—'

My eyes flickered past his shoulder and across the pool.

Eliot glanced over his shoulder to see where I was looking: Alice's room.

He folded his arms. 'What's going on, Loretta?'

I considered lying, but Eliot could always work me out. 'It's Alice. I only found out tonight.'

'Found out what?'

'Oscar. He's been coming to her room.'

'When you were there?'

'This evening. I hid in the wardrobe.'

'You *what*?'

It did sound kind of silly when I said it out loud.

'Alice insisted!'

'You girls!' Eliot began to pace the room, raking a hand through his hair. 'This is getting insane. It's not safe. I'm . . . I'm calling the studio!'

'You can't.' I went to shut the door, turning to lean back against it. 'We only have another day of filming. This is your movie we're talking about, Eliot. Your script – you're this close to an award. Are you going to throw that away?'

'I don't care enough about a script to see you two placed in personal jeopardy! Christ, Loretta, don't you get it? I'm not that kind of man. You shouldn't be hiding in wardrobes!'

'It's fine – don't worry about it.'

'It's not fine.'

Well, it wasn't, but I wasn't in the mood to agree with him. 'They wouldn't want to do anything, anyway. It would only hurt us – all of us, you included! Definitely, not him.' I couldn't bear to say Oscar's name out loud.

We both knew that what I said was true. At his silence, I began to shake my head. 'It's all my fault. I should have done more. I should have known.'

'It's not your fault, Loretta.' Eliot came and steered me towards the bed. 'Here. Deep breaths.'

I stared at my feet. 'I abandoned Alice. I should have argued our room allocations.'

Eliot took hold of my arms. 'This isn't your fault, Loretta.' But I barely heard him. My mind was scrolling faster and faster, back into the past.

I began rocking. 'I should have stayed.'

'Stayed where?' asked a voice.

'I left Enid to deal with everything on her own.' The argument on the stairs. My fault, all my fault. My rocking quickened, in time with the scrolling – and then suddenly arms were around me and another body rocked with mine, until we finally stilled. I blinked once, twice and looked up. Eliot.

When he spoke, the words came out slowly and carefully. 'Who's Enid, Loretta?'

I stared at him. 'My sister.'

The person I loved most in the world. I'd thought I could forget, but I hadn't, not really. Not at all.

I gave him a watery smile. 'The two of them are so alike. You know the way that Alice is always that little bit slow to get the joke?' I said. Eliot smiled and nodded. 'Enid's the same.'

Eliot let go of me and placed a hand over mine.

'Not everyone's as strong as me,' I told him. 'I need to look after them, you see.' Except, I hadn't. I'd failed.

'You can't look after everyone, Loretta.'

'But I can look after Alice,' I said, hardening.

The past was the past, but the future – that was something else entirely. I could see that I'd worried Eliot, but there was nothing he needed to be anxious about at all.

I was fine, absolutely fine, and besides, we only had one more day's filming. Just one more day.

'We really should get some sleep.' I stretched my arms above my head.

Eliot looked reluctant to leave me on my own. 'Will you be all right? I could stay here, on the floor?'

'Don't be silly! Tomorrow's a big day and you need your rest.' I took his hand and led him to the door.

He paused. 'What's she like? Enid, that is.'

'Just imagine the opposite of me.'

'I'd love to hear more about her one day,' he said.

'Sure, I'll tell you all about her. One day.'

'And I can tell you more about ... you know ...' *Agatha*.

I inched the door open and peeked outside. 'All clear!' I whispered.

Eliot slid through the gap and was almost gone when he turned back to me. 'What were you doing in the bathroom earlier?'

I fixed a smile on my face. 'That's no question to ask a lady!'

'You had something in your pocket. When you came back out it was gone.'

I thought quickly. 'Oh, just a handkerchief!' Well, it was half true. 'I dampened it to cool myself after my walk. That OK with you?'

Guilt flashed across his face. 'Sorry.'

I flapped a hand at him, turning it all into a joke. 'Shoo! Get out of here!'

He gave me one of his little salutes and I watched

until he'd disappeared back into the hotel. Then I shut the door and locked it, using the chain as well for good measure. Then I propped a chair against the handle. Then I turned into the room.

It was time.

I stalked into the bathroom and whipped the shower curtain down, spreading it across the ancient lino. I pulled on the cotton gloves and tied a silk scarf across my nose and mouth. Then I knelt on the floor to unknot the handkerchief. As carefully as I could, I plucked the flowers, one by one, tearing them apart until petals, stamens and pollen gathered in the bottom of the mortar bowl. So virginal, so pure.

I took the pestle and began pounding. My jaw clenched tight as my hands moved with a steady grinding motion, shifting the bowl around at intervals. The work was calming and it was a relief to finally feel my mind clearing of the drama of the last few hours. I began singing one of Ma's soothing nursery rhymes. The pounding became harder and quicker. The snow-white blooms became a yellowish pulp, and as I reached the last line, I sat back on my haunches, staring into the bowl. '*Chop, chop, chop. The last man's dead.*'

As the words faded away and my pounding ended, the room fell silent.

I'd have to strain the pulp – that was fine; I had an old pair of stockings somewhere, waiting to be darned. I climbed to my feet and carefully carried my work over to the bedroom table. I realized I was sweating slightly and went to wash my face in cold water, holding the flannel to my temples. Afterwards, I gazed at myself in the mirror above the sink, and felt calmer, more reasonable. If I was ever going to change my mind about what I was doing, this was the moment.

I turned and went back to my work.

By now, I was able to mix Oscar's make-up by rote; I didn't even need to glance at his chart any more. The ingredients were simple – talc, wax, pigment – but the real secret lay in the proportions. A little less wax, a touch more talc. Everything was mixed together in a cup, then placed in a warm water bath fashioned out of a spare wine bucket. I carefully set the arrangement to one side and peeled off my gloves, dragging the scarf down from over my nose. A job well done. I crawled into bed without even bothering to get undressed, pulling the sheets up to my chin. Within moments, I was dead to the world.

58

The next day's filming began like any other. This time, Alice travelled next to me on the bus out, her hand held tight in mine. When we arrived on set, Eliot gave the actors notes on some last-minute finesses to the script, as the crew set up for the first item on the shoot list. Oscar sat at a stony distance, sulking. A thread of gold hung above the far horizon – and the wind was picking up, the silk neckerchief at my throat whipping back. The relentlessly fine weather had finally broken.

One of the crew gazed uneasily into the distance. 'Storm's coming,' he predicted.

A coyote stood on a rock, his nose pointed in the same direction we were looking, then it gave a whine and leapt away, tail tucked between its legs. A crew member laughed uneasily. 'He knows.'

Any other time, we might have considered postponing the day's shoot, but this was our last day; we didn't have any choice but to push on.

I rubbed my arms. An ancient, skeletal tree stood proud against the buffeting of the wind, a twisted limb pointing in my direction. This desert – it got under your skin.

'Right, everyone!' Riki called us together. 'We need to beat this weather. I want us all ready by . . .' He glanced at his wristwatch and gave us a time that made my stomach roil.

As the crew dispersed, Riki crooked his finger at me and Alice. We went over. He pointed from one of us to the other. 'I don't want perfect; I just want done. If you two drag it out, the whole day's shooting is out of whack. Understand?'

So respectful of our art.

Dutifully, we nodded and moved off to our trailer, me keeping close to Alice as we picked our way between boulders.

'Did you sleep all right?' I asked.

She seemed surprisingly chirpy after last night's events. 'Like a baby! You?'

'Mmmm.'

Inside, I laid out my station. Make-up to one side; brushes to the other. Sponges beside them. There was only one space sitting empty. I glanced round to check on Alice – she was already settling an actor into her chair, safely on the other side of the room. Oscar wasn't getting anywhere near her on my watch. Not ever again.

I turned back to my counter and, reaching into my pocket, withdrew a small screw-lid jar and placed it down beside its companions. Petraś or Arvella might have noticed that it wasn't one of our usual pots, but neither of them was here. I pulled on my white jacket, and as I fastened the buttons, a sudden headache throbbed and my vision blurred. Maybe it was a tension headache from the brewing storm or maybe it was something else. Was I prepared to go through with this – like, really go through with it? What was the sentence for murder these days? Death?

A noise came from the door. When I looked up, Oscar Romero was there. He threw himself into the salon chair and only then did he take me in with a look of pure loathing. Oh, yes. He knew that I knew all about him and Alice.

'Good morning, Mr Romero.' I pulled the drape around him, knotting it at his throat, cocooning him. He was all mine now. 'How are you?'

'Get on with it.'

I set to work, marvelling that this was the last time I'd ever get to study Oscar Romero up close. I tracked the details of his face. Around his hairline I could make out the tide of colour that indicated a dye job; a few greys were starting to grow through. I wondered if he did it himself, locked away in his marble bathroom, or if he had a hairdresser come to his home. His cheeks were ruddy, and even though he'd had a close shave, his stubble dragged against my palms. There was that slight scar across one eyebrow where the hair didn't grow any more – easy enough to cover up. The full lips and cleft in his chin were as dramatic as ever; he was a handsome, young man. I massaged cold cream into his skin to remove any oils before commencing the make-up. My fingers laced and spread, laced and spread across his cheeks, pummelling. In the mirror, he watched me closely as I worked, his lip curled in a sneer.

Without warning, he caught hold of my wrist. 'You know Stanley, don't you?'

Knew the man? Oh, sure.

Oscar's grip tightened. 'My party. You were there.'

I stepped back, pretending to study his face. Alice was looking over. I gave her a tight little nod. *I've got this.*

And I did. I really had this. There was nothing Oscar could do to frighten me any more.

'I don't recall.' I pulled my hand away.

'Hogwash.' Oscar's eyes flicked to my face with fierce intent. 'You're the one who got away.'

'Now, if you'll just close your eyes for me.' I held the tip of his chin and waited, staring into his burning eyes. I itched to slap him, but managed to control myself. After a few more seconds, he did as he was told, and I pulled on my cotton gloves. Discreetly I held my hands out before me and waited for the shaking to stop. There. Then I began to spread pancake across his face. The one that I'd mixed, especially for him.

'I remember,' he whispered out of nowhere, making me jump.

Remembered what? What was he talking about? As if in reply, there was a movement from beneath the drape and then I felt the sensation of hot, clasping fingers between my legs, catching hold of my thigh. Bile rose in my throat. Any other time, I'd have screamed out but I couldn't, not today. I forced myself to keep working. His other hand moved beneath the drape and there was the faint hiss of a metal zipper. 'Keep going.' The hand inside his trousers set to work. His eyes screwed tight as he tugged away. 'Describe what happened,' he grunted. 'In my bedroom.'

So. I had the answer to my questions now. He remembered me from that night.

'The door handles were solid gold.'

'And what did you wear?'

An oatmeal two-piece. I swallowed. 'My wedding outfit.'

I drew long, smooth strokes across his face. 'Your friend held my wrists.' The tugging became faster. More images flashed behind my eyes. 'You bent me over the bathtub.'

By now, he was well into his fantasy. I stroked his face; he tugged. We were working in some awful tandem.

Oh, cherished love of mine.

Your face is so divine.

Those lyrics, those awful lyrics. I leant close to Oscar's ear. 'You forced me, remember?'

There was a moment's pause and then he let out a pathetic '*ngh*' of delight and his body melted into the chair. I placed the lid firmly back on the jar, screwing it nice and tight.

I came back down from where I'd been floating, close to the ceiling. The memories shrank away like wisps of smoke being sucked into a box, the lid slamming shut. I waited as he took a moment to compose himself, his hand re-emerging. Then I went to remove his drape and hastily bundled it up.

'All done.'

When I looked back up, someone else was standing there. Eliot.

'Everything OK in here? Only, Riki is asking when we can start.'

'Hunky dory,' I said.

Oscar swished a hand down his body and stood up. 'Let's get on with it, then.' He left without even looking back.

'You're welcome,' I called after him.

The French have a fancy saying for this, don't they? *La petite mort.*

59

Riki got his final wish. Everything moved real fast after that.

There was no going back now. Alice had already headed outside with her actor and I could hear the set coming alive as people found their marks and the cameras took position. I dropped the jar back into my beauty case, locked it and slipped the little gold key into my bralette. Then I strapped on my belt, pockets full of brushes, and went to the trailer door.

I stepped out beneath the flapping awning. Eliot ran over, hands in pockets, to stand beside me, glancing nervously at the darkening sky. Already, they'd started filming one of the key scenes, Alice standing close by as Oscar's character picked an argument with the student he was secretly in love with. The scene suited him well – he could take out all his anger and frustration on the poor kid acting opposite him.

'How was he?' Eliot whispered nervously, as we watched the acting. 'Everything OK?'

You don't want to know. 'The usual,' I said. 'Sulky, morose, stubborn.'

'Oh my God!' Alice's shriek could have been heard from ten miles away.

There was an answering noise from the sky – a

rolling, warning grumble – and suddenly the heavens opened with violent sheets of rain.

'Jesus!' Eliot sprinted out from beneath the awning, immediately drenched as he went to join the actors crowded round in a huddle. Rain lashed down. Lights toppled over, crashing into the dust. Sand flurries danced around like devil spirits as jackrabbits and rats raced for cover. The air turned yellow. Everything was movement, including the crew who were all running towards a single figure, lying in the dirt.

I took a faltering step forward into the rain. It was like a million tiny hammers pummelling my skin. It was an odd sensation – not quite pain, but not far off. It felt . . . right. Like something I deserved. Someone ran past me. I chased after him, slipping and sliding in the dirt. I didn't want to see, and yet I had to.

There was Oscar, writhing against the ground. It wasn't pretty. His eyes rolled back in his head, but then they seemed to settle on something, someone.

Me.

By this stage, the crew were going mad. Grown men weeping. I stood there and simply watched. A witness. But then I felt myself drawn closer to look at the legend that was Oscar Romero, prostrate in the dirt. My sister's voice circled in my head.

Bloody hell, Margaret. What have you gone and done now?
Killed a man, Enid.

Anyone could see the struggle and pain. Riki point-lessly attempted to bring his star back to life, hands slipping around as he pumped up and down on Oscar's chest. He looked like he was going to break a rib. My glance drifted back up to Romero's face. Make-up ran in chalky rivulets down his cheeks and through his hair to disappear into the sand. I bit my lip as all the evidence was washed away.

'What happened?' I asked uselessly, blinking the rain out of my eyes.

'He just collapsed!' someone said.

'No, he didn't,' another protested. 'He swayed around a bit first, starting blathering about something.'

'I think he was praying!' someone else whispered dramatically. I sincerely doubt that Oscar Romero had ever said a prayer in his life.

Riki was still pumping. He looked up desperately. 'Someone! Take his pulse!' His eyes fixed on me. 'You!'

I lowered myself down, grit hurting my knees. I took his hand, fingers pressed against his inner wrist. My gaze settled on the middle distance. I felt the faintest flicker. Faint but distinct.

Eliot sank to his knees in the dirt over on the opposite side of the body and tested another pulse.

'Well?' Riki demanded.

Eliot waited a beat. 'Nothing.'

Riki's pumping slowed and then stopped. His hair was plastered to his skull beneath the rain, revealing the beginnings of a bald spot. Stiffly, the three of us got to our feet.

'The fucker is dead,' he said, dragging a hand through his wet hair. 'Why do these things always happen to me?' He looked at me across the body, his face accusing. 'You were the last person with him,' he shouted above the rain. 'What happened?'

Every face turned to me. Talk about judge and jury.

I swallowed. 'Nothing.'

'Something must have.'

'Hold on, hold on!' Eliot said, raising his hands into the rain. 'This isn't Loretta's fault.'

I realized I was trembling.

There was a movement behind me, and Alice stepped into the circle. 'I saw it! I saw everything!'

'Alice—' I began.

'No! Don't try to defend him, Loretta.' She placed a protective arm around my shoulders. 'He was masturbating beneath the drape. It was disgusting.'

Everyone stared at Oscar's body afresh. Everyone except Eliot, who was staring hard at me.

'Is this true?' Riki asked sharply.

I hesitated, then nodded, my eyes downcast. Alice hugged me tightly.

An expression passed over Riki's face, as though everything suddenly made sense. He looked at the corpse as though he wanted to kick it. 'He gave himself a heart attack, beating the meat. Unbelievable.'

Eliot cleared his throat, his face pale. 'Shouldn't we . . . get him to a hospital, or something?' His glance flashed to mine.

'Yes, yes. You're right.' Riki dug a hand into his pocket and tossed a set of keys over to Eliot. 'Take my car. Take her with you, too. They'll want to ask her stuff, I'm sure.' His glance slid around; the rain showed no sign of easing. 'We need to get the set down before everything is ruined.' He gave abrupt urgent instructions and the crew ran after him, only a few of them pausing to throw one last look at the corpse.

Already, Oscar's face was turning blue beneath the rain. He looked nothing like a matinee idol now, muddy pools forming around his body. Riki's assistant knelt and tried to close Oscar's unseeing eyes, but they just popped right open, staring vacantly. I turned into Alice's arms and listened to the men talking around us, saying, 'Let's get him to the car.'

Riki's assistant took his shoulders; Eliot took his feet. Alice and I helped support the weight. Somehow, between us, we made it to Riki's car. The roof was down and the upholstery already soaked.

Eliot grunted as he backed into a door, then we wheeled Oscar's body round and tipped it onto the rear bench. His legs stuck out over the side of the motor car. The assistant swore quietly and shoved them until the knees buckled and we could cram them inside. Oscar lay on the back seat, but his feet still dangled over the edge, nothing more than a slumped pile of limbs. He couldn't have frightened a mouse now and the warmth of that knowledge went some way towards stopping the panic that kept rising in my chest.

'There's a hospital behind the hotel,' the assistant, Jack, said. He gave us hasty directions.

'Let's go.' Eliot nodded towards my trailer. 'You need to bring anything?'

I ran back to the make-up trailer to strip the sodden

white jacket off me, grabbing a cardigan. Within seconds, Alice had followed me inside, shutting the door behind her.

'You didn't mind me telling them, did you?' she said, her face beseeching. 'What he did?'

Jeez, did I not mind. I shook my head.

'Good, because I feel terrible.' She was pacing the trailer. 'I should have done something to stop him, and then the words just blurted out of me!'

'No one could stop him, Alice.' No one but me. 'Don't blame yourself.' I caught hold of her as she made to pace the same tight line one more time. 'You need to calm down.' Alice would make a terrible accomplice.

'A man just died!' she cried. 'And you were the last person to be with him, alive!'

My breathing slowed down. 'What do you mean?'

She flung her arms out. 'I don't know! I feel so terrible that you had to see all that.'

Alice was being naive again and, clearly, I needed to save both of us from that.

'Just calm down. It wasn't anyone's fault; stuff happens.'

'*Stuff!*' Alice glared at me and she never did that.

I took hold of her arms. 'A man died. It was his own fault.'

She shook her head. 'It feels *wrong*, Loretta.'

I had no choice. Emotional manipulation. 'It felt wrong when Sally died. Did you know how close I was to her?'

Alice nodded.

'Well, then. These are stars; this is what happens. Sure, he was too young – tragically young – but that's neither here nor there.'

She looked up at me. 'You sound so cold.'

A shiver really did pass through me then. 'I'm not being cold; I'm just being real. This has nothing to do with either of us. Remember that.'

'I don't like it,' Alice muttered. 'It's too much.'

'It's Hollywood.' I shook her again. 'You get that, right? It's not our fault,' I repeated. *Not any woman's fault.*

She gave a watery smile and then the tears came. 'I don't know what I'd do without you, Loretta.'

Another voice rang through my ears. *I couldn't do this without you, Margaret.* I squeezed my eyes tight shut at the memory, determined not to start crying myself. I wasn't the crying type and wasn't about to start now.

'I have to go with Eliot to the hospital.' I spoke slowly, giving Alice time to process. 'Will you be OK on your own?' She nodded and I pulled her into a hug. Her entire body was trembling. I kissed the side of her head. 'I have to go now.'

'I'll tidy up in here,' she said, wiping away the tears with the heel of her hand.

I glanced at my beauty case and grabbed it. 'You do that,' I said. 'I'll see you later.'

Back at the car, I clambered in beside Eliot. Steam rose from the tarmac, rain already burning off in the day's returning heat.

'See you back at the hotel?' a runner asked.

'Guess so.' Eliot stared straight ahead, a muscle

twitching in his jaw. He turned the key in the ignition and pulled out with the lazy and redundant orange flicker of an indication light.

We headed towards the watery horizon, leaving Alice behind, along with the rest of them. I didn't look back and neither of us spoke for the entire journey. I kept my gaze firmly trained on the unfurling ribbon of road ahead, the beauty case at my feet as I tried not to think too much. Not to think at all.

60

The hospital receptionist's eyes lit up with excitement.

'My goodness me!' She reached blindly for a telephone, craning her neck to stare out into the parking lot where Oscar was still in the motor car. 'Is he OK?'

'No, he's dead.'

Orderlies came running out within moments, pushing a wildly swerving trolley between them. The receptionist emerged from behind her desk and the three of us watched through the glass doors as there was an undignified tussle to lever him out of the car and onto the trolley. She scrambled up her sleeve for a handkerchief and sobbed quietly into it as he was wheeled inside. I guessed that she'd be on the phone to her pals the moment his body disappeared out of sight. She'd probably have a social at hers that evening, so that they could hear all the gory details over jugs of margaritas. *He looked as handsome as in real life! Even though he was, you know, dead.*

Dr Price checked that Oscar was most definitely, quite certainly dead. We explained what had happened as he listened unashamedly, morbidly fascinated. The heat of desert filming. Oscar's drinking and sudden imposed sobriety. The masturbation in my make-up chair. Collapsing. Heart attack. The story told itself.

'Where is he now?' I hadn't seen the trolley since the orderlies had wheeled it down a corridor.

'They'll have taken him to the morgue,' Dr Price explained. 'We'll need to do a post-mortem. Establish cause of death.'

'But . . . but we told you,' I countered.

He smiled. 'It doesn't quite work like that.'

How dumb could I have been? Of course there'd be a post-mortem. My thoughts whirled. There might still be traces in his system.

'So, what? Do we just . . . leave him here?' Eliot's question interrupted my thoughts.

Dr Price nodded. 'We'll need to inform his next of kin. They can decide what to do with the body after that.' Next of kin? Surely someone like Oscar didn't have people who actually loved him.

'How long will this all take?' asked Eliot.

The doctor shrugged. 'A day or two.' He smiled. 'We're kind of quiet around here.'

'And you'll send us the results?' I asked.

He looked at me oddly. 'We'll send the family the results.'

I swallowed. 'What if there is no family?' I looked at Eliot for support. 'I've never heard of any family, have you?'

'No,' he said after a moment. 'Not that I can remember.'

'Listen,' Dr Price reassured me, 'when a movie star dies, there's always family. Don't you worry – they'll come crawling out of the woodwork.'

In a daze, I got to my feet, and the doctor led us out to the reception desk. I looked back over my shoulder. It felt odd to leave Oscar like that. The great star, the host of Hollywood's grandest parties, all alone in a chilly hospital morgue.

'We'll take good care of him,' Dr Price assured us, shaking my hand and then Eliot's. 'You don't have to worry about what happened here. We'll get to the bottom of it.'

Back in Riki's car, we sat in silence.

'Can you believe it?' Eliot said.

I shook my head. 'No.'

'Better get back.'

'Yes.' I flumped back in my seat. 'Thank you for—'

'You don't need to thank me,' he said abruptly. 'Someone had to get him to the hospital.'

'I don't even know what to think,' I said.

'Neither do I,' Eliot said, his face tight, staring straight ahead above the wheel.

'Look, Eliot—' I began.

'Let's not talk,' he said, cutting me off. 'I'm exhausted.'

'OK.'

I pulled my scarf up over my head and we drove back to the hotel in silence.

61

You never saw a place empty as quickly as Dow Hotel, everyone desperate to escape the taint of death.

'Keep your mouths shut and pack up,' Riki said, as we gathered in the restaurant for one last time. He had put his own hand in his pocket, which was just about unheard of, and bought everyone in the crew a drink. He raised his glass. 'To Oscar.'

Dozens of glasses flashed in the air. 'To Oscar.'

As shots were thrown back, I placed my glass untouched back on the bar. Shortly after, the hotel manager waved us off, standing among the stringed lamps that lined the little gravel path.

'You'll be OK?' I asked Alice, just before she climbed onto the bus.

'Sure.' She didn't sound certain.

'You don't want to drive back with me and Eliot? Like we did the first time? It was fun, wasn't it?'

She avoided my glance. 'Nah. I think I'll travel with the crew.'

I watched as the bus pulled away in a cloud of dust. Eliot and I hit Route 14, driving back past ranches and parks until the outskirts of town began to reappear, his car coughing and spluttering past all the landmarks we'd driven past before, seeing them all backwards now.

The cacti shaped like dinosaurs. Clusters of sand-blasted orange boulders that hid secret caves. The odd abandoned hut, windows broken and ragged lace drapes blowing in the wind. They'd lost their mysterious air. Now they seemed brooding, watching, knowing.

'We can talk, if you'd like,' Eliot said, as though reading my mood.

I tensed. 'I'm not so sure—'

'A man died, Loretta.'

'And?'

His hands shifted on the steering wheel. 'And . . . men seem to have bad streaks of luck when they're around you.'

My heart was beating like a drum in my chest.

'I think I felt a pulse,' he said all in a rush. 'Did you feel it, too?'

'I . . . Well, why didn't you say anything?'

He took a deep, shuddering breath. 'So, you did feel it. Oh, God, he was still alive.'

I snorted. 'Barely.'

He glanced over at me. 'Loretta, don't you feel anything at all? I know he wasn't exactly nice, but—'

'*Wasn't exactly nice?*' I exploded. 'Are you joking? The man was a monster!'

'Are you saying he deserved this?'

'Well, you didn't raise the alarm!'

'I didn't say anything because I thought that—'

I thumped my seat. 'What? What did you think?'

He didn't respond but stared straight at me. His eyes bored into mine.

'It's all very unfortunate,' I said gingerly after a while.

I stared back at the reddish horizon. Then a hand reached over and pressed against my thigh. 'I know that what he did to you was bad, very bad, but . . .' I waited, still rigid with tension. 'You need to be careful, Loretta.'

'I'm always careful.' My beauty case jangled against my feet. 'Eliot, I—'

'Forget it.' He cut me off and took his hand back, turning the steering wheel into a sharp corner as we entered a boulevard, causing my body to rock against the side door. 'We're good.'

He drew up outside my building and pulled on the hand brake, turning to rest an arm around the back of my seat. 'Well, it's been a riot.'

'It's been something,' I mumbled, getting out. He put out a hand to stop me. 'Loretta, I'm sorry, it's only that . . . I care about you. Surely you know that by now?'

'I do.' Shame flushed through me. None of this was Eliot's fault. 'I really do.'

'Shall I call you soon? Once we're settled back in.'

'Sure.' Even I could hear that I didn't sound that convinced. This whole journey back home had rattled me; I needed time to think. Before he could say anything else, a figure appeared at one of the windows of the Hacienda Arms, waving madly.

'You're back!' It was Primrose, her hair in rollers.

'You'd better go say hi to your friend.' Eliot came out to help me remove my belongings from the trunk, and passed me my suitcases. The lipstick samples rattled.

'I'll come over to yours!' Primrose's voice called out

again, and she jabbed a finger in the direction of my apartment.

'I'll see you soon,' I said, avoiding Eliot's gaze.

As I turned towards my building, I heard the sound of his engine driving off and I didn't look back. What was the point?

62

Primrose had found some beers in the fridge and popped a couple of them open against the side of the counter to welcome me back. 'I saw Eliot drop you off.'

We went to our usual perch on the windowsill.

'Yeah, we fell out.'

'No!'

'Yes.'

'About what, for heaven's sake?'

I didn't want to go there. 'Oh, the usual.'

'Oh, I know the usual.' She was clever, noticing that I didn't want to talk. She turned her head out of the window and the corners of her mouth pulled down.

'You OK, Primrose?'

She rubbed a hand down her arms. 'I don't know. This place.' She gave a shudder and pulled the silk kimono up her arms. The tassels were frayed and grubby. 'It's getting to me.'

'You're not thinking of leaving, are you?'

'Maybe.' She pushed a hand through her curls. 'Someone I know has a cattle ranch. He ... he wants me to marry him.'

'Married? You?' As soon as the words left my mouth, I felt guilty. Wasn't this just what Primrose had said to me, when I'd been so certain about Raphael? Primrose hadn't judged back then.

'Do you love him?' I prompted.

Primrose's face lit up. 'Like no one else! He's called Arthur; he's a real Texan gentleman. You know, that fella who rescued me from Peter.' I did remember now, but Primrose was talking so quickly I didn't dare interrupt. 'He wears cowboy boots and everything and he's just adorable! Besides . . . I've already said yes.'

'You have? Well, that's just wonderful!'

'Are you happy for me?' She gave a hopeful smile. 'I'll have my own horse, and the ranch has three bathrooms!'

I gave my bravest smile. 'If you're happy, I'm happy.'

'Well, that's good, then.' She brought out a package that she'd been carrying and handed it over to me. 'I think it's time, don't you?'

Maybe it was. Maybe it really was.

Primrose swept me up in an embrace and I hid my face in her hair, breathing in the scent of her. When she pulled away, her eyes were brimming with tears. She patted my hand. 'Now, tell me all about you and Eliot.'

I was stunned. 'Me and Eliot?'

'Sure! The two of you have to be courting by now, surely. Come on, Loretta. Don't kid a kidder. Indoor picnic!'

'That doesn't mean anything!'

She looked at me fondly. 'You know, Arthur took me for a picnic.' She sighed with pleasure. 'It was in Griffith Park, by the zoo. That was where he proposed.'

I wasn't often nearly speechless, but this was one of those times. 'How . . . romantic. But listen. Eliot and I, we're not like you and Arthur.'

'Oh?'

'He's not even tried to kiss me.'

'Huh.' The ends of her mouth turned down in disappointment. 'I could have sworn you two were in love.' Then she seemed to shrug off the entire topic and got to her feet. 'Well, I'd better get going.'

I walked her to the door, pretty happy to forget the whole subject myself. 'When do you leave?'

'In a couple of months.'

'What will you do with the business?'

'Find someone to buy it off me as a going concern. Great location, discreet, accommodating girls – who wouldn't want it?' She grinned.

'Go on. Get going,' I told her. 'You have a wedding outfit to pick out.'

'I know!' Her eyes near about popped out of her head. 'Little old me!'

Happy for Primrose, I leant against the door jamb and watched her disappear down the stairs, singing a melody to herself, happy as a songbird. I listened until the main door swung shut behind her and the sound of her voice faded away.

I stood on the doorstep, all alone. Eliot, in love with me? What a crazy idea.

63

After that weekend, it was time to get back to the studio. I picked out a pure white *broderie anglaise* summer dress with a little collar, and paired it with matching belt, shoes and lips in a coral pink.

Biff waved his peaked cap. 'Hey, the Lip Girl's back in town! Get over here!'

I weaved between motor cars. 'How are you, Biff?'

'All the better for seeing you, sweetheart.'

A man in a suit pointedly cleared his throat as he sat at his wheel, waiting for the gate to be raised. Equally pointedly, Biff ignored him.

He looked searchingly into my face. 'How *are* you?'

'Fine, Biff. How are you?' I glanced nervously at the man in the car. 'Shouldn't you—'

'Are you sure?'

'Listen, Biff.' I wriggled out of his grip. 'I have to go, or I'll be late.'

He gave a mock salute. 'Understood, captain!'

I pretended to laugh and saluted him back.

The driver held a hand to his brow. 'Can I go in now?'

Biff reached to raise the gate and I ran off. Nerves fluttered in my empty stomach. I no longer needed to search for the beauty studio; I could trace the path there from memory.

'He's waiting.' Klein greeted me at the door, a cigar rolling between his teeth.

'For me in particular?' I asked, my mouth suddenly dry.

'Who else?' The wig-maker pointed his cigar down the corridor.

I wandered in a daze, keeping my mind determinedly blank.

The office door stood open.

'Come in. Take a seat.'

I shut the door behind me.

Petraś waited for me to be settled. 'So, what's been going on?'

I tried to muster up my trademark sass. 'What would you like to know?'

He steepled his fingers against his chin. 'Why don't you start with Oscar Romero?'

I shrugged. 'I don't really . . . I mean, where would you like me to start?'

'Maybe, with the truth?' He reached into a drawer and slapped a copy of the *Daily Variety* onto the desk.

LIVER THE SIZE OF A BASEBALL! the headline trumpeted.

I read quickly, my eyes scanning back and forth. *Dramatic collapse . . . renowned alcoholic . . . disturbing behaviour . . . autopsy results . . . liver and heart disease.*

'They did an autopsy already?'

'Things move quickly in Hollywood.'

They sure did. A whole autopsy and then the scribes finding out, all over the weekend? Someone was talking. Without a word, I slid the paper back across the desk.

Petraś let out a sigh. 'Why didn't you tell Arvella?'

'I didn't know he was going to die!'

'Yes,' he admitted. 'It all sounds very . . . dramatic.' He paused. 'Did anything else happen while you were out there?'

'What do you mean?'

He nodded at the paper. 'Disturbing behaviour.' He hesitated. 'This is serious, Loretta. This is only your – what? – second or third movie, and there's a death on location.' He suspected something – he did, he did! Had Eliot said something? He hadn't so much as picked up the phone to me since we'd got back.

'This isn't what I want for any of my girls,' Petraś said, more softly. 'If you have anything to share, now is the time.'

I pasted a shaky smile to my face. 'You don't need to worry about me.'

'You keep saying that, Loretta, but I do.' He gave a sigh. With a creak of his chair, he walked round the desk and leant back. 'The Lip Girl's Lipsticks. Nice name. I like it.'

I closed my eyes in resignation. 'Arvella.'

'I'd suggest that in the future you don't leave a list of ingredients lying around.'

Not just anyone. *Arvella!*

'You know, Loretta, you may find this difficult to believe but Arvella's actually doing you a favour.'

'Meaning?'

'There's a reason I've been away in New York.' He folded his arms, looking ever so smug.

345

'Go on.'

'I've been looking for a new launch,' he said. 'Something aimed at a younger market. Teenagers. You heard of them?'

I gave him a long, hard look. 'I was one, not so long ago.'

'Exactly! And when I came round your apartment that time? I saw what you were doing.'

'I never did any of that on your time,' I rushed to say.

'You don't need to explain yourself to me, Loretta.' He went back to his chair and sat down. 'I'll invest for seventy per cent of the stake.'

'You'll . . . what?' Conversations sure *did* move fast in Hollywood.

'I'd like to help. My money, your name,' he continued.

I did some quick sums in my head. 'And I give up *seventy* per cent?'

His eyes turned hooded. 'Do you have any idea how much it costs to launch a make-up range?'

My face flushed as I remembered Arvella scoffing at my maths. 'But they're my recipes,' I stalled.

'You could have the best recipes in the world.' He took a patient breath. 'But what about production? Ever been inside a cosmetics factory?' He waited for the shake of my head. 'Of course not. What could you possibly know about water-jacketed vessels, or the exact temperature at which to keep them? And that's just the start.' He began to list off considerations on his fingertips. I swallowed, unable to speak.

'I'm not saying this to be cruel, Loretta. I'm helping

you understand. You need me.' He gave me a look that seemed to encompass everything that was racing through my mind. 'We need each other.' He threaded his fingers again and waited.

'Fifty per cent,' I said quickly. 'You can have fifty per cent.'

'Don't you understand? I'm offering to make you wealthy.'

We stared at each other. I took in his silk tie, his mahogany desk, the gold fountain pen: everything that he had been and what he was now. The immigrant, the self-made man, the person who could spot an opportunity and turn it into a fortune. The person who thought I had it in me to do the same.

An assistant burst into his office. 'Mr Petraś, sir!' she said all in a rush. 'Mr Klein says please will you come now? Marilyn is getting very particular about the shade of blonde.'

'All right, thank you.'

The girl disappeared, and in silence we listened to the sound of her retreating footsteps. After a moment, he let out a resigned sigh.

'Klein and his wigs. Sometime soon he'll demand that they have their own Academy Awards.' He gave me a smile. 'Would you like to think about it, at least?'

I swivelled round to watch him leave.

He turned and began to walk backwards out of his office to address me one last time. 'I was thinking sixteen shades! You know, sweet sixteen!' He held his fingers to his lips and punctured the air with a French kiss. My overworked heart felt near about burst. 'And that's just for the start!'

Then he disappeared through the door.

I flumped back.

'Yes, yes,' I could hear him say from out in the corridor. 'Now, what seems to be the problem . . .'

Sixteen. I stared at the door where he'd disappeared. Then I glanced around his office – at the awards, the photographs with stars, the leather ink blotter, the row of pens in their stand . . .

Sixteen fucking shades.

64

Eventually, we settled on fifty-one per cent to Petraś.

'Now we have fun,' he announced, after we both signed the paperwork drawn up by his lawyer.

The very next weekend, he invited me over to his mansion so that we could begin. A maid met me at the door in a pristinely starched apron and black uniform with a cute, scalloped collar. She introduced herself as Mary. 'Mr Petraś is waiting for you in the kitchen.'

I followed her through the house, forcing myself not to stare. Standing in front of the landscape windows that opened out onto the rear garden were Petraś and another man. They wore silk paisley dressing gowns, cravats tied loosely at their throats. Petraś's companion was strikingly handsome, cheekbones carved from granite, his chin carrying the perfect little dimple. He was a Greek god, slumming it with us mere mortals. I spotted a look of intimacy pass between them that made my stomach tighten.

And you thought he and I were fucking! Sally's voice taunted. *What a doozy!*

'Loretta, meet Paulo.'

I swallowed hard, as Paulo reached out to shake my hand. I sensed him watching me intently. I took his hand and gripped it hard. 'An honour to meet you.'

His face relaxed and he turned to Petraś. 'You're right. She's one of the good ones.'

My boss gave a smile. 'Oh, trust me, I know.' He pulled out a stool. 'Come on. Sit down. Make yourself at home.'

Home. I mean, if white marble pillars, a triple garage and separate guest annexe could be described as homely, I guess that's what this place was.

As the maid retrieved something from the stove, Petraś came to sit beside me and Paulo went to help Mary turn a sponge out onto a tray. These three were like a little family.

Petraś reached into his pocket to pull out a heart-shaped box.

'This is for you,' he announced. 'Today is a very important day, after all. Your last day as a make-up artist before becoming an entrepreneur.'

'What is it?'

'A little something to mark the occasion.' Petraś nodded at the gift box. 'See for yourself.'

Paulo looked fit to burst.

There was a pink satin ribbon tied in a bow, and I pulled on the end, enjoying the satisfying hiss as it slithered loose. The box's brass hinges creaked as I eased open the lid. On a raised bed of pink velvet sat a heavy-looking gold lipstick tube.

I looked up again, guessing but hardly daring to. 'No!'

Petraś nodded.

I lifted the tube, hefting the weight of it in my hand.

'Solid gold,' he confirmed. 'Turn it over.'

Engraved on the other side: *The Lip Girl.*

'This is too much,' I said, but that didn't stop me from easing the lid off to twist the lipstick up.

'Call it a sample,' Petraś said, looking immensely proud of himself. 'Go on. Put it on.'

There was a little hinged mirror attached to the tube and I flipped it up to gaze at myself in the reflection. I hardly recognized the young woman gazing back. My face had plumped out and something that had looked so haunted was gone from beneath my eyes. So much had happened since I'd left Ma and Enid behind in a small house by the sea.

'Try it.'

I swiped the lipstick across my lips. 'How do I look?'

'Killer,' Mary whispered, joining us.

Paulo nodded as Petraś placed a hand on my arm. 'You deserve everything that life gives you, Loretta.'

My smile faltered as thoughts flashed back to Oscar's body prostrate in the desert rain. I really hoped that wasn't true.

65

'Reminds me of the old days!' Petraś rubbed his hands together, watching greedily as I brought out my home-made pigments.

We'd gone into his dining room, where plastic sheets had been laid out over the long table to protect it. Petraś went through what I'd already mixed, rejecting at least half of the shades with a few damning words – the brown wasn't warm enough, or there was too little blue in the red. I had to admit, I didn't know what I was doing at all!

'The sixteen shades need to be a cohesive whole,' he explained. 'Not just some random pick 'n' mix, Loretta.'

I was still struggling with this part. There were so many colours to choose from. 'But how do you know?' I wailed.

'You're telling a story, Loretta. That's what all true make-up artists do. Lizzie Arden and her red door. Bourjois and their little round pots. Max and his Hollywood glamour. Now, what's your story going to be? Come on, Loretta,' he coaxed.

I pulled a chair out and sat down, chin in my hands. Who *was* the Lip Girl? A daughter and sister. A black-mailer. An English immigrant. A wife, a make-up artist, a friend. And someone, most definitely, with secrets.

It isn't pick 'n' mix, Loretta. Something stronger?

I thought about all the actresses I'd admired. Who had brought me out here. The strong ones. Lauren Bacall, Elizabeth Taylor, Lana Turner. Lucille Ball, for Christ's sake! *I Love Lucy* had only recently premiered, but it was already the bomb and she'd worked with her Cuban husband to build it! The list went on and on. Finally, I was finding my inspiration.

'So, we model our shades on strong women,' I said at last. After all, isn't this what we'd done with Sally?

He inclined his head, considering. 'Keep talking.'

Oh boy, could I talk! 'Young women don't want to look like their mothers any more. All that thick pancake. What are we? Clowns?' My voice gathered pace, along with my thoughts. 'People want something else.'

I started to look around the range of colours, excitement flooding my veins. Raspberry, coral, all those teenage shades . . . No, fuck them! We needed something more deliberate. Suddenly the story came together. Elizabeth's violet hues. Lana Turner, in *The Postman Always Rings Twice*. Film noir, baby! We didn't want to be ourselves; we wanted to be something else entirely. We wanted to be movie stars, no matter how young we were.

'OK, I get it,' I said. 'Go bold or go home.'

'Right!' Petraś was in. Maybe I was teaching *him* something for once!

We cast around, grabbing jars. From that moment, we knew we were onto something good. We kept scrupulous notes as we weighed and mixed, tweaking here or there by milligrams. Magenta! Scarlet! Cherry! Soon, we had our first six launch shades and I learnt an important lesson that day. Creatives needed friends.

One afternoon, we were playing with a particularly striking shade that reminded me of Grace. It would look perfect on her. I cast my mind back to her beau, James Luke, and the fact that both their careers had turned awfully quiet. I'd only received the one postcard from her back in the desert, and hadn't heard from her since.

'You ever know anyone who's been blackballed?' I asked, from where I was bent over my work.

Petraś didn't even look up. 'Is this about your friend Grace?'

My mouth dropped open. 'How did you . . . ?'

'Arvella told me that you two are thick as thieves. You're not as subtle as you think, Loretta.'

'Oh.'

'Listen, I know you two are close, but you mustn't get involved.' My face clearly betrayed me. He pointed the end of a spatula at me. 'Whatever's going on, stay out of it.'

'I don't even know what is going on!'

'Good. Keep it that way.'

'But it's prejudice!' I blustered. 'She's not allowed to date someone because he's . . . what? A Nip?'

Petraś glared at me. 'Wash your mouth out!'

I felt the rage flood through me. 'That's what they're all saying – you know I don't mean it! You think I'm going to stand by while Grace gets run out of town?'

He took a deep, shuddering breath. 'Don't you ever accuse me of standing by.'

'Well, what *are* you doing?'

'Trying to make it better, Loretta! Like I've been doing my whole life, like I'm doing for you.' He slammed the flat of his palm against the table. I'd never seen his composure shattered so. 'But we can't fix everyone's problems.' Another shuddering breath. 'Besides, Grace is clever.'

'You called her bland.'

He shot me another warning look. 'I was wrong.'

He did know something. 'What's going on?'

'You'll find out.'

'When?'

'Soon enough. She and her beau, well . . . you'll enjoy the news.'

'Why don't you just tell me?'

'That's down to the gossip columnists, don't you think?'

'Gossip columnists, my arse. You know something!'

As I beat my fists against his chest, he held me off, laughing. 'Everyone needs their secrets, Loretta.' His voice sounded final, determined to share absolutely nothing. He went back to his work and I watched, the nastiest feeling crawling all over me like those cockroaches in my apartment. This was all a joke to him, but it wasn't to me.

Sure, *everyone needs their secrets* – but if he knew something about Grace, did that mean that he knew about me, too? If that were the case, he wouldn't go into business with the real me . . . would he? There was, however, one bigger question that made me feel even more uncomfortable. Who *was* Loretta Darling?

66

I should have guessed. Dr Price had been right all along, and not just about the relatives. Oscar Romero's memorial service turned out to be the social event of the year.

Oscar's family sat in a small cluster on one of St Clement's front benches, the women hiding their faces behind black veils. They looked disturbingly ordinary, all badly cut suits and purses peeling at the corners. I was up in the cheap seats, which suited me fine. Father McCoy was an hour late starting. While the rest of us waited for the main event, I occupied myself with star-spotting below.

Hedda Hopper was seated beside Petraś, a row or so from the front. Arvella was placed a discreet few spaces along. Shame. She wouldn't be able to share any gossip. There was brooding Brando, Elizabeth Taylor – looking divine in a little two-piece and a black veil that only served to accentuate her violet eyes – and nearby was the soon-to-be star Grace Kelly in a Christian Dior New Look suit that hugged her nipped-in waist.

Eventually, Father McCoy made his appearance. He gave us a long speech about what a talent Oscar Romero had been – the usual hokum about his abilities with scripts, which must have given Eliot a laugh. Where *was* Eliot?

I squinted around. I'd never been inside a Catholic church before. It was very different from the damp, plain Methodist chapel I'd been dragged to every Sunday morning. Jesus sagged from a dozen different crosses, his face distorted in various expressions of exquisite pain. There was a lot of gold and what Ma would have called showing off.

At last, my gaze settled on a figure across the way. Eliot. He wore a black suit, which, you know – heat! – and leant forward to watch down below. I observed him over the top of my hymn book, then our eyes caught as my lips were moving silently along with whatever hymn it was – all about shepherds or sins or something. I tried desperately to judge the expression on his face. Might he be ready to make friends again, or was that too much to hope for? As we reached the final verse – so many verses! – he began to sing in an exaggerated manner, crossing his eyes and playing the clown. I had to hide my laughter behind the hymnal. He must have been able to see my shoulders shaking, and when I peeped over the top again, he was grinning at me. I couldn't wait for the service to be over.

As I emerged – finally! – outside, a shadow passed over me.

Hedda flipping Hopper.

'The Lip Girl!' Why was she bothering with me? 'How *are* you?'

'I'm . . . fine.' I looked around for someone to rescue me, but there wasn't anyone. 'How are you?'

'Obviously, I'm devastated. Arvella was kind enough

to give me an invitation. Such a tragedy. So!' Out of nowhere, she produced a notepad and miniature gold pencil. 'You did Oscar's make-up, I believe? On *The Misbelievers*?'

I stared at the pad, her pencil hovering. 'Er, yes.'

'There's going to be an inquest into his death, right?'

I had to pause for a moment to gather myself. Thankfully, over her shoulder, I spotted a familiar face. I waved madly. 'I'm sorry, I have to go.' I ran over, dodging movie stars. 'Hey! It's so good to see you!'

'Hello.' Eliot glanced past me at Hedda. 'Problems?'

I nodded, and he steered me to the side of the church where I sagged back against the door. 'Thank you.'

'You're welcome.' He checked round the corner before ducking back. 'We're good.'

'Not so good. Hedda Hopper!' I blurted. 'She's talking about an inquest into Oscar's death!'

His face creased in a frown, but before he could say anything Riki appeared, slapping Eliot on the back. 'Hey, fella!' He spotted me then. 'Oh, hi, Loretta.' He turned back to Eliot. 'Coming to the rushes?'

'You go ahead,' replied Eliot. 'I'll catch you up.'

Riki nodded reluctantly. 'Good to see you, Loretta.' He gave me a quick peck on the cheek. 'Don't be too long,' he said, with a final nod to Eliot.

'You should go with him,' I urged, as Riki walked off. 'Don't hang around for me.'

Eliot raised his eyebrows. 'Seriously? You don't want me to hang around?'

'Like a bad smell?' I prompted.

'You know, a person could take offence.' He crossed his arms, holding his body stiff. As though I was going to fall for that!

It was so good to have someone to tease again. I crossed my arms back and we had a staring competition. He was the first to look away, shaking his head and swearing softly under his breath.

'God damn you, Loretta Darling.'

'Thank you!'

He looked up at me. 'Wanna grab something to eat?'

'I'm starving!' Churches do that to a person, don't you find?

Eliot reached out the crook of his arm. 'Come on, then.'

There was only one problem. When we walked back out, Hedda Hopper was talking to Arvella.

67

'At least they didn't see us!'

'Who?' asks Eliot.

'Hedda and my friend, the bitch.'

'Loretta, do you seriously think they care about us? We're nobodies!'

Eliot was right. I stared up at the hoarding. This was the first time in a long time that I'd been back.

'You don't like Van de Kamp's?' he asked. 'We can go somewhere else?'

'No, no.' I shook myself. 'Come on. Let's go in.'

The waitresses were scurrying about in those pink-and-turquoise uniforms, though I didn't recognize any of the new faces. The short-order cook was the same, though.

'Hey, Loretta!' Jake cried. 'How's tricks?'

I gave him a wave. 'All great, Jake, just great. How are the eggs?'

'Ha! All over easy.' He pointed a ladle between me and a waitress. 'Apple pie on the house.'

Eliot looked at me quizzically.

'I used to work here,' I explained. 'When I first came out.'

His eyes slid around. 'So, this is where it all began? They should put up one of those memorials.' He drew a hand through the air. '*The legendary Lip Girl once served pie here.*'

We slid into a booth. The waitress – her embroidered name informed us she was a *Judy* – came to take our orders. We asked for black coffees and a side order of ice cream for the pie.

As soon as she'd left, Eliot folded his arms and leant across the table. 'So, let's talk. What's all this about Miss Hopper?'

'She's on to us.'

'Us? What do you mean?'

'There's going to be an inquest! Oscar's family. They're not buying the whole exploded liver thing.'

Eliot's face paled. 'His liver didn't explode?'

I flung myself back on the bench. 'He was always going to die! The man was a walking chemistry lab!' I picked up a paper napkin and then threw it back down again. 'Oscar Romero died in the desert. What else is there to understand?'

He leant across the table. 'You tell me. You're the person all agitated about an inquest.'

I widened my eyes. 'His pulse. In his wrist. You know, the one we felt?'

'Well, I didn't . . . I don't.' Genuinely, he looked confused. Too confused.

I looked away. 'It doesn't matter,' I said, waving a hand. 'Just forget it.' I could feel the pinpricks of sweat in my armpits. I'd thought we were compatriots, and now . . . this?

Eliot watched me for a few moments, then sat back.

'All right. No one panic. Whatever it is we're meant to be panicking about.'

'Nothing,' I said grumpily. 'Absolutely nothing.'

'Well, that's great, then. Because I have a suggestion for you.'

'Go on.' I pretended to sound sulky, but actually I couldn't wait to hear what his next words might be.

'First, I need an apology.'

'A what?'

'Now, Loretta.'

I stared at the table. 'I'm sorry,' I muttered, though I had no idea what I was meant to be apologizing for.

'*I'm sorry, Eliot. I'm sorry that I sulked and I'm sorry that I ignored you and I'm sorry that we haven't even spoken for weeks,*' he dictated.

'Yeah, sure. All of that.'

'Wow,' he said. 'And you're single right now? Really, I'm astounded.'

'Who said I'm single?'

'You're not single?'

I sighed. 'I'm single.'

'Good.'

'OK, OK, I'm sorry. I'm sorry, I'm sorry, I'm SORRY!'

Diners were starting to look round.

'Great. Real humble. That's what I've always liked about you.' He took a breath. 'Do you want to hear my plan or not?' He leant forward and threaded his fingers between mine. All the other noises fell away. 'We trust each other, right?'

I squeezed his hand back. 'Always.'

'Well, then . . .'

And then he started talking. About a plan for both of us. A plan that would take us far, far beyond Hollywood and its sneaky lies and gossip columns, where everyone knew everybody. A plan that meant a fresh start. Frankly, I couldn't wait to escape.

68

Eliot's motor car had given up its last gasp – again! – so instead we hailed a cab to his place. Silently, we sat in the back of the taxi, hands gripped together.

As we stepped into his hallway, Eliot knelt to ease off the shoes that had been sending pains up my calves all day. I stepped out of them, one by one, and then he straightened up to look into my face. As our eyes met, I felt a cascade of emotions down my body and limbs. Was this for real?

'Can I mix you a drink?'

'No.'

'Snacks?'

'We just ate.'

He looked confused. 'I can't do anything for you?'

I took his hand and led him to his bedroom. I knew the way by now. A bedside lamp sent out its welcoming glow.

'What's going on here?'

'We're going to have sex, Eliot.'

'You make it sound so romantic.'

'You could undress me, you know?'

And so it began. The hooks and eyes that he had to release. The hiss of the metal zip. The slow, murmuring slide of the stockings. My thighs heated. My chest felt ready to explode.

Eliot stood back and looked at me in something that was like awe and I felt my insides melt, even though I was trying to stay in control.

'You going to get undressed now?' I asked, keeping up the act. Well, one of us had to. 'Because I don't think we can make this happen, if you don't.'

'You know, Loretta, it's been a long time since—'

I unfolded my body back across his bed.

He stared at me. 'OK, look, if I'm going to do this, I need some music.'

'What are you, a stripper?'

Ignoring me, he ran out to the living area and I clasped my hands behind my neck, listening. Soon enough, there was the sound of Ella Fitzgerald on the turntable, her voice coaxing. He reappeared in the bedroom carrying two tumblers of whisky, before gulping down one of them. 'Dutch courage.'

'You're not going to war, you know.'

Doubtfully, he looked down at his body.

'Start with the shirt,' I suggested.

One by one, he undid the buttons, a cuff catching on his silver wristwatch as he tugged in desperation.

'Oh, honey,' I murmured. 'You really are the best.'

'Shut *up*, Loretta!'

I smacked a hand over my mouth and with my other made a zipping motion across my lips. After that were the trousers, the pants, the vest . . . Jeez, men nearly wore as many layers as us women!

He approached the bed and lay down next to me, resting his head in my armpit. 'Thank God that's all over!'

He sank back against the mattress, and I climbed on top of him, my face turning serious as we pressed against each other, the heat coming off in waves.

'You wanna do this?' I asked.

'I really want to do this.'

The next few moments weren't *entirely* straightforward. His hands caught in my hair. He told me when my body was too up or too down or anything in between. Lots of talking, lots of instructions. Lots of kindness. Lots of intimacy.

I looked into his face, as I took in the scent of his body and the way his hands travelled down my curves. My own desire for him that was like a hunger in my belly. The rest wasn't clean, or even sophisticated, but it was caring.

Afterwards, we lay on the mattress, side by side, our limbs flailed out like starfish.

'Points out of ten?' Eliot asked, as we stared at the ceiling.

'Oh, men! Why do they always demand a scoreboard!'

'We can't help it. It's written into our DNA.'

I leant up on my elbow and studied his face, tucking that constant stray lock of hair away from his brow. 'Hmmm. Let me think. Are we talking Olympics?'

'You tell me.'

I started to count points off my fingers. 'Mounting, seven. Athletics, six.'

'Six!'

'Oh, come on. You fell off the bed at one point.'

He nodded. 'Accepted.'

'Performance . . . ten.'

He grinned. 'You're just indulging me now.'

I shook my head. 'Oh, Eliot. I can promise that I will never, ever indulge you.'

He reached out an arm to his bedside table to light a cigarette from a marble lighter. 'I knew it.'

I kicked him then, hard in the shins to make him yowl, and climbed on top of him, pinning his arms back so that my chest was pressed against his and my hair draped over his face, his cigarette hastily abandoned and spluttering in the ashtray. I leant to kiss him. 'You will never, ever get a better woman than me.' I pushed my hands harder into his. 'Right?'

He craned his face up to kiss me. 'Right.'

I sat back up on top of him, scooping my hair up into a messy knot. 'I need to go.'

He pushed me off and scrambled over his side of the bed. 'What? Why?'

'Academy Awards tomorrow, remember.'

'You can't be serious!'

'Oh, I am. Things to do. Sleep to get.'

He glanced at the bedside clock. 'It's not even midnight!'

'Oh, come on.' I nestled my head against his neck. 'It's only until tomorrow. We both need our sleep.'

'And we can't do that together?'

'Listen,' I said, giving him a kiss. 'You have a good night's sleep and I'll see you tomorrow. We've both been through a lot, and we can't make up for it all in one evening with a diner and sex.'

He pulled back to search my face. 'Anything on your mind?'

'Oh, not you.' That sounded harsh. I threaded my fingers between his. 'I'm sorry, I didn't mean it to come out that way.' I paused. Memories had come flooding back. To be this intimate with a real man – and Eliot was one of the real ones – it reminded me of all that I'd missed out on.

'You wanna tell me about it?' Eliot asked, seeing something in my face.

'About what?'

'Loretta, if we're going to go through with my plan, don't you think we should at least be honest with each other?'

'Right now? Like this?' We were both still entirely naked.

'If not now, then when? Look, we are going to have this conversation sometime, whether you like it or not.' I didn't like it, not one little bit. 'Come on, get back in bed.'

He went to pour us a couple more whiskies and put a new record on.

'You don't have to look so scared,' he said, leaving my drink on the bedside table. He came to sit on the other side of me and plumped our pillows.

'So . . .' he began, folding his arms.

'So.'

'OK, pretend I'm your therapist.'

'I've never been to one.' Honestly, out here they were

all obsessed with the goings-on inside their heads and how to pay for someone's honest opinions. Didn't they have any friends?

'Sessions usually start with the parents.' He closed his eyes. 'Talk to me. Pretend I'm not here.'

I swallowed hard. Maybe I could – for once – be honest. With myself *and* Eliot.

'Well, my mother was a traveller.'

'Traveller?'

'You know, Gypsy.'

He nodded. 'Got it.'

'Da took her on and she was always meant to be grateful for that. It made her weak.'

'Go on.'

'Da had always been cold, but then after the war he changed.' My hands gripped my whisky glass. 'He'd get drunk and would come home angry.' I gave a sort of laugh. 'I'm sure you've heard this type of story before.'

'Every story is unique,' he said, eyes still closed. I appreciated the fact that he wasn't trying to look at me. 'Siblings?' Of course he already knew, but I let him off that one.

'A younger sister, Enid.'

'And how did you feel about her?'

That was possibly one question too many. Love blossomed in my chest, overwhelming and threatening to spill out. How to find the words? 'I loved her.' My voice caught. 'Enid was the best of us.' I meant it.

'That's good,' he said.

It was. She had been.

'I needed to protect her,' I said. Pain spiralled down my spine.

'Must have been difficult.'

I thought back to that narrow landing and the handrail that had come loose at the screws without any of us realizing until it was too late. The dim overhead light. Enid, with the baby in her arms. Da, drunk and angry and wanting something – or someone – to punch. Such a shabby little home. Barely any home at all. But a family that I'd needed to defend – until I'd abandoned them for myself. What did that make me?

Suddenly I felt exhausted and laid my head against Eliot's shoulder. 'Can we stop now?'

The two of us lay in silence.

'You're not going to put this into a movie script, right?' I asked, poking him in the ribs. I really didn't need him to put any of me into a script.

He kissed my brow. 'Your secrets are safe with me. Will you stay the night, please? Keep a man company?'

I snuggled down against my pillow. 'If you insist.'

'Pastries in the morning?'

I nodded, then turned over and reached out an arm to switch off the bedside lamp. I was glad that he hadn't suggested more sex, because I wasn't sure that I was up to that.

An arm curled around my waist and turned me over so that we could lie side by side, legs tucked around each other.

'I'm so glad that you'll be here in the morning,' he whispered, kissing my ear.

'I'm glad, too,' I murmured.

It was only as I switched off the bedside lamp that I noticed . . . The photo of Agatha was still there. It would have sounded strange to anyone else, but I didn't mind. I remembered Enid, and Eliot still remembered his wife. We were both taking care of people, and I don't think that made either of us so different or wrong. All we were doing was caring. For the people who needed to be remembered.

69

I hadn't entirely told Eliot the truth. Yes, I'd been invited to the twenty-fourth Academy Awards – but not to attend. To be in the powder room. Petraś had a long-standing deal with the Academy. A nice extra touch that he supplied gratis. In return, he collected favours that he'd trade throughout the year. Of course, it helped that us girls all loved the chance to come within spitting distance of such an event.

On the day itself, Debra's father dropped us off in his Buick extra early so that we could take everything in before the attendees arrived. The Pantages Theatre lived up to its lavish reputation. Row after countless row of red velvet chairs – hundreds of them. There was more gold leaf than I'd ever seen before. Even the little ashtrays on the rear of the seats dripped with gold. I tipped my head back and gazed at the expanse of ceiling. Howard Hughes was rumoured to have his offices somewhere up above those chandeliers.

'Loretta, look!' Alice skipped past the rows of folding seats, peering at their undersides and the names taped to the bottom of each seat. Oh, the names! We walked past each row, calling out to each other.

'Debbie Reynolds!'

'Humphrey Bogart!'

Debra slowed down. 'I'm just gonna find a payphone,' she called over to us. 'I'll meet you in the powder room.' Then she ducked backstage.

'Who does she need to call so urgently?' Alice asked, as the two of us met at the back of the stalls.

'Her dealer?' I joked.

'Oh, Loretta! Debra doesn't do narcotics!' Alice said cheerily, linking an arm through mine. 'Come on, let's see the powder room.'

I allowed her to lead me up to the mezzanine bar. The powder room was large enough to hold about thirty people at a time, everything decorated in a dusty pink. We had an open, carpeted area with one wall lined in mirrors above a Formica dressing counter, with silk drapes. It was our job to give female guests a treat: topping up their powder and flourishing a swipe of lipstick. Of course the stars would already have had their make-up done at home by the studios' teams, ready for the flashing bulbs as they arrived.

Alice and I each chose a station and put down our beauty cases, then wandered around. Even the toilet handles were gold! When there were no further lamps or brocade stools to gasp over, we went back down to watch the preparations.

Staff were floating about – mainly out-of-work actors pretending to be ushers – making sure that everything was in order or sneaking another cigarette while the orchestra set up in the pit. As violin strings were plucked and drum skins vibrated, we worked our way from the grand lobby, back towards the stage.

'Where is Debra, anyway?' I asked, climbing the steps up to the main stage. It was so huge, my footsteps echoing. Soon, real-life stars would be up here, collecting their awards. I gazed out across the sweep of chairs, wondering if Eliot might stand on this stage one day, clutching a gold statue.

Alice had sat in one of the chairs, swinging her legs. 'I'm Marilyn Monroe!' she cried, pointing a finger to the underside of the chair and the name label. This was probably the most rebellious thing Alice had ever done in her life.

I ducked between the wings and looked around. Down a corridor leading towards the dressing room, I saw Debra leaning against the brick wall, still talking into the phone, her back to me. What was taking her so long?

She was standing beneath a lamp, reading out from a scribbled note. I crept closer.

'. . . and Ingrid Bergman is sitting in row two, next to Humphrey Bogart. I think that's everything! Or as much as I could get, at least. Don't forget the tip!'

There was a faint answering voice at the end of the line and then Debra planted the headphone back into its cradle and turned round. The smile dropped off her face like a rock off Mount Whitney.

'Loretta! What are you doing, creeping around?' Hastily, she scrunched her notes up in her fist.

I shook my head as understanding dawned. 'And they call *me* the Lip Girl. It was *you*. You're the sneak who's been feeding information to Hedda!' All those stories. The 'coconut crash' after I'd fixed Clark Stuart. Raphael falling ill on set. Oscar's death.

She started to back away from me, holding up her hands. 'You know, it's really none of your business.'

'It's none of yours either!' I couldn't understand it. She came from money; she didn't even need this job. 'Why?'

Debra rolled her eyes. 'Oh, don't be such a banana brain. How do you think this town works? We do each other favours. I feed Hedda information; she helps my career.' She looked me up and down. 'You know, Loretta, you could have done the same yourself if you'd had half an idea.'

'I don't need some gossip columnist to help my career. I'm doing pretty well on my own.'

'*On your own!*' She hooted with laughter. 'Don't give me that. You're so busy looking up at Petraś that you must have neck ache.'

'What are you two whispering about?' Alice had come up from the stalls, her gaze switching beneath our furious faces. 'Is something wrong?'

I took her hand. 'Everything's fine, Alice.' I stared at Debra and she stared back. 'Just fine. We need to get to our stations. *Debra* has made us late.'

We headed back to the main foyer, which was a whole spectacle in itself. Two staircases led up to the balconies – perfect backdrops for posing in a dress beneath the vaulted ceiling. There was a sudden commotion outside the doors and we ran, crowding together to peer through the panes of glass.

Motor cars had started to arrive, windows open as familiar faces peered out. The crowd heaved forward against barriers from the temporary bleachers set up on the sidewalk. My gaze scrolled along the line of security guards. There was Biff! I knocked on the glass and his cheery face turned round, before we shared a thumbs up with each other.

Above us, the sky bled into a deep black, searchlights making it impossible to pick out the real stars. Skirts lined up like a row of boudoir dolls, and gentlemen steered their partners with a hand that hovered just clear of the small of a back. Ma would have moaned with jealousy at all the furs. It really did look like everything it was meant to be. Glamorous, beautiful, graceful. Until a drunk broke clear of a rope and stumbled onto the red carpet, calling out abuse to one of the actors.

Debra straightened up. 'We should get going.'

Up in the powder room, Debra extravagantly sprayed herself with perfume, leaning into the mist. It was as though she'd already forgotten our conversation entirely. I had to give her points for bare-faced cheek.

'Jeez Louise! Don't let Arvella catch you!' Alice warned.

'I'm not even called Louise and that gossip can kiss my ass!' But as the door opened, she gave a little yelp and hurriedly placed the perfume down with a clatter.

It wasn't Arvella, though.

It was a young woman in a neat little blouse. Her heels sank into the carpet as she clapped her hands together. 'How darling!'

'Would you like your make-up touched up?' Debra asked promptly.

The woman dropped onto the nearest pouffe. 'I can't believe this! I really can't!'

Before we knew it, there was a line stretching out of the door. The excitement caught like wildfire, and the powder room became thick with perfume as gossip floated above our heads. Debra started doing something annoyingly impressive with an eyebrow pencil. Everything was so exciting that I was almost ready to forget her betrayal with Hedda. 'Oh, my goodness!' her woman cried. 'I feel like a queen!'

Just then, there was an announcement, and the lights were switched on and off again to indicate the ceremony start. 'Ten minutes. Ten minutes, people. Take your seats.'

Debra's client shot up. Women grabbed each other's hands, flooding out, skirts crushed in a froth of silk.

'Guess it's started, then,' Debra quipped.

I guessed it had.

70

If anyone had looked to the back of the mezzanine they'd have seen – one, two, three! – faces peering through a gap in the velvet curtains.

'Reckon we can sneak over?' Debra nodded to an empty space by the balcony rail.

'No!' Alice whispered. 'It's—'

Too late. Debra grabbed her wrist and the three of us crept down the far aisle to kneel beside the balcony, our skirts billowing around us in taffeta clouds. Debra was still annoyingly fun to be around, even if I did hate her loose lips.

Danny Kaye gave a hilarious opening monologue before a giant golden Oscar, with white columns setting off the stage. A few of the less important awards were presented and then the dancing girls came out. The three of us passed around a tiny pair of diamanté-studded theatre binoculars that Debra had borrowed from her father.

A Streetcar Named Desire stole the evening – twelve whole nominations! There was a short, tasteful tribute to Oscar Romero that I hadn't been expecting, presented by Stanley Hughes. He got through his speech well enough, but I couldn't help feeling happy about how uncomfortable he looked up on stage.

After that, there were the other posthumous awards.

The Witch had become Sally's masterpiece: the one nobody had seen coming. Except for her, of course. There was a sad little speech – 'brilliant actress . . . one of a kind' – and the audience rose to a standing ovation, which she would have adored. I found myself clapping furiously. No sign of Eliot, though.

After several more hours during which I wondered if my bladder would hold out, the mutual back-slapping was done. Debra nodded towards the velvet curtains and we crept back to the powder room before the audience flooded out from their mezzanine seats. As we did so, we bumped into the most unexpected person.

'Grace!' I rushed to embrace her. She was wearing a diaphanous gown of powder-blue silk and looked more beautiful than ever.

'I didn't realize you'd be here!' she gasped. A man came to her side.

'This is my beau for the evening,' she said. 'James Luke.' *The* James Luke! He was handsome as anything, with a dimple in his chin and an open face. He was *almost* as perfect as Grace. 'James, this is Loretta.'

'Ahh – the Lip Girl.' He reached to shake my hand. 'I've heard a lot about you.'

'All bad, I hope.'

'Terrible.'

I liked him already.

'What are you up to right now?' I asked.

I braced myself for Grace looking all sad and downbeat, but instead her whole face lit up. She shared a look with James, and he gave a discreet nod.

'Don't tell anyone, but we're going to New York!' she gushed.

'New York?' That was interesting.

'Yes, don't you remember? When you borrowed the wig for me? We were off for an interview that day.'

James took over. 'Television Land. They heard about the two of us being a couple and they've commissioned a vehicle especially for us. A series.' He looked at me pointedly. 'I'm not one to brag, but let's just say it's a very big deal.'

'I thought the two of you had been off on a date!' I gasped.

Grace placed a hand on my arm. 'Oh, bless you. You're so cute!'

I couldn't believe it. I'd been played by a player greater than me. Welcome to the table, Grace Riley!

Grace's smile quirked as she explained further. 'Well, we were blackballed and—'

'You knew!'

'Of course I knew! I'm not dumb, Loretta. So, James and I figured – what is it you Brits say? – in for a penny, in for a pound.' She laughed. 'We had our agents make a few discreet calls but I couldn't let the studios know. I'm sorry, that meant I couldn't tell you, either.'

Petrás had already known this, I guessed. I couldn't help feeling a bit hurt that he hadn't told me.

'You don't get if you don't ask,' James said.

'Well, isn't that the truth?' I said, hugging Grace again. 'You clever bean,' I whispered into her ear.

She pulled back and took me in her arms. 'You should come out to see us!'

I smiled. 'Maybe I will.'

Grace reached into her clutch and drew out a business card, her address in beautiful copperplate on thick, cream paper. 'Look me up.'

As I pocketed the card, James put an arm around Grace's waist.

'Oh, we have to go, Loretta,' she said. 'Some of the gang are throwing us a farewell party.'

'Well, have fun. I'm so glad we bumped into each other.' I really was. Between them, they'd stuck two fingers up at the entire system. The studios, the executives, the money men . . . all the people who'd behaved like Hollywood czars. Grace had told them all what they could do with their so-called power. Likely it meant she could never come back again, but she didn't seem to care one jot, throwing herself into the next adventure – and New York sounded like one hell of an adventure.

Suddenly a head poked round a velvet curtain. 'Loretta, come on!' Alice called. 'We're about to blow a gasket in there!'

I followed her back to the powder room. Sure enough, it was busier than a beehive. Everyone was getting ready for the after-show parties. It was a delight to do their make-up one more time, knowing everything I did now. So many more adventures!

After what felt like several more hours on my feet, my legs ached and I was just about ready to call it a night.

Carrying my beauty case, I walked down the grand staircase to find someone else standing in the foyer.

My stomach dropped somewhere in the region of my shoes.

'Arvella.'

'Loretta. I hear you're leaving us,' she said. It was almost as though she'd been waiting for me.

My mind scrolled back through every moment of hatred that the two of us had shared. Some obvious, some less so. Raphael's 'allergic reaction'. The leaks that had escaped the Dow Hotel when Eliot's movie was going down the pan, and Arvella turning up just at that moment. Arvella and Hedda, heads close together. Arvella's total reputation as a gossip! But that sneak Debra had proved me wrong. I could hardly believe it, but I'd actually overestimated Arvella. Would I admit my wrong suspicions to her? Damn, no! They could stay among the rest of the sins I was already piling up.

'So, you've heard the news?' I muttered instead. 'You'll be glad to see the back of me, I expect.'

She gathered a fur around her shoulders. 'Yes, I have. Well, good luck. Loretta. Here's a tip from me.' Her mouth twitched. 'You don't want any baggage following you out there.'

'I have no idea what you're talking about.' I wasn't going down that road now. She was so nearly out of my life, and I wanted to leave it that way.

'You have any friends in New York?' she asked, after a moment.

I thought about Grace, and other people, too. I wasn't

as alone as Arvella thought I deserved to be. 'Actually, I do.'

Her face pinched narrow. 'Well, keep them close. You'll need them.'

Then she turned away towards the lights that had been turned off, the empty stands and the abandoned sidewalk, covered in litter – just like that time I'd raced out of a hotel room with Raphael. This city was all she'd ever known, one to be forgotten and ignored in while other people built their dreams. Even – maybe – people had believed the wrong things about her. But that wasn't my fault. I watched from behind the glass doors, as she climbed into the back of a cab.

'I'll miss you,' I whispered.

I never in my life could ever have dreamt that I'd say that. Then I turned towards home. Back the way I'd come. Back to where it had all started. I'd said so many goodbyes this evening and now there was just one more I needed to say.

71

I made it out as far as Vine Street, the evening air cool on my face. I figured it would be a long walk home, but I didn't mind that. I'd be glad of the time to think and take in my town for one last time. My town. I wondered when I'd started thinking of it like that.

The sidewalks were unusually empty; everyone was at one party or another. I must have struck an odd figure in my silk dress and silver evening shoes. Damn, these shoes were killing me! Maybe a bus was a better idea.

But then there was the sound of scuffling and when I turned round I saw Eliot arguing with a security guard outside the theatre. I gave a sigh and went back to find out what the fuss was about.

'If you can just let me past,' Eliot was saying as I drew up. 'Hey! This is the one I was telling you about!'

The guard narrowed his eyes at me from beneath his peaked cap and looked me up and down. He grunted. 'I see what you mean.'

I placed my hands on my hips and stared from face to face. 'What am I, a slab of meat?'

The guard sniggered. I noticed then that he had hold of Eliot's upper arm, but when he saw me looking he let go.

'What's going on here?' I demanded.

'All I did was try to slip through the security railings to try to—'

'You unclipped two of them, sir.'

Eliot rolled his eyes and began again. 'All I did was unclip two sets of railings so that I could slip through and catch up with you.'

'That's a breach of security, sir.'

'Oh, come on! There's no one here any more. What do you think I was going to do? Ask the ghost of Lucille Ball's presence for an autograph?'

I took a sharp intake of breath. Being sarcastic with a security guard? Didn't Eliot know that was asking for trouble?

He slid a look at me. 'Can you vouch for this gentleman, miss?'

Oh, there were so many jokes I could have cracked. Eliot's eyes bulged at me, silently pleading for help. 'Yes, I can vouch for him.'

'You're free to go then, sir.'

Eliot adjusted his tuxedo. 'Thank you.' He hesitated for a moment, then slipped through the gap he'd created as the guard discreetly looked the other way.

I took hold of Eliot's hand and the two of us moved away.

'Free to go?' Eliot muttered. 'What was he going to do, arrest me?'

'Now, now. Just keep walking,' I whispered, keeping my face fixed straight ahead.

'My car's just down here.' We turned a corner, and once we were out of sight, Eliot began running. 'Come on!' he called back. 'While we still can!'

I burst out laughing and chased after him. Scott Eliot flouting rules! And who said miracles didn't happen? We arrived beside his car and sagged against it, catching our breath.

'Where were you headed, anyway?' Eliot asked between gasps. 'I didn't see you all night and then there you were, strolling down the sidewalk.'

'Home,' I said. 'There's something I needed to get.'

He frowned. 'Your place? You know you were headed in the wrong direction, right?'

Oh, lord – thank goodness for Scott Eliot. An idea occurred to me. 'Hey, give me a lift?'

'Sure.'

We moved round the car, and I climbed into the passenger seat as Eliot settled himself before the steering wheel. As we pulled out into the road, I rested my arms on the open window and lifted my face to the breeze as I watched the street unfold, taking us further and further out, leaving everything behind.

72

After a quick trip to my apartment, the two of us stood outside the gates of Forest Lawn Memorial Park, still in our evening outfits. Not quite the usual attire for a cemetery, but there wasn't anything ordinary about what we were about to do.

I took in the six-foot fence, the gates locked, then moved along, testing my foot against a picket rail, judging its weight. 'I think we can do this.'

Eliot stared. 'Do what? You're wearing kitten heels and an evening gown.'

I reached to grip the top railing and then looked down at him. 'Leg-up. Please?'

'You're kidding.'

'I never joke about a leg-up, Eliot.'

'What is it with me and fences tonight?'

He shook his head and then cupped his hands beneath my foot. 'Remind me, again. Why are we doing this?'

'You'll see.'

Eliot launched my body into the air so that I tumbled over the fence to land in a heap of limbs on the other side. I scrambled to my feet. 'You, now.'

Eliot gazed from one side of the fence to the other. He didn't have anyone to offer him a leg-up.

'Remind me why you brought me here,' he said warily.

'Because we're in this together, aren't we?'

'I suppose.'

'Could you stop being so romantic?'

The two of us walked either side of the fence, looking for something – anything! – that could help. After a few steps, we came across a tree stump on his side.

'There you go!'

'There I go,' Eliot muttered. 'You overestimate me.'

Still, he tried. It wasn't easy. I had to stuff my hands into my mouth as I watched him wobble, skinny legs scaling.

'If I lose my manhood, I'm blaming you, Loretta Darling!' he groaned, as he reached up and pulled himself over. He fell so hard that I wondered if we were going to have to call an ambulance, but I helped him to his feet, patting down his limbs.

'Good, good, not so bad, good.' I straightened up. 'Look at you! You're practically an Olympian!'

He brushed the soil out of his hair. 'I hate you.'

'No, you don't. Now, come on.'

The air misted around us, my hair inevitably ruined. But as we walked further into the grounds, I remembered again why we'd come here. The winged cherubs with their pouty cheeks. Sad angels and carved gods. The graves and, oh, the tombstones. We weaved between them, mist swirling around our ankles, dew soaking the hem of my dress. Our jokes fell away as I glanced at the sky. Dawn was breaking

'What are we doing here?' Eliot whispered again.

'I need a ceremony,' I said. 'A sort of last goodbye.'

We arrived before Sally's tombstone and I felt a sudden plunge of guilt, realizing that this was the first time I'd been here since her funeral. The grass was trimmed short and movie fans had left a maudlin remembrance of candles and gaudy bouquets. I knelt beside them, no longer caring that my gown was getting sodden with dew and mud. Reaching into my evening bag, I pulled out a package – the one that Primrose had returned to me. Primrose had tied it up in the most beautiful buttercup-yellow tissue paper, all with hospital corners and silk ribbon.

Eliot knelt beside me. 'What do you have there?'

A tumble of postcards spilled out as I untied the ribbon, along with a note in familiar clumsy handwriting:

We don't need to see this any more. It's upsetting. Please stop.

Please stop. Just stop. Nothing more.

The two of us watched as damp crept up the corner of a postcard and began to blur the ink where I'd written Enid's name.

'What . . . what is this?' Eliot asked.

There was a movement beside me, as he turned the cards over, one by one, reading the messages. *Your loving sister, Margaret.* Eliot was the only other one who knew me by that name.

He took in the stamps and postmarks, then looked up at me. 'These are . . . these are the stories of your life, Loretta.' I liked that he used my chosen name. Not so new now. 'But why do you have these?' He turned one back over and squinted at my blurred handwriting and the postmark. *Dear Enid . . .*

'My sister,' I said.

'But why did she return them?'

I swallowed hard. 'She didn't.'

'I don't understand.'

'She's dead.' I couldn't carry on once that expression spread over his face: pity. My own heart flooded, and I realized how much I'd needed this – some sort of sympathy, no matter what it looked like. But, quickly, I gathered myself. 'Got any matches?'

Eliot began to pat down pockets, finally reaching to draw out a red matchbook.

I gathered the postcards and arranged them in a pyramid.

'You sure about this?' he asked, guessing.

I nodded, then took the bunch of matches and lit them all at once against the striker, rushing to tuck the flames beneath the cards. The two of us knelt back, and watched the postcards start to burn, flames licking at the corners, smoke billowing. I leant down and blew, just like I used to do against the coal fire. The flames spread, growing orange, and we watched as ash flew into the air, caught by a rare Californian breeze dragging them apart until their messages disappeared into the ether.

'It's done. It's over,' I said.

'But, Loretta . . . if your sister's dead, how did the postcards come back? Who were you sending them to?'

'It had been such a rush to leave. I couldn't let myself believe it was true. But Ma didn't want them any more.

Sent them back.' The sister who'd filled my heart so full of love it hurt. The mother I'd left behind.

'It's cold,' I said, climbing to my feet. 'Let's find somewhere else.'

We wandered over to a bench and Eliot drew me into his arms, a hand stroking my hair. I kicked off my shoes and tucked my feet up, folding my skirts around my ankles.

And so the real story began. Finally.

'Da wasn't . . . He wasn't the best.' Now that I was letting them in, my mind flooded with memories. The way he'd come home drunk as far back as I can remember. His slurring words, his bulging eyes, his face puce. Him, picking a fight with Ma because the baby was crying again. Me shushing Enid, curled up around her. Replaying over and over again. Until there was Enid, her belly swollen. The baby who never stopped crying. Da, drunk again and brawling. Ma, too broken to help. Me, on my own. Fighting. Always fighting. Scared but fighting. Me, protecting Enid. Always protecting her.

The fall. The bodies. The limbs. Eight of them.

'How did . . . how did Enid die?'

'I was too late. By the time I found him at the top of the stairs, he'd already done his worst.' I'd tried to stop it, but in the tussle . . .

'The baby?'

'Ma looks after him. Or tries to. I dread to think how they're getting on.'

'It must have been difficult to leave.' I checked his

face out of the side of my eyes, relieved to see that the only expression there was one of concern.

'I needed to. It was impossible to stay any more.' The place of ghosts. 'People were talking. Neighbours. They'd heard the fights, put it all down to me. The difficult one. Besides . . .' I sat up on the bench. 'There was my career to launch! You know, the Lip Girl.' I gave my bravest smile.

'Ah, the Lip Girl,' Eliot repeated, mirroring my smile. 'What would we ever do without her?'

'Be happier?' It was a joke, but not much of one.

He pushed the hair out of my face and straightened the dress around my legs, tidying me up, pulling me back together again. 'Well, I could be.' His mouth twitched. 'But then who needs happy when they could have Loretta?'

'You lowlife!' I punched him in the shoulder, and he pretended to wince. 'You mocking me?'

'As though I could ever take you anything less than seriously.'

Together, we turned and watched the last of the flames flicker out from my small funeral pyre, the one that had been lit too late. It was time to leave Enid behind. Da, too. Maybe even Sally.

Don't you dare. I couldn't help laughing.

'What's so funny?' Eliot asked.

'Oh, not much. Just Sally. You know what she's like.'

There was a sound from a tree where the birds had been nesting, and one of them took to the air. The two of us watched in silence, then Eliot angled his wristwatch beneath the moonlight.

'You know, there's still a chance to catch a party.'

I pulled a face. 'I never want to go to another party again in my life.'

'Come on. Let's see if we can get out of here.' Eliot took hold of my hand. 'Fancy another road trip? We agreed, right?'

I pulled a face. 'In your car?'

'Hey! It's not that bad.'

'Oh yes, it is.'

Hand in hand, we walked towards the front gates where someone was unlocking them. It was the funeral director who had laid out Sally.

'What are you doing in here?' he said, glaring. 'Hey, don't I know you? You're the one who followed Petraś around, right?' He looked me up and down, taking in the mud around my ankles, bare feet from where I still carried my shoes.

'I did, once upon a time,' I said. 'But not any more.'

73

The next morning after zero hours' sleep, it all ended with me alone on a sidewalk, looking for a friend. Just as it had begun. Except this time, something sleek and glamorous slid round the corner.

'You have to be kidding me!' I said, as a brand-new Cadillac pulled up, the soft roof down. I'd spent all night packing and, as it turned out, it didn't take that long to empty an apartment. My life here had felt so big, but now it felt small again.

I gave a low whistle and Eliot watched with a grin on his face as I walked round, taking in the entire motor car. The paint job was a pale pink; there were show-off fins on the rear, and chrome just about everywhere.

'You said I had to get rid of it if I ever hit the big time!'

'You've hit the big time?'

'Well, I have a first big pay check, at least.'

'You serious?' I said.

'Well, the land of television is.' He rubbed his thumb and forefinger together. 'Moolah, baby! You ready for a road trip?'

'Only with you, sweetheart.'

We both laughed at that last word; it was so unusual between the two of us.

'We should write a romance novel together.' He laughed. 'It would be a masterpiece.'

'Do they get to kill each other at the end?'

'Yes, in a deeply tragic romantic pact. Now come on, get in. We can't stand around whispering sweet nothings all day.'

As we drove out of town, I spotted a store with a rack of postcards outside. 'Could we pull in a moment?'

'Seriously, Loretta?' he grumbled. 'We've only just started!'

'Oh, come on. I'll be quick, I promise.'

Eliot parked haphazardly. 'Don't be too long.'

I ran over and plucked out the first postcard that my hand landed on. 'That and a stamp,' I told the person behind the counter, scrambling in my bag for a pen. But the only thing I could find was an eyebrow pencil. I turned the postcard over and scrawled.

It's over. It's done. It will end now, I promise. I paused and then signed: *Loretta.*

Licking the stamp, I went out to the mailbox on the sidewalk and gazed up at the towering palm trees, the clear blue sky and everything that I'd come here to find. A sense of who I could be. Not the shop-counter girl or the person a fella could drag into a doorway, not a daughter who killed and shamed. I'd wanted to be someone who relied on no one other than herself. But I had come to rely on so many people – Primrose, Alice, Petraś. Eliot.

'How long is this trip actually going to take?' I asked, as I climbed back in.

'Five . . . six days. We'll need to go through Pasadena and then hit Route Fourteen.'

Eliot swung the car round. The roads were quiet. As we passed the big houses, I had a fleeting moment of doubt. What was I doing, leaving all this behind? The swimming pools and rolling lawns, the drive-in restaurants and the beaches . . .

I leant back against the seat, still rich with the scent of new leather, as we cut through the town. I took in the cinemas, the drag joints, restaurants and hotels. Where would it ever end?

A young woman sashayed down the sidewalk past a shoeshine, clearly dragging herself home after some party or other. She wore a gold satin dress, her feet bare.

'Look after yourself!' I called, waving madly out of the window towards the stranger.

'You, too!' she called back.

I turned to Eliot. 'So, tell me. Is New York really so different to Hollywood?'

He grinned from behind his brand-new steering wheel. 'Oh, Loretta. You're gonna love it. And they'll love you, too! The place where we can rebuild our dreams. You as an entrepreneur, and me as an award-winning television writer. Sounds like a plan, right?'

I sank back into my chair. 'Sure does.'

Television Land, here we come.

Eliot nodded at the stretch of tarmac ahead. 'You ready?'

'Oh, I'm not sure.' I let out a long, fake yawn. 'Maybe we should just turn back and forget this whole thing.'

'Who even *are* you?' Eliot asked, a wry half-smile lighting up his face. 'And what have you done with my girlfriend?'

Girlfriend. I liked that word.

Then he pressed his foot on the accelerator and we sped forward, the engine throwing us back against our seats as we laughed with the exhilaration. I whipped the scarf off my head and tossed it into the air. I was done hiding.

'I'm the unforgettable Loretta, darling!' I cried, lifting my face to the sky. And I could do anything I damn well pleased.

THE END

Bibliography

Anger, Kenneth, *Hollywood Babylon*, second edition (The Book Club/Cassell, 1975)

Davis, Gretchen, and Mindy Hall, *The Makeup Artist Handbook* (Routledge, 2008)

Eldridge, Lisa, *Face Paint: The Story of Makeup* (Abrams Image, 2015)

Graham, Sheilah, and Gerold Frank, *Beloved Infidel: The Education of a Woman*, British edition (Cassell, 1958)

Lamparski, Richard, *Lamparski's Hidden Hollywood: Where the Stars Lived, Loved and Died* (Fireside Books, 1981)

Marsh, Madeleine, *Compacts and Cosmetics: Beauty from Victorian Times to the Present Day* (Remember When, 2009)

Ponedel, Dorothy, *About Face: The Life and Times of Dottie Ponedel, Make-up Artist to the Stars* (BearManor Media, 2018)

Powdermaker, Hortense, *Hollywood, the Dream Factory: An Anthropologist Looks at the Movie-Makers* (Little, Brown, 1951)

Woodhead, Lindy, *War Paint: Helena Rubinstein and Elizabeth Arden – Their Lives, their Times, their Rivalry* (Virago, 2003)

Young, Louise, and Loulia Sheppard, *Timeless: A Century of Iconic Looks* (Mitchell Beazley, 2017)

Acknowledgements

It all began in a meeting room just off Piccadilly Circus, where fifteen nervous writers sat round a table and introduced themselves and their stories. My sincere thanks to our Curtis Brown Creative tutor, Simon Wroe, for encouraging us to dream, and to Jennifer Kerslake, for cheerleading those dreams. My fellow students have become friends for life and have read many – too many! – extracts from this novel. Particular thanks must go to Helen for her historical knowledge and eagle eye. Also, to Diane, Natascia and Suzanne who all kindly read my first full draft. (Or was it my second? So. Many. Drafts.)

Thanks, too, to our CBC guest tutor, Kerry Hudson, for suggesting the orgy!

Janene Spencer helped during my submission to agents and has been a friend through books and sewing for more years than I care to remember.

Thanks to Katie Greenstreet for reading my manuscript overnight and making me an offer of representation that would change my life. I am so proud to be a part of Paper Literary. Melissa Pimentel supplied notes on the story that fundamentally changed it for the better.

Brilliant editors come like buses: you wait ages for one, and then two come at once. Vikki Moynes of Viking and Sara Nelson of HarperCollins US gave me all the support and wisdom that any author could ask for – I've learnt so much. A special mention must also go to my copyeditor, Wendy Shakespeare, who saved me from several howlers, and to Natalie Wall, my brilliant editorial manager.

Any book involves multiple people working hard and often unseen – many thanks to cover designer Charlotte Daniels, proofreaders Mandy Greenfield and Sarah Barlow, and all the wider publishing teams who made this novel happen.

Josette Reeves is my better half at Speckled Pen and read many, many versions of Loretta's story. Probably she never wants to read this book again! Clare Whitson gave me her editorial expertise when I needed it most.

Alex Allan and Tracey Turner have provided me with love and laughter for the best part of three decades. They didn't let me down as I wrote draft after draft, cheering me on. Thank you for your friendships. Also, Egle, who has seen first-hand how messy an author's office can get.

Raj is the best boyfriend I could ever have asked for and didn't even mind as I crept out of bed at 5.30 a.m. to write.

Finally: to my mum, who taught me to read and always made sure the childhood home was filled with books; to Dad for his stoicism, surrounded by so many women ordering him about; and to my sisters – Amanda and Tracy – for their kindness and solidarity.